THE DUNGEON MASTER'S WIFE

BOOK ONE: THE UNDERDARK

KATIE MESSICK

Layout design and Copyright (C) 2020 by Next Chapter

Published 2020 by Shadow City – A Next Chapter Imprint

Edited by Elizabeth N. Love

Cover art by Cover Mint

ACKNOWLEDGMENTS

I need to take a moment to thank my cat. Without her snuggles and constant demands for attention and food, this book would not have been written. I guess I could also thank my outrageously supportive husband, Gary, who feeds my cat every day so she can be there to support me.

I also need to thank Leah Fletcher, my first reader. She slogged tirelessly through the worst grammar known to man and came out on the other side with wonderful comments and edits. Comments that empowered my cat to empower me to believe in my own writing.

And last, I need to thank my beta readers. Through your eyes, my cat was able to refine my words into meaningful combinations of meows and purrs for all to enjoy.

NOTES ON DUNGEONS & DRAGONS

You do not need to have ever played *Dungeons & Dragons (D&D)* to enjoy this book. It is intended to be balanced between flavor text for those of us who play and explanations for anyone who does not. However, this section gives an overview of the game, if you are confused or would like the basics. You can also find details of Aaron's thought process and his drawings in *The Dungeon Master's Notebook: Aaron, The Underdark* (DMN), available on Amazon now. At the end of chapter headings, CS# corresponds with the chapter title in the DMN.

D&D is a fantasy role-playing game where groups of people get together to experience and create stories. The game is created by the Dungeon Master (DM), who helps steer players through a story. However, players are given free will and often do not understand the DM's clues and just do whatever they want. The DM must then adapt, rewrite, and create new stories as players make their own terrible – er different – decisions.

The trick to this is that all decisions, actions, and even, to a certain extent, your characters are controlled by dice. Because if we could all make our own choices every time, we would never fail, and most of us would believe we know everything. If players want to know more about something, they can roll to see if they know. If you want to stab something with a sword, you need to roll to see if you can hit it. If you want to scare someone, you need to roll to see how scary you can be. Character sheets give bonuses to rolls so that everyone is better or worse at different skills.

Unless otherwise stated, the higher you roll, the better the result. Eighty percent of rolling is done on a twenty-sided die often referred to as a D20. Most *D&D* players keep at least two sets of dice of different colors with them, as you often need to roll two or more at once.

All of the rules, restrictions, and calculations for *D&D* are located in the various *D&D* Player Guides. These books also contain lore about the world, the classes, and what abilities you can and cannot use. Because let's be honest, if you could create magical people who could do anything, would you give them limits? I certainly wouldn't.

D&D as a system is very controlled so that no one character is more important than any other – in theory. However, the fantasy aspect makes it incredibly flexible. Often referred to as "home brew" the DM can really do whatever they want, and players, with the permission of the DM, can also create anything they want within the system's rules.

After everything is created and the game is being played, characters grow, just like people hopefully do in real life, by leveling up. DM's keep track of how much experience people have, and at each level, characters get more complicated and have more powerful toys, bodies, brains, and hearts.

Far from a complete list, brief descriptions of races and classes used in this book are below.

Your <u>Race</u> is the people you were born to. Kate Messick is a human.

Dwarf (*Lilly*) – A short and stocky people, dwarfs often spend most of their lives underground, are extra hearty, and are known to enjoy their ale.

Orc (*4aDeer*) – Strong, broad, and often green-skinned, orcs are not known for their intelligence but rather for their strength and fighting skills.

Gnome (*Poppy*) – With an average height of three and a half feet and a vast range of looks, gnomes are naturally very intelligent and generally good-natured.

Drow (*Eismus*) – The dark side of elves, drow are tall and thin with pointed ears and dark complexions. They are known to be very intelligent and usually evil.

Elementaling (*Craig*) – This is a made-up (home brew) race with ideas from different games. These tall, broad creatures have rock-like skin and bodies that are heavy and dense. They are innately powerful but slow to interact with the world around them.

Your Class is the job you have chosen in your life. Kate Messick is a word engineer.

Bard (*Lilly*) – Charming, inspiring, or distracting, the bard is usually more assistance than damage. These musicians and storytellers are known for their knowledge and diversity.

Fighter (*4aDeer*) – Often the ones charging headfirst into combat, fighters are heavily armored combatants, skilled in the use of all weapons, large and small.

Druid (*Poppy*) – Connected to nature, and often knowledgeable in medicine and animals, druids are incredibly versatile and have the ability to shape change and use nature magic.

Sorcerer (*Eismus*) – Sorcerers are arcane spellcasters with magical abilities, in Eismus' case, his were bestowed on him by a dragon. They are often mysterious, solitary, and hungry for power.

Earth Mage *(Craig)* – A homebrew class, the earth mage is a cross between arcane and nature spellcasters, able to cast spells from both origins.

Last, but most important, I do not own *D&D*. *Dungeons & Dragon's* was originally written in the seventies by Gary Gygax and Dave Arneson and published by TSR. It has gone through many different versions and rewrites, and most recently published by Wizards of the Coast with an open gaming license so that everyone can be creative, enjoy it, and add to it. If you want to learn more, you can find all the technical details in the official player's handbooks and through your local search engine.

Who is who in the Campaign

PROLOGUE

VOWS

The sun kissed everything it touched – the golds and reds of the fall leaves glowed and peacefully rustled in the breeze. A brook babbled nearby, adding to the ambiance, its cheerful song a memory of the past as it moved toward the future.

Rachael glowed. Her long brown hair was piled artfully on her head, and elegant pearls dropped off her ears and accented her long neck. Her face was painted and powdered, her blue eyes wide and exaggerated with color. The top of her strapless white dress was covered in delicate lacing and beads. A thin white bow tied under her bust started an empire waistline, and layers of white skirts fell to the floor. A bouquet of red and orange, accented with rich green leaves and bright yellow, was clasped gently between her hands.

A photographer did his best not to draw attention to himself as he captured every moment of her day. The harp started playing, the performers' deft fingers adding to the serenity. Rachael walked, unaccompanied. Her feet, never more sure, seemed to float as they traveled the little path in the grass marked only by the heads of white baby's breath scattered by the little flower girl who had gone before her.

Despite being surrounded by family and friends, Rachael had eyes for only Aaron. He looked incredibly dashing. His traditional suit was accented with reds, and he wore a red bowler cap to keep the sun off his bald head. The red brought out the red highlights in his neatly trimmed goatee.

She stopped to hug and kiss her parents, seated front and center, before walking the rest of the way to stand across from Aaron. They didn't touch, just gazed into each other's eyes as the minister started the ceremony. His words were traditional – Aaron's family was traditional, and family was extremely important to him. It was the act and not the words that had meaning to Rachael. The minister's syllables blended into the moment.

"The couple has written their own vows." Rachael swallowed down her nerves. And watched Aaron take a piece of paper out of his pocket, a slight tremor in his hands the only sign that he shared her state of mind. He cleared his throat.

"Rachael," his voice was strong and confident. "You are the most patient woman, and I can't believe it took eight years for us to get here." A few chuckles. "But the last eight years have been like nothing I would have ever thought possible. You have helped me study, nursed me while I was sick, changed flat tires, and even, once, admitted that I might be right. Your laugh makes even my darkest moments light up. Your constant support and love mean everything to me, and I vow to love you, to listen to you, and to support you because you are my world and hold my heart."

Rachael felt tears well in her eyes and her heart filled with more love than she knew it could hold.

Her voice wavered, unable to contain her emotion. "I will never have your eloquence," she stated. "Or be as prepared." She motioned to his piece of paper. A few giggles from her closest of friends. "But I will always be there for you. I wasn't being patient – I was loving every good and bad moment we had. And I vow to keep loving them. To keep your heart as safe as you keep mine."

The rest of the ceremony went by in a blur, and then Aaron, her Aaron, to have and to hold forever, was kissing her. His hand supported her back as he dipped her dramatically to the sound of their family and friends whooping and cheering. The beginning of her happily ever after was perfect.

1

UNDERDARK

LILLY

The Underdark is an underground realm of realms. It's polished black walls swirl with dark plum purples and weave massive caves, tiny nooks, and sudden ends together like a spider web. The low hum of power never quiets, and the endless glow of timeless magic is ever-present.

— AARON – DUNGEON MASTER'S NOTES, CS2.

L illy's thick red dreadlocks fell to one side as she cocked her head, her green eyes narrowing.

"And what will you give us for doing this?" she asked. Her voice was a low alto and she spoke the common language with a light dwarven accent. Dwarven being the language of her people and Common the most spoken language of the world.

"Let's just say, it is in your best interest." The fey priest's hands came out of his sleeves in an expansive gesture; his long, thin fingers reminded Lilly of a spider. Lilly couldn't help the cold shiver that crawled down her back.

"I guess we are doing this. Everything on your list, for information." Lilly held out her hand for the list. With an oily smile, the fey priest dropped the small roll of paper into her hand. "Agreed, agreed, agreed."

She turned to the elementaling behind her. Craig had been human hundreds of years ago, but now his body had been mostly replaced with brown rocks of all sizes, his features large, exaggerated, and indistinct. Round green human eyes looked out of deep sockets, the only remaining tie to his mortal past.

"Time to go," Lilly said to Craig.

"Wait, hold up," Martin interrupted the game. "Did you just accept a quest on behalf of the party for no reward?"

"I am playing a young, naïve bard... so yes?" Rachael answered sweetly.

"We really are not getting anything?" Tom asked. He looked right at Aaron the Dungeon Master, or DM for short.

"Don't look at me. No one else who came to the temple spoke up," Aaron said happily. "Back to the game."

Lilly, with Craig trailing behind, left the gaudy Temple of the Fey, its Greek gold-and-red-patterned walls blurring in her haste to feel the eyes of the fey off her back. She rested her hand on the top of her pony keg drum as she walked, her main instrument. She had designed it herself. It held about 17 pints of ale, and the drum changed pitches as she poured herself pints out of the spigot at the bottom. Her hand caressed the side of it, calming her, despite it having been empty since they had been brought to the Underdark.

Craig sensed her nerves and easily slid in closer to match her small steps. His protective, literally rock-hard presence reassured her. Craig was not tall, but his steps boomed with the weight of his mass and his broad shoulders were ridged all the time.

Craig and Lilly found the rest of the party in the market. Other than being in the dimly lit black and purple gloom of the

Underdark, it could have looked like any market. Stalls, filled with goods and lit with lumen crystals, popped up on the edges of the little square located in the middle of Elm City. As far as they could tell, Elm City was located in the middle of a giant cavern. The air was musty from lack of circulation, and the occasional cold and biting drip from the roof of the cavern, far above, was one of the many reminders that they were very, very far from home.

4aDeer's muscle-covered orc frame was tense, his tusks extra visible against his green lips as the poor merchant he was speaking with once again explained that heavy plate armor was expensive. Eismus was crouched down, making flames appear and disappear for some wide-eyed children. The action looked sinister coming from his dark grey, scaled hands that peeked out of billowing dark blue robes. He had a long nose and slightly pointed ears that gave away his partial drow heritage, though his scaled skin identified his branch of sorcery as draconic. And finally, Poppy, the three-foot druid gnome who had somehow managed to get on top of the herb traders table to haggle. Her slender frame swam in the dull red, ill-fitting leather armor she wore.

Lilly and 4aDeer also wore ill-fitting armor. The dull brown leather was patched in the usual spots, and the material of 4aDeer's strained around his large frame; it was just a little bit too small. Lilly wished she had her old clothing back. But it had disappeared along with her old life. She had been performing for lodging at a tavern when everyone was magically put to sleep. She and all the other people had woken up naked and imprisoned just a few days ago. They had quickly made their escape, finding some armor along the way, but only 10 people survived.

She looked over at Craig, the elementaling made of rock. He had found them wandering the caves and brought them here, to Elm City. Lilly found herself drawn to Craig. As a mountain dwarf, she was an expert in all things geological, but this earth mage was an enigma. A story waiting to be drawn out.

"Are we going to tell them about the quest?" Craig asked awkwardly.

Lilly's face flushed as she realized she had been staring right at Craig for an inappropriate amount of time. She shifted her gaze to her keg drum. She thanked her god Milil that her drum, along with most of the party's personal effects, had somehow ended up with a merchant in Elm City. They had bartered, spent, and traded everything they had to get them back.

"You might want to hold off on those," Lilly said during a lull in Poppy's haggling. "We have a quest from the Temple of the Fey that includes getting a list of stuff. We might find it on the way."

"Ohh, very nice. Well done, Lilly, and what is the reward for getting everything on the list?" Poppy happily moved her attention to Lilly, sensing a possible upper hand in negotiations. Lilly smiled brightly.

"Information!" Lilly said proudly. "And maybe he will be our friend."

Some of the brightness left Lilly's smile as her announcement was met with silence.

"We are not getting paid or anything? Not even expenses?" Poppy, still ignoring the herb trader, exclaimed.

"Lilly, we have the clothing on our backs and a few days' rations to our names, and that is it," Eismus added.

"I didn't think it was a big deal," Lilly shrugged. "Anyway, it is something to do in this odd world, and maybe we will find something worth money along the way. Maybe some armor for 4aDeer."

"Armor? Where!?" 4aDeer's attention suddenly spiked.

"Not here, buddy," Eismus stated, putting a hand on 4aDeer's huge arm to calm him.

"The quest has been accepted, let's rest up, so we are ready to go." Craig's gravelly voice was almost lost in the busy market.

Lilly let herself fall to the back of the party with Craig as they headed off to the tavern they had secured lodging at. They were an eccentric group brought together by circumstance and powers beyond their understanding. But they needed each other if they were going to survive in this new world and maybe even find a way home.

2

FORT COLLINS

DINING ROOM

"And we will call it there for the night," Aaron said. His bald head and goatee ducked behind the DM screen to take notes.

"You could have at least asked for a shrubbery," Tom shook his head. He was not tall like his character Eismus, but they were both thin and wiry. His long, deceptively youthful face currently held a grimace and his long blonde hair was pulled back in a ponytail at the base of his neck.

"You never know when you could use a shrubbery," Greg laughed. Where Craig was made of stone, Greg was made of muscles. Biceps threatened to tear the rolled-up sleeves of his button-down, and his chiseled, hairless chest peeked out of the unbuttoned collar. Even his face had muscles.

"I don't think the Knights of Ni are in the Underdark," Debby added to the Monty Python quote. Debby's hair was bright electric green this evening, her clothing a spattering of yellows, greens, and oranges that worked well together because of their purposeful clashing. Seated at the table, she could meet the eye of anyone, but standing, she was not so lucky. Maybe not quite as short as her character Poppy, Debby just barely managed over four feet in height.

Little conversations started up around the table as alter egos returned to the small stacks of papers that housed them. The numbers and personality traits that guided the characters were listed in detail on character sheets that came out for the game each week. Martin, seated on Rachael's right, immediately started talking about the skills he wanted to take at level two for his fighter, 4aDeer. Martin was the oldest in their campaign. In his mid-forties, his hair had gone completely white and he kept it cropped short. It looked good on his tall, thin frame. Rachael half-listened, a little tipsy and very happy, adding her own plans for Lilly.

Her dining room had a big window facing the street, with large bushy trees obscuring part of the view. The window was flanked on either side by bookcases. The majority of the dining room was taken up by a huge oak table stained a rich dark brown that matched the bookcases. D&D handbooks, dice, and printed out sheets were strewn about the table's edges, with Aaron's famous 3D homemade terrains neatly arranged in the center.

She stood and picked up the few plates mixed into the mass of papers and dice and walked to her kitchen. Absently, she loaded the dishwasher.

"Can I help with anything?" Greg asked. His hand brushed against Rachael's as she closed the dishwasher door. Little tingles of excitement pulsed where they brushed, and Rachael laughed a little awkwardly. Greg was Aaron's brother. They had similar heights and the same soft brown eyes, but the similarities stopped there.

"Nope, just got done putting them in. Nothing really to do," she responded. Hopefully, he assumed her awkward laugh was because of his poorly timed question. Greg was an enigma, much like his D&D character Craig. She didn't know when their first accidental brushing had happened, but she had come to look forward to them. A little excitement never hurt anyone.

"Sorry, maybe I should have asked earlier." Greg didn't sound sorry. "Hey, Aaron says we are already most of the way to level two. Any thoughts on multiclassing?"

"This is my least favorite part of role-playing," Rachael sighed and immediately missed the glass of wine she had not quite finished, sitting next to her character sheet. Leveling consisted of number crunching and picking new abilities that you were then stuck with if you made the wrong decision. As characters – toons as they were sometimes called – moved through the game they gained experience. These gains were reflected by getting better at things and learning new things. Just like real life, Rachael supposed.

"It's my favorite," Debby added in her thick southern accent. She moved in front of them to put her Diet Coke in the recycle bin. "Poppy will get to shift into animal forms at level two!! I can't wait to be a dire wolf. I have felt super useless so far. Although I do love my little gnome."

"That's because she is short like you," Greg teased. In her late twenties, Debby was the shortest, roundest, and happiest person that Rachael had ever met. She died her hair a different color each week and always did her nails and make-up to match.

"Hey, no short jokes, remember?" Debby shot back playfully.

Lilly felt a little squeeze in her chest and wrinkled her nose. Why would listening to Greg and Debby flirt give her any reaction at all?

"I am leaving now." Debby looked at Rachael's nose. "Something smell bad?"

"Sorry," Rachael mumbled. "Random thought that I didn't like."

"Yup, those happen to a lot of girls when there is a hot guy around. Greg, you are walking me to my car." The question was a playful demand. Greg gave a theatrical stage wink at Rachael

12

and gave Debby his arm. Rachael didn't watch them leave. Instead, she headed back to her character sheet and her wine glass. She finished the last bit of wine in one swallow.

She and Aaron had bought their house together right after they got married. The layout of her house was ideal for hosting. It was two floors, with two bedrooms on the top floor. The bottom floor was basically a circle around the stairs leading up to the bedrooms, and there was a bathroom on each level. The kitchen was long and opposite the front door, though you couldn't see the front door from the kitchen. The kitchen had an arched entryway, hiding the counters and appliances from view while not cutting off sound or flow to the dining room, and, if you poked your head around far enough, you could see into the living room as well.

Rachael and Aaron had fairly minimal tastes. A few pictures on the walls and some mismatched second-hand furniture. The pictures as diverse as the collection of furniture. The only things that matched were the beautiful oval eight-seat dining room set and the bookcases; it was easy to see where their priorities lay.

Rachael enjoyed having people over, especially for role-playing nights, and her husband was an excellent DM. His campaigns were nothing short of legendary, and this one was looking to continue the legend.

In D&D, everyone created characters out of their own imaginations and rolled dice to balance them. All the characters together formed a party that worked together on puzzles, adventures, and battles in a world created by the DM. She loved the way this party was shaping up; this new character was becoming one of her favorites. Lilly Thunderbeard was a single, young, and lovely dwarven bard. Short in stature but still strong, Lilly was especially calm with high charisma but very naïve – so opposite of Rachael in real life. Lilly had so much to learn.

"Why would you accept a quest for nothing?" Tom asked, bringing Rachael out of her musing. Tom was Aaron's best friend. They had both moved out here for college, and, with some bumps in the road, never looked back.

"Get off it, Eismus, I was just playing my character," Rachael responded as playfully as she could manage. She decided then and there that when Tom was being especially annoying, he would get called by his drow sorcerer's name.

"I think you would have made the same deal on any character. I don't think it was good role-playing at all," Martin added to the conversation.

"Thanks for the vote of confidence," Rachael said flatly.

"No, I'm not saying it was bad. But we all want to improve our characters, and I just feel that rolling a naïve toon is not super difficult for you to play," Martin explained.

Rachael bit her lip. Aaron stayed silent and Tom looked almost excited to see how this would play out.

"I'm not saying you are naïve," Martin suddenly rushed. "All I am saying is that naïve is easy to role-play and leaning on your lore as a bard might help you and the party in the long run."

"And you playing a giant, hulking, illiterate fighter isn't easy?" Rachael was not pleased.

"It is hard for me because I know more than everyone here – except Aaron – about what is going on, and I have to say to myself, I know this but would 4aDeer?" There was a tense and heavy pause. "But I do understand what you are saying. I won't bring it up again, but I do think you should think about it."

Martin closed his player's handbook and picked up his trash to toss in the bin on his way out.

"Maybe if you wrote out Lilly's backstory it would help," Aaron both recommended and chastised. Everyone in the campaign had to write out their character's backstory and put it in an online file system that the group shared. Lilly's backstory was the only one missing.

"I will," Rachael said. "It just hasn't come to me yet. Lilly is out of my comfort zone."

"Well, it will come. Thank you two for hosting as always. See you next week." Martin had to duck to get through the door.

"I'm off as well," Tom stated, picking up his bag. "For level two, Eismus is just picking up more damage spells."

"Sounds great, Tom. See you this weekend." Aaron waved absently as Tom rushed out the door. There was a bit of a scuffle as Tom seemed to be leaving as Greg was coming back in.

"What are your leveling plans for Craig?" Aaron asked Greg.

"I will email you an updated sheet. Nothing exciting," Greg easily answered. He and Aaron had been participating in and running all sorts of role-playing games since they were kids. Greg's character was filled with home brew and number crunching to make him as powerful as possible, but also complicated to see if Aaron caught errors and imbalances. They had an odd sibling relationship, close as two brothers could be but fiercely competitive at the same time.

"What are you two up to this evening?" Greg asked, flopping down in one of the recently vacated seats.

Rachael gave a little silent jump for joy at the question.

"We are having a quiet night in," Aaron answered, as he looked up from his organizing of papers behind the DM screen. Rachael could feel her body slump. Right, quiet night. She avoided Greg's eyes.

"Are you sure?" Greg asked.

"Yes, I spent most of the week preparing for tonight, and I think it is time to pay attention to my wife," Aaron chuckled. Rachael perked up a tad – did he have a plan? She looked over at Aaron, who smiled at her encouragingly.

"Ok, man, as long as you two are doing something fun. It is Friday night after all!" Greg acquiesced, disappointed.

"Of course," Aaron said as if confused by Greg's question.

"Now get out of here. I have to see you all week at work. I don't know what possessed me to get you that job. Give me a night off, would you?"

"Alright, I'll see you Monday," Greg responded with a chuckle. His eyes moved to catch Rachael's. "Call me if you need anything."

"We will," Rachael said with a skeptical smile and walked Greg to the door. His shoulders brushed hers as he passed, and once again she felt little tingles of excitement. She absently brushed her shoulder and watched his very pleasing ass as he walked to his car. He didn't look back.

"So, what is the plan for the evening?" Rachael tried to keep the excitement out of her voice as she rejoined Aaron in the kitchen. It had been a while since Aaron had last planned for them to do something together. Three weeks and five days, to be exact.

"There isn't one. I just didn't feel like going anywhere," Aaron said, putting the final parts of the game on their designated shelf. Rachael felt her lips straighten out into a line, and she took a steadying breath.

"I know that is your calming breath," Aaron said to the room.

"I was just excited to do something, and when you said you wanted to pay attention to me, I was just hopeful," Rachael said, put out.

"I do, we can snuggle on the couch and watch something," Aaron said as he came around the table. Rachael couldn't help smiling when he smiled. Even 11 years after their first date, Rachael still found him handsome. He had gotten a little rounder over the years, and his mostly trimmed goatee was frosted with white. It balanced the top of his head that had just a shade of hair left – probably because his brains pushed out the rest. Rachael swore he was getting smarter as he aged.

"What are you smiling about?" he asked as he put his arms

around Rachael's waist and pulled her to him. Rachael had to look up just a little to plant a kiss on his very pink lips.

"You," Rachael stated. They kissed again.

"Would you like more wine to go with our movie?" Rachael asked.

"No," Aaron answered. Rachael felt the twist of disappointment but added her wine glass to the dishwasher. She didn't like to drink alone.

"I will get our show cued up. We can just watch an episode or two and head to bed," Aaron said.

"Ok," Rachael tried not to let disappointment fill her voice.

"Don't be disappointed." Aaron came up behind her and squeezed her bum. "I know you love cuddles."

"I do. Go get the show set up. I'm just going to start the dishwasher," Rachael stated, but Aaron had already headed toward the living room. Rachael paused before pressing the start button. She needed to give Aaron some credit. After eight years of dating, and now three years of marriage, he did know her better than she knew herself at times.

She felt her lips flatten out into a line on her face again. The dishwasher beeped, and the swish-swoosh of the prewash cycle filled the kitchen. It would have been nice to do something on a Friday night.

3

FORT COLLINS

DIRK AND DIRK REALTY

"**Y**our weekend could not have been that bad," Karen stated, sitting down at the little white breakroom table with her coffee in hand. Karen's face was meticulously painted, her shoulder-length platinum blonde hair perfectly arranged in banana curls around her shoulders. She was dressed much like Rachael, dark dress pants and blouse, white and light green, respectively. Karen's blouse showed more cleavage than Rachael would have let out, and she had delicate two-inch black heels on her feet instead of Rachael's black flats.

"It just wasn't really good, either." Rachael wrinkled her nose. "We didn't do anything. Friday, we watched a show together, but then Aaron spent Saturday working on some project on his computer that he stayed up way too late working on and then slept 'til noon on Sunday."

"But then you had sex, right?" Karen made her voice sound dirty as she asked.

Rachael blushed a little. "We like our Sundays for that." It wasn't every Sunday anymore, but she and Aaron at least still had that going for them.

"See, it could not have been that bad. I have been coming up

18

dry for two weeks now." Karen started her rant. "There is not a decent man in Fort Collins. I had three dates – two on Saturday! FoCo is just full of students and technology brats. My first date on Saturday. I swear he was 12."

"He could not have been 12," Rachael exclaimed.

"Ok, maybe not 12, but he definitely lied on his Tinder," Karen continued. "And was most definitely looking for a more mature woman to stick it in." Karen's turn to wrinkle her nose.

"A little visual, but I get your point," Rachael responded.

"You are so lucky not to be in the dating scene in the twenty-first century. It is just a bunch of dicks and hookups. And even when that is what I am in the mood for, the buildup is often better than the sex. Hey, speaking of built up. Who was that that dropped you off this morning? There is no way that was Aaron."

"Greg does have a lot of his brother's looks," Rachael stated.

"Greg is Aaron's little brother. With the economy the way it is and so much tech moving to Colorado, Aaron got him a job."

"Little brother? He looks bigger than Aaron." Karen's eyes seemed to glaze over a bit. Rachael gave her a moment with her imagination. Greg and Aaron were the same height, but Aaron had gotten the brains and Greg had gotten the brawn. He spent hours at the gym every day, lifting and exercising. Where Aaron was soft, Greg was chiseled. All the way to the shape of their jaws. Somehow Greg had been gifted with the hair gene – he kept the sides and back short with a long top that was dark brown, peppered with red and black. You couldn't get dye jobs as good as his natural hair.

However, this strongly reinforced Rachael's theory that Aaron's brains had pushed out his hair. The brown, red, and black could still be seen in his mustache and goatee. What weight Aaron had on him, Rachael and Aaron had put on together. He filled out well from stringy computer geek to his adult body, as Rachael called it. Though the two of them might have indulged a little more than their adult bodies needed.

"Is he single?" The question brought Rachael out of her comparison.

"I think so." Rachael was unsure.

"You don't know? How old is he? What does he do? Spill, girl," Karen pressed.

"How about both of you work?" The manager's voice was clearly not amused as he poked his head into the breakroom.

"We are on break," Karen shot at the manager. A clean-shaven face sticking out of a matching suit and tie appeared in the door.

"Break's over – at least according to my watch," he said as he pointed at his wrist.

"It wasn't when you interrupted us." Karen put her hands in the air, palms up. The man shook his head and moved to the coffee pot.

"You are going to get us fired," Rachael hissed. "I am sorry. We are getting back to work." Rachael grabbed Karen and pulled her out of the breakroom.

"What a dick. He must be new. I didn't recognize him, and he didn't recognize me," Karen said, not quietly. She was one of the three human resources managers at Dirk and Dirk and usually knew everyone. "How many general managers does one realty company need?"

"All of them, apparently," Rachael mumbled. "Don't we have three HR managers?"

Karen gave her a small smile.

"Are you going to the gym at lunch?" Rachael asked.

"No, you ask me every day. But I might come watch you run like a rat in a trap if you promise to tell me more about Greg." Karen purred.

"Sure." Racheal turned for her desk before Karen could see her face. Karen was really nice, but she could not see her and Greg together at all. Rachael sat at her desk in her little cubicle. She had a few pictures of Aaron and her together; a photo of her late cat, Richard the III; and a picture of her and her best friend, Vicky, from her hometown in California. There wasn't room for much more.

Rachael's family wasn't close. Her older sisters left town the moment they could, and her parents were supportive and happy for her but were enjoying their well-deserved empty-nesting stage of life. She missed Vicky horribly and many of the familiar faces and comforts of California, but she was adapting to Colorado. Aaron was so happy here; she could be too.

Her fingers flew across the keyboard as she logged on and began researching and reporting. She didn't mind her job. She had very little interaction with customers – mostly doing research for the sales team and data entry. It kept her mind just busy enough that she couldn't think of other things, but not so busy that she needed to take any baggage home with her. It was ideal, really.

Karen did not find her for her little workout. Just 20 minutes of cardio and a few weights to keep the body healthy. It was actually Aaron who got her started on the routines – apparently, he learned them from Greg. She smiled to herself, remembering the feeling Aaron's hands on her arms as he helped her position the weights correctly the first time. "I actually hate this, but mathematically, exercising for 30 minutes every day will keep us both happy," Aaron had admitted.

He wasn't wrong. Rachael felt changes in her body right away the three or four years ago this had started. Was it really that long ago? She mused. They didn't do their workouts together anymore. And she wasn't always good about doing them on her own. Aaron's job was across town from hers and had an amazing gym in the building that she just couldn't get to. And Aaron had a good point that it was only 30 minutes, so he might as well take advantage of the perks of work. They would do something else together instead.

But they didn't make the effort to fill that 30 minutes. There just seemed to be a lot of practical reasons that their lives didn't involve each other as much as they used to. Maybe it wasn't the 30 minutes of fitness that made her happy, but the time with Aaron.

Was there a state of happiness that wasn't happy? Kinda like a state of fitness that wasn't really fit? Was that called complacency? If you could run five miles but never ten, were you still athletic?

4

GOOGLE DRIVE

4ADEER'S BACKSTORY

Written by Martin

I don't remember my mother. My only family were the others in the fighting pits. When we were too young to fight, we dragged off bodies, fed fantastic beasts from around the world, and cleaned. Endless cleaning. Surfaces that would never come clean of the grit, blood, and suffering that covered them.

Orcs come into their size young, and I tore the limbs off my first animal, a warm-up show for the real pit fights. I think it was a wolf. They start you with starved animals before you move to smarter creatures. Creatures more like yourself. I lived and breathed in my cage. Let out to fight, to practice, and eventually to breed with other captives, the masters always looking for the new biggest and best bloodline.

Apparently, my father was one of the best before one of his wounds became infected and he died in his cage. I wouldn't die in my cage like my father. I was regularly taken to a big female –

she had yet to bear fruits from my seed – when I found my opportunity for escape. She wanted to come, but fear held her in place. I left her with one more chance at a coveted child and never looked back.

I was pursued, but I left my pursuers in piles of bloody body parts and ran until even I didn't know where I was. I was lucky, passing a caravan that was being attacked by filthy goblins. In my memory, green greedy goblin faces, watched me fight. Taking bets but never offering up a fighter of their own. I charged in to defend the caravan, and, with my help, the goblins were run off without a single lost life. Goblins don't count.

Evan, the caravan leader, feared me but also respected my skills. He taught me how to survive, to live outside the pits. He gave me work until his work ran out. And then I was on my own. To wander, to survive, to live and learn. Someday I will be wise enough to start my own clan of Orcs. I will have honest victories over the villains of this world, and I will protect innocent life. Because that is the only thing worth protecting.

5

UNDERDARK

4ADEER

The first sign that you have changed realms in the Underdark is the air. Your usual dry pulls of the stale, slightly metallic substance change as your taste buds and lungs fill with the fire of memories and hope for the future.

— AARON, DUNGEON MASTER'S NOTES, CS3

4aDeer's triumphant roar echoed off the walls of the massive cave, all but silencing the rabble that had surrounded the party.

"*Holy shit, Martin,*" Tom exclaimed. "*Two natural twenties in a row.*"

"*I told you,*" Martin was matter-of-fact. "*It is what my character is meant to do.*"

"*OMG, you just exploded an enemy that wasn't really supposed to die. Stop gloating and role-play this out,*" Aaron demanded.

4aDeer's grin was almost lustful as the echoes of his triumph rolled into the distance. He took a step toward the leader of the mercenaries and felt his muscles quiver painfully. His victory had come at quite the cost. As if hearing his thoughts, he felt warmth surround him and smelled earth. A heal from Craig, no doubt.

"We have defeated your best," Lilly started. 4aDeer paused. He didn't like the word "we," but it was Lilly speaking, and Lilly had saved him long before he was pulled into this world with any of these other fools. "We will pass unmolested."

4aDeer dropped the head of his giant axe, making a ping against the ground. He might not be literate, but he could add to whatever show the bard was putting on. And a huge, muscled, greenish orc currently covered in leather, weapons, and the blood of enemies was pretty intimidating.

"Yes, that is the bargain we struck." The leader of the mercenaries was not a large man. The purple tone to his skin implied that there was something more than human hiding behind his stature. "But you better watch your back. We will not forget you."

Although he answered Lilly, his eyes locked with 4aDeer's. 4aDeer grinned. "I not forget. I dance victories on your grave."

The mercenary didn't take the bait but shrilly whistled. The band slowly moved off, back toward Elm City.

"Well done, 4aDeer." Poppy came to him and started cleaning up his many wounds and binding them so they would stop bleeding.

"If we didn't know this already, we have enemies in the area," Eismus stated almost carelessly. 4aDeer once again questioned Eismus' allegiance to the party but chose not to voice it. He would just keep a close eye on Lilly. She was too trusting and was starting to take a leadership role. 4aDeer hoped to lead one day, but one must have many victories to gain the confidence. All his victories were in fighting rings, and he was learning that life was much more.

"You can fight everyone everywhere!" 4aDeer didn't notice he was talking out loud until Poppy patted him on the arm.

"I think he might have lost more blood than we thought. Does anyone have another heal?" Poppy asked.

"I have one, but we should probably save them and rest for a bit before continuing," Lilly responded. Her hands quietly began beating a pattern on her pony keg drum, the song of rest.

4aDeer sat heavily, not that he would admit he needed it, and accepted a ration from an unidentified hand. Lilly's drum pattern helped soothe his wounds. He watched Lilly sit down on Craig; her hands didn't miss a beat. Craig had reclined against a wall near the entrance; his rock form did make an inviting place to sit. The rest was short, but 4aDeer felt much stronger. He hefted his battle axe and double-checked his large pack before purposely moving into line behind Lilly.

"You do know that we're looking for things, and with you two in front and behind me, literally all I see is the two of you," Lilly complained cheerily.

"Do you not like what you see?" Craig somehow managed to wiggle the big slab of rock that made up what would have been the behind of a human. The little green loincloth, hiding much speculation, fluttered with his movements.

"We are in a cave; it is like the perfect camouflage for you," Lilly laughed.

"What we looking for?" 4aDeer asked slowly.

"Mushrooms," Lilly answered. The small cave they were walking through suddenly opened up, their torches swallowed by the vast darkness of the cavern's size.

Do elementalings have dark vision? Tom asked. *Dark vision was the ability to see in the dark that most magical races had, all but Craig included. Greg's toon, being not a standard D&D race, was still fairly unknown to the party.*

"No, they do not," Greg answered. *"But the general glow of most of the caves is enough for me to see shapes and get around."*

"You can hold onto Lilly if it is too dark," Rachael offered.

"Ha, I can see that now," Tom laughed. *"You will hit your head on everything over four feet tall."*

"Could we please have this conversation in character? I'm going to start making penalties if too many conversations happen out of character," Aaron stuck in.

"I can see that now," Eismus laughed into the gloom. "You will hit your head on everything over four feet tall."

4aDeer shuttered, as he could swear he felt the eyes of God roll. He quickly crossed his axe arm to ward off curses.

The party wandered a little way into the cave but halted as Poppy's feet squelched against something moist. With a finger to her lips, she motioned for all torches to be put out. It took only moments for 4aDeer's eyes to adjust to the gloom that was not quite as dark as he first thought.

"It's beautiful." Lilly's voice was breathless, and 4aDeer nodded absently in agreement. The middle of the cave was filled with mushrooms of all sizes and shapes, some of them giving off a faint glow. The ground was a blanket of purples, greens, and browns. If not for the squish of Poppy's feet, 4aDeer would have tried to lay down — it looked so soft.

"Ok, we should spread out. I feel like that would be the most effective way to search an area this big," Eismus expressed.

"Don't split the party," 4aDeer said. He felt like he had seen that movie already.

"Would 4aDeer know that?" Rachael almost hissed.

"Are you still angry about the last session?" Tom answered before Martin could even get a word in.

"Why are you even talking, Tom?" Rachael did hiss this time.

Martin looked back and forth between Rachael and Tom. "Lover's quarrel?"

Greg's laughter shattered the tension. It was so hard he had to wipe a tear from his eye. "Sorry, guys, I have obviously missed something, but continue."

With the moment over, Martin cleared his throat. "Yes, I believe that 4aDeer would know that as it is basic tactical strategy. You see how hard it is to play him?"

Greg's laughter filled the kitchen again, and this time he got up and got a tissue and another beer. "Anyone else want one while I am up?" No one turned him down — other than Debby, who didn't drink — and Rachael quickly got up to help and get out of Tom's line of sight. Debby filled up the silence with out-of-context questions that Martin and Aaron did their best to answer. When beers were again full and on the table, the game resumed.

"Don't split the party," 4aDeer repeated. A sudden small boom followed by the sound of stifled laughter came forth from a pile of rocks lying on the ground that looked a lot like Craig.

"Moving on," Lilly's voice had a slight edge to it. "I agree with 4aDeer. I think we should just pick a direction. Poppy, will you stay in the lead? We need to spread out a little bit so we can see, but stay within eyeshot."

Without hassle, the party spread out, their noses to the ground. They had not gotten far when a piercing wail cut through the sounds of their squishing feet. Mindless of his own safety, 4aDeer ran toward the sound but stopped short, moving his head to one side.

"The mushroom is screaming?" he exclaimed, asked, and commented, as he wasn't even sure.

"We need shriekers!" Lilly whooped "Get it."

4aDeer didn't need much more encouragement as he took out his axe and bit into the mushroom's trunk. He pulled it out to swing again when he heard Eismus yell, "Look out!"

Two tall mushrooms with long, bark-like faces appeared out of the mushroom forest; their little feet seemed to scurry quickly in juxtaposition to their massive frames and large caps. He hesitated just long enough that the first mushroom arrived and jumped on Poppy. He wasn't worried, though. Poppy could take care of herself. He saw her body start to change before he had to focus on the second mushroom.

A drumbeat started behind him, and he could feel the power of Lilly's magic as it enhanced the party. As he freed his axe and prepared to face the nearest attacker, three fire bolts flew over his head, one missing and the other two slamming into his target. With a battle call, he charged the mushroom, which was quicker than it looked and dodged the biggest part of his axe. Another fire bolt flew over his head, slamming into the mushroom and lighting part of its cap momentarily on fire. Using the distraction, he swung his axe in an arc, intending to chop the mushroom in two, but he didn't quite have the angle, and his axe got stuck halfway.

The little whips from the mushroom stung as they dug into the flesh of his arm, and he cursed, one of his earlier bandages falling away.

"Down," Eismus' voice was commanding. 4aDeer dove for the ground and the mushroom exploded with Eismus' final spell. 4aDeer and his axe hit the damp ground with a thud. A muffled boom sounded from behind him, accompanied by the sound of laughter and squished mushroom.

"Did you just sit on it?" Lilly's voice giggled. She stopped her drumbeats, still watchful for more attackers.

"It makes a lovely chair," Craig grinned. "Care to join me?"

"Oh my god, how can you flirt with that awful wail still going on?" Eismus demanded with more venom than strictly necessary.

"Bark bark," Poppy's dire wolf form commanded.

"The sound is going to bring more." Lilly fought back her giggles.

"On it," 4aDeer said. He ran up to the shrieker and, with one fell swoop, finished it off. The screams died on its lips, and the party strained their ears for sounds of more enemies. 4aDeer picked up the mushroom carcass and moved it toward the party and away from the stem planted in the ground. Just in case.

"We should move," Eismus stated calmly after a few minutes.

"Agreed," Lilly echoed.

"If no one else is coming and the screaming has stopped, maybe we should at least fix up wounds and make sure no one is poisoned first," Craig added.

4aDeer did not miss that Lilly first looked at Craig before nodding and making her way over to him. Craig was too new. 4aDeer and Lilly had done a job together a few years ago before getting pulled to the Underdark. He liked and trusted Lilly, but he didn't quite trust Craig, or Eismus for that matter. Poppy, on the other hand, was a druid of moon, dedicated to nature and animals. 4aDeer had sworn to protect life after he escaped the fighting pits of Hebdenic. Poppy's druid nature embodied life and he felt that Poppy was under his protection.

"Craig can't be poisoned," 4aDeer deadpanned.

"We don't know that, and he is still sitting on a mushroom. It never hurts to check," Lilly explained. 4aDeer didn't like it, but he nodded and let Lilly rebandage him. "You don't look poisoned. How do you feel?"

4aDeer stood. He felt fine and stated as much. Poppy, still in dire wolf form, just whined and lay down on her belly.

"Teeheehe." 4aDeer, now standing, spun.

"Do you hear that?" he asked. He briefly looked down at Lilly as the laugh came again.

"Teeheehe."

"I did that time," answered Lilly. The dire wolf whined.

"It's a fey," Eismus stated. "But where is it coming from?"

"It is always above you," Craig answered, and the entire party looked up. Nothing.

4aDeer looked at Lilly.

"Why is it always above you?" he heard her ask...but he didn't see her mouth open.

"Lilly, ask above?" 4aDeer asked. Lilly shook her head, a spark of fear coming into her eyes.

"I wish Craig was nearer." Lilly's voice again, but her mouth didn't open.

"Teeheehe."

"Who's there?" 4aDeer roared as loud as he could, throwing everything he had into it.

"No need to yell," a tiny voice in his mind said. 4aDeer thrashed about looking for the source of the voice. He didn't notice his companions backing up from him in fear.

"Teeheehe."

He looked right at Lilly. Craig had come up behind her and wrapped an arm protectively around her upper shoulders.

"You got what wanted," he said, confused. Was Lilly scared of Craig?

"What?" Lilly asked. She drew further back into Craig. No, she wasn't afraid of Craig; she was afraid of 4aDeer.

"You wanted Craig closer to you, and he came," 4aDeer stated.

"Teeheehe."

4aDeer started wildly looking around again and swinging his axe.

"She didn't say anything about that out loud," Eismus said, puzzled.

"But I thought it," Lilly said, her voice gaining confidence. "We can't see where the voice is coming from because it's in our minds."

"Teeheehe. Not as dumb as you look."

"Who are you?" 4aDeer thought as loudly as he could. Suddenly many voices were speaking inside his head at the same time. He involuntarily dropped to his knees and put his hands over his ears. "Too much. Too loud. One at a time."

The voices vanished.

"I am Minksey," a little high-pitched voice said into the new silence. A slightly glowing ball appeared out of nowhere. As eyes focused, it quickly became clear that the ball was not really a ball, but a very small elf with wings. Maybe a foot tall, her dress was a bright blue matching her hair and her very large eyes. Little toothpicks for fingers, almost impossible to see, danced as she spoke.

"You have been so entertaining!"

"What?" Eismus asked.

"We have been lacking entertainment for months! Watching you stumble around here is lovely. How long do you plan to stay?" Minksey's voice was delighted.

"Umm, we're not. We are looking for mushrooms," Lilly thought slowly. "I don't need to say that out loud, do I?"

"Teeheehe. Nope," Minksey laughed.

"Why have you just been watching us stumble around and get attacked?!" Eismus' thoughts even hurt 4aDeer's head.

"Too loud," 4aDeer whined.

"If you are going to yell at us, we are going to leave." Minksey started to fly away.

"Wait, can you help us?" Lilly asked.

"We don't help," Minksey stressed the word don't.

"Could we purchase your services?" Lilly pressed.

"Ohh, we like things. We like shinies."

"We just happen to have some shinies," Lilly sounded genuinely surprised. 4aDeer peered at her.

"Are you surprised we have shinies?" he thought. Lilly turned her head to him and shook it.

"Teeheehe. Hard to keep your thoughts to yourself." Minksey giggled.

"Help us find mushrooms, and we will give you shinies," Lilly thought.

"Deal!" Minksey jumped on it.

"No deal," Eismus and Poppy's thoughts rang loud and clear at almost the same time.

"Hey, you can understand me as a wolf," Poppy thought.

"Lilly, hand me the list. I think we need specific things," Eismus demanded.

Lilly handed Eismus the list. "Damnit, we have a shrieker but this one is the wrong color." Eismus' glare could have withered stone.

"Leave her alone. We all passed around the list right after we got it," Craig came to Lilly's defense. A thought started to come from Lilly, but it was bit off before it could form. 4aDeer blinked, unsure of how to describe the sensation in his head.

He didn't really listen as Eismus worked out some deal with Minksey to guide them. Though any deal with the fey was a bad one — what else could Minksey be other than fey? 4aDeer looked up and blinked to see if anyone reacted to that thought… he was unsure if he was thinking just to himself these days.

"And we will stop there for this session," Aaron concluded. "I will assume you take a short rest while we finish up the social encounter with Minksey."

Everyone was already grabbing their stuff as Aaron spoke. Martin couldn't usually do weekday sessions, so it was nice to be able to have this one. He traveled the longest for the game and he enjoyed being home before midnight.

"I'm sorry I questioned you." Rachael held out a hand to Martin.

"I shouldn't have been telling you how to play your character." Martin took her hand and shook it. He liked Rachael. She was wise beyond her years and passionate about her knowledge but always prepared to admit that she was wrong.

"You shouldn't have been, but you also had a good point. I need to think more about what Lilly would do, not what I think a naïve person would do. I look forward to Friday," Rachael said.

"Me too — but I am off now before the wife makes me sleep on the couch." Martin picked up his player's handbook and shoved it into his bag.

6

FORT COLLINS

DIRK AND DIRK REALTY

"So, he is single, hot, employed, and the same age as you, 33." The speed with which Karen stirred her coffee increased as she spoke. "You have to set me up."

"I really don't think it's a good match," Rachael said. Although she wasn't sure why, her brain just didn't like the idea of Greg seeing anyone.

"Is there something wrong with him?" Karen flat out asked.

"I just have this feeling," Rachael said vaguely. "He is super competitive, and so are you," she added lamely.

She really didn't want to set them up. Last night, Craig had come to her defense when Eismus started picking on her. She had taken a moment to pointedly look at Aaron, but he seemed oblivious that she wanted to be defended.

"SET ME UP!" Karen's voice was commanding and brought Rachael back from the campaign.

"Fine," the response was automatic, and she regretted it the moment it came out of her mouth. But it was for the better, especially if they hit it off. Why was she daydreaming about Craig? He didn't even exist.

"Fine, fine, fine, fine. When are you free? Give me a few

choices." Rachael wrote them down as Karen began to rattle them off.

Twice Rachael found that her mind drifted back into the caves of the Underdark. By lunch, she had still been completely unproductive. It had been so nice to be defended by Craig. Her words to Martin were sharp because in her heart of hearts she was still upset about playing a bard. She usually played a paladin. A character that put him or herself into harm's way to protect the party. But playing a bard put her in a more vulnerable position. A position where she didn't always have to be strong and on the front line. And she was surprised that she enjoyed being protected.

Rachael was like everyone. "We all have a sob story," Rachael's mom used to say. Her parents had split when she was young. She didn't like her stepparents. But really, life hadn't been so bad. She had some tough growing up moments and she found that kids were cruel, but she had waded through it with a few close friends and a high enough GPA to see her through a local liberal arts college. Not that a college degree meant much anymore. Not in this economy, but it helped.

Nothing had ever really been handed to Rachael. She had to fight, struggle for every grade, every achievement, and even for Aaron. She met Aaron at a party. Smart, good looking — if a little scrawny — and well-spoken, he had no issues with women. The night they met, he made her feel special, giddy, and adored.

Her first night with Aaron had been incredibly steamy, and the next day came with the bliss of kids in love. Dating taught her that Aaron was not as free and ready for a relationship as she originally thought. And thus began the game of love and romance that ended with her taking home the grand prize, Aaron.

She smiled to herself, her mind drifting back to the first time Aaron brought her home to his family's house for dinner. She had been nervous; it seemed too early to her. The relationship was still too fragile to survive the drama of family. But Aaron had told her she was amazing and strong, and that his family would love her.

It had not worked out exactly as well as Aaron described, but he had stood by her the entire night as his family asked every question under the sun. He even deflected a few questions that he knew she wasn't ready to answer.

It was her strength he loved. But especially recently, she just wished her strength wasn't assumed. That maybe he would step back and make her feel special and protected once more.

7

FORT COLLINS

LIVING ROOM

A ll the cold showers in the world would not have helped. Between her daydreams about being protected and her memories of her first weekend with Aaron, Rachael was quite worked up by the time she got off work. Aaron was always home late, but consistent, and she decided to surprise him. Not much for sexy lingerie, Rachael put on her cleanest, laciest set that mostly matched. She put together an easy salad for later and popped open a bottle of wine. With a skip, she asked Alexa to turn on sexy jazz and waited.

Aaron came in the door a few minutes early, and Rachael jumped up and put her arms around his neck. He barely got his lunch bag on the table before Rachael leaned into him, kissing his neck.

"Did you have a good day." Her voice was husky.

"It was a day," Aaron monotoned.

"Would you like it to be a better day?" Rachael started moving her hips back and forth with the music. Aaron put his hands on them and moved with her a little bit before bending down to kiss her, his tongue quickly exploring the inside of her mouth. Rachael moaned and moved her body, grinding against his. He pulled away first.

"Alexa, stop," Aaron said. "Did you make dinner? I'm starving!" His hands moved off her hips while steering Rachael off to the side so he could come into the kitchen.

"I did," Rachael said. "Would you like to play with me first or after?" Really, she thought she was being obvious. But maybe he needed words.

"Let's see how dinner goes. I had a long day," Aaron answered.

Rachael turned around, trying to hide her disappointment.

"And don't be disappointed. I love you lots and lots." Aaron's hands traveled down her body, tracing the outline of her breasts against her shirt before ending at her hips. She turned her head so he could kiss her from the side as he pushed her away to fetch his dinner.

One hand slid under the blankets, retracing the path that Aaron's hand had lit up with sparks earlier that night. It paused, making a slow circle on Rachael's tummy before moving down between her legs. Rachael bent one knee to the side, careful not to bump Aaron's softly snoring form. She was so horny, and Aaron had just gone to his computer after dinner, his mind focused on everything that wasn't Rachael.

A moan caught in her throat as her fingers began slowly touching and rubbing the top of her clit, each rub moving her inner lips aside and adding layers of moisture to her fingers. Her body warmed up quickly, but her mind not so much, still hurt by Aaron's focus on his computer instead of her. She didn't want it to, but her mind drew her to the Underdark — the caves where a man made of stone looked out for her and protected her.

Does a rock man even have a penis? A large, rock-hard one. Rachael almost had to stop and giggle but stifled it by slipping one finger into her own opening, her palm still rubbing gently against her clit. Her eyes closed. Her body started to very minimally move as her mind-built Craig, or a more chiseled version of him. "The puns have got to stop, or I am not going to be able to orgasm," she thought.

Craig was seated on a rock, his not-punny figure sculpted like a Greek god's. Muscled legs braced his built body, and his chiseled abs formed an imposing backdrop for his fully erect shaft, which twitched in anticipation for her. And when she came to him, one strong hand pressed against her lower back, guiding her onto his lap. His other hand flicked against her breast, the nipple standing in anticipation. Rachael's breath was shallow, she slipped another finger inside herself, and in her imagination, she rocked hard against Craig's shaft. His hands slid from her waist to her upper back and pushed her breasts into his face. His tongue, firm but soft, was relentless on her cherry nubs.

She pushed herself forward again, her clit pulsed with anticipation. Craig's wide hands moved to her waist, supporting her motions as she slowly sheathed herself and began rocking slowly, squeezing at the top of every pulse. Her breasts bounced; Craig's tongue occasionally snuck forward to tease a nipple when it came close enough. Her motions increased in size and rhythm as moisture and heat built in her core. She looked down at Craig, his brown eyes looked up at her like she was the only woman in the world. Rachael opened her mouth to moan as her body reached its apex and ecstasy crashed through her being. She quickly moved her arm up to her mouth to stifle her sounds of pleasure. She turned to look at her husband, who remained undisturbed and snoring next to her.

It took a few minutes to catch her breath. She pulled the blankets off of her as a small trickle of sweat beaded between her breasts. Without thinking, she got up and washed her hands and face.

This was not her first orgasm; this was not her first orgasm next to her sleeping husband. But this was her first orgasm to someone — not Aaron — with a face. And the face her mind gave Craig looked too much like Greg's.

8

FORT COLLINS

DIRK AND DIRK REALTY

"When is my date?" Karen didn't even wait for break this time. Rachael yawned into her first cup of coffee for the day.

"What?" Rachael mumbled.

"My date. You promised you would set it up!! I need to know, because I want to fill the spots he has not taken."

Rachael took another sip of coffee and looked down at her phone, hoping that it hid the color coming to her cheeks. She had forgotten to call Greg and set something up for Karen. Ugh, she had been hoping to avoid him completely until Friday — usually easy, as Aaron and Greg didn't have much more than work in common. And role-playing. They both grew up with it.

"I will call him at lunch," Rachael promised.

"You better," Karen mumbled as she left. To Karen's credit, she brought Rachael another cup of coffee before break. Karen wasn't really bad. She just had abrasive moments.

Work was blessedly easy to focus on, as a new project came in almost with her second coffee. The morning passed quickly. She practiced a few things she was going to say to Greg while she did her cardio and then skipped some weights to make the call. He picked up after a few rings.

"Hi, Greg, it's Rachael, Aaron's wife."

"I know who you are, you don't need to explain how you know me," Greg laughed.

"I just don't normally call you," Rachael said awkwardly. The only reason she had his number was because she did the scheduling for D&D nights.

"No worries, is everything OK?" Greg sounded concerned.

"Yes, yes. Everything is fine," Rachael rushed. "But one of my coworkers saw you drop me off at work the other morning and she has been pestering me to set you two up."

Silence from the other line.

"I honestly don't know if you are even dating at the moment, but she is very pushy and insisted."

"No, it's fine. I'm just surprised. I'm not really dating at the moment." Pause. "But if you would like to have coffee with me and tell me about her, I might make an exception."

"Coffee?" Rachael repeated the word as if it was a foreign concept.

"Yes, that stuff that you suck down like water. You usually have equal parts coffee to liquor during the campaign."

"Right, sorry. I've had a lot of it today. I just didn't expect you to really consider it."

"Anything for you." Did Greg's voice sound lower?

"OK then. How about today right after work, OK? What time do you get off?" Rachael asked.

Greg laughed. "Well, any time I want to." Greg seemed to pause, looking for a response. When it didn't come, he continued on. "But usually by 4:30 p.m. Meet at the Starbucks on College Ave and Stuart?"

"I will see you at 4:30 p.m.," Rachael confirmed as they hung up. For a moment, Rachael just looked at her phone, the screen dimmed before going to sleep.

"This will not be weird," she said out loud before heading back into work.

9

FORT COLLINS

STARBUCKS

Rachael spied Greg's car in the parking lot as she walked up from the bus stop. She took a deep breath. Greg didn't know about her not-on-purpose fantasy, and the only person who could make this coffee weird was Rachael. She sent off a quick text to Aaron letting him know she was meeting his brother for coffee. He wouldn't get it until he was out of his work building, but it was the principle that counted.

Greg waved her to a table, two coffees in front of him.

"Matcha Green Tea Crème Frappuccino?" Greg pushed the drink toward Rachael.

"Thanks, and good memory. What are you drinking?"

"Just a regular black coffee, no cream for me."

"Why?"

"Have you looked at my body? My fat is at twenty percent. This…" Greg's hand moved from the top of his head down to as low as his arm would go, "…doesn't happen with cream."

"Oh, sorry." Rachael wasn't sure if she was sorry for asking, sorry for his lack of cream, or sorry she didn't know.

"Don't be! I'm glad I could fill you in. And I am NOT judging you for your drink."

"I didn't feel judged, but I guess I do now." Rachael scrunched up her nose.

"No, no, um, let's...." The color drained out of Greg's face as he started to backpedal.

"I'm kidding. Aaron has told me all about your fitness craziness," Rachael said as lightheartedly as she could manage. "But telling people you're not judging them is the best way to make them feel judged."

Greg put one of his beefy arms behind his back and scratched at it. "That is a good point."

Awkward silence. "Why is this so awkward?" Rachael thought.

"My friend, Karen. She has a nice heart but she can be very blunt. She is a little shorter than me, maybe five-foot-seven, wavy blonde hair that she does something with to make it rather shiny, and blue eyes that she always accents with pretty colors."

"Do you have a picture?" Greg asked.

"Right, that would have been a great idea. Yes, we are friends on Facebook. Give me one minute to pull her up." Rachael quickly got out her phone. Karen wasn't too bad about posting on Facebook often, but she was a daily offender. At least we would know if she was ever kidnapped.

"Here you go." Rachael handed the phone to Greg with Karen's profile up. Rachael took a drink of her Frappuccino and let her eyes wander around the room. It looked like probably every Starbucks in America did, if not the world.

"Well, she is conventionally very pretty," Greg eventually said, handing the phone back to Rachael.

"Conventionally?" Rachael said.

"I'm honestly not really interested. I like a little meat on the bones, if you know what I mean." Greg blushed a bit and Rachael felt her heart flutter.

"Karen is pretty thin, although she has pretty big boobs for her build," Rachael said a little too cheerfully.

"Hence conventionally. I don't mind a little makeup, but that is just a lot," Greg expanded.

"Have you dated since moving out here?" Rachael asked. "You have been here for over a year now. Does it feel like home?"

"Well, I've made some friends and had a few very casual dates, but I'm not sure exactly what I'm looking for. And it's starting to feel like home. I miss Mom and Dad and the beach — Colorado has so little water. I miss my old gym buddies back in Manhattan Beach. Weird bunch, but we got each other. I haven't really found that here yet." Greg didn't sound as happy as she had hoped.

"I'm sorry, I didn't know you were struggling." Rachael reached out and squeezed his forearm, his coffee lightly gripped in front of him.

He smiled back at her. "Don't be sorry. It has its perks, too."

Rachael realized that she was still holding his forearm and quickly moved her hand back.

"Maybe you just haven't found the right gym."

"I have thought that, too. My gym membership is up next month, and I'm set up to try out some different ones."

"Have you tried out 24 Hour Fitness?"

"No, I tend to prefer something a little more — what's the right word — exclusive?"

"Ah, ya, it is cheap. They let anyone in there. Not to bring up Karen again, but she says that the cheap places are where it's at in the town because 'Fort Collins is filled with rich, techy twats.' Just something to think about."

Greg laughed. "Maybe Karen isn't so bad."

Rachael took another sip of her coffee. It was almost out.

"I shouldn't stay too much longer. Aaron gets home around seven and I like to have dinner on the table for him."

"I hope he understands how lucky he is."

Rachael couldn't help the twinge of pain her in voice. "I hope he does, too."

Rachael didn't want Greg to respond. She didn't want to get into the insecurities she was having in her marriage. She didn't need to be on *The Jerry Springer Show*.

"Rachael." Greg's voice was both a command and a question. Rachael pushed down on the straw and noisily sucked up the last of her Frappuccino to distract herself. Whatever the moment had been, it quickly became that horrible sound of a straw just sucking up air from the bottom of a plastic cup.

"If you ever need anything, just let me know. I will see you on Friday, OK?"

Rachael didn't trust herself to take the straw out of her mouth. She just nodded and ran.

10

GOOGLE DRIVE

POPPY'S BACKSTORY

Written by Debby

I never felt at home with my family. We were a small family for gnomes — two parents and seven kids. I was the baby in every respect, coddled, given special treatment and every toy any other girl had gone through in my family. Gnomes love stuff, and my family was no exception. Our family business was trading goods, so I was surrounded by things, always.

Despite all this, I was never truly happy. When I was 20, I fell into a hole at the base of a tree. A fox den, I thought it would be the end of me. But no fox parents were home and the babies were fearless. They played with me and let me pet them until I lost all sense of time.

I didn't even notice when the fox parents came back, and they didn't notice that I wasn't a fox. I didn't think this was odd until I heard my family calling for me. I crawled out of the hole, covered in dirt and smelling of foxes. What I didn't know is that my natural magic had emerged in that hole, that my skin had darkened and my blonde hair had turned as green as the roots of the tree. The innocence of the foxes had awakened druid powers in me.

My family turned their backs on me. No longer favored, but still loved, they gave me to the Temple of Mielikki, the forest queen. There, I spent my years studying, tending, and training until I was ready to heal the world. I took my oaths and began my missions; the order always had work. People so easily ignored nature around them. I spent years doing good for the earth, stopping conflict, balancing soil, defending the forests and much more.

Recently I returned from restoring a forest, ravaged by a war long forgotten, and was told by my order leader, the great druid Enkrana, to travel to the Temple of Silvanus to receive his blessing. I cannot wait to advance through the ranks of our order. The higher your rank, the farther out and more important missions you're sent on. I want to help nature and all of her creatures.

And if I happen to collect a meaningful bit or two along the way, no one will judge me for that. I am still a gnome, after all.

UNDERDARK

POPPY

Although saturated with ancient power and memories, the Underdark must bend to the powers of the elements. Water has slowly carved out its own network, its own paths. And where there is water, there is life.

— AARON, DUNGEON MASTER'S NOTES, CS4

"OK, so it looks like if I get out of a 30-foot range of you, you can't hear me anymore," Poppy concluded. Somehow being in the presence of Minksey, the little fey fairy, was enabling them to communicate mind to mind.

"And this flippin' Minksey so far has run us in circles for 45 minutes, as far as I can tell," Eismus added.

"Not quite a circle, but the only mushrooms we've found that we needed are the death caps...and I am pretty sure those were by accident," Craig added, his voice frustrated.

"No, she definitely pointed in this direction for death caps.

Eismus, you are the one who wasn't more specific about mushroom location," Poppy accused.

"Now, I never stand up for Eismus, but we don't know how far apart these mushrooms are," Lilly added, giving Eismus a glare while standing up for him.

"Maybe that's what we should have started with." Eismus glared right back, though his words were directionless.

"No argue. Just find mushrooms," 4aDeer cut into the conversation.

"Bah, just keep walking in the direction the stupid fey led us, eventually we will either find the mushroom or a wall. This cave has to end," Poppy said. Her dire wolf form had run out shortly after their short rest last session.

The group was spread out as before, with Poppy in the lead as the best tracker. She chose to save her animal forms for another battle, and her very short legs led for a slow journey. Eyes to the floor, Poppy soon started noticing little paths. It was obvious that even though they had not come across many creatures, this cave was pretty heavily inhabited and had some sort of an organization system.

Not only that, but the patches of mushroom were not as scattered and random as she thought. They were currently walking through an area mostly made up of the shorter mushrooms, but "mushroom forest," for lack of a better term, seemed to cluster together in pods, their texture denser and more diverse.

She had stopped to run her hands along a chain of little blue mushrooms in the ground when she heard in her head, "Don't move."

"Why?" she thought back. The voice might have belonged to Eismus, but the wolf heard voices differently than Poppy, so she wasn't sure.

"Two green shriekers — I can't believe they didn't see you yet." Definitely Eismus.

"Does anyone have a way to cut it down other than 4aDeer's big axe?" Lilly asked out loud. Poppy thumbed through her spells, but she had nothing.

"I think the best bet is just to rush them," Lilly continued. "4aDeer heads in first, and we will be ready for anything that jumps out at us. 4aDeer, you must focus on getting both the shriekers down and then run with them back the way we came."

"Why back the way we came?" Eismus whined.

"Because we know what is there." Poppy agreed with Lilly. Eismus just looked around like the world was too stupid to understand him but didn't respond.

"Ready, 4aDeer?" Lilly was excited. Poppy could hear it in her voice. "One." Lilly began to count.

"So, is it on three or after three?" Greg asked.

"It is always on three," Tom huffed. This was not the first time this conversation had happened.

Poppy could hear Craig moving. She watched as the big rock man moved slightly behind Lilly in a very defensive stance.

"Two." Lilly continued. Poppy once again wondered if something was happening there, but before she could think too hard about it…

"Three!" Lilly yelled. 4aDeer was running like a dog after a bone. Poppy would have laughed, except two shriekers were much worse than one. She paused to shake out her ears, possibly some dire wolf hearing left over.

The pause may have saved her life, as a little black mushroom shot out of the mushroom forest and blocked her path, two more joining it.

"HELP!" she yelled as she cast a quick thorn whip. The trio of little beady-eyed shrooms were not big and the thorn whip managed to catch the closest one and pull it back. Her little gnome legs pumped as hard as they possibly could to reach her party.

"Why did you bring us more?" Eismus cried.

"Because I am a tiny fucking gnome at the moment. I can't do jack shit on my own," Poppy yelled back before transforming into a dire wolf. A bolt of fire whizzed past her head, completely taking out one of the little black ones. Her dire wolf form gave out a deep growl as she plunged into the fray, ignoring the little mushrooms that had jumped her and aiming straight for the biggest shroom, another of the tall ones from the first fight.

She managed to sink her teeth into it just after one of Craig's earth spells stuck it to the ground.

"Leave it alive if you can," Lilly's voice came through over their mental link loud and clear. Her drums beat rhythmically. If Poppy could hear the drums, 4aDeer was probably done with at least one of the shriekers. She felt a sudden burst of power and speed as Lilly's chant increased her abilities. With the big one contained, she could smell three more. Two of the little ones that followed her and another of the big variety — though a bit smaller.

She heard the drums falter and guessed that Lilly was in need. She spun on her hindquarters and leaped for Lilly, who was attempting to dodge attacks from the two small mushrooms. Poppy landed with a thud right on top of one, unsuccessfully biting at the other. Lilly's drums stopped as she flipped the hand axe she had been drumming with onto its pointy side and swung at the one pinned down by Poppy.

"I guess decapitating mushrooms is just as successful out of the kitchen," Poppy threw out.

The remaining little black one took a final swing at Lilly before Poppy took a bite too big for the mushroom to recover from. She quickly began spitting.

"Water," she croaked through the mental link, and Lilly was quick to start emptying out one of the water skins into Poppy's mouth.

"When did the shrieking stop?" Lilly breathed next to her.

"Got to go..." 4aDeer said as he jogged past them with the two green shriekers.

Lilly and Poppy both looked around for Craig and Eismus and found them already on the move with what looked like a forest of movement behind them.

"Run away!" said Poppy as she dug her paws into the soft floor and sprang in the opposite direction of the shrooms.

"Run away!" the phrase was echoed a little bit more than strictly necessary by everyone in the party.

They didn't run far or for long. It was quite obvious that the shrooms behind them didn't intend to chase. Lilly seemed to be having the most trouble catching her breath.

"Really, Lilly?" Eismus exclaimed.

"My legs are half your height. Leave me alone. We are all here and with only two mushrooms left to go," she wheezed.

"We are better off than we were before," Craig agreed. "What direction were the brown shriekers in?"

Eismus vaguely waved and Craig nodded.

"Same order. You are a better tracker as a dire wolf?" Lilly said and asked.

"Yup!" Poppy said, excited to be tracking as a wolf. She took the time to smell the green shriekers before bounding off toward the direction Eismus pointed. With Poppy in the lead as a wolf, the course was much truer, and she stopped just out of range of the two brown shriekers this time. She lay low on the squishy ground; her nose once again found the chain of little blue glowing mushrooms.

"Hold up, I want to check on something," Poppy said into the mental link. "I found these blue mushrooms near the other shriekers, too." She pointed them out with her nose, loving the mental communication, before following the line in the opposite direction of the shriekers.

She didn't get very far before a bloodcurdling cry came up from behind her.

"What the fuck!" she projected before bounding back toward her group. Eismus was standing out of range of the blue line but had clearly cast some fire spell toward shriekers. The foremost one was now burned to a crisp, and the one in the back was screaming the mushroom's version of bloody murder.

4aDeer started running. It almost happened in slow motion, and Poppy stopped to watch his feet cross the little blue line of glowing mushrooms. Immediately, more mushroom people jumped from inside the blue line to rush 4aDeer. He was thrown back from the force of their motion.

Not a second too late, Lilly's chanting reached a climax, and three of the four mushrooms that burst out of the forest stopped moving. Asleep, maybe. Poppy didn't wait to find out. She rushed the one still moving and pinned it to the ground.

"Get the shrieker, 4aDeer," Lilly yelled. 4aDeer ran past Poppy and her pinned mushroom and started chopping. The sound of Craig's massive steps found Poppy's ears. She waited until the last moment to get out of the way, as Craig simply sat down on her pinned enemy, the soft mushroom body crushed under his bulk.

"This is fun," Craig's wide, misshapen rocky mouth rumbled. Poppy yipped her agreement.

"I've got it," 4aDeer called as he picked up the chopped shrieker. Several of the mushrooms were still not moving. Her original guess that Lilly had cast sleep was correct, and they slept soundly still.

"Don't kill the sleeping ones!" Poppy exclaimed, as she stepped in front of Eismus.

"Why ever not?" Eismus asked, his voice curious. It was rare that Poppy told anyone what to do.

"I have a theory. I think that they are just defending their homes. I don't know if the shriekers are alive or not, but I think they are part of an alarm system, and as long as we stay out of their territory, they won't attack us." Poppy started backing up the way they came, and the party quickly followed, listening for noise. Nothing followed.

"I'm right," exclaimed Poppy.

"Maybe we can make friends," Lilly added. Poppy turned to nod and was surprised to see Craig, once again, right at Lilly's side. Lilly didn't seem bothered; they weren't that big a party. It could just be chance. "We need one more, as our fourth brown seems to have come into contact with some fire."

"I had forgotten about that," Poppy said through the mental link while shooting Eismus a special look reserved just for him. She hoped it was still clear in her dire wolf form. "But if my theory is right, we can skirt the blue circle and see if they have another alarm up."

"Right, lead on," Lilly said. Knowing what they were looking for and what to avoid made the last brown shrieker easy to find, but it was still on the wrong side of the blue. But now they knew if they could get in and out fast enough, they could possibly avoid the added combat.

"It will be the chop to make all chops," 4aDeer promised. "One swing."

"What do I need to roll to get that?" Martin asked Aaron.

"I'll give it to you on a 12 or higher. You have some experience chopping down mushrooms at this point."

"Sorry, I don't usually ask, but I wanted to put some good energy into the dice this time."

4aDeer strapped all his gear onto Poppy, lightening his load to almost nothing. Lilly had inspired him during the last fight, and he had not used it yet. He let the energy flow freely through him. Even Eismus crossed his fingers. "Last one without a fight, you can do it 4aDeer," Poppy whispered into the mental link.

As if that thought got him going, 4aDeer sprang into action, his muscled body charging the mushroom, axe at the ready. The shrieker started shrieking and...

"Is that a one?" Aaron blinked.

"It's these dice," Martin started saying.

"I'll let you use your bardic inspiration as a reroll," Aaron said.

"I feel like that's cheating, but I'll take it," Martin said, and he shook the dice to roll it again. *"You have got to be kidding me."*

"Ouch," Rachael said. *"I'll grab another round of beers. Aaron, please don't kill our fighter."*

"A three won't kill him, a one would have, but a three…well Martin, would you like to tell the party how this goes?"

Poppy watched 4aDeer's buildup in wonder, waiting to see the mushroom go down in one fell swoop. But in almost comic slow motion, 4aDeer missed… and not only did he miss, but he fell forward, face-first into the soft mushroom earth, his axe flying further into the mushroom forest.

A moment passed. Even the shrieker seemed to forget how to shriek, and then all hell broke loose.

"My axe!" 4aDeer yelled. The mushroom forest suddenly seemed to be moving forward as a wave of angry fungi charged. Poppy watched as 4aDeer scrambled up and barreled through the line. His set shoulders, butt, and then legs disappeared as the mushrooms continued moving toward the shrieker.

"Shit," polite Lilly swore. Hefting her own smaller axe, she looked to beeline for the shrieker. Poppy hesitated as she tried to decide who needed the most help. The first round of fire flew over her head and landed like a bomb in the oncoming wave. She bound forward into the hole Eismus created in the line, looking for 4aDeer.

She found him a little way in, cuts covering his body, wildly swinging his axe in circles at a group of mushrooms. They were actually staying pretty far away from the erratic ball of death. In her mind she shouted "4aDeer, to me." It took him another round of wild swinging before he found her direction, and then his steps were not as sure as they should have been — either from blood loss or dizziness, she couldn't tell. He curled his hand painfully into her fur, blood leaked into his eyes.

"Can't see well," he stated.

"Lean on me," Poppy projected. And as quickly as 4aDeer could go, she dragged them through the line of mushroom people. "Lilly, we need a heal or two. 4aDeer is with me... assuming we get to you," Poppy projected. She could feel little spikes of pain biting into her hindquarters as she half ran, half limped toward Lilly. The sounds of magical explosions bombarded her ears. Eismus was still not in view but she could hear the madness of his battle rage as he launched spell after spell blindly right behind the shriekers, holding back the line from Lilly, who was madly chopping away with a hand axe.

With a final push, Poppy jumped through Eismus' bombardment. Poppy felt fire singe her shoulder as one of Eismus' spells grazed her before hitting 4aDeer square in the chest, lighting his leathers on fire. He was conscious enough to stop, drop, and, well, he just stayed on his chest. But the fire was out. She could see his body fighting for air; otherwise, he didn't move.

"Lilly," she projected. The dwarf left the shrieker and ran toward them, casting her heal. A mushroom broke the line and struck Lilly hard across the face. She kept her feet and hit it full-on with her battle axe, keeping herself between the trying-to-stand 4aDeer and the glowing-eyed fungus. Poppy's hackles went up, but before she could charge, the earth began to rumble beneath her. The mushroom stopped attacking Lilly as Craig's low voice finished its spell. A 20-foot wave of stone and mushroom flooring careened toward attacking mushrooms. The mushrooms were thrown back, their attacks briefly halted.

"We have very little time. Cut down that shrieker, Lilly!" Craig bellowed. Lilly snatched the battle axe out of 4aDeer's hands and sprinted the few steps she needed to take. The mushroom that had attacked her nailed her backside as she retreated. Craig had turned from his destruction and barreled into the mushroom. It exploded under Craig's weight. The shrieking stopped as 4aDeer's axe finally bit the rest of the way through the shroom's base.

"I can't carry both," Lilly stated, looking between the mushroom and the axe.

"I've got it, baby." Craig scooped up the mushroom and, at the slowest run Poppy had ever experienced, the group limped away from the battle and across the line of blue mushrooms.

FORT COLLINS

DINING ROOM

"Martin, how many hit points do you have?" Rachael asked, referring to the numbers on the character sheet that equaled the character's health.

"Two, I had to make two death checks before you healed me." Martin looked pained.

"I'm glad you were holding onto your big spell. 4aDeer almost wiped the party," Debby said to Greg.

"What about me single-handedly holding off an army of mushrooms?" Tom gloated.

"Props," Martin said sincerely.

"Really good rolling and spell choices," Rachael begrudgingly agreed.

"You did build a berserking glass cannon. Did you buy magic bombs at the market with the group money for supplies?" Poppy accused.

"Well, I feel everyone having rope is excessive, and if we need to sleep overnight, I will just share a bedroll with Lilly," Tom said offhandedly.

"What makes you think you can do that?" Rachael asked.

"Just a feeling." Tom's look was nothing short of lewd. "You did make a naïve character who says yes to more and more things when she drinks."

"I would make you roll for every single thing," Rachael said with narrowed eyes. She let the tension ring for a moment before adding, "With Martin's dice."

"That is so mean." Martin's voice was lost over the laughter from the rest of the table.

Rachael stood and gathered up the remaining plates, her ritual to let her guests know it was time to move on. Greg stood with her, grabbing the few near him. As always, people turned and had short discussions as they gathered up their things. Aaron answered what questions he could. He always stayed put to keep an eye on his coveted items and plans hidden behind his DM screen.

Rachael put the dishes on the counter and opened up the dishwasher. It was still full of clean dishes. She wrinkled her nose, but before she could make a decision, Greg's thick hand came down. "So, where do these go?" he asked. Rachael felt her face light up and she motioned toward items' homes. Their hands brushed as he fumbled around her kitchen and both of them laughed as they went for the same thing multiple times.

Dishes came in and out fast with two working on the project, and the minute they were done Debby demanded an escort to her car and helped herself to Greg's arm. Rachael smiled and waved her off before sitting down at the table and finishing her drink.

"Would you like to get beers tonight?" It was obviously the tail end of a longer question that Tom was asking Aaron.

"Actually, that sounds great," Aaron said.

"Are you joining us, baby?" Tom's voice dripped in sarcasm.

"If I am invited. And Aaron," Rachael turned to her husband, ignoring Tom, "whether I go or not, I had a chat with Greg yesterday and I really think we or you should invite him to more social stuff. He is just not fitting in as well as we assumed."

"You think so?" Aaron asked softly.

"I was trying to set him up with my coworker, Karen, and we had a long chat about that stuff, and he misses his old friends and the beach." Rachael kept her voice down, waiting for Tom to say something mean. But people are full of surprises.

"I have not been the nicest of people," Tom admitted. "I have a pretty grating sense of humor. Let's have a guy's night for beers. You OK with that, Rachael? We can call it party bonding. I feel like I am becoming the odd man out sometimes anyway."

"I am totally cool with that," Rachael responded. "I think bonding would be good."

13

FORT COLLINS

BEDROOM

Rachael was not really "'cool with that.'" She was overdue for a night out. She wanted one so badly, especially if it was with Aaron. But Greg deserved to make friends and Tom had spent the better part of the last 10 years being a third wheel. Another night in would not hurt her. Or if she was really feeling it, she could go out alone, or maybe not.

It was also already 11:30 p.m. The guys would only be out for a few hours. She settled into her comfy 'PJs and picked up her Kindle, the most recent page of her fantasy book always saved, but she struggled to focus on the story. Her mind began wandering back to Aaron's campaign.

Craig had called Lilly "baby" tonight. And not like an infant, but like someone he cared about. Rachael and Aaron didn't have pet names. Did most couples have pet names? Rachael, except for the rare occasions when she added something to the end, like "Aaron-bear," or the occasional "sweetie," never really used them herself.

"Baby," Rachael said it out loud and put her book down. She closed her eyes; her imagination conjured a sexy version of Craig. His brown stone coloring stayed, but his body compacted, his indistinct features molding into corded muscles that ran the length of his body. His cut stomach tapered into a trim waistline. She ran her hand up her PJ-swathed body, feeling the rough cotton material pull up a little as it moved against her skin. Her hand traced the line of her neck and chin and ended on her own lips. She ran a finger over their soft surface before sticking the middle one in the side of her mouth and licking the tip, nibbling.

The lights in the room were controlled by an app, and she easily flicked them off, moving herself under the bedsheets…but Aaron wasn't home. Why would she need to stay under? Why did it need to be dark, anyway? She flicked the lights back on and shed every stitch of clothing she had while walking to the full-length mirror behind the bedroom door.

She took a minute to study herself. She was tall and broad for a woman; her wide shoulders underplayed her double-D breasts, but also kept her top half proportional. She carried most of her extra weight around her stomach. She absently stuck her finger into her belly button, doing little circles before slowly inserting it and pressing gently. She had a little of an hourglass figure, but mostly only if you look straight on.

Her hand absently started tracing the old stretch marks that almost looked like oddly colored fire across her stomach. Going all the way down and disappearing into a mass of fur between her legs.

Absently, she moved her hand to her slit, the moisture barely being held in by her inner lips. She let her fingers dip briefly before moving her hands up and up, slowly bringing her breasts together and twisting each of her nipples. She dropped her breasts and worked her hands up her slender neck, really the only thin thing about her, and traced her lips again. Her face was wide, the features a little small to be conventionally beautiful, to steal his word. Her eyes were very grey tonight, and her just-past-shoulder-length brown hair fell straight and boring.

She stuck the finger that had just been between her legs in her mouth; the other hand returned to her nipple.

Was it Lilly being called baby that turned her on? Or was it just the attention in general? She had to fight with Aaron to get him to unload the dishwasher. And Greg just did it — why was that hot?

Rachael walked to the bed and threw the covers off it. She lay down, taking just a moment to flick off the lights; the Underdark's dimly lit purples swirled around her. Craig's hands wandered, exploring. His hands would be smooth, the surface worn with his years of experience. He moved slowly at first, his hands exploring her curves. He traced from her stomach down before sliding and teasing her legs apart. His fingers ran across her slit, once, twice, then the heel of his hand slowly pressured her clit before coming up for more tracing. Her mind was not done with Craig. His body, his support, and his protection were waiting for her.

She pushed her face into her pillow, her butt coming as high into the air as it could without leaving the constant pressure of her fingers. In her mind, her face was in the warm, earthy smell of the mushroom forest. Craig was above her. His hands rubbed her shoulders and came around to cup her breasts; his fingers played with her nipples until they were almost sore. She moaned as he dragged his impossibly smooth hands down her waist. His mouth drawing a slow line down her spine, ending with a nibbling kiss at its base. Craig kneeled behind her, his hands played with and caressed her hips and bottom before his powerful hands gripped her waist. He pulled her to him, her butt pushed into his stomach, and she moaned with pleasure. His erection, not yet inside her, but stiff and strong, slid back and forth, teasing her sex. She rocked her hips forward, feeling spikes of pleasure as the heat inside her body started to build. Rachael's knees slid further apart on the soft blanket of moss as

Craig entered her, his manhood filling her and then sliding and teasing the outside again.

"More," she pleaded. He entered her again and began slowly thrusting his hips. His small circles matched her rhythm perfectly. Too soon, her body tensed; she felt her fingers inside of her as her walls pulsed with released pressure, and she moved them out, resting the heel of her hand against her clit as it throbbed in after-orgasm ecstasy.

She didn't get up this time to wash; she just threw the covers over herself and fell asleep, like a rock.

14

FORT COLLINS

COMPUTER ROOM

Rachael sipped her coffee as she scrolled through Facebook. She had missed her spin class, sleeping right through the beginning. Aaron had not woken her up when he came in. He was passed out, one shoe still on, and mostly still dressed. She must have been sound asleep if he was that drunk when he came in.

Baby pictures were the big thing now. So many baby pictures. It was like when women turned thirty, one just magically popped out. And if you had been trying, it was number two that popped. Of their own volition, her hands typed in Greg's name and she took a moment to scroll through his page. A selfie with Tom and Aaron from last night was the first thing to pop up.

Aaron hated selfies and was obviously hanging back, although enough liquor had been had at that point that his face was fighting a drunken grin. Tom looked like Tom. His thin nose matched his long face. Strands of his long blond hair had escaped their ponytail and a tiny shadow of peach fuzz, probably two days' worth of growth, was barely visible on his chin. Rachael could imagine him standing on his tippy toes to get his head into the pic. He had a few inches on Debby, but that wasn't saying much.

And then there was Greg. Greg was at the front, taking the selfie. His brown eyes were glowing with liquor, white teeth came out of his wide mouth, the lips the same pink as Aaron's. His hair tussled more than usual, as if he had been running a hand through it. It looked like they had had fun.

Rachael glanced at the tag — 1:45 a.m., taken at The Drunken Monkey. So, they had gone downtown. She scrolled down. Greg didn't post too often. It was mostly selfies of things he was doing. A few gym pics and articles from his old buddies about California and weightlifting. Honestly, if it wasn't for their coffee adventure, Rachael would have moved him in the douchebag category in her mind after looking at this. She didn't really know Greg.

Aaron didn't talk about him much, but when Greg needed a job, Aaron came through for him. And the one time Rachael had something negative to say about Greg, Aaron had cut her short and defended him fiercely. Greg could do no wrong in Aaron's eyes, it seemed.

Greg had a degree in business — as generic as a person could get. Aaron had gotten him a job in the sales department, where he seemed to be doing well. He was renting a nice apartment downtown and was obviously getting out.

plink Facebook chat request. Rachael clicked on it. "Speak of the devil," she whispered.

Greg: Thank you for chatting with your brother, but I wish you had come out with us.

Rachael: No, Tom wanted a boys' night out. You had more fun without me.

Greg: Not possible, but it was a good time. I have never really seen Aaron drunk before.

Rachael: LOL, it doesn't happen as often anymore — he says that hangovers are worse after you turn 40.

Greg: What did you do?
Rachael hesitated, heat coming to her cheeks as an image of her wet pussy sliding across the impossibly hard but soft surface of Craig's made-up dick filled her mind.

Rachael: Nothing, just cleaned up a bit and went to bed.

Greg: That was a long pause for nothing.

Rachael: I was trying to think of something that would make me cool. Like going to a biker rally. But it was taking too long to google if one was happening or not.

Greg: LOL

Rachael: How's the hangover?

Greg: Not too bad — drank a lot of water and took some Aspirin before I went to bed.

Rachael: Good planning, got to keep things flowing so that body fat percentage doesn't go up.

Greg: Indeed. Speaking of which, I am headed out to the gym soon. Would you like to join me?

Rachael: Haha, funny. I think that sleeping through my spin class was a sign.

Greg: You spin?

Rachael: Just the one class, Saturday.

Greg: We should spin together.

Rachael: Nope — I will look like Lilly after our sprint last night. And I can't fall from your graces like that.

Greg: I don't know, I think you would look amazing covered in sweat.

Rachael: No one looks amazing covered in sweat.

Greg: You only think that because you haven't watched me glisten.

Rachael thought about that and it sent a small shiver of anticipation down her back.

Rachael: Go to the gym and stop bothering the married ladies. You are a menace.

Greg: ^_~

15

FORT COLLINS

DIRK AND DIRK REALTY

"I can't believe he said no. You showed him my selfies from Facebook?" Karen's voice was grating.

"I did everything you told me to and more. The man is in love with California and the gym and probably himself. I don't know what else to tell you," Rachael responded calmly.

"Well, fuck him then," Karen almost spat.

Rachael just took a sip of coffee. Karen seethed in her own thoughts for a minute, sipping her own coffee before asking, "How was your weekend?"

"Fine," Rachael responded tiredly.

"Didn't do anything?" Karen pressed.

"Yup," Rachael said. "We are just stuck in this rut and I am so frustrated. This morning, the barista at Starbucks told me my scarf was a nice color and I was ready to drop my pants for him I am so desperate for a compliment." Pause. "My weekend — the highlight, *D&D* on Friday followed by time with my fingers. Saturday I even missed my only event for the day, spin class, and then played *Zelda* by myself until Aaron got hungry, and then we ate separately while each working on our own things. Sunday, I cleaned the house while Aaron painted miniatures and then we played board games with other people until it was time to go home and go to bed."

"Sad. I thought Sunday you would have at least gotten some playtime," Karen tried to joke, but Rachael was just not in the mood.

"Ya, me fucking too. I'm going to beat *Zelda* before I get to have sex again at this rate. I don't even know what the fuck he is working on. And when I ask, he just says 'stupid videos on YouTube.'"

"It probably is just that. Men are simple creatures," Karen stated. "Well, break time is over. I'm headed back to my desk."

"Hey, Karen, thanks for listening. Sorry I ranted."

"I know we aren't really close friends, but it sounds like you need someone to talk to. I am here for you."

"Thank you, that means a lot." Rachael gave Karen a quick hug before heading back to her desk.

FORT COLLINS

OPEN HOUSE

Dressed in a grey pencil suit and low heels, Rachael smiled at people and handed out flyers as they left the property that one of her sales agents was currently showing. She didn't usually work directly with customers, but Mr. Johnson was shorthanded and asked Rachael to fill in.

The day's showing was for a large condo in one of the new complexes a mile from Old Town. It was a modern building with every amenity. Clean, eggshell white walls were decorated with simple crown molding. Most of the house was covered in wood floors or tiles of brown, red, and blue. Even though Rachael wasn't really part of the sale, she was proud of it.

"Don't forget a flyer. Thank you again for coming," she said cheerily.

She looked around for her next victim and was surprised to see Greg walking down the complex hall. He must have been on his lunch break. His dress pants were black, his button-down white and blue striped. The sleeves rolled up to expose half his biceps.

"Greg," she waved. He smiled charmingly at her.

"Hey," he said. "I didn't know you were showing this place."

"I'm not, really," Rachael corrected. "I am just helping Mr. Johnson. He is short-staffed today and my workload is the lightest. Are you in the market?"

"Not really," Greg laughed. "But I am thinking about it, so I have been going to some open houses to check out my options."

"Cool, would you like a tour?" Rachael asked.

"That would be great," Greg answered. Rachael put the flyers on the little folding table with bright decorative flags, making it easy to see. When she looked back at him, he had put out his arm. She folded hers around it and started guiding them around the condo, periodically pushing him away to go look more closely at bits and rooms.

As she pointed out features, she remembered back to buying her house with Aaron. They had looked at probably 50 places before picking the one they lived in now.

They had not been married for long when Aaron landed his job in Colorado. He had loved his university days out here and jumped at the chance to come back. Especially as his best friend Tom, they had gone to school together, never left.

Rachael had been in Colorado for some of her degree but had transferred a few times. Struggling to find the right fit. She had not been as excited as Aaron to move, but his joy had been tangible and she wrapped herself in it.

"We looked at some condos too," she said to Greg. "There was this one out by the stadium that was covered in dog poop."

"What?" asked Greg.

"Really!" Rachael laughed. "The renters just let the dogs poop inside and the owner never checked on his place. We were the first showing. The realtor had no idea! We ended up spending the entire time documenting the damage to the condo."

"That doesn't sound very appealing," Greg said.

"The dog poop wasn't," Rachael responded. "Although it didn't smell as bad as I would have guessed. But making the memory with Aaron was appealing. Life isn't about what goes right, it is about the memories you make along the way." Rachael smiled to herself. They had so many of those, but not as many memories recently. She felt her smile drop.

"And this is the master bedroom," she said. She made a little twirl with her arms up. As if the motion could help her shake off her negative thoughts and regain her earlier excitement. Her twirl ended facing Greg; she met his eyes, which had watched her spin, and he smiled.

"Go investigate," she commanded, making a shooing motion with her hands. She broke their eye contact. Her smile back in full force.

She watched Greg poke his head around and rattled off some obvious facts about the space. His body moved with purpose. His clothing fit like a glove, black shoes shined like new against the hardwood floor. She could see every muscle move in his shoulders and corded neck. His inquisitive face was clean-shaven and his hair styled, not a piece out of place. Sunglasses sat spun around backwards on the back of his head.

Rachael stifled a giggle and turned to face the window. Her imagination drew a little mouth and nose below the sunglasses. Now Greg was two people! His front sharp and human, his back the hairy monster from the deep. Both sides still hot as hell.

Greg's warm hand on her shoulder sent a shiver down her spine. How long had she been looking out the window?

"Are you cold?" Greg asked, concerned.

"No," Rachael stepped away and covered her flush with a rush of information. "But the air conditioning in here is brand new! Ready to see more?"

She held out her arm for Greg to take this time. And Greg barked out a laugh and took it. She guided them through the last two rooms, the condo tour over much sooner than she wanted.

"This has been much more fun than looking on my own," Greg said as they got back to the front door.

"It has been fun playing real estate agent with you," Rachael responded when they were back by the door. "But I need to get back to work. Here, have a flyer."

She watched his backside walk down the hall. It really was a good view.

GOOGLE DRIVE

EISMUS' BACKSTORY

Written by Tom

I never knew my parents. As a baby I was found, abandoned, and taken to the village of Temling in the elven forest. One of the few villages where humans and elves lived together peacefully. It should have been a haven for an abandoned child. But drow blood runs strong even in half-breeds like me. And the universal hate for the drow runs stronger still. I was surrounded by distrust, disdain, and prejudice. A haven it was not. I was tormented by those my own age, bossed around by adults. My own adopted family tried to limit my education, to contain my abilities and expanding mind.

As soon as I was able, I left. I wandered, my budding limited talents with magic allowed me to put on street performances to feed myself and steal when I could not. I was on the outskirts of elven land when I saw my first true sorcerer. It was from a distance, his grey-scaled skin reminded me of my own drow grey, and I followed him as if in a trance.

It hadn't occurred to me that he was leading me somewhere. I was too young and too stubborn to think anything bad would befoul me. He entered his house, leaving the door open. I hesitated only the amount a young teenage boy would. I thanked the cursed gods that created me for my good luck. An opened door would be easy pickings.

It would be 20 years before I left that house. Twenty years I don't care to recount. But 20 years later, I emerged. My skin scaled, my power crackled within me, and the bloody corpse of my mentor, teacher, and abuser now cooling in my past.

My control over sorcery is absolute, but my power is limited by my knowledge and body. My old mentor told me stories of the Dragon Temple to Zoindinth, the elemental dragon of fire. I will find this temple; I will increase my power. And I will learn the spells that will let me lay waste to the hometown that should have protected me. I will rebuild it in my own image.

18

UNDERDARK

EISMUS

No one knows who first discovered the Underdark. But traders were the first to utilize it, to find its shortcuts and lands unknown to mortals. Few survived at first, but those who did became wealthy beyond imagining. They established routes and small towns to aid them along the way.

— AARON, DUNGEON MASTER'S NOTES, CS6

The party was seated at a large table in the only tavern in Elm City. Weeks ago, it seemed like a lifetime to Eismus, they had been enjoying themselves at a tavern on the elven and dwarven border. All the patrons, the party included, were mysteriously put to sleep and woke up in cages in the Underdark. Only 10 people had survived and escaped the cages. Their party of five, four simple folk, and the tavern keep, Steve, who had surprised even himself with his fist-fighting abilities.

The simple folk had all gotten jobs in town to make ends meet and Steve now worked at the tavern. They could use all the money they could get, especially with Lilly making so many bad deals. Eismus watched Steve return to his place behind the tavern bar before digging into breakfast. Mushroom porridge, again. He was getting tired of the lumpy beds and the bland food this tavern had available.

"Look, I just think we should make a party preference rule," Eismus said around bites.

"What?" 4aDeer asked as he fingered the head of his always shiny axe. Eismus was pretty sure he even polished it in his sleep.

"When two people of the same sex…" Poppy started to say.

"No, definitely NOT any of that," Eismus interrupted. "I just feel like the party occasionally struggles because personalities are being valued over skills. Also known as Craig obviously has a crush on Lilly, but Lilly is more resilient than me and I should be protected first."

"But I healed your ear," Craig said, pointing to Eismus' left ear. Eismus flushed. The last two ingredients on their list had not gone to plan at all. Lilly ended up making a weird, small troll thing, called a boggle, laugh until it cried. Craig had found wood and insisted on bringing it back with them to sell. Then, getting back, they were attacked by slavers just leaving town. But this time, 4aDeer was low on energy and unable to surge into battle. Craig wouldn't drop his wood and started laughing every time someone asked him to. He was asked a lot and did not do much other than laugh.

It was Poppy's wolf form that saved them, but not Eismus' ear, because Craig stepped in front of Lilly instead of him during the fight. Not once, but twice. He lost his ear on the second hit. Craig had fashioned him a new one out of dirt and breathed life into it. It wasn't quite the same color, but he could still hear.

"I need to be protected. Lilly is a dwarf; she is stout and wearing leather. I should be getting the first line of defense. My damage is what leads us to victory in battle," Eismus elaborated, fuming, his power crackled in the air around him.

"I'm sorry," Lilly finally said, a little sadder. "I can't make decisions for Craig, but personally I don't trust you, drow."

"What?!" Eismus seemed genuinely surprised. He distractedly glanced down at his hand, the grey scales clearly visible there as he knew they were on his face. The drow as a people were a mix of elven and dragon magic. They were powerful and very well known for shifty alliances. But that was racist.

"Burn mushroom. Only helpful when the going gets tough," 4aDeer deadpanned.

"Poppy." Eismus turned toward her, looking for defense.

"What? I don't trust anyone of you people. As a druid of the forest, I am literally trapped away from the sun in a world that gives me no light. If I knew how, I would abandon all of you all just to see the sun once."

"Well, at least we are in the same boat," Eismus sneered. They might not trust him, but they had taken him into their party. And they listened when he spoke, mostly.

"Look, we are trapped down here for the time being. Let us return to the temple with the last of the list and see what the fey priest has to say," Lilly begged.

The group, now all healed up and rested, walked the gathered mushrooms and remaining quest items to the Temple of the Fey. 4aDeer and Poppy waited outside the entrance. The bright red walls with gold leafy branches decoratively painted had not changed, though in places the details were so intricate that they almost looked like they could have been fluttering in the breeze. A large, lifelike gold tree was both built and painted into the wall — the start of all the gold leaf branch patterns. Eismus felt a little bit of sweat trickle between his shoulder blades underneath his robes.

They were led from the alter to a back room, just as richly painted but with a giant mahogany desk in the middle. The fey priest's chair made a terrible noise as it scraped against the stone floor in his haste to stand.

"What took you so long? Why did you not bring these last night!" the fey priest demanded. Assuming this was permission to approach the desk, the party moved forward. Lilly happily took the items out of 4aDeer's pack and handed them over to the fey priest, who in turn handed them to an underling, its small size allowing it to completely hide behind the desk. "It doesn't matter. Return to me this evening to ask your questions."

"No, that wasn't the deal," Lilly voiced.

"I also said 'time is of the essence, child,'" the fey priest met her eyes. "If you so badly need something to do while you wait, I need some letters delivered, and I am expecting a delivery later today that will need to be unloaded."

"You want us to deliver your shit after not paying us for your shitty job?" Eismus asked incredulously.

"This one has a mouth on him," the fey priest stated. He turned to Lilly.

"Here, child, I will pay you 15 obsidian for each letter delivered and three iron for each person helping unload my delivery."

"That sounds...." Lilly started.

"Like cheap labor to me," Eismus cut in.

"All my best, Lilly, but you really are bad at making deals," Craig stepped in front of her and next to Eismus.

"You give us some information now, in good faith, and tell us more about these letters before we agree to deliver." Eismus pushed his pointer finger against the priest's desk for emphasis.

"I will kill two birds with one stone," the fey priest declared as he pulled a map out of his desk. It was very simple on a plain cloth, and just from a glance Eismus would have guessed it was of the town.

"This is a map of the town," the fey priest stated.

Eismus felt movement off to his side and was surprised to see Lilly pull up beside him...though on second thought, Craig's bulk did take up most of the side of the table.

"My letters need to go to these locations," the fey priest said. He marked Xs on six spots in town and drew an arrow going out one of the tunnels. "The seventh one," he pointed at the arrow, "will be down this tunnel and should be obvious. It is not on the town map because it is technically not in town. But the way to this delivery is clearly marked."

"What are the letters for?" Lilly asked.

"That is presently none of your concern," the fey priest sneered.

"Presently?" Eismus repeated.

"Look, hard times are coming. This is a peaceful community — one of the last neutral territories in the Underdark. I know you just want to get home, but your arrival time is fortuitous." The fey priest looked hard at Eismus.

"Fortuitous?" Disbelief filled Craig's words.

"Maybe 'bad' would have been a better choice," Eismus picked up Craig's tone of voice. "You do know that we were pulled here from our world against our will and with everything we owned ripped from us? 4aDeer had to kill someone with a splinter."

"And Lilly had to see Eismus' dick," Craig added.

"At least I have one," Eismus mused, fully agreeing with Craig's sentiment, if not his example choices.

"The letters," Lilly broke in. "You are looking for people to help you defend the town."

"I am," the fey priest responded. "And I am willing to pay to get these delivered to the right people. You can keep the town map regardless of your choice to take the job or not — my show of good faith." The fey priest almost choked on the last words. Fey loved to make deals in everything but good faith.

"Ten water chips for the day," Eismus suddenly said. "That

gives you all the labor you need and guaranteed delivery of the letters, assuming their recipient is physically present."

"Five. Ten is too rich for my humble establishment," the fey priest automatically responded.

"This desk is worth a fortune; how can that be true?" Lilly exclaimed.

"That question is why you are staying quiet, Lilly. Ten is already a bargain but I will throw in a song during the unloading. Our bard here can make physical tasks go faster and with cheer. It will not only be us, but everyone involved who gets the benefits."

"I would like to hear that. Ten is the agreement, 10, 10, and 10. And said thrice the deal is sealed." The fey priest turned to Lilly and handed her six envelopes in a bunch and a seventh on its own. "Now, these six go to the Xs in town. However, this one in your left hand can only go to Grogith Gotlittle, the cave troll who lives down the path marked on the walls. Try not to scare him. He ate my last delivery man."

"We didn't ask where his normal delivery guy is. Or about the people that we are delivering to." Eismus couldn't tell if Craig's gravelly voice was crying or laughing.

You are not any better at this than me," Rachael shot at Tom. "We should have rolled this out instead of trying to match wits with Aaron."

"No one in our party really has high charisma and we are dealing with fey, a charisma based being." Martin pointed out the low odds, in this situation, of relying on dice rolling. "But on principle, I agree with you. We should not be matching our wits against Aaron; Eismus should have been verbally sparring with the fey through dice."

"Ten water doesn't even cover the damages we took during the first job, and now we are possibly facing a cave troll. What level is that, like 10, and we are two?" Debby was annoyed.

"If you live, you might get something out of it," Aaron stuck in. "I will try to be better about asking for rolling social encounters. But it

works both ways, you can also ask to roll a skill and we will play it out based on your roll."

"I think we all need to be better about remembering to roll our social skills," Rachael added. "I love how in character we are staying but dealing with the fey is starting to sound like my conversations with Aaron about who is doing laundry. And Aaron hasn't washed his own underpants in seven years. So, we know how that goes."

"I don't do mine either," Martin added. "I just thought it was a girl thing."

"It most certainly is not; no one likes to do laundry." Debby shook her head dramatically.

"How much did we get for all the wood again?" Tom redirected the party to the task at hand.

"Almost five mithril," Greg answered.

"I vote that we just grind wood and drink until we meet someone who knows the way out. We will be rich in no time," Tom recommended.

Laughter from the entire table. "That is not a bad idea, but let's leave it as a last resort. I say we give this fey priest two chances. If both jobs don't pan out by the end of today, we will either check out the other temple or grind wood until we are rich." Lilly said. "All in favor?"

Ayes were heard around the table.

Aaron's grin turned absolutely malicious "Then let the mail delivery begin!"

"I say we split up," Eismus said, the map now spread out on one of the tavern's tables. All seven letters sat next to the map. "Each of us delivers one letter in town — I will deliver two — and then we can meet at the cave entrance to do the cave troll all together."

"I don't want to split the party," Lilly immediately said.

"Why can't we just get along?" 4aDeer said tiredly.

"What do you recommend then, 4aDeer?" Lilly asked sweetly.

"Two groups, deliver on west side first," 4aDeer motioned to the left side of the map. "That way same area, call if trouble."

"Actually, that is a killer plan," Poppy nodded.

"Let's do it," Lilly said.

"Craig, with me," Eismus divided up the group. "Let's leave 4aDeer to protect the ladies."

"I was thinking if there was a lady in each delivery party it would make us seem less intimidating," Craig said. He looked directly at Lilly.

"Good thinking," Eismus looked back and forth from Craig to Lilly. He took a breath and purposely split up the budding couple. "Poppy, with me and Craig. 4aDeer and Lilly have worked together before, so it should be smoother this way." Eismus frowned as Lilly and Craig slowly stepped away from each other. He didn't like it. He didn't like it at all.

"It's OK, Lilly, I have protected you before," 4aDeer said slowly, not quite understanding the holdup. Lilly and Poppy each took three letters; Lilly grabbed the one labeled Grogith Gotlittle as well.

"I know, I have no doubts in your skills, 4aDeer!" she exclaimed. And the two of them set off, but not without Lilly's eyes coming back to meet Craig's one more time.

"Stop for a moment," Aaron halted the game. "I am going to give both Greg and Rachael inspiration for that because A) you split up for the sake of the party and B) I'm even starting to think a spark might be there. And please remember there isn't a traitor in the party."

"You are giving them inspiration?" Tom asked slowly.

"Yes. Did you not think it was good role-playing? Rewarding good role-playing is the point of the inspiration system in D&D fifth edition." Aaron nodded enthusiastically, excited to try out new game mechanics.

"Did you two think it was good role-playing?" Tom asked carefully.

Rachael's face turned pink and she had to try twice to defend herself. "I did, I guess I got really into my character and forgot that the

DM is my husband for a minute there, though. I am assuming that is your outrage, Tom."

"I thought it was quite good as well," Martin added. "Very fitting for the young, naïve female bard. I think it's extra brownie points because this is only your second time rolling a female toon? Right, Rachael?"

"Yup, but this is making me blush. Could we just go back to playing?" Rachael mumbled.

Although dulling slightly, Poppy was a nature druid. Her flawless brown skin glowed and was accented by a thick, braided lock of forest green that almost trailed on the ground. Her build was very slender for a gnome, but her face was round, with wide trusting features and green eyes flecked with orange and gold.

Having the three-foot gnome deliver the letters was a no-brainer. The first three letters were delivered with ease. Doors opened with some suspicion, but then as eyes finally wandered closer to the ground to see Poppy beaming up at them, doors were quickly opened. Eismus and Craig hung back, ready to jump out if anyone attacked Poppy.

"No, I'm sorry, I can't come in for tea. I am on the job," Poppy responded on the last delivery.

"Ready to go, gnome?" Eismus showed himself and purposely walked toward the opened door to speed up her exit. Shafulb, the ugly mutt of at least three different races, blushed and bashfully looked down at the ground.

"I'm glad she is not alone, though good choice to send her in first," Shafulb said to the ground.

Eismus acknowledged Shafulb's words with a nod and let his long-scaled arm dangle so Poppy could grab onto it.

"For the trinity of Elm City." Shafulb straightened as he said it, his hand made a fist in front of his crotch.

"For the trinity of Elm City," Poppy repeated carefully as they turned to leave.

"Is there a salute or something I missed?" Eismus asked as they headed toward the merchant district. The rendezvous point was at the plate armor stall so 4aDeer could have another drool. It was also on the east side of town so they would be close if there was trouble.

"No, and he was the first one to do that," Poppy added. She described the "for the trinity of Elm City" for Craig, who had joined them once out of sight of the delivery house. "I think it is something to take note of, though I don't know if it is important."

Lilly and 4aDeer were already at the stall. Eismus couldn't help but notice a superficial but long cut on the orc's lower jaw.

"Everything ok?" he enquired.

"Peachy," Lilly answered brightly. "Are we ready for our last delivery?"

"What happened to your face, dude?" Craig asked.

"Would an ancient elementaling earth mage say dude?" Aaron cut in. "It is the third time you have done it."

"Craig is a bro," Greg answered. "When you are that old you just don't care anymore."

"Fine," Aaron grumbled.

"I am not stupid," 4aDeer stated as if that answered everything.

"He didn't say you were stupid. He said the letter was stupid. And I still can't believe how good you were!" Lilly stuck in. Eismus didn't like it that she sometimes seemed to talk to 4aDeer like he was her pet dog. Not that 4aDeer was much smarter than one, but he didn't need to be talked down to.

"I didn't hit back," 4aDeer sounded shocked.

Eismus was shocked. "Whoa, a guy hit you and you didn't hit back or even defend yourself?"

"Murgphy was not excited to receive a letter from the temple. Well, honestly, he was just really grumpy about everything. But superficially when we tried to give him the letter. He didn't even touch it. Just told us to take our devious temple rhetoric and leave; 4aDeer decided it would be a good idea to push it into the man's hands so that we had fulfilled our end of the deal." Lilly took a calming breath. "At this point, Murgphy decided to use the letter as a weapon."

"You can crit with a papercut?" Tom couldn't help the giggle that came out of his mouth.

"I can crit anywhere, anytime. Except when I want to," Aaron said magnanimously.

"Didn't think would hurt," 4aDeer added. "Then Lilly pulled arm. Talked about armor and now here."

"And now we are going," Craig added. "One more delivery."

Eismus motioned for Poppy to take the lead, and the party easily found the cave opening that the fey priest had marked with the arrow. Words and a picture had been carved into the wall. The picture was of what could have been a cave troll, though it looked more like a stick figure with a big head. The markings reminded them of a DANGER BEWARE sign, but in a different language, so they were unsure.

"Cave troll," Lilly mumbled, irritated.

"Cave troll," 4aDeer repeated, excited. Eismus could see his hand flexing as he tightened and released his grip on the axe.

It was a good 30-minute walk, passing a few openings along their path. Lilly was at the rear and chalked the walls to speed up their retreat if needed. Cave trolls were big, ugly, usually unfriendly, and illiterate. What this one needed a letter for was beyond Eismus.

"May I see the letter?" Eismus asked as they walked.

"Nope," Lilly didn't even stop. "We are under strict orders not to read them. And I can't think of another reason you would want it."

"Hold up." Eismus stopped the line. Poppy stopped as well, looking behind her. "I'm not going to read it, Lilly. I just want to be the one who hands it to him."

"You are lying," Lilly stated.

"*You are using deception on your own teammate?*" Greg was surprised.

"*Lilly doesn't trust Eismus anyway,*" Tom stated, shaking his dice. "*And I think I want to tag my aspect and use my inspiration for an advantage.*"

"*Explain aspects to me again?*" Tom asked Aaron.

"*I don't remember aspects in fifthED at all,*" Martin added.

"*They are not in it. I stole the concept from the FateCore,*" Aaron said. "*In D&D, characters have traits and skills that we utilize through numbers on our character sheet. Aspects take that concept but add in a role-playing flavor. When we made our characters, I had each of you write up a good, neutral, and bad thing about them. When you want to do something, or I want you to fail at something, you or I can tag an aspect for bonuses.*"

"*So right now,*" Tom said, "*I am tagging my aspect 'shifty alliances' to get to roll two dice instead of one, and I get to use the higher number.*"

"*Exactly,*" Aaron responded. "*But remember, you have to earn your inspiration and you can only tag an aspect if you have an inspiration. Use them wisely.*"

"*Like to trick your own team into doing something bad,*" Debby said sarcastically.

The dice rolled into the dice tray. Seven and fourteen. "*Including my base stat bonus, that makes a seventeen for deception.*"

"*Rachael, roll insight,*" Aaron said, initiating a roll off.

Rachael quickly rolled her single D20; saves didn't receive bonus stats. Twelve.

"I'm not lying, Lilly," Eismus purred, coming in close to her. "I just don't want you to get hurt. Your arms are really short, and I don't think the cave troll cares about the difference between men and women. They probably all taste the same."

Lilly had to look up to see his face. "I'm sorry I accused you of lying." She handed him the envelope. "And those are very good points. I do not want to be eaten."

Eismus took the envelope quickly before Lilly could change her mind and turned away from her, pulling out his eating knife. The tunnel floor was still the smooth purply rock, and he quickly mumbled the incantation for light and kneeled down on the floor.

"What are you doing?" Lilly asked, honestly curious.

"I am just making sure the envelop hasn't been tampered with," Eismus answered as he studied the wax seal.

"Bullshit," Craig's grinding voice was right behind him.

"Look, we need to know what is going on. One guy basically gave a secret salute, and another reacted violently to the letter. All we know about the fey is that they are tricky, and this fey priest especially," Eismus reasoned.

"You are going to open the letter!" Lilly suddenly realized with a start.

Eismus mouthed the spell to heat up metal and easily and cleanly pried open the seal with the tip of his warm dagger. The wax would be easy to melt back on. Eismus glanced behind him to make sure Lilly wasn't causing trouble. She wasn't. Craig had one hand on her shoulder, obviously holding her in place just in case.

"You know, if anyone finds out, we will throw you under the bus," Poppy said, her voice pitched low but obviously just as curious.

"What is a bus?" Eismus asked as he pulled out the message.

"And this is what you find," Aaron stood up behind the DM screen and put a strip of paper in the middle of the table.

"See, we were not supposed to follow the rules," Tom almost cheered his victory.

"Aaron is just really thorough," Rachael shot back, giving Aaron an approving smile.

"It is just a bunch of pictures," Poppy stated, coming around to peek under Eismus' elbow.

"It has to be code, or a puzzle," Eismus said. "But nothing even looks familiar to me. Does anyone have a way to copy it down? Do we have a bard that collects lore in the party?"

Lilly stubbornly didn't move.

"Boring. For the good of the party." 4aDeer had started pacing, itching for a fight.

"I know he lied to you, but 4aDeer is right." Craig's eyes softened as he moved his hand off her shoulder and onto her back to help her take off her pack.

"Fine, flipping fine," Lilly said, taking out her writing tablet to copy the images.

"Oh, really, now I roll an 18." Rachael glared at her dice.

"Wow, if the surface of the paper wasn't different, I'm not sure if I could pick out the original," Eismus said happily as he carefully put the original back in the envelope. The hot knife melted the back of the wax again. He fumbled slightly getting the seal in the exact right spot, but it could easily just look like the priest was in a hurry when he sealed it.

"Let's get this over with," Lilly sounded unhappy despite Eismus' praise. It made Eismus happy to see her unhappy. She moved in front of him in the walking order, staying close to Craig. It was only two more gentle turns before they came to an opening blocked with a giant round door. Really, a cave troll had a door?

"The door is made of wood," Poppy said, confused, as she gently touched it. "Wood and iron, I believe."

BOOM, BOOM, BOOM.

Eismus jumped.

"Bored," 4aDeer stated, his hand still poised in its knocking. They could hear the footsteps behind the door long before it opened. As it opened, the smell of rotting veg and the tang of unwashed bodies assaulted their noses. Eismus went so far as to cover his face involuntarily.

The cave troll was at least eight feet tall, its skin a blue grey — lighter than the rocks around it, but similar. Oddly enough, it was wearing a giant white apron covered in stains of various greens, yellows, browns, and reds.

"We have a letter for you," 4aDeer stated. "Do you want it, or should we fight?"

"Depending on who it is from," the cave troll's voice was even and lightly accented common. "I think I would prefer the letter. Orc meat is a little tough, and I already have someone slow cooking in my cauldron."

Eismus hastily handed the letter to 4aDeer, whose shoulders had slumped in disappointment, though he didn't move his other hand off the axe.

"From Temple of the Fey," 4aDeer said as he handed it over.

"Thank you," the cave troll said.

"Did you just say thank you?" Lilly asked.

"I did, though I will say 'eat you' next if you don't leave my doorstep. Did no one ever teach you to say, 'you're welcome,' and leave when obviously dismissed?"

"That's so many big wor...ouch." Eismus looked down at Poppy, who must have just used all of her body weight to jump onto his naturally armored foot.

"You're welcome," Poppy said sweetly. "We will leave you to your cooking."

4aDeer stepped back as the heavy wood door slammed in his face.

19

FORT COLLINS

HORSETOOTH RESERVOIR

"What a beautiful day," Rachael was purring she was so happy. She had a lovely little picnic packed up and Aaron had just parked their car at the trailhead. "I promise we don't have to walk far. I just thought it would be nice to get out."

"You are probably right," Aaron admitted, visibly not as happy about this as Rachael.

Rachael decided not to push her luck and kept her mouth shut. She grabbed Aaron's hand as they walked toward the single-track path.

"I am loving your campaign," Rachael said, to start up conversation. "I liked the details on the cave troll's apron. And the visual of a cave troll in an apron."

"I thought that would be fun," Aaron's voice pepped up. "I hope Martin is OK with the lack of combat last night. But it is what the story needed."

"Martin has DMed his own campaigns. I am sure he understands," Rachael pitched her voice to carry forward as she matched pace behind Aaron. Little beads of sweat were already forming on his bald head. It was unusually warm for April, but the sun was almost always out in Colorado and the winter had been mild, so the warm day was not unexpected.

"Signs of global warming," Aaron stated as he mopped his head with a bandana.

"I was thinking something similar," Rachael agreed. They fell into a comfortable silence, the single track winding a lazy path across the front of the reservoir. The path didn't go all the way around, as the rock walls were sheer. It would go up in a bit and get wider, ending at a lovely lookout.

When the path did widen, Rachael scooted forward, putting her hand in Aaron's. Why weren't their silences at home comfortable like this? Her mind wandered, trying to remember the last time she and Aaron had a moment.

"Where did you go?" Aaron asked, his voice soft. He pulled on her hand, moving her off to the side of the trail so a family could pass them.

"Honestly, I was trying to think of the last time we had a moment," Rachael said.

"A moment?" Aaron asked.

"Do you remember when we got back together after our breakup and you would have takeout waiting every Wednesday when I had that horrible afternoon shift?" Rachael asked, smiling at the memory.

"I do," Aaron's answer was more guarded.

"I am worried about us," Rachael started. She looked into his brown eyes.

"Why? I am so happy." Aaron's other hand gently cradled the side of her face and pulled her to him for a brief kiss. He released both his hands and stepped back. "It's too hot for touching," Aaron said. Disappointed, he turned back to the trail.

"I'm not." Rachael wished she could shove the words back into her mouth.

"You are usually warmer than me when we walk. I am

surprised you are not hot." Aaron continued his slow walk up the hill to the lookout spot.

"Right," Rachael said. Now that the words were out and misunderstood, she wanted to say them again. But they wouldn't come out a second time. "I am sure I will overheat like usual on the uphill."

The silence was not as comfortable, both of them breathing hard by the time they reached the top, but the view was breathtaking. The sky was a vivid powder blue, the sheer dark red and brown cliffs imposing as they vanished into the still and sparkling water of the huge reservoir. A few small white boats dotted the surface. Rachael pulled out her phone for a quick selfie. Aaron put on his best fake smile, humoring her.

"We should take a vacation," Rachael suddenly thought out loud. She squinted at the selfie on her phone in the bright sun, unable to clearly make it out.

"I can't get time off right now, Rachael," Aaron said quickly. Rachael stopped looking at her phone to face him. "I told you about the newish project we have been working on." Aaron's face and voice lit up. "I forgot to tell you that I need to go in tomorrow. I am actually really excited. I am one of the leads for the program this time and it is something totally new the client is asking for."

"You need to work on a Sunday?" Rachael's voice was not excited. "I am glad you are excited. I know you love new puzzles," she added quickly.

"Speaking of puzzles, I wonder if you guys are going to get the one in the campaign."

Rachael tugged on Aaron's sleeve to start them walking back down. She went along with Aaron's blatant change in topic. She was slower than Aaron on the downhills, and they walked together enough that he automatically stepped in behind her.

"Don't give me any hints," Rachael demanded, carefully

studying her footing. "Or Greg. I am glad the two of you are doing dinners once a week now."

"I am, too," Aaron said, and then more teasing, "and I won't give you hints, not unless you ask really nicely." His hands shot out, tickling her sides a bit. A smile forced its way briefly onto Rachael's face.

"Tom is good at puzzles, as is Martin," Rachael added. "Although I noticed you were careful to make sure no one could take the letter home, so obviously the internet has the answer."

"The internet has all the answers," Aaron responded dramatically.

A hysterical but short laugh ripped out of Rachael's chest. "Does it now."

"I think it does. It is a mingling of knowledge and opinions. With enough data, anything can be solved. Although the degree of correctness might vary."

"The degree of correctness might vary," Rachael repeated the statement. Aaron chuckled.

"OK, maybe an understatement."

Rachael's shoe squished in some mud and she stopped to wipe it off. They didn't walk often enough to warrant good walking shoes. The ground was the rich brown-red of clay. Short bushes, often starved of water despite being this close to the reservoir, were mixed in with massive boulders. Many of the boulders sprouted, like clown feet, the bright red or blue matts the free climbers used to fall if needed. She didn't actually see any climbers at the moment.

She turned to the water. It sparkled in the sun, a few small boats making lazy circles in the center.

"There was a town here before they built the dam. I was reading that the foundations of houses are still there, just hidden by the water," Rachael said.

"See, the internet tells all. Food time," Aaron declared, taking the lead again.

"Food time," Rachael echoed. She hesitated before following, her eyes scanning the surface of the reservoir. She wanted to dive in and swim down to find those foundations. The 'Fort Collins' from before. Maybe that Fort Collins still ordered takeout once a week because it wanted to make its people happy, even if it wasn't necessary anymore.

20

FORT COLLINS

COMPUTER ROOM

"My head is sunburned." Aaron's complaint sounded like an accusation.

"I'm not bald," Rachael responded. "It didn't occur to me to bring a hat or sunscreen. If it makes it any better for you, my nose is quite pink. I'm going to take a quick shower. You joining me?"

"No, I think the water will hurt my head," Aaron responded. Rachael wasn't surprised or disappointed. Although she was disappointed that she was not disappointed. So, she was disappointed? Aaron often joined her, and she loved the intimate touches and the results they often led to. But even when it wasn't sexual, which was most of the time, they had a large shower and it was just nice to have someone wash your back.

She quickly washed the dirt and sweat off and changed into comfortable house clothing. Aaron was not at his computer, but she could hear a rustle from the living room. He was probably painting miniatures or game pieces or whatever.

Rachael sunk into her computer chair and woke up her PC. With the unconscious ease of long-formed habits, she cycled through her email, double-checked her calendar for the day, and ended on Facebook.

"Great walk at Horsetooth Reservoir today," she captioned her selfie, tagging Aaron and Horsetooth. She scrolled through her own page, glancing at past posts. She looked so happy on social media. Maybe if she looked at it enough, she would feel as happy as she looked.

plink

Greg: Nice selfie, did you climb any rocks?

Rachael: Do I look like I climb rocks?

Greg: You look like you can do anything you want to.

Rachael: Har har, laying it on a bit thick there. Do you need money?

Greg: Nope

Rachael: Do you need power?

Greg: Nope

Rachael: Do you need fame?

Greg: Nope

Rachael: You know what you need?

Greg: Nope

Rachael: A kick in the shins. Why are you messaging me?

Greg: I need a kick in the shins and I think you are the woman for the job.

Rachael: Nope

Greg: Ok ok, sorry. I just got back from the gym and saw you online and wanted to chat.

Rachael: Lonely?

Greg: That word just makes me sound so sad.

Rachael: Better sounding sad than being sad.

Greg: Aww, was your day not as beautiful as the weather?

Rachael: Something like that. Aaron has to work tomorrow and our walk was just short today, and now he is working on his projects again.

Greg: Lonely?

Rachael: I see the tables have turned, sir. Round two?

Greg: Tomorrow, over lunch. My treat?

Rachael's hands stopped and lay flat against the keys. She could feel her pulse quicken and peeked over her shoulder. But Aaron was still in his own little world in a different room. Why was she even looking over her shoulder at all?

Rachael: Brb

Rachael dragged one hand along the wall; it drifted with

nothing to trace as she crossed the front of the stairs before landing on one of the floor-to-ceiling posts that decorated the entrance to the big living space on the other side of the house.

Aaron was bent over his miniature table, his dorky glasses that magnified what he was painting made it look like he was trying to see into one of those old projector toys.

"Hey, since you are working tomorrow, mind if I get lunch with Greg?" Rachael asked. Her mind began to scream, "Say no, tell me you don't want me spending time with anyone, start an argument — say SOMETHING to make me feel like you know I am here."

Her hand wrapped around the pole; she leaned away from it, swinging slightly, and waited patiently. It was rare that Aaron didn't hear her, but he wasn't really capable of answering until he could pull his focus away from what he was working on. He looked up, his eyes huge in the glasses. Rachael couldn't stop the chuckle.

"I don't mind at all. I'm sorry I won't be home. You two have fun, tell him lunch is on me." Aaron was already dipping his brush in paint again before he even finished speaking.

"Great," Rachael breathed out. She pulled herself straight slowly, watching to see if Aaron sensed her disappointment, but she might as well have not been there.

21

FORT COLLINS

OLIVE GARDEN

"Olive Garden?" Rachael said as they were seated.

"Why not? Endless soup, salad, and breadstick lunch. Casual, but nice, and halfway between our houses. If we drink too much, both of us could almost walk home," Greg listed off.

"Wow, you really thought about this," Rachael commented.

"What can I tell you? I am a thoughtful person." Greg gave a cheesy smile.

Rachael rolled her eyes and wiped the sweat off her palms onto her napkin, still nicely folded on her lap. She was nervous.

The day was not as warm as the day before, a hint of winter still clinging to the breeze. Olive Garden was in the middle of strip mall city, as she called it. The inside was as bland as the Starbucks they'd had coffee in.

Aaron had already left for work when Rachael got up, and she was ashamed to say that she had changed her clothing three times before settling on her tightest pair of light blue jeans and a low-cut eggplant purple blouse with no sleeves. The shirt could only be worn with the one bra, and she hadn't done laundry in a while, so she only had her lacy underpants available. They didn't match the bra but they made her feel quite sexy.

Not that that was a good thing in this situation. Greg was Aaron's brother and not interested in her like that. It was nice to have an excuse to feel sexy though.

Greg looked very handsome. He had met her at the door in light blue jean shorts and a white short-sleeve button-down that showed off his arms nicely. A masculine gold necklace sparkled on his chest and matching gold sparkled on his left wrist. His sunglasses were propped up on his spiky hair. It looked like he had just shaved. She usually saw him at the end of his workday with his five o'clock shadow.

"You look stunning," Greg had said. Greg usually saw Rachael at the end of her work week as well. She was often already in game night comfy clothing — sweatpants and a sleeveless tank top, and this time of year she had her favorite zip hoodie pulled over the tank top.

"I made sure you had low expectations," Rachael answered. Her body physically responded to the compliment. She knew she was blushing a little.

"And what about me?" Greg pressed. Thankfully, he either didn't notice the blush or chose to ignore it. She was still sunburned.

"You clean up well. I almost didn't recognize you without the stubble. You look more like how I imagine Craig without it." Rachael realized what she said just as she said it. But Greg laughed. She felt his large hand fit into the small of her back, guiding her though the open door and to a table that he had reserved. His hand had sent fire through her sorely neglected lady parts.

"Earth to Rachael," Greg waved a hand in front of her face.

"Oh, sorry, Craig. I spaced out there," Rachael said absently.

"Really? I couldn't tell," said Greg. A slight hesitation, and then, "I just ordered us a bottle of wine and the lunch special." The comment was both a statement and a question.

"That sounds lovely," Rachael responded with a nod. The waiter left and was back quickly with a bottle of something white. Greg was confident in his swirl and sip and quickly approved the bottle. Rachael once again wiped her hands on the napkin. Was it hot in here? Why was she nervous? Maybe because even last night as Aaron slept, Lilly and Craig had explored more of her Underdark.

"OK, now you are grinning. I feel like I am watching a conversation," Greg laughed. Rachael felt the heat on her face increase and knew she was probably the same color as a tomato.

Greg stopped laughing. "Are you ok? I mean, you are little sunburned, but it literally just doubled and we are inside."

"Yes, I am fine. I was just thinking about Aaron's game and am embarrassed I spaced out again," Rachael muttered, her lips flattening out. "Focus, girl," she thought to herself. "Greg is just Aaron's brother, NOT Craig."

"No worries — I figured that when you just called me Craig," Greg said.

"I'm sorry, again!"

"Don't be. I sometimes think of you as Lilly in my mind," Greg answered. Rachael blinked and wrung the napkin under the table. This was getting odd. "Greg is Aaron's brother," Rachael repeated to herself.

"But we can chat about the game later," Greg started, and as it turns out, Greg was an excellent conversationalist. Although she should have guessed that based on their few chats on Facebook and Aaron's own charisma — these things often ran in families. He never pressed for information but always shared something of his to make Rachael feel more comfortable sharing. She quickly forgot her nerves, her hands moving to help her articulate her points.

And the best part — he never asked about Aaron or what

was wrong. She didn't notice they had moved onto a second bottle of wine. The food had stopped coming a while ago.

"You have a picture of Craig in your head?" Greg suddenly asked, changing topics.

"Don't you? I love the escape of role-playing. I can close my eyes and just see the world and the people." Rachael closed her eyes for emphasis, seeing more worlds than just their current campaign.

"I am pretty good with the worlds — I have been doing this for years — but I usually just see people as versions of who they are," Craig responded.

"What about when people play the opposite sex?"

"Same thing, I just laugh more."

Their slightly intoxicated chuckles blended into the quiet of the restaurant. Few other patrons were still around, and bland music softly played out of a hidden speaker system.

"I guess when I imagine Craig, I see more of you than other toons," Rachael admitted.

"I don't see Lilly as a dwarf. I just see you." Greg's voice lowered a bit as he spoke. His brown eyes met hers and held them. She felt his fingers find her hand on the table. It was an intentional movement, not an accidental brushing or an easily misinterpreted message. Greg was asking if she was interested.

Rachael was frozen; she could see her reflection in Greg's wide, clear pupils. Was she interested? The thought of cheating on Aaron was painful. She had never done it. But Aaron had not been interested in her for a while now. Her lack of action encouraged Greg; he moved his hand further into hers, his thumb rubbing a circle on her palm. His brown eyes, so like his brother's, remained locked with hers.

"Can I get you anything else?" the waiter asked.

Rachael moved her hand out of Greg's and looked down, the moment broken.

"No, just the check," Rachael said. If Greg was disappointed, he didn't show it.

"I think that was the fourth time they asked us if we wanted the check," he moved on as if nothing had happened.

"Was it?" Rachael was not moving on as easily. "I need to use the facilities."

Her napkin fell to the floor in her rush to go. She did need to pee, but more than that she needed to look herself in the eyes. Her underpants were damp with juices. Her body had been responding much faster than her mind and heart with their complicated ties and emotions.

"What am I doing?" she asked her own reflection as she washed her hands. And then her face.

Craig. Greg was hot. He made her feel special. He had taken control of every aspect of lunch. God, there was nothing hotter than a man taking control and making decisions. Would he do the same in the bedroom? Is that what she wanted?

Aaron wasn't passive, but time and balance had made them complacent. Rachael had to make the first move. Rachael picked their meals. Rachael had to plan their activities. Rachael was just Aaron's manager. And she wanted to be more, to be something else.

But no matter how much Greg made her body want, he was Aaron's brother. It wasn't right. She washed her face again, quelling the yearning in her body and strengthening her heart. This was not right. All the wine in the world couldn't make it right.

Greg had vacated the table and was waiting for her by the front door. He held it open and put a possessive hand once again on her lower back as she went through before him. He walked by her side along the building and toward the parking lot.

"Where is your car?" Greg hadn't moved the hand off her back and she hadn't asked him too.

"I took the bus. We only have one car." Rachael's voice sounded cold even to her.

"Rachael." Greg stopped and moved toward her. She took a step back, her heel hit the side of the building. Greg didn't stop moving. If it wasn't for the building, she would have fallen. Instead, her back landed with a little thud against it as Greg's lips claimed hers. His body was not as hard as Craig's in her fantasies, but it pressed her hard against the building and it was real. His tongue wiggled, begging to be let in, and she obliged. His mouth was so big. And it was odd not feeling the tickle of facial hair.

Rachael's hands moved of their own bidding, feeling his tapered waistline and the line of his hips. She moaned into his mouth as his cloth-covered arousal pushed into her jeans. His hands pulled her hips toward him, his fingers squeezed the soft round cheeks of her backside.

It felt so good to be wanted. To feel the heat of new lust and the excitement of another person.

Time stood still as she rocked her hips against whatever surface Craig was providing her. And when he pulled away, a low groan of frustration escaped her kiss-swollen lips.

The sunlight seemed brighter with Greg's body no longer trying to combine with hers.

"No, no, no, no, no." Rachael didn't recognize her own voice. She was still leaning against the building.

"Rachael, I'm not apologizing." Greg's voice was husky with lust and a little out of breath. "You are a jewel. He doesn't appreciate what he has." Greg's voice was angry, anger she hadn't picked up on before. Her mind repeated his last words, their meaning emerging like a swimmer in a pool of Jell-O. Greg was jealous of Aaron. As much as she wanted this to be about her, it wasn't. It was sibling rivalry; it was their constant competition.

He didn't move, just stood waiting as Rachael collected her thoughts.

"I'm going to call you an Uber home," Rachael said slowly. A small gust of leftover winter chilled her as she pushed herself off the sun-warmed wall. He started to come closer and she put out a hand. Not trusting herself.

"I want you," Greg said lamely.

"I know," Rachael answered.

FORT COLLINS

DUNGEONS & DRAFTS

Rachael got out of her own Uber, her body thrumming with sexual tension, self-loathing, and self-pity. The Uber ride had been short and quiet, the driver already taking another fare. Greg hadn't said another word, getting in his own separate Uber without taking his eyes off her.

She couldn't go home. Greg knew that Aaron was working today and he knew where she lived. And Rachael didn't have the self-control to say no a second time. She felt oily as she opened the door as little as possible to get into Dungeons & Drafts. She needed to think. But to think in a space where her decision had consequences.

Sundays were always a big day for the pub, Sunday being a popular game day. It took moments for her eyes to adjust to the lights, though as a gaming pub they kept most of the lights bright. The only mood lighting was around the bar and in the back corners and hidey-holes that dotted the edges and upper balcony story. The balcony story was unique and gave the large room almost a tournament-like quality, though the balcony itself was closed at the moment.

Dungeons & Drafts was Aaron's second home and Rachael

found herself here often. The pub was built to look like an old medieval English pub, as cheesy as possible. It hosted everything nerdy and had a great selection of craft beer. Sunday afternoons would be finishing up *D&D* Sundays where local game masters took turns running one shots. More than half of the big tables in the middle were full.

She got a pint of water and a single glass of white wine and searched the room for faces she knew. She recognized a few, but none of them well enough to take an interest in her arrival. Which suited her nicely. She headed for a dark corner in the back with a good view of a game going on nearby. She slowly settled in; her body had been shaking but she wasn't ready to think about it yet. She made herself finish the pint of water before taking her first sip of wine, still tipsy from the extended lunch. Usually one of her favorite feelings.

She closed her eyes and listened to the sounds of the pub. Of games being played and fantasy worlds. She was surprised to hear a Scottish accent from nearby. She took another sip of wine and focused on his voice. It was low and smooth; it would have been hard to pick up from any other table.

"The forest continues for a long way. Roll perception." The sound of dice rolling and voices calling out numbers. "You don't see jack shit. It still looks like the same forest you have been bumblin' about in for the last hour."

Rachael smiled, her frayed emotions centering at the familiar sounds of dice and people. Time passed and eventually her wine glass was out. Feeling better, she went back up to the bar with the same order.

"You look a lot better," the bartender made small talk. She didn't know this one.

"Thanks, I find the sound of world descriptions and dice very calming."

"Do you want to start a tab?" He was obviously either new or just a stand in. Rachael hadn't been asked that since the first time she and Aaron did a two-day marathon of the legacy game, Seafall. Had she paid for her first drink?

"No, I think this will do me, though if anyone is waiting tables today, I'll leave a tip for one more glass of water in about 20 minutes."

"I will let it be known," the bartender said dramatically with a wink. Rachael cracked a smile, paid in cash, and went back to her booth. She sent a quick text to Aaron letting him know that after lunch she had decided to get drinks with some girlfriends and wasn't sure when she was going to be home. Her stomach pinched at the lie. She didn't like lying and was terrible at it, but she just wasn't ready to face anything yet.

She downed the water and closed her eyes. The Scottish voice walked his party through a few adventures in the forest. The party seemed new, as he had to stop and explain a lot, as well as correct some impossible things on character sheets. Rachael's mind wandered to her first game with Aaron. He might have grown up playing, but she had never played before. Her centaur had been amazing, until the party used her as a shield and she failed her third death check — you only got three of them.

"Do you want another water?" Rachael opened her eyes, confused, as it seemed the Scottish voice was suddenly very close and asking her a question.

"Yes." She had been dozing a little, her second wine barely touched. She sat up in her booth and ran a hand through her hair and pulled at her shirt to straighten it. "Sorry, I was dozing. Rough day."

"Don't apologize, you looked upset when you first came in," he said soothingly. He set the water in front of her.

"The bartender noticed too. I must look terrible." Rachael looked down at herself.

"Scott, the bartender tonight, is just extra observant of moods. Mind if I sit?" he asked.

"No, go ahead. Sorry, you don't work here?"

"Ah, you caught me. No. I am new to town. I was actually just helpin' out with the generic one shots the pub puts on."

Rachael drained what was left of her now warm white wine, followed by more water. She was sobering up a little, but it was making her thoughts worse. She looked over the newcomer. He was probably the same height as her, brown bushy hair matched his brown bushy eyebrows. He was clean-shaven with a strong chin. His well-built frame was covered in jeans and a t-shirt with a dragon on it. Strong arms came out of his sleeves, although they were nothing like Greg's in the muscle department.

It was hard to see too many details in the low lighting in her hidey-hole. She had picked it to have enough privacy to think.

"My name is David Douglas," he said.

"I am so sorry; I am Rachael. And I am poor company at the moment."

"Misery loves company," David repeated the old adage.

"What brings you to FoCo?" Rachael forced out the question; she really didn't want company. To her surprise, David shook his head.

"Work, but I didn't come over here to force you to chat. I know when a lass needs an ear."

Rachael felt tears well up and then it was like a river. She didn't care that he was a stranger. He was just a person willing to listen. David moved next to her and wrapped his arms around her as she did her best to drench his shirt. She didn't know how long it took her to control herself, but once she had a voice, she started talking. And once it started, she couldn't stop it.

Years of pent-up self-pity, held back emotions, and misplaced tension came out in what was probably not even an intelligible order. Her loneliness at being separated from her hometown. Her hurt at being ignored by Aaron, the reason she moved. How tired she was of fighting for everything. And how confused she was on what she wanted. She cried about little things like socks on the floor, and her anger blazed at Greg. Her stupidity at thinking he was just a man interested in a woman.

Someone had brought David another beer and her another glass of wine, an extra big one, that she took an extra big drink out of.

"I think I'm crying all the water back out." It was her first joke in probably an hour. "Oh my god. You must think I am insane. I can't believe you are still sitting here."

"I really didn't have any plans for my Sunday evening." David's voice was full of comfort and humor. His Scottish accent giving even the most benign word a flourish.

"Just keep talking," Rachael said. She wiped her eyes and drank half the glass.

David laughed and said in a mock Yoda accent, "Like the accent, you do."

Rachael nodded, feeling a smile crack her face. But then smiling made her think of Aaron and another tear slipped down her cheek.

"No more of that." David's hand cupped her face; his thumbs erased the salty drop.

Rachael found that trying to stop crying made it worse.

"You are wonderful and you are loved." David moved forward and kissed her on the forehead. Rachael started crying harder. "That was supposed to make it better." Rachael buried her head in his already wet shoulder. Her tears were slower, her mind grasping more of her surroundings. David smelled of leather, clove, and man. His arms were long and wrapped around her gently.

"I think we need a change of scenery." David tugged at her to get up. Rachael wiped her eyes again but followed, draining her glass before she got up. Air would do her good.

The sun was low — she had really lost track of time. She

quickly checked that her purse and phone were with her. She checked the phone. 6:15 p.m. No messages, not even from Greg.

"I feel like I am invisible," she croaked.

David's arm wrapped around her as he guided her to a little park directly behind the pub. They didn't talk, just breathed in the fresh, cool spring air and walked. Rachael shivered.

"Should I call you a cab?" David offered. Rachael thought of her house. Of the chances Greg was there and the knowledge that even if Aaron was, she couldn't face him.

"No." She wrapped her arms around herself.

"This is where I offer you my coat but all I have is my t-shirt." David paused. "I do live nearby if you are avoiding someone." Rachael looked at him, new tears coming out of her eyes.

"I am going to assume those are grateful tears now?" David looked at her face as if it was a puzzle. "I am really getting tested on my tear types today."

Rachael's laugh sounded more like a sob, and David put an arm around her again and led her to his apartment.

The apartment was on the top floor. Unpacked boxes were still stacked up in corners of the big living space that had a trendy modern kitchen on one side. Some furniture seemed to be purposely placed but much of it was just about. The room was lined on one side with glass windows glowing with the first pinks and purples of sunset. There was just enough light streaming through the big window to see.

"I picked this place for the view." David's voice came from right behind her and his warm hands started rubbing her arms. "You are still cold." She could feel his breath on her ear. She just wanted to feel loved, wanted, alive. She turned around and his hands once again went up to her face. He held the sides of her head gently and kissed her forehead. She closed her eyes. His strong lips kissed each closed eyelid as if trying to banish the tears. When she opened her eyes, his face was very close, his blue eyes were intense, and she didn't shy away when he very, very gently kissed her quivering lips.

Rachael didn't pull away; she didn't think of Aaron or Greg. In fact, she didn't think at all. Her body molded itself to David. His hands released her head and slid down her back, quickly caressing her cloth-covered butt before they wrapped around her waist and pulled her forward. The kiss developed from gentle into something rich and demanding. Rachael's lips parted, and for the second time today, her mouth was invaded. David's tongue was both gentle and insistent , feeling for hers, eliciting a dance.

Rachael felt his hands move, restless as they explored. Her own arms, wrapped around his waist, were still. David absently tugged at the top of her pants before sliding his hands under her blouse and resting momentarily on the bare skin of her curved waistline. She pulled away just long enough to pull off her own shirt, David doing the same.

Their mouths met again; his hands explored up and down her backside, eventually finding and easily releasing her bra strap. She felt her breast swing forward; David stepped back to catch one in his hand, gently rolling the handful. She didn't notice the bra fall away as David subtly moved them back toward his couch, his mouth falling on her bouncing breasts, his fingers leaving heat where they kneaded and squeezed. Rachael moaned as his ministrations of her nipples made her core flare with heat.

She pushed him back, hooking her thumbs in his waistband, deftly undoing his belt buckle. David's hands undid the top of her pants; his hand dipped down, feeling the lace of her panties and briefly pressuring her wet clit. She stifled her moan by kissing him again, and David growled into her mouth. His hands moved to relieve her of her pants. But the tight jeans she had squeezed herself into didn't want to come off.

"Fuck," she breathed, looking down at the offending garment.

She looked up just as his hands grabbed her belt loops. He pushed her onto the couch. His strong arms slowly peeled her pants, panties and all, off her body, mostly. She reached down herself to finish freeing her feet. Once free, she propped herself up, her knees sinking into the couch cousins.

While she had been struggling with her jeans, David had dropped all his layers and easily stepped out of them. Rachael absently played with her own nipples as David's naked body stalked toward the couch. His posture, even naked, was impeccable. It accented his shapely chest and shoulders. Confidence seemed to radiate from him as he approached. His hand pushed hers away, rolling her nipples between his fingers.

His other hand cupped the back of her neck, tilting her head up. Smoldering green eyes looked into hers. Unlike his posture, his face was tender and filled with lust. His eyes devoured every bit of her. He dropped his mouth to hers — the kiss was deep. His teeth scraped against her bottom lip as he pressed his large and hard bulge against her stomach.

Before Rachael could catch her breath, they were moving; his fingers dug into her hips as he sat down hard next to her and pulled her up and then back down, her legs straddling his hips. His hard dick rubbed up against her slit, and she involuntarily rocked, looking for more. Rachael's hips moved against his rigid shaft as his hand traveled up her stomach, kneading her breasts again, and then back down. His hips thrust up as she pushed down on top of him. His dick seemed to try and reach her breasts.

"I need you." It was the first time either of them had spoken, and Rachael wasn't sure who said it. She helped him as his hands guided her up and then back down. She went slowly. He was much bigger than she was used to, and his groan when he was finally sheathed made her walls tighten. They just stayed that way for a moment before Rachael began rocking her hips forward, slowly at first, her clit rubbing against him at the end of every movement. Her breathing became shallow and she could feel pleasure pulsing as they moved together. It wasn't fast. Speed had never gotten her anywhere. But when he finally remembered that her breasts were at eye level and put the first nipple in his mouth, that was all it took.

The build had been slow, but the sudden rush of blood and pleasure from her pinnacle left a rush in her ears. She felt David's arms encourage her tense body to move up and down, still sliding on his pulsating dick to extend the waves of heat. She felt him swell and explode inside her. She couldn't stop her little bits of rocking; her sex pulsed.

David was breathing hard underneath her, his dick slowly going soft in her sensitive walls. She could feel all their juices starting to pool and run but she didn't care. This wasn't her house or her couch. She collapsed down on David, beyond tired, and let herself slide off him. The smell of leather, clove, and sex filled her senses

This wasn't her husband.

Rachael didn't have more tears. Tonight had been for her. With someone she would never have to see again. Someone who made her feel special, loved, and taken care of. Everything would be all right now.

23

GOOGLE DRIVE

CRAIG'S BACKSTORY

Written by Greg
Short version edited by Aaron
See archived email
"I am going to make you read all of this"
for full backstory.

I was not born of stone, but of flesh and blood. I am sure I was raised by a loving family; at least I have no bad memories or ill will toward families. But I also don't remember much of my life before stone. I was reborn. My senses awoke, hundreds of years ago now, to a world where time has no meaning. When I am hungry, I eat, when I am tired, I sleep, and when I am near the earth and its stone, I can recharge.

I did not awake alone. My brothers and sisters that were also reborn awoke with me. Together we talked about our new world. We discussed its meaning. Our reason for becoming stone. But we could not remember. Directionless, we wandered, slowly dwindling in number as we found individual meanings and tasks. Until I was alone. I did not like being alone.

Before he left, one of my brothers spoke of a realm dedicated to earth. A realm where I could find answers. I wandered the earth. I made the occasional friend and helped the odd traveler before I despaired. This realm I was searching for, this rumored "God of Earth" or "Demon of Rock," was a myth. My brothers were scattered to the wind. I was alone.

I climbed to the highest mountain I could find, and there I met an elemental earth dragon who spoke to me of the Underdark. A realm of realms. He claimed to be the Demon of Rock I was searching for. We stayed together for a time, but he was as directionless as I. He could not be what I was searching for. And so, I left him. I was alone again.

But my loneliness was purposeful this time. I will find this Underdark. And it will lead me to a purpose. A god. A home of stone and magic.

24

UNDERDARK

CRAIG

The Underdark itself has no magic; it is purely stone and memories. But the realms do. And they shift to etch their marks deeply into the smooth polished surface of the Underdark's timeless existence. For, in the end, memories are all that matter.

— AARON, DUNGEON MASTER'S NOTES, CS7

The world moves slowly for the being of earth and rock. This constant need to be "doing" is a difficult concept. Craig didn't know what to make of Poppy as she bounced around excitedly, or Eismus with his hands or mouth constantly moving. He liked 4aDeer. Like Craig, he was often thoughtful. Smarter than anyone gave him credit for.

The rock felt his heart beat a little quicker when he looked at Lilly. Her dwarven body was soft and round. Her dirty blonde hair came down in waves to her shoulders. Her laugh was like water to a starving person, and the way her face lit up when she smiled at him made him wish the earth didn't move quite so slowly.

"Craig, you coming?" Eismus asked, bringing Craig out of his musings.

"Yup," Craig answered and followed along in the back. Lilly did not drop back to walk with him. Craig tried not to frown. They had received their reward for mail delivery and the unloading of what turned out to be fertilizer for the mushroom garden in the courtyard in the middle of the temple. After that, the fey priest jerked them around for a bit longer, not that Craig minded. Time was meaningless, but it bothered Lilly, so by association, it bothered him. However, at the end of it, the fey had created a potion that would protect them from something big and nasty that was in the area. And most likely the reason for the town's current unrest.

The fey priest had given them vague information and then spent the next hour being thoroughly questioned by the entire party. Elm City had three factions. However, all were underhandedly fighting for control without using fists, as the city was a haven with no violence.

They were back at the tavern after a supply run that had mostly run them out of funds. It had gone well. Still no plate armor for 4aDeer, but they added some ranged weapons to their arsenal and now had a collection of interesting potions to try out. It was time to decide what to do next.

"We know the first two factions are the Temple of the Fey and the Dragon Temple," Lilly explained. "I, personally, believe that both temples have good intentions. But it is doubtful they will ever get along. The third faction is the unknown and probably the faction taking people. BUT we also can't forget that this is a huge trading port, and slavers come through here often."

"We also know that the fey priest made us drink something that supposedly protects our minds," Eismus picked up. "The fey can't lie. We know for sure that he is fey, so there is that. But can't lie doesn't mean squat if he can just leave things out or tell partial truths. If it does more, we will find out."

"Right, I hate that part," Lilly said. "I just want to believe that he wants to help us."

"The world never works that way," Poppy said soothingly. "And even if he does want to help, he is not helping himself or us by not letting us know what our minds are being protected from."

"Something bad," 4aDeer said.

"Maybe he IS protecting himself," Craig added. "Maybe if we know we ruin everything."

"Right," Eismus added, looking sideways at Craig.

"So, with all this, our goal is still to get home," Poppy added bitterly. "And to do that, we need a guide that costs, well..." Poppy drew out the word. "A lot more than any one of us has seen in our lives. I need to see the sun." Poppy's bitterness left a sour note in the air, and the group sat silently listening to the lull of the tavern.

"We start making money and finding contacts," Craig finally said into the silence.

"Craig right. Start now, maybe more comes up," 4aDeer agreed.

"I still would like to know why we were pulled here in the first place," Lilly stated, not looking Poppy in the eye. "What we know about our involvement," Lilly began listing. "An entire tavern full of villagers and adventurers was pulled here from the surface and were being sacrificed for some reason. We killed the man in charge and stopped the sacrifices before stumbling into Elm City. Elm City is a magically protected neutral zone that is having political unrest and mysterious disappearances. All of which appear to be recent. And the leader of the Temple of the Fey is looking for help, bad enough that he is asking strangers."

Craig nodded supportively to Lilly's summary.

"Something is happening down here. I don't think we can

get out before shit hits the fan," Eismus added. "We need to figure it out and pick the winning side, and fast."

"All of that sounds like I am not going to see the sun for a very long time," Poppy responded.

Poppy pulled a rolled-up sheet out of the pack 4aDeer usually carried and spread it out over the table.

"Is this a map?" Lilly asked, excited.

"Sorta," Poppy responded. "It is a map I have been working on, since maps are so expensive and hard to get down here."

"Well done." Lilly bounced with excitement.

Craig calmly nodded his thanks and approval to Poppy before bending down as much as he could to peer at it. It was quite obvious that Poppy had just picked up this skill, but also quite obvious that she had an eye for detail.

"We have two quests from the Temple of the Fey and more information on their opinion of things than anyone could need." Lilly pointed at the room they had found before that had the path to the fey realm. "The two quests have rewards of money and armor and probably whatever we can pick up to sell on the way home. More wood, if possible."

"And the wood grinding begins," Eismus said, mimicking a maniacal laugh.

"I think we should also go to the Dragon Temple and see if they have quests for us," Craig added.

"What about this third faction?" Eismus asked. "We don't even know where to start there."

"What about it?" 4aDeer answered. "Not asked to do anything. Just told about. Leave others' problems to themselves."

"The priests did just give us an info dump," Eismus slowly confirmed.

"I thought he talked about the third faction," Lilly stated questioningly.

"We literally just sat here for 22 minutes while Aaron lectured us... did you forget that already, Rachael?" Greg asked. "Because I timed it."

It was the first time he had addressed her specifically this session. She had been avoiding him since Olive Garden — all 50 Facebook messages and 22, and counting, text messages.

"Yes, I forgot everything, Greg," Rachael deadpanned.

"Um, moving on," Aaron said, looking at the two of them strangely.

"It was information overload," Eismus agreed. "But it is good to know. We know what to watch for now. But we need to go to the Dragon Temple next remember; somehow, all of this is going to come together, and we need to pick the WINNING side. Maybe the reward will be a guide out of here. Who knows?" Eismus put his hands in the air and attempted to make eye contact with God. God ducked behind his DM screen.

"I don't think we need to pick the winning side," Lilly took Eismus' bait. "We need to find out what is going on and help those most in need."

"AND I JUST WANT TO GO HOME," Poppy yelled. The tavern fell silent briefly around them, and then conversation resumed like it had never stopped.

"Right now, no matter our goals, we need to take action." Poppy brought the group back on task. "To the Dragon Temple to see if they have any quests for us?"

"Information," Eismus agreed.

"Stop talking and go," 4aDeer huffed and got up. Poppy had to rush her map back into 4aDeer's pack as he made orc equivalent of whining noises until the party was moving. "Everything takes too long."

Craig waited until he was the last one out the door. Lilly was just in front of him and he hurried as much as a being of earth and rock could hurry so they were side by side. She didn't acknowledge him but she didn't move away either.

They slowed down as they approached the Dragon Temple. Its imposing walls looked like the walls of a fortified castle, and the double doors at the front looked a lot like the ones on the cave troll's house. Lilly pointed out the obvious and Craig was quick to agree.

"They probably just have the same maker." Eismus didn't give anyone much credit.

"No matter, going in!" 4aDeer pushed open one side of the doors and the party filed in behind him. The inside was dark, the walls painted black with silver ornamentation. The floors were the same stone as the outside. Rows of benches, all made of stone, faced an altar. As the party walked forward, Craig noticed the altar was made to look like a dragon's claw, and the claw was attached to an oversized dragon that looked like it was carved into the wall itself...part of its scaly body even patterned with silver where it connected to the wall.

"Can we help you?" said the voice of a woman. Craig ripped his eyes away from the altar to find a young human woman in robes of black looking at them questioningly. Something about her made Craig uneasy.

"We are new to town and looking for work," Eismus spoke up. Odd, usually Eismus had something to say after everyone gave their opinions. Mostly so others could be wrong and not him.

"A drow, looking for work here?" The human woman's eyes sparkled. They were bright purple. Craig suddenly realized, not a human woman at all.

"A half-drow draconic sorcerer, looking for work with his companions here," Eismus added, his tone serious. Craig eyed Eismus again. There was something going on here. He had suspected it from the beginning, they all had. Honestly, you couldn't not. Eismus was very excited about whatever secret he had been keeping from the party.

"I see," the not-human woman said. "My name is Isa. Come with me."

Isa's walk was flawless; her hips rocked from side to side as her feet seemed to hardly touch the ground. Craig glanced over at Lilly, feeling guilty for looking, but she was watching Isa just as much as he was.

"I don't think she is human," Lilly pitched her voice just loud enough for Craig to pick up the comment. He nodded once but didn't try to change the order of the group. Isa took them to a side door and told them to wait.

The wait was short. Apparently Eismus' presence there was interesting enough for them to get admitted immediately. So immediately, in fact, that a group of robed men was just leaving the room as they came in. Craig looked hard at each of them, trying to commit their faces to memory. You could never have too much information.

"Come in, come in. Let me take a look at you," the dragon priest said cheerily, his demeanor completely opposite the drab setting. Eismus walked a little faster than the rest of the party so that the dragon priest could get a look at him. "And you are here for work?" the priest questioned again.

"We are. My name is Eismus. We," he stressed the word we, "are looking for information and currency in exchange for our services." Eismus worded his answer quite specifically.

"I see." The priest nodded. "Are you looking for a specific amount?" he asked, then paused. No one in the party filled in the empty airtime with answers; they didn't know how much a guide cost exactly, and even if they did, saying it would give away their hand.

"Well then, on that note. I have three jobs that I need done. One of them, the pay is not good, but I am currently low on manpower. The other two, instead of putting a final pay on them, I would instead ask what your time is worth to complete the tasks."

"Why are you low on manpower?" Lilly asked.

The dragon priest blinked and looked down his nose at Lilly. He seemed unsure of how to answer. "Two of my apprentices have gone missing. Not that it is any of your concern...um, dwarf. You are a dwarf, right?"

"Yes." Lilly brightened, probably missing the priest's unease completely. Ah Lilly, always seeing the good in everything.

"Um, do the robes these priests are wearing look familiar?" Debby interrupted the game to ask.

"Why, yes. They certainly do." Aaron's eyes crinkled.

"Didn't we kill two black-robed priests when we were escaping in the first session?" Tom began flipping through his notes.

"Are you asking your party that in front of the dragon priest?" Aaron asked.

"No, he is not," Martin said. *"But we did gouge out one of their eyes for the Temple of the Fey."*

"So, we are the reason they are low on manpower," Greg concluded. *"And the Dragon Temple is responsible for bringing us here, or at least our original captivity."*

"One more out-of-game word and I will count this entire conversation as having happened in front of the high dragon priest." Aaron ended the chatter and refocused the group on the game.

"Eismus," the priest turned back to the drow. "My other task requires someone who can leave the temple and journey to another realm."

"We can do that," Lilly said. Craig smiled and nodded at Eismus' pleading look. He moved next to Lilly and put a hand on her shoulder. She flinched but didn't move. He put a finger to her lips. She stopped talking and moved his hand away from her face. Eismus and the priest resumed their conversation.

Craig didn't listen. He never did to these parts. He was here for Lilly. He had originally joined the party when he found them wandering around mostly naked, lost and running out of what little supplies they had managed to pillage from their captors. He had brought them to this town, though he had never been here himself. His people came from a different world, a world he had left so long ago he could hardly remember it.

The party promised to help him find answers. Lilly was especially passionate in the beginning and he found himself drawn to her. Maybe because dwarfs were so connected with stone themselves.

"Does the party agree?" Eismus turned around, double-checking with the group. Craig nodded as if he had been listening.

"I choose Lilly for the binding," the dragon priest said.

"I don't agree to that." Craig's rock body tried to move to protect Lilly, but he was too slow as the binding spell had already been cast.

"Craig, it will be ok," Eismus said. "Lilly is the best choice, although I do wish she had been able to verbally agree first."

"Lilly will be fine," 4aDeer deadpanned.

Craig turned to where Lilly still stood, her eyes closed and head drooped. "Lil?" he questioned.

Slowly, her head came up. One green and one purple eye looked up at him.

"Hi there, rock man." Lilly's voice was odd, as if two voices were speaking at once — Lilly's low alto and something softer and lighter. Lilly put her hand out and Craig took it in his.

"We've met before. My name is Isa," she said.

"So how does this work?" Rachael asked. "I am possessed?"

"You are not sure what is going on," Aaron explained. "You feel a second presence inside of you and you find that you're moving and speaking without telling your body." Aaron put a weird energy meter in front of Rachael. "You can feel your bardic magic like it's trapped inside a part of you. You know you are not yourself."

"I am not Isa," Lilly said, immediately after telling Craig she was Isa, and removed her hand.

"I am Isa," Lilly said, smiling again and putting her hand back in Craig's.

"I am Lilly," again with the hand snatching back.

"Stop, we get it. You are two people," Eismus growled.

"I am Lilly?" Lilly's lip quivered. "We are Lilsa!" Isa giggled.

Craig looked uncertainly at Lilly, wanting to comfort or fix whatever was happening with her mind.

"She'll be fine." 4aDeer came up beside him. Craig looked over at the big orc, his arms crossed over his chest. He looked imposing. "Isa will keep her safe. They want to know the job is done right."

"That they do," the dragon priest smiled. "And she will. If Lilly dies, Isa dies, so honestly, she is probably the safest one in the group. I am still over the moon that you accepted. We have never had anyone who tried this come back alive."

"What?" Poppy said.

"Oh, nothing," the dragon priest smiled brightly. He placed a small pack over Lilly's shoulder. "Isa knows the way to the Ice Dragon's Realm and will lead you. Isa can only stay in Lilly's body for three days. After that, if she is not extracted, Isa will force her way out, probably turning Lilly into a vegetable. So, my suggestion is Not. To. Doddle."

The party, with Lilsa in the lead, left the way they came in.

FORT COLLINS

DINING ROOM

"Dark, very dark. I LOVE it," Debby said. "Great session, Aaron. I really feel like we are getting into the story now."

"Thank you — I'm loving running it. Thank you all for playing and getting so into your roles. It is my favorite way to play." Aaron was practically beaming. He was also happy with the way the session went. Greg was sitting and drumming his fingers on the table.

"Two sessions in a row with no fighting," Martin complained. "Why did I roll a fighter?"

"I would bet that there will be A LOT of fighting going on in the future, Martin." Debby's voice was full of humor.

Rachael didn't want to get up. Greg always helped her with the dishes, and she didn't even want to look at him. It had been hard enough trying to play out Lilly while still having a crush on Craig. She felt so much relief when Isa "possessed" her. She had no idea that was going to happen. Sometimes Aaron dropped hints during the week, but not this week. Even if he had wanted to, she had hardly seen him.

"Hey, Rachael, I have had a crazy week. I brought my suit. Could I use your hot tub?" Debby asked.

"Of course. I'll go put mine on and open another bottle of wine." Rachael was beyond relieved. She just left the dishes. She would get them later or they could just sit out for days…that would be OK. Things didn't always need to be cleaned up. One hand clenched and unclenched trying to pick up her plate. But one glance at Greg and she got control of her hand and fled.

She was in her little forties vintage swimming suit — the fabric black with cherries on it — in no time. She peeked in the kitchen. Greg was still here and in view of the wine. Debby didn't drink anyway. The hot tub lid was off already when Rachael stepped out. The evening was chilly. It was still spring, and once the sun was gone the heat didn't stick around.

She did a quick chemicals check. They were close enough. She would put more in when they got out.

"Can I get in?" Debby asked.

"Oh yes." Rachael jumped in first, leaving the stairs for her vertically challenged friend. She absently picked two rubber ducks out of their bucket and set them floating in the water.

"No new ducks?" Debby asked.

Rachael shook her head. "We would have to go somewhere for that," she said bitterly. She bought a new rubber duck every time they traveled. She had about 12 in the bucket, a few of them gifts from family who missed the point of the collection.

"Is that why you never offer the hot tub?" Debby asked.

"We said anyone can use it any time the first time you came over! That was months ago," Rachael defended.

"It still would be nice to hear the offer again every once in a while," Debby said, pressing the buttons for the jets. Rachael let it rest. The session tonight was short; it was only about 10:30 p.m. Aaron must have been too pleased and wanted to end on a high note. Or possibly out of material. His workweek had been very demanding.

Rachael closed her eyes and relaxed.

She was both pleasantly and unpleasantly surprised by her lack of guilt about David. The pent-up emotions had needed to come out and the sex was phenomenal. She felt the lightest and freest she had felt in the last year, at least.

She had picked up Aaron's favorite pizza on the way home from David's place. She had carefully planned out an explanation, but by the time she got home around 7:30 p.m., he still was not home. And the uncomfortable transition with David's smell still on her was avoided. She took a long, leisurely shower, threw out her underpants, and put her outfit right in the wash.

She got a text around 8:15 p.m. saying that he was glad she was out and was having a quick beer with his coworkers before heading home.

He got home safely in a great mood and was extra talkative about his work project. He beamed when she handed him his favorite pizza, reheated in the oven, and gave her a big hug and a kiss before having a few pieces with a big glass of water.

"I'm going to head to bed early tonight," Aaron said. "I'm just going to watch a few videos to wind down. This is going to be a long week, but the client comes on Friday, and if all goes well the project should be good for lift off."

"Did you have a good lunch with Greg and a good time with your girlfriends?" he asked.

Rachael took a steadying breath. It was time to be honest.

"Ha — he does that to me too!" Aaron chuckled. "He can make me so mad, I have to take a break to calm myself before talking about it. Thank whoever I need to thank that he enjoys RP; otherwise we wouldn't even speak to each other."

"Exactly." Rachael couldn't do it. He was in such a good mood.

"Just be careful. I know you always want to help out the underdog, but Greg had some issues growing up," Aaron confessed. "You know I would do anything for him, but he has been jealous of me my entire life."

Rachael's ears piped up. Aaron so rarely talked about his family. And usually, when he did, it was all rainbows and sunshine.

"What kind of issues?" Rachael pressed.

"Nope, not saying. He has a clean slate out here," Aaron said. "I shouldn't have said what I did. But the look on your face — I didn't want you to feel like you needed to beat around the bush."

"Right, thank you. I never hear much about your family," Rachael stated.

"Because there is not much to tell." Aaron laughed. "And the future is much more interesting than the past. Computers are getting so small. My program..."

They had talked for maybe 20 minutes before talking about his work made him think of an article he needed to read. And that was that.

Rachael felt the warm water jetting against her back and shook her head, clearing it of her week. Rachael was done crying, she was done with self-pity, and she was done feeling invisible. David had broken open a dam, a well of anger and emotions she had been holding back for years.

"Here I come," Rachael said, feeling a new sense of self-awareness and joy fill her spirit.

"Where are you going?" Debby asked.

Rachael's eyes were filled with the stars. Fort Collins wasn't so big that its light washed them out, and on clear nights, the heavens opened up. This was one of those nights.

"Wherever I want to."

DIRK AND DIRK REALTY

"Someone is in a good mood," Karen said.

"What?" Rachael asked.

"You are in a good mood. You just put two sugars in your coffee and you are humming something," Karen accused.

"Sorry," Rachael said. "It's probably whatever song was on the radio on the bus this morning."

"Still only have one car?" Karen asked.

"Yup, but I think I'm going to save up to get my own," Rachael mused.

"Hold up — that is a rather independent statement. Am I talking to Rachael, Rachael Chambers?" Karen asked with dramatic flair.

"Yup. Do you want to go get drinks after work tomorrow?" Rachael asked.

"What? Did you just ask me to go out for drinks on a work night?" Karen exclaimed.

"Well, I mean, we can wait 'til Sat…" Rachael backpedaled.

"No, no, no, no. Girl, let me cancel on my Tinder date. What are we wearing and where do you want to go?"

"I was thinking a cocktail dress." Rachael blushed a little as she said it. "And I was reading an article about two-for-one martinis at Elliot's. I have not really explored much of FoCo since moving here, honestly, and I think it's time."

Rachael was pretty sure Karen's screech could be heard through the entire office. "I need to send an email," Karen said dramatically. "But not so badly that I am willing to leave break two minutes early. Here, we will do another pot of coffee."

"So, really," Karen said after the pot was bubbling away, her voice calmer and at a more reasonable level. "What is going on?"

"I am just tired of doing nothing, and I don't need Aaron to have fun." Rachael hoped she didn't blush too much, a vivid memory of sex in a stranger's apartment in her memory.

"All right, don't share," Karen said as she refilled both their coffees and headed off to her cubical.

Rachael slowly made her way back, the junction of her thighs pulsing slightly from the memory. She put her headphones in and sat up a little straighter than absolutely necessary to start her data mining. And if she rocked further forward in her chair while "dancing" to her music, no one would say a thing.

26

FORT COLLINS

COMPUTER ROOM

Plink

Greg: I just want to talk.

Greg: Please.

Rachael: You are right. I am avoiding you.

Greg: So…you read all my earlier messages.

Rachael: Almost 50 messages, Greg. You must have something better to do with your time.

Greg: I want to do you with my time. *joke*

Rachael: I will block you.

Greg: Sorry, I just wish we were back on our old terms.

Greg: I miss our conversations.

Rachael: Greg, I love your brother. I want us to be friends for the sake of him, but that is it.

Greg: I understand that. I would like to be friends, too.

Rachael: Are you capable of treating me that way?

Greg: Yes.

Rachael: Ok.

27

FORT COLLINS

ELLIOT'S MARTINI BAR

"Who are all these people?" Rachael asked.

"Sweetie, all these girls work at the same office we do. You just never look around," Karen chastised. Some ladies were in their office clothing. Others had brought a little dress to change into. Rachael felt self-conscious. Even in her slightly thinner twenties, she had mostly frequented pubs and little mom-and-pop shops. Martini bars and little dresses were not really her thing. But that was the point.

"Stop pulling that thing down," Karen said, swatting at Rachael's hands. "And honestly, I would have worn that to a funeral. We need to teach you what a martini dress is."

"I think I did wear this to a funeral," Rachael laughed. "I didn't have time to buy a new dress between deciding to do this and doing this. At least it is black and formal-ish." Karen gave her the stink eye anyway.

Rachael didn't care. The dress had long sleeves, a high neck with little chrome buttons that went down one side, and some ruching that hid her belly and accentuated what little hourglass she had. The bottom hugged her hips before ending in a little flare. She was still just wearing her black office shoes — maybe not perfect, but baby steps. She left her hair up in its work bun. It helped balance out the high collar.

Karen spent a few minutes introducing everyone around. There were six of them out tonight, and Karen said if it went well, she hoped it could become a weekly or every-other-week thing. Rachael often forgot that Karen was one of the heads of Human Resources. She knew everyone and everything. She had a mind like a steel trap and loved Dirk and Dirk. It was why she got away with speaking the way she did to the managers. Often.

"Ladies..." Karen paused for dramatic effect. "Let's get our drink on."

Elliot's was maybe half full at 5:30 p.m., mostly of people in business casual. Although a few people had beers, the number of martinis in hand was reassuring that this was the place to go. She followed Karen and her coworkers up to the bar.

The three bartenders rushed to take their orders. Rachael watched to see what others were ordering before heading up last.

"I was looking at your menu and, unless you think there is something better, I would like to start with a Bad Bitch. A double please. And then I want a Midnight Express, also a double."

"I am legally only able to make one drink at a time," the woman at the bar said. "But I will write down your order and see what I can do. Starting a tab?"

"Oh yes, although only those two drinks will be on it," Rachael answered.

"We gotcha," the woman winked, taking her card and putting it in a box behind the bar. "You are tab eight."

"Thank you," Rachael said. She leaned on the bar and watched the woman pour liquors into a shaker. She threw some of the bottles into the air, caught them.

"They are pretty good at that," a low Scottish accent.

Rachael jumped, nearly peeing herself. "Jesus."

David lay a steadying hand on her back. "Steady," he said, his head very close to her ear again. His voice melted her insides and heat flooded all the parts of her body it shouldn't have.

"Rachael, who's your friend?" Karen came over quickly, looking at David with a skeptical eye. "How long has your drink been on the counter?"

"It can't have been long," Rachael started. "They were still making it when David startled me."

"David? Mister Handsy has a name?" Karen looked at the woman behind the bar. "Have you taken your eyes off that?" she asked, pointing at the martini.

At the nickname of Mister Handsy, David quickly drew back. Rachael couldn't decide if that was a good or bad thing.

"I just put it down. It hasn't been touched," the bartender said.

"Good, I can't believe we left you at the bar by yourself." Karen's cheerful voice was back. "First time out and we abandon you. Don't think badly of us. We have the table by the window."

Rachael didn't look for or at David. David was in the past. And like Aaron always said, it was the future that mattered.

28

FORT COLLINS

LIVING ROOM

Rachael bit her lip to keep herself from moaning. One of her hands rubbed her lower stomach while the other one controlled the vibrator that had just arrived in the mail today. It was smaller than she thought. There was a joke in there somewhere, but at the moment she didn't care.

The device was a simple, vibrating, vaguely penis-shaped plastic rod with a little fork-like thing that vibrated against her clit. And that it did. Rachael had never had sex standing up. And so, it was time to give it a try. Her pants were partway pulled down. A buzzing noise filled the living room. She first rubbed the vibrator against her tummy and then down. Letting just the tip rest just above her clit, the vibrations sending tiny pulses of pleasure before she inch-by-inch pushed it up into herself. She rotated it around until the little fork gave her its own special buzz.

She bit her lip again, this time moving the little machine in and out, just enough that she lost contact with the fork and then gained contact again...the total vibrations never stopping. She tried to lose herself in the sensation, but after a bit, she took it out and turned it off.

She needed something to focus on. A story, a situation. A woman half-dressed with a dildo was not hot to her mind. It made her feel sad.

Especially sad because Craig was gone, never should have existed really, not even a fantasy she wanted to touch. And David. David was real, and real things always got messy.

Angrily, Rachael threw the dildo back into the box it came in. She looked at the little discrete package containing the dildo and a few other toys that had seemed interesting online. She was tired of being pent-up. Ten years ago, Aaron couldn't get enough of her. And just because his libido was slowing down and hers was speeding up shouldn't keep her from experiencing new things.

She just needed to find a new situation, a new mental plaything that had no relation to anyone she possibly knew. Maybe she could develop a celebrity crush — those seemed to be all the rage.

29

GOOGLE DRIVE

LILLY'S BACKSTORY

Written by Rachael

I grew up happy, loved, and cherished. The middle child of 10, I was never old enough to take care of anyone or young enough to be taken care of. My family was and is unreasonably happy, supportive, and helpful. I did my best to take up the family mining business, but I often wandered and found a passion for music.

My family didn't mind and helped me find my dream. Although no tutors could be found in our village, the local tavern always had a traveling minstrel and troubadour, storytellers from faraway lands. By age 15 I had stretched my first skin over one of my father's beer steins, and by age 30 I had designed a series of functional pony kegs that changed pitches as you drank.

By age 40 — dwarfs are a long-lived people, and this would be my late teens if I was human — I not only was learning from the musicians at the tavern but playing with them. It was in my local pub that I met 4aDeer, and together we adventured for my lyre from the god, Milil, Lord of Song. With my lyre and drums, I decided to leave my family for the first time to find my own stories and songs.

I cried, my family cried (cue Disney music). But it was time. I have been on the road for about five months now. I have not been bothered. My easy manner and innate musical talent have kept me fed, dry, and blissfully unaware of many of life's trials I have yet to experience.

30

ICE DRAGON'S REALM

LILLY

The Underdark is connected to everything. The realms of light and dark. Of powerful creatures and of wastelands long destroyed. It is aware of everything, but everything is not aware of it.

— AARON, DUNGEON MASTER'S NOTES, CS8.

"We're following the leader, the leader, the leader," Lilsa sang tunelessly in that odd double voice.

"Would you stop that?" Craig asked.

"Stop what?" Lilsa asked.

"Making noise," Craig said lamely.

"Ah, no. That won't be happening any time soon," Lilsa said. "You might have Lilly under your thumb, but I'm a part of her now. And as a powerful sorcerer, I sing what I want."

"I think she is doing it just to bother you now, Craig." Poppy's voice was sympathetic, but her eyes danced with laughter.

"Are we close, Lilsa?" Eismus asked.

Lilsa stopped singing and walking. She drew the group around her. "Actually, we are. We probably want to be as silent as possible here soon. The cross to the Ice Dragon's Realm is just a few bends ahead. And we need to put on our warm gear. The Ice Dragon's Realm is cold, obviously."

They had left town later than expected. After almost an hour of bickering, mostly between Craig and Eismus, the group had finally decided to get another day's worth of rations and warm clothing, draining the last of their finances and owing a debt to the general store.

"One more time," Eismus said. They had sketched out a plan.

Lilly piped up, "We are stealing a gem out of the ice dragon's hoard for the Dragon Temple. Isa knows what it looks like and has described it for us. We need to get to the hoard and steal it as quickly as possible and get to the exit.

"We are playing magic maze!" Rachael exclaimed. *"I love magic maze."*

"Stay in character, please," Aaron sighed. *"I'm glad you are in a good mood, Rach, but really, these interruptions need to stop."*

"Are there any areas that give us extra time?" Lilly asked.

"No," Isa answered. "Technically, you don't even have to do it at all if you don't mind losing your mind."

"Sorry I asked," Lilly said.

"It's so weird watching you have a conversation with yourself," Poppy added as she slipped on her last layer. "We need to get there soon or I'm going to die of heatstroke."

"Almost done," Eismus, or what used to be Eismus, said. Poppy laughed at the ball of layers that might have contained a drow. "I'm naturally cold-blooded," Eismus snapped.

"Sorry." Poppy spread out her hands in innocence but didn't stop laughing.

They were soon off. Lilsa in the lead with Craig close behind her and 4aDeer bringing up the rear.

The transition from the Underdark to the Ice World was instantaneous — a chill in the air their only warning. A world of blinding white and howling wind. Even with the extra layers, Lilly felt the cold down to her bones. Isa shrank back from Lilly's physical form, cutting off her ability to feel cold, and Lilly felt her own consciousness take complete control of her body once again.

She didn't talk to the party, just kept them moving as fast as possible, an almost deadly pace, the screaming winds ripping the heat from their bodies. She lost track of time. Isa occasionally nudged her in the right direction.

"We must find shelter to rest," Lilly said to herself. The only answer was a nudge toward her left. She led on, not breaking pace.

"Look, a cave." Lilly heard the voice over the wind. Her pace doubled almost to a run in her excitement to get out of the wind. Inside, the howling was much worse, but the cold was less. Lilly stamped around with her group, getting feeling back in her feet.

"Are we alone in here?" Eismus asked.

"I have no idea," Lilly answered. "Honestly, I was too cold to think to check, and Isa is basically hiding in a corner so she won't have to feel it. Do we have any way to detect weather patterns? Is this normal for this world?"

"It is not normal," Isa answered. "I can't do anything about it or tell you how long it is going to blow."

"I have basic weather magic. It comes from knowing the earth," Craig said absently to himself. "But it has been so long."

"Give it a try," Lilly asked. She easily rested a hand on his arm. Craig looked at the hand and smiled.

"I will do my best." Craig went back out into the snow, the only one of them not uncomfortable. Stone didn't feel the cold.

The group waited, some more patiently than others, for Craig to return. It was agreed that they would stay close to the entrance with no fire until they knew what the weather was doing. Craig's booming footsteps could be heard even above the screaming wind. Lilly filed that information away for later.

"The storm is at its height. It will blow itself out over the next five-ish hours," Craig explained.

"It will take about three hours to reach the middle of this world. It is not very big," Isa added helpfully.

"We have time." Poppy relaxed a little. "I say we explore a little of the cave and light a fire and see if we can get some sleep. We don't need it now, but we will need it later."

"Just a bit of the cave." 4aDeer's teeth were still chattering. They had the hardest time finding layers for the broad orc.

"Just a bit," Poppy repeated. "Just far enough to block out the wind," Poppy agreed. Without prompting, 4aDeer started walking. Craig and Lilly hastily followed after with Poppy, Eismus trailing behind.

It didn't take long for them to feel the wind completely stop, and the cave was blessedly empty.

"We don't have anything to burn for a fire," Poppy suddenly realized.

"That is not a problem," Isa said. "4aDeer, bring me the biggest rock you can find."

4aDeer nodded and headed off down the cave.

"Don't go alone," Poppy softly yelled, her little feet pumping to catch up with the big orc.

Lilly continued to stop and rub her own arms.

"I wish I could warm you up," Craig said sincerely.

Lilly was cold enough that she would have let Hitler warm her up. "Me too."

"AAHHHHH," they heard the yell before they saw Poppy's little form hoofing it. Odd to see Poppy first. Then Lilly spied 4aDeer loping along with a rock twice the size of his head above him.

"Didn't want to give up rock," he yelled. A pack of white

four-legged creatures was right on his heels. The creatures were short, maybe three and a half feet, and they moved like gorillas, but their front arms were unbelievably long. Blue eyes with no pupils glowed out of dragon-like eye sockets.

Lilly watched as one of their very, very long arms swiped at 4aDeer, almost taking him out.

She had just gotten feeling back into her hands and she beat out a rhythm on her drum, hardening the air directly behind 4aDeer. It landed solidly, slowing five of the creatures.

"That won't hold them for long," Lilly shouted.

"Drop the rock and get down, you idiot," Eismus shouted before his fire spell rolled off his lips.

4aDeer threw the huge rock ahead of him and to the side, rolling in the opposite direction as bolts of fire hit the three closet attackers. Lilly started to ready a spell when she felt Isa take control of her body. Suddenly she was feeling her lips move of their own will, her hands adding gestures.

Poppy cast thunder wave, shaking the very walls of the cavern, knocking all but one of the slowed creatures down. 4aDeer managed to get himself up and threw a small axe. The axe buried itself in the side of the only creature still standing.

It cried out in pain as Lilly heard the pitch of Isa's chanting change, and a black ooze erupted from the middle of the group of creatures. The smell of burning flesh and fur filled the cavern as the creatures tried to get out of the oily substance now eating at their bodies. 4aDeer readied his axe but was smart enough not to chase through the spell.

"When do I learn that?" Eismus asked. Lilly felt sick. Some of the creatures were still alive, being slowly eaten by the magical acid. Their dying moans getting weaker by the minute.

"When you are ready and begin your studies again," Lilly heard Isa answer. "The power a dragon priest wields is unimaginable."

Lilly didn't want to see her own face, because if it mimicked the lust for power that she could see in Eismus, she was going to be sick.

They ended up compromising with the wind, keeping a small amount of it at their backs to try and relieve the smell of melting hair and flesh. No one else came looking for the stone, and Isa easily spelled it to generate heat. Lilly watched, confused, as the strange carvings in the stone glowed brighter at first before disappearing in the heat.

She tried to come to the surface of her own mind to point it out, but Isa was having none of it. And she and Eismus bent their heads together and spoke of power and spells. The stone went forgotten and unobserved.

The hours passed slowly, but the storm did lessen. Lilly didn't know if her body slept, though her mind went in and out, sometimes listening. Her ears perked up when she heard the name of the tavern they had all been in when they were originally taken.

"We felt the spell there," Isa said. Eismus leaned closer.

"I placed it. I still don't know what went wrong, but I am here," his voice was barely audible.

"She is listening," Isa said before she faked a laugh as if Eismus had told her a joke, and the conversation stopped.

Lilly mentally blinked. She had missed the beginning, but it sounded like Eismus wanted to be here? Was he the reason they were all stuck in the Underdark? Lilly let her mind circle the possibilities until it wore itself out and she slept.

When she awakened, the storm was almost out. The occasional flurry of wind and blown snow howling from the entrance. Blinding bright light peeped through the turns in the cave. She hesitated, the need to confront Eismus forefront in her mind, but this was not the time or place. They needed to work as a team to complete the quest.

"Let's go," Lilly felt Isa return to her corner, avoiding the discomforts of the journey. "Remember to wrap your eyes in the dark mesh," Lilly said as she wrapped her own face. It was hard to see with it on, but Isa had said it was necessary in the world of blinding light.

Lilly paused as she wrapped her head. Isa had not told them to put the gauzy material on back in the Underdark. She must have known about the weather, but then why not wait or warn them? Before she could even take a breath to speak, she felt her lips snap shut — Isa's will.

Anger simmered inside Lilly. This is the second time Isa had tried to silence her, and Lilly would have none of it. She pushed hard against Isa's control, focusing on prying her own mouth open.

"Roll a D8 for your meter," Aaron asked Rachael. Rachael picked up her favorite D8, a red one with swirls of white and gold, and tossed it into the dice tray. It stopped on a 3. Aaron looked down behind his screen.

"Isa remains in control of your body and mouth. Please move your meter down by three," Aaron asked.

"I see, I have a limited amount of ability to fight Isa." Rachael wrinkled her nose. The meter was already down by 25%.

"Isa is a powerful sorcerer," Aaron stated with a shrug.

It was Lilsa who got the party moving. They stumbled through the cave. It was too dark to see details in the cave, but where the sunlight started to peek through, reflecting off the pristine white, the snow was blinding. Their eyes adjusted slowly. The snow was at least a foot deeper than when they came in.

"The irony," Poppy wailed dramatically.

"Huh?" Craig rumbled.

"All I have wished for this entire miserable time in the Underdark was sun. And now the sun is so bright and it's so cold that it can't touch my skin, and I need to see it through a cloth," Poppy explained before wailing dramatically again. "The irony!"

"We head that way." Isa ignored Poppy, pointing the direction they needed to go.

"Take turns breaking trail. Snow too deep for short ones," 4aDeer responded. "I will start."

And with that, they were off. With little to no wind, the cold was not quite as biting, and Lilly could see little sparkles on the snow through the dark cloth. Hopefully, they could take it off to search the dragon's hoard. But she was surprised by how much she could see in the bright despite the cloth.

The march was tiring but uneventful. Miles and miles of rolling snow in every direction, with the occasional rock outcropping to break up the view. Nothing seemed to live in this world of white. Lilsa led them steadily toward a huge mound of snow, which was, in fact, a mountain, the side of it sheer and the top rounded like a mushroom cap.

"That doesn't look natural to me," Poppy stated. She had spent most of the walk with Lilly. The two shortest legs had to stick together.

"Me either," Lilly added.

"Because it's not, you chattering fools," Isa said. "The dragon built it centuries ago out of ice and snow, and every year the ice and snow builds. The walls are said to be 3 kilometers thick — probably more now."

"How do we get in?" Eismus asked.

"There is only the one entrance, the dragon's entrance. We need to see if the ice dragon sleeps or wakes and make a plan from there," Isa answered. "The entrance is off to the left a bit. We will walk for another mile and then I will need to lead."

And so they did, rotating Craig to the front to save their strength. Upon arrival at the entrance to the dragon's mountain, they took a quick rest, catching their breath and checking weapons.

"Who has the highest stealth?" Tom asked.

"Um, that would probably be Poppy," Debby answered. *"But I*

would need to turn into something else. Something sneaky. And I still don't have flying, not until level eight."

"A cat," Tom said. *"Everything else will move too slowly through the three km walls, assuming they are three km thick."*

"I do like cats." Debby grinned.

"Craig, would you be so kind as to carry my bags while I sneak in and see if the dragon is sleeping?" Poppy asked sweetly.

Craig nodded, taking the tiny pack from Poppy and placing it inside his big one. Not a second later, a little brown and black house cat wiggled its way out of a pile of clothing. The cat gingerly padded toward the entrance and disappeared inside.

"If she is not out in 30 minutes, we go in," Lilly said.

No one responded, though Craig picked up Poppy's clothing and shoved it in his pack. Most of it stuck out of the top. It took Poppy about 20 minutes to return.

"It sleeps." Poppy gratefully accepted her warm layers, back in gnome form. "The ice and snow layers also make it darker inside, so we won't need the cloth. It is also warmer, but I don't want to leave anything outside in case we need to bolt."

"Night will fall soon, and we will need our layers and shelter," Isa added.

"One step at time," 4aDeer said quietly.

"Craig, you need to stay out here and guard the door," Lilsa instructed. "We can hear your footsteps from some ways away. You will wake the dragon. Lilly and 4aDeer will go left, and Poppy and Eismus will go right once in the room."

"I can't leave you, Lilly," Craig was matter-of-fact. Lilly grimaced. "You must get over this, Craig. We will find you a place to belong. We promised, and I intend to keep it, but we can never be together, together. Under any circumstances."

"Not even as friends?" Craig's voice was so hopeful.

"Of course, as friends," Lilly's answer was too quick. "But only friends."

"Good friends." Lilly wanted to scream as Isa pushed the

words out of her lungs that she didn't want to say. "But we need to go now. Stay at the door. Be ready for us."

"*Really, Aaron?*" *Rachael asked. Aaron was role-playing Isa's part.*

"*I think it is a fun aspect to the storyline,*" *Aaron laughed.* "*And even if I didn't, Isa's motivations are unknown to you.*"

"*I think she is pretty clearly up to no good,*" *Martin added.* "*She is probably trying to cause strife in the party.*"

"*Let's just play,*" *Rachael huffed. She refused to look at Greg's happy, grinning face across the table.*

As quietly as possible, the group slowly walked through the walls of thick ice. Isa was correct about the way it was built. Layers upon layers of ice and snow. It was stunning — so pure, the ice was tinged with blue. Finite cracks ran through some parts where the weight of the roof was straining. But others were so polished you could see your own reflection. Although everyone just looked like ninja Michelin Tire mummies at the moment.

Lilly struggled to not burst into song to hear the acoustics, her bard nature being held in check by Isa and fear of the dragon. It seemed to take hours, but eventually, they saw a glimmer of yellow and the hallway opened up to a vast chamber. The biggest pile of gold and gems of all sizes that she had ever seen filled most of the room. On top of that slept a snow-white dragon. Each of its claws was as big as Lilly.

The party split, going their separate directions. Lilly heard herself chant under her breath as her arms lifted and gestured across the treasure pile. Isa immediately clamped her lips shut tight. Lilly didn't know what she just did, but without the ability to communicate it without waking the dragon, she just went along. Isa stayed mostly in control of their shared body. They slowly walked, eyes peeled for a clear, perfectly square diamond with a red and black heart suspended in the middle of it.

Assuming the dragon didn't wake, they were to meet in the back and search each other's side with a fresh set of eyes. They were about halfway around when the sound of a distant coin clinked. That turned into more coins that eventually became a crashing avalanche of treasure.

She didn't move but slowly looked up. One giant blue eye, the iris just like a cat, looked back at her.

FORT COLLINS

KITCHEN

"I thought we chatted about this." Greg brought the one plate he had managed to steal off the table before Rachael's desperate grab for them all finished. He gently set it in the dishwasher. Rachael sent out a silent thank you that she had remembered to empty it that morning.

"And then you continued to try and flirt with me through chat." Rachael did her best to sound like an adult. "I have asked you to stop. We need some distance. Olive Garden never happened, do you understand?"

Greg narrowed his eyes.

"Hey, Aaron," Greg pitched his voice to carry. Mind if I stick around a bit for tonight? The sky is supposed to be clear and I would like to use the hot tub."

"Oh, it is lovely. I have a thing in the morning so I can't stay, but I am planning on bringing my suit again next week," Debby added helpfully.

"You are always welcome to it." Aaron was much too nice. And as always, not moving from his coveted position until everything was put away and people off.

"Thank you for running; I can't wait to fight the dragon next week," Martin said as he ran out the door. Hopefully, his wife didn't give him too hard a time. It was going on 11:30 p.m.

"It's late. I'm going to head to bed," Rachael said evenly.

"But you love the hot tub. And I'm not working tomorrow," Aaron said suggestively. Rachael brightened. If Aaron was with her, Greg would behave himself.

"You are joining us?" she asked Aaron.

"Why not?" Aaron said. "It's my hot tub and I have had a crazy week. The client approved our concept. We have started programming a little already, but pieces will start coming together on Monday. I am on call, but not nearly as busy."

"Wonderful!" Rachael said, honest happiness coming from both relief and time to snuggle with her husband.

"Sounds good to me," Greg said.

It took about 10 minutes to get settled, but soon Aaron and Greg had beers and Rachael another glass of wine. The jets on the hot tub happily churned the water and bubbled away.

Rachael took another sip of wine and looked up at the stars, her hand in Aaron's. This was nice. Why didn't Aaron want to do this more often? She slid down a little farther in her seat and felt a jet brush her nether region. She pulled it back. A time and a place. When Greg was gone she would have some time with Aaron. Maybe she could talk him into some time with her back against a wall.

The sound of the hot tub and the clear night filled Rachael's ears and vision. The trio enjoyed each other's silent company.

She slid down again as tension started to leave her body, the stream just changing the water direction enough. A little warmup never hurt. She closed her eyes as the water direction became more pressure. Good pressure. Unconsciously, she moved her hips forward, wanting to feel more of it. She squeezed Aaron's hand.

"Did you have fun tonight?" Aaron asked.

"I did," Rachael's voice was throaty and relaxed. The perfect amount of arousal seeped into her very being. Not wanting, not truly horny, just lovely awareness. "I wish we could have kept going." Her words had a double meaning at the moment.

"Me too," Greg's voice was much closer than expected. Rachael opened her eyes. Greg had moved to almost right across from her. His face studied hers. The pressure on her honeypot increased and pulsed, no longer the easy relaxed arousal. She felt her body start to respond and she bit her bottom lip. Her eyes closed briefly.

"What was your favorite part?" Aaron asked. Rachael looked over at him. His eyes were closed, his beer half empty. Guilt filled her but she didn't move. Was it a body part? A tool? Or just water? Rachael couldn't tell, though it felt like more than water. The soft pulsing continued, and she began rocking her hips, the water displacement lost in the jets.

"I liked the dragon the best," Greg said. "Although I have no idea how we are going to bring next session to a climax." His eyes hadn't left her face. It was Greg doing this. It had to be. Rachael should move, but she didn't want to. She had promised herself that she would have new experiences. And it might not be Greg. He might just know about the jets or be able to read her face. Was it turning him on?

"How about you, Rach?" Aaron asked. Three quick pulses right on her center. "Rach, are you ok?" Aaron was drinking his beer. He still hadn't turned to her but squeezed her hand. She squeezed back and then let go of it to push some damp hair out of her eyes.

"Yes, sorry. I am just really relaxed." Three more pulses. She set her wine down on the edge and used both hands to keep her in place, her head slightly above the water. Her hips began to move. The "jets" felt a little harder and began a steady pulsing.

"I think..." more pulsing "my favorite part..." the pulsing was fast now, and she could feel herself on the edge. "Dragon." She almost moaned the word as the warm water and pulsing sent a small wave of pleasure over her brain and body. Her arms that had held her to the seat gave out and she let herself go under, her small climax moan turning into bubbles. She came up breathing hard, Greg's strong arms keeping her head above water.

"I must have had a little more wine than I thought," Rachael eventually sputtered. Greg let go of her arm and she ignored his lude smile. She paddled over to Aaron, who had sat up to watch Greg fish her out of the water. "My favorite part was the description of the dragon's lair and playing Lilsa! I know she is evil, but she is kinda badass."

Aaron smiled and pulled her into his arms, one finger absently fingering her breast under the bubbles.

"That is why I love you so much, you always love my details," Aaron said, giving her a squeeze. Rachael held eye contact with Greg until he looked away. It was Greg who left first, showing himself out.

"Hello, mind helping me with some boxes?" Rachael called out to the bar at Dungeons & Drafts. It was 9:45 a.m. on Sunday and Aaron had decided to do some clearing out in the middle of the night, apparently. He was sound asleep but had left a note next to the bed with his request that the boxes get dropped off this morning. Too bad he hadn't done any Rachael cleaning. Rachael wished her most recent, be it small, orgasm had been with Aaron and not a hot tub jet. Definitely a hot tub jet.

She was not dressed for a day out and wanted to get this done before too many people enjoyed the view of her little PJ shorts and her favorite hoodie. Of course, her most comfortable flip flops finished the outfit. At least she had put on some hoops and piled her hair on top of her head, a few strands coming out to frame her face. As long as you had on earrings, any outfit was complete.

She set down the box she had in her hands and headed back out to the car to get another one. She tried to juggle two boxes, but she just wasn't coordinated enough.

"Here, let me get one of those." Scottish. She didn't jump this time. But she did turn abruptly, forcing David to take a step back or get thoroughly thumped. He gingerly took the box from her. "I see you still have lost the ability to form words. I can make you a potion for that."

"Just the two boxes." Rachael hated how much her voice squeaked and the hot blush that filled her face. David balanced his box with one arm and helped close the trunk of the car with the other. Rachael led the way inside.

"Hi, Rachael." Bob was the owner of the pub. "What did you bring me today. And have you met David?"

"Um, yes. He is very helpful." Bob didn't pick up on David's snort. "And I'm not actually sure. When I woke up this morning, Aaron had left a note on them saying to bring them by. I know he has been super into his miniature painting recently. But he just got over his landscape spell so it might be all the leftovers of those."

"I will get Bobbie to go through them this afternoon," Bob said. Bobbie was Bob's son and co-owner of the pub. Bob and Bobbie really looked like older and younger versions of themselves, aside from some key distinctions. Of average height and build. Bob kept his blonde hair cropped short from his military days, though his stomach told the story of how long ago those were. Bobbie never quite recovered from his goth phase and kept his hair dyed black and lived in his black wrist guards.

"David, do you mind helping us move them to the back? Careful now, Aaron does amazing work and never asks for anything, so we treat his stuff with care."

"Happy to assist," David said. Once the boxes were settled on Bobbie's desk, Rachael made to leave. She got to the door and out the other side before David's deep voice lowly rumbled, "I don't think so." He came out right behind her. "I don't have some of the hottest sex of my life after a three-hour cry-a-thon just to let it vanish a third time."

"I'm sorry," Rachael began awkwardly.

"I can make you sorry," David's voice lowered, his Scottish getting a little thicker as he stepped toward her.

Rachael blushed as her stomach did a little flip. She wanted him to make her sorry. But she couldn't, shouldn't, and wouldn't say that. David was in the past.

"Can we go somewhere more private?" she finally asked. The pub opened at 10 a.m., with games starting at 10:15 a.m. Rachael looked at her watch — the parking lot was not private.

"Let's go for a drive," Rachael said, motioning to her car. David let himself into the passenger seat, and Rachael drove the car to a no access service road at the far end of the park they had walked the other night.

"David," Rachael started. "I am happily married. The sex. It was hot…"

She didn't get to finish as David stepped out of the car, closing the passenger door behind him. Rachael watched him walk across the front of her car. He held his square shoulders back, his posture impeccable. His well-rounded ass looked great in his jeans, although the top was hidden by his untucked black button-down. This was a bad idea. David opened the driver's side door and held out his hand. She took it, his rough hand collapsed around hers and he half pulled her out of the car.

"Look," she started again, calm. But didn't get any further as David's warm mouth was once again on hers. His tongue demanded entrance, his hand pushing on her hips almost painfully. She wanted it, her body wanted it. Why the fuck didn't Aaron want it?

"Stop," she pulled her mouth away from his and he pulled back, breathing hard, his hands still on her hips. "I decide if this happens or not," she breathed. Her hip moved subtly under his grip, the sounds from a distant busy road and the birds the only thing in their ears.

It was like a car race flag suddenly came down. David's hands were everywhere, his mouth moved from hers to her neck and back again. Her hands reached under his shirt. Her fingers explored his flat stomach before she stuck a few fingers in the waistband of his pants and tugged open the top button. The zipper glided down with a single motion. His erection freed of the tight fabric seemed to leap in anticipation, peeking out of his tartan boxers.

She wrapped her hand around the tip and slowly pushed the material away, squeezing at the bottom, before lightly running her hands back up his length. His mouth hummed in pleasure, vibrating the skin at the base of her collarbone. His kisses moved down her chest, one hand unzipped her hoodie and exposed her breasts, trapped in place by her favorite beat-up bra. He dove face-first into her breasts, lips kissing and nipping at the mounds of flesh. His hands moved down her sides and dipped into the elastic waistband of her PJ shorts.

They didn't need much encouragement to fall to the ground. David kissed back up her neck. One of his hands ran down her hip and the outside of her thigh before circling around and coming up the inside. She stepped out of her shorts, opening up her legs to give his hand better access. Her own hands draped over his shoulders.

She was already wet. He slid two fingers inside her and pressed her clit with his palm, pulling everything slightly upward. She moaned. Encouraged, he did it again harder, and a third time. She hissed on the fourth, this time moving to take hold of his throbbing cock and steering it between her legs. She pressed against him, bending her knees and squeezing his dick between her thighs and crotch.

David grunted, one hand possessive on her hip, the other guided her legs apart. Rachael put both her arms around his neck as he guided as much of his dick as he could fit into her. His other hand returned to her hip before he thrust again, pulling out and using big, rough strokes. Rachael felt the hoodie still hanging onto her arms bunched-up in her lower back. The pressure increasing as his strokes pushed her against her car. She could feel every part of him, his low grunts as he thrusted rumbled in his chest. Rachael squeezed her eyes shut as she felt his dick swell and burst. Her own walls squeezed in response. He moved more gently a few more times before pulling out. He rubbed the head of his quickly deflating penis against her quivering clit.

A small cry escaped her lips as that last rub surprised her with an unexpected but enjoyable little wave of pleasure. She stood for a second, fluids dripping down her legs. David was breathing hard; he unbuttoned his top and pulled off his undershirt, motioning to her to clean up with it. She did as he replaced his top layer and accepted his now soiled undershirt back.

Redressed, she slid down the side of her car and sat.

"I feel like I need a cigarette," she said. "But I don't smoke."

To her surprise, David sat next to her, his back also against the car.

"I shouldn't have done that," David stated. "I haven't been able to stop thinking about that night. I don't care that you are married and mentally unstable. I'm not looking for anything. But if I can help you again. If we can make each other feel good, even for a short time." He paused. "It felt good to be needed. That is all I wanted to say."

Rachael didn't know how to respond. She felt aroused, violated, frustrated, guilty, and almost everything in between. The two of them just sat side by side against the car, listening to the birds and each other's breathing.

He couldn't have sat for long. Without a word, he stood and walked back toward the pub, a phone number written on one of Dungeons & Drafts business cards left in his spot.

FORT COLLINS

DIRK AND DIRK REALTY

"So, it was hot?" Karen asked.

"How do you know if I have had sex or not?" Rachael glared at Karen as she walked into the break room. "And why are you late?"

"HR meeting. Shit's going down and I will go to the grave with my secrets," Karen said. "Now spill."

"It was different," Rachael finally voiced. "It was..." she groped for words other than "it was not with Aaron."

"Did you two have a fight? Was this fighting sex? I love fighting sex, I just have trouble picturing Aaron..." Karen trailed off. "Well, having any sex."

"He is good at it when he does it," Rachael defended.

"When 'he' does it does not sound like good sex to me," Karen deadpanned. "But I don't want to get into it with you. To each their own. I had this Tinder date on Saturday."

"Karen, all we ever talk about is sex and men," Rachael interrupted.

"What else would we talk about?" Karen asked.

"I don't know," Rachael thought for a moment. "Current events? Do you have any hobbies?"

"You should know me better, Rachael." Karen actually looked offended. "The world is run by people we will never meet and policies we can never change. And hobbies, do I look like I knit? Please. I love to work, gossip, and help the people I do meet…if you know what I mean." Karen gave Rachael a little wink. "Besides, sex is a hobby. Maybe not a socially accepted one. But a hobby nonetheless."

Rachael didn't completely agree with Karen, but she understood.

"Now, my date on Saturday…"

FORT COLLINS

COMPUTER ROOM

"VICKY!" Rachael said as Victoria's picture appeared on Skype.

"RACH!" Vicky responded, just as excitedly.

"How are you? I miss you so much. Talk to me about home." Rachael talked fast so that Vicky wouldn't pick up on the waver in her voice or the fat tear that slid down her cheek. Vicky was her best friend. They had grown up playing together, and although she had really gotten into music in high school and Rachael hadn't, they remained close. Vicky was her maid of honor over her two sisters.

"I am really good. I miss you, too. I am still seeing the same guy and I still have the same job. I actually really like this one, the job and the guy. The administration is pretty good about supporting the staff, although it is an inner-city school so some of the kids are rough around the edges." Vicky was a music teacher and amazing at it. Rachael spent the next 20 minutes listening to her stories and genuine love for her job and life.

Rachael had loved her life; she still did, right? She let Vicky's stories blend into her memories of past Rachael and Aaron. Her mind watched their victory dance after weeks of trial and error when they had finally beat the video game *Divinity*. Aaron's love filled her heart as he came home from a long day at work, a single red rose, just for her, held between his teeth. She felt his arms around her as she had started crying during the fireworks at Disneyland, the princesses' happy endings the path she was so sure she had been on.

Rachael could see the little picture of herself in the bottom corner of the screen. She could even see the reflection of the screen in her glasses and remembered why she preferred her contacts.

"Didn't we take a class that said, in movies when people are shown in reflection, it is symbolic?" Rachael asked as Vicky's stories began to slow down.

"I think so," Vicky said, obviously trying to figure out the sudden jump in topic.

"Do you remember what it is symbolic of?" Rachael asked.

"Honestly, I really don't. I could google it," Vicky responded, already pulling her keyboard toward her.

"Let's do that." Rachael did the same.

"Well, this is bringing up a lot of specific examples and poetry." Rachael could hear the click-click of Vicky's searching and was sure she was sharing the same sound.

"Well, just a quick scan says duality," Vicky finally said.

"Ya, the movie *The Shining* came up in two different searches for me too and said the same," Rachael added.

"Why did we just google that?" Vicky asked.

"I am looking for a new hobby," Rachael said absently. Did she need a new hobby? She needed something to change.

"Games not enough for you? You could learn a musical instrument!" Vicky sounded excited.

"I need a change of pace. Not to feel like an idiot all over again," Rachael laughed. "I want to build on something I already know and something that is independent."

"Independent?" Vicky questioned.

"I have most of my hobbies in common with Aaron. Especially since moving, I just…" Rachael trailed off.

"I get you," Vicky smiled. "Just because you are married doesn't mean you need to share the same life. I have been telling you that for years. It's not even healthy. You have been too emotionally dependent on him, and Aaron just isn't really a giver. Remember, I watched you two date for years. I know what I am saying." Vicky paused in case Rachael wanted to get a word in, but Rachael wanted Vicky to finish her point.

"You two are head over heels for each other, but Aaron has a special mind. He gets focused and you get hurt, and when you were here, we had non-boy stuff to distract you. I wish you lived closer. I know something's wrong and you just don't want to talk about it. You look like you could use a hug."

"You have no idea." Rachael felt another fat tear slide down her cheek. She wiped it away. "I am not crying again. Vicky, I made some bad decisions, but they made me happy at the time."

"Rach, there are no such things as bad decisions, just lessons in our past," Vicky said, her hands fluttering, trying to virtually hug Rachael. Rachael took a deep breath and controlled herself.

"You're right. Aaron says something similar." Rachael was happy there was just a little waver in her voice. "I'm going to go. I love you and miss you."

"Wait, Rach. If you ever need to talk about it, I am here. I love you, too," Vicky said before Rachael ended the call.

Rachael listened to the sounds of her house, the spinning of two computer fans, the occasional click from unknown pipes, and the low sounds of Aaron's music coming out of his headphones from the other room. Her computer faded to black, going into sleep mode.

***P**link*
Rachael looked down at her phone. She had a new Facebook message. She didn't use Messenger for much, so chances were it was Greg.

plink *plink*

Rachael finished looking through the rack she was on before taking her phone out of her back pocket. Surprise, it was Greg.

Greg: Coffee?

Greg: Lol, jk. I know you wouldn't get coffee with me.

Greg: But I am surprised to see you shopping for dresses.

Rachael put her phone down and looked around.
plink

Greg: Aaron doesn't care what you wear, so who could you be getting this for?

Rachael: There are two of us in the marriage and I have been getting into dresses.

Greg: Fair, although I like the idea that you are getting one for me.

Rachael put down her phone and shook her head. She wasn't justifying that with a response.

plink *plink* *plink*

She didn't look at her phone, but she definitely didn't want to be dress shopping if Greg was watching her while she was doing it. What a weirdo. She should have gotten out of the hot tub. It probably had been him and now he was encouraged. Even if it hadn't been him, he had watched her face and she hadn't said anything.

plink

Rachael looked around for him one more time before heading out the closest exit and flipping open her phone.

Greg: I would love to see you in blue.

Greg: With a matching little hat.

Greg: Look at your phone.

Greg: Look at your phone.

Rachael wished she hadn't looked at her phone. She was suddenly uncomfortable waiting around for the bus and called an Uber to pick her up from the Chuck E. Cheese's a few blocks away. Greg was probably just at the mall the same time she was and was trying to make a game of it.

plink

Greg: Look at your phone.

FORT COLLINS

COMPUTER ROOM

Rachael smiled as she watched a slideshow of pictures on her computer. An earlier version of herself and Aaron gazed into each other's eyes in the corner of the picture. In the background, the still water of Bear Lake reflected the rich pine forest that surrounded it, and the tall mountain peaks, tipped with white, seemed to gaze down at the world from above. The weather had been unbelievable, the sky crystal blue.

When she and Aaron had first moved to Colorado, they had driven their car up to Rocky Mountain National Park with some camping equipment they bought on Craigslist. The camping had been a disaster. Rachael's first time and Aaron's first time without a more experienced camper with him. They had forgotten things, discovered that the tent was missing a pole, and ended up spending the night in the Stanley Hotel.

The hotel had inspired the horror novel *The Shining* and happened to have a channel dedicated to playing both versions of the movie on repeat. The unsuccessful day of camping left them too drained to be willing to sit down for a formal dinner and, with takeout in hand, they had watched both versions — the old and the remake.

Rachael laughed out loud as the picture of her almost falling over came up. After watching the movies, in the dead of night, the two of them had wandered the haunted hotel taking pictures and looking for ghosts. They didn't find any, but Aaron had hidden behind a bend and turned the flash on the camera and scared Rachael half to death.

She was still laughing when she heard the front door open and close.

"Aaron," she called. "I'm in the computer room."

"Be there in a minute," Aaron's voice drifted back to her.

The slideshow went through a few more pictures of random parts of the hotel before changing into pictures of the little tourist town of Estes Park and then of the label of a wine bottle — Snowy Peaks Winery, Oso White.

"How was dinner with Greg?" Rachael called out as she paused the slideshow.

Aaron's arms wrapped around her shoulders and he gave her a hug and kissed the top of her head.

"You need to look at pictures of wine too? Did we run out of wine in the house?" he asked playfully.

Rachael swatted at him.

"No, this is the slideshow from our visit to Estes Park," Rachael responded. "I haven't checked the wine rack in the last hour though, so hopefully no one came in and drank it all."

"Dinner with Greg was good," Aaron answered. "We really should have been doing it when he first moved here. Most of our hobbies are different, but it is great to talk about role-playing and our younger selves."

Aaron kissed her head one more time before heading to his own computer. Rachael swallowed down a little nervous lump in her throat. "Did you talk about me?"

"Why would we talk about you?" Aaron asked back.

Rachael hesitated. "Greg was sending me messages while I was shopping the other day. It seemed like he was watching me."

"He did mention that he saw you at the mall," Aaron said. "He said that he was trying to be playful, but it might not have come off well and then he had to run."

"It didn't come off well at all," Rachael agreed.

"We are working on it," Aaron said. "We don't really talk about you, but we are talking a lot about girls and communication in the 21st century. He is an amazing sales rep but, boy, does he say some dumb things when he is not at work."

"Wow, he is telling you about them?" Rachael was surprised.

"Ever since his injury in high school we have had a completely open and honest policy," Aaron said. "I still don't want to get into it, but it was my fault. I didn't notice things I should have, and we agreed then and there that we would not keep things from each other."

Rachael absorbed that for a minute. Her kiss with Greg replayed in her mind. "And you believe everything he says?"

"He has never given me a reason not to." Aaron's voice was flat. This was dangerous ground. "Even when I got him the job out here, he was straight with me about why he wanted to leave California."

"And why was that?" Rachael asked quietly. She turned to face Aaron, who was not looking at his computer, but across the room at her.

"He was having relationship problems." Aaron's eyes were hard. "And if he would like to share more, that is his right. But I don't believe in talking behind anyone's back, especially family."

Rachael nodded. The conversation closed.

Rachael slowly turned her chair back to her computer as Aaron's attention drifted to his own computer screen. She hit play on her slideshow. A picture of her and Aaron clinking glasses in the little tasting house came up and then vanished, leaving behind a black screen with the words "Press the Esc key to exit slideshow."

Rachael' could see her shoulders rise and fall as she took a deep breath and reached for the escape key on her keyboard. Everything should come with an escape key.

ICE DRAGON'S REALM

4ADEER

Elemental dragons are extremely solitary and intelligent immortal beings who value wealth over everything but their own lives. Their realms are each unique and crafted by their innate magic. Despite their solitary nature, dragons are often wistful for entertainment. They have been known to align with smooth-talking, powerful individuals with promises of valuables.

— AARON, DUNGEON MASTER'S NOTES, CS9.

4aDeer didn't hesitate. No dragon would sleep through a treasure slide. It would need to investigate, count, and congratulate itself. It's what 4aDeer would have done. When the first coin dropped, he had looked up and watched as the three sets of eyelids slowly pulled back one at a time and the slits of pupils dilatated, adjusting to the light.

It took him four striding leaps; his feet seemed to fly as they sent showers of gold down below. It took all the strength he had to reach the dragon's head and his swing was true. Eye juices squelched as his war axe bit right into the center of the eye. There was a moment of shock, both from 4aDeer and the dragon, and then the dragon roared, bashing 4aDeer's body and sending him flying with his snout.

4aDeer tightened his grip on his axe, waiting for the impact of the wall. But when it came, it was soft and he hit the ground with a thud. He opened his eyes to see Lilsa with her hands pointed behind him, some cast on her lips.

"We have it. RUN!!" Poppy's high-pitched scream was almost inaudible over the dragon's cries of pain; its head and one good eye thrashed about as it looked for something to kill. 4aDeer felt hands grab his arm and pull him back toward the door. They were Lilsa's. He was lucky the dragon hadn't thrown him further back into the cave.

"I smell a dwarf; a gnome; an orc; and a dirty, dirty drow," the dragon bellowed. It spun, and treasure sprayed everywhere. 4aDeer felt something thud against his chest, leaving a little dent in his leather armor.

"Ouch, we need cover!" Lilly was bleeding from a cut where some pieces of treasure had hit her cheek. She tugged on 4aDeer and pulled him toward the pile.

"Lilly," 4aDeer started to warn, but as they got closer to the edge of the pile, the spray of projectile wealth lessened. They ran now.

"This is my kingdom. You may get out of this chamber, but you will never leave here alive." The sound of a huge amount of air getting sucked in by massive lungs was terrifying. 4aDeer's long legs outstripped Lilly and he sprinted for the exit. He was relieved to see Eismus and a white bear of some sort loping ahead of him.

The sound of air being sucked in suddenly stopped. A bellow, half roar and half high-pitched hiss, filled the cave. 4aDeer dove forward as cold hit his backside. He rolled several times before lurching to his feet. Instincts told him to keep running, but his mind screamed, "Lilly!"

Against his better judgment, he turned. The entrance to the cave was sealed off. A wall of blue and green dragon ice sat cold and impenetrable in front of him. He pressed against it. The cold burned his bare hands.

"Lilly," he yelled. He could see her blurry form through the ice — her eyes wide. Then she mouthed something to him and disappeared.

4aDeer's mouth copied the shape Lilly's had made and he repeated her word. "Dorom." Dorom was dwarven for run. Lilly had told him to run; Isa didn't know dwarven. 4aDeer had no choice. He ran. He ran as the wall shook with the dragon's rage. Sharp points of ice dropped from the ceiling. One sliced through his left arm. Another made him dodge right or be impaled.

Craig was waiting at the entrance for him. The wind was beginning to pick up again.

"Where is Lilly?" Craig's words were fast for a rock monster.

"Trapped. Run," 4aDeer said.

"You left her?" Craig demanded.

"No choice," 4aDeer said. 4aDeer placed his hand on Craig's arm, his green blood dripping onto the cold rock, sizzling slightly before freezing to the stone. "Isa in her. We come back."

The cry of pain and rage that ripped out of the rock mage's chest sent a shiver of fear through 4aDeer. But, as he turned to run, he heard the thumping steps of the rock mage behind him. They followed their old broken trail until it branched off, a set of bear and boot prints going in different directions. 4aDeer could feel himself shivering violently as his adrenaline left his system. The wind had picked up again and it cut through his sweat-filled layers. It was getting hard to see.

"Craig, can you see?" 4aDeer asked.

"I can see fine." Craig's voice was tired. "But the sun is going down, maybe if you took off the black mesh…"

4aDeer reached up and pulled off the mesh. He could see fine. The sun was just losing its hold on the world.

"I am sure they split to hide the trail from pursuers. So, where are they hiding and how are we supposed to know?" Craig mused out loud.

"Lilly," 4aDeer simply stated. She had spells to help them follow. They studied the trail for another few seconds.

"I have to keep moving or I will die," 4aDeer stated.

Craig nodded. "Then we make a third path directly between them and pray." 4aDeer slipped in behind Craig as he began once again breaking trail through several feet of snow.

"I see smoke ahead and to our left," Craig said, already adjusting course.

4aDeer hugged himself. He couldn't feel most of his body and just assumed that because he was still moving, his feet were still there.

The snowbank had been getting taller as they walked. The smoke was gone. 4aDeer felt his body stop shivering and he smiled, enjoying the sudden warmth.

"Warm," he said, taking his arms out of their hidey-holes.

"I don't think you are supposed to feel warm," Craig said, concerned. He seemed to think for a minute and then made a decision. His fingers moved as he mumbled something and pointed at the deep snow in front of them. A green light emitted from his fingers and the earth rumbled. He opened his hands, and a hole began to form in the snow. Just wide enough that they could see. On the other side of the bank was a clearing and the rosy glow of a fire.

"Who's there?" Eismus demanded.

"It's us," Craig yelled back. "4aDeer doesn't have much longer."

"Shit," Eismus said. "Stand back."

4aDeer saw the fire burst from the snow but just giggled as it hit him. It was warm. But he was already warm. Craig's stone hands pushed him toward the hole the fire just made in the snowbank.

"Crawl for your life, 4aDeer," Craig rumbled. And 4aDeer crawled, because what else was there to do? At some point, he checked for his axe. The hilt felt warm against his hand. For a second, he realized that it was dragging in the snow...it would get dull, but he couldn't hold onto the thoughts. He felt another push from behind and then suddenly he was in a clearing.

"Where is Lilly?" Poppy's voice.

"With dragon," 4aDeer giggled.

"Shit, he is delirious," Eismus spat. "What can we do? All we found is this clearing."

"We need to warm him up. Craig, on guard duty. If anything was following us, you led them straight here. Fill in that hole you made in the snow if you can," Poppy instructed. "Eis, keep the fire going and strip him. Put anything wet by the fire and give us your top layers."

"My top layers? Why?"

"Because you are warm, you selfish prick," Poppy snarled. "I am going to change into a bear and wrap around him and then you need to cover us with as many dry blankets as we can spare."

"Must get Lilly," 4aDeer mumbled. He was having trouble keeping his eyes open.

"Hurry!" Poppy said, and then 4aDeer let his eyes close.

"Isn't that bad?" Rachael asked. "Does that mean you have hypothermia and are not going to wake back up?"

"We are using it for dramatic effect and not spending eight hours role-playing out 'keep the orc awake,'" Aaron answered. "Or we could spend the rest of the session and next playing that out..."

"No, no. I'm good. Anyone else?" Rachael said innocently, looking around the table.

"Good then. You aren't here," Aaron stated. "You are back in a dragon cave. You are like Schrödinger's cat at the moment. Stay quiet and contemplate your quantum superposition."

"You successfully get 4aDeer warm under blankets and bears. But you will not know his condition until you wake up the next morning," Aaron explained. "Wake up when you are ready."

Everything hurt. Even seeing through his eyelids hurt. But he was warm. 4aDeer felt something small in his arms. It tugged at a memory buried down so deep he couldn't access it. He pulled it closer.

"Ouch, I need to breathe," Poppy's voice. 4aDeer tried to sit up but couldn't. "4aDeer, are you OK?"

"Can't move." 4aDeer started to panic, but it didn't register in his body.

"Don't panic and don't move too much. The sun is back up, but we will lose the heat. I am surprised Eismus hasn't woken yet," Poppy said.

"I have," Eismus stated. "But I feel my current position is undignified and I refuse to acknowledge it."

Craig laughed as he put more of the soggy wood on the smoldering fire. It was drying quickly; the fire must have been lit for hours to be that hot.

"Lilly," 4aDeer said.

"We don't know," Poppy was quick to answer. "Nothing has changed other than we all lived through the night. Literally in a dogpile on Poppy in bear form with every piece of dry clothing on top of us and the wet ones on top of those. Thank you for taking care of us, Craig," Poppy sniffed. "If you don't mind, I am assuming our clothing is dry at this point. If you could pass it to us…"

"Me first," Eismus demanded.

4aDeer felt the man move against his back and was

relieved that he could feel even if he couldn't move. He didn't know how to respond, so he watched and waited. Poppy dressed first and tossed Eismus his clothing before getting rations out of the pack, along with the collection of random potions they had bought. Most were labeled, but they had picked up a few at discount that were not. Poppy opened one and smelled it.

"This one is either a sleep potion or poison. I think we will wait on it." She sniffed a few more.

"Ah, here is the one that we bought the lot for." Poppy brought it to 4aDeer and opened it up. "I can't believe someone made this and didn't label it. It is one of the most powerful healing tonics in the world. Drink all of it, and when you can move, dress and join us at the fire so we can figure out what to do next."

4aDeer needed some help but got all of it down; it didn't take long for the magically imbued potion to travel the length of his body, but he was loath to leave the warmth of his blankets.

"I have to roll to get out of blankets now?" Martin asked.

"You nearly died of hypothermia," Aaron stated. "4aDeer has a new aspect. Would you rather fear cold or just hate it a lot?"

"I don't feel that 4aDeer would fear anything that almost killed him, growing up in the fighting pits and all. But I see what you are saying. Hate the cold is fine...does it replace my current negative aspect?"

Aaron laughed. "Nope. You just get to have two now."

Three times it took him to finally face the cold morning, but Poppy had brewed something warm, and the fire was burning cheerily.

"We got what we needed," Eismus stated, patting his pocket. "And Lilly has one-and-a-half more days with Isa — assuming she is alive."

"Until I see a body, she is alive." Craig's voice was cold and hard. It left no room for discussion.

"I'm just saying," Eismus concluded that thought but didn't elaborate.

"We know what you are saying, but we will not abandon her," Poppy shot back.

They broke camp with the tentative plan, squinting in the bright light but unwilling to compromise their vision.

"Everyone takes one damage," Aaron said after double-checking their choice.

"What?" Greg exclaimed.

"It's really bright. I described it for you and gave you protection for free," Aaron defended. "If you choose not to use it, the environment will damage you."

No tracks added to their own as they squinted their way back to the dragon's lair. It was really quite close. When the snow was not deep enough to hide their heads, they crawled, and Poppy once again shifted into the light-footed cat. She was back all too soon. Using the meow once for yes and twice for no, they quickly discovered that their tracks were being guarded by something near the dragon's entrance. But something Poppy felt they could take.

"What positions?" 4aDeer asked. The little cat rolled onto its back, its front paws pointing to the edges of the trail.

"I will take the one on the left." 4aDeer stood and charged, Poppy barely flipping over and getting out of the way. He didn't wait for the others to divide it out. This group was too much talk. The fight was short and brutal. The two guards were more of the odd, white-furred things. Their blue blood stained the pristine white snow as the party dragged their bodies back in a vain attempt to hide them.

"Do you think," Eismus started to ask, but was interrupted by a rush of wind and a deep dragon's hiss.

"I can smell you, thieves. And I will eat you for breakfast." The dragon landed with a boom on the snow in front of them, his mouth open, ready to freeze them.

"We will bring you something better." It was Eismus who spoke up.

"Something!? One something. You steal three of my prized possessions and a power crystal, and you offer me a thing?" The dragon's outrage was almost madness. Its tail whipped the snow behind it, sending a dramatic wave of sparkling white into the air.

4aDeer gripped his axe, but Eismus pushed past him and stood in front so he wouldn't be able to draw it. They needed to talk their way out of this. Especially as, to 4aDeer's knowledge, they had only stolen one thing.

"This land is troubled," Eismus said dramatically. "We did not come to take but to give."

"Taking is what you did." The dragon's cold hiss bit through their layers of clothing.

"Only in an effort to see." Eismus was struggling to sound confident. "Have you spoken with our bard?"

"The dwarf amuses me," the dragon said. "I was going to eat her…but she might be a treasure worth keeping."

"She is doomed to die," Eismus said theatrically.

"All little mortals do." The dragon was unimpressed and began sucking in air to breathe ice again.

"Then take me, too," Craig suddenly yelled. His rock arm easily shoved both 4aDeer and Eismus out of his way. "I don't want to live without her."

The dragon hesitated.

"You are a creature reborn of earth, hundreds of years old." The dragon craned its remaining good eye around.

"Yet, I am in love," Craig's voice was soft and rang true.

"You are." The dragon looked puzzled. But its mouth shut. 4aDeer tightened his muscles for a spring…ready to take out the other eye. Wait, the first one was healed already, cloudy still, but it looked days old. What was going on?

"I have lived long and could use some entertainment. And

187

you are not wrong. My minions have been dwindling. Something is not right in my land." The dragon paused and then lifted its head up, looking above them.

"Lilly is safe and sound in my most secure of vaults. Find her, bring me the head of whatever is killing my minions, return my treasures, and I will only take one of the Orc's eyes for my payment. I will even give you a one-hour head start to leave my land before I hunt you down like the filthy thieves you are."

38

FORT COLLINS

DINING ROOM

"The dragon's maniacal laughter fills the air as hundreds of minions begin to lope into view," Aaron described. "Die here or face my challenges!"

"I guess we know what we are doing next week," Tom said.

"I would hope; I have made the path pretty clear." Aaron nodded happily. "Although, the love story — I did not expect that. Really. Everyone will start next session with a bonus. I think this is one of my best campaigns ever, for role-playing."

Rachael smiled prettily at him but groaned on the inside. That is what Greg needed, more encouragement. To her surprise, it was Tom who started grabbing dishes and walked her to the kitchen.

"Are you OK?" Tom asked.

Rachael blinked. "Why are you asking me?"

Tom opened the dishwasher, efficiently loading it.

"Because I can feel Greg's eyes boring holes into my backside," Tom answered. "Honestly, Aaron told me he has been worried about you. You are suddenly acting differently, and he said you were crying when you were talking to your friend on Skype the other day."

"I am going through some stuff." Rachael had forgotten about the plate in her hand, and Tom took it from her before she could drop it.

"I grew up with Greg and Aaron," Tom continued. He had run out of things to put in the dishwasher, but he kept his hands busy with the towel. "I am Aaron's best friend, not just from here, but from childhood. You know that. Family is everything to Aaron, and he wants Greg to have a clean slate here. But I don't think that should be at your expense — that, in the end, will be at Aaron's. It is not my place to tell you anything. But if Aaron isn't listening...if Greg gets out of hand."

The offer was clear, even if Tom couldn't finish the sentence. Tom didn't like Rachael. He tolerated her because she made Aaron happy. If nothing else, Rachael was happy the two of them were on honest terms.

"Thank you," Rachael said. "But I can handle it."

"If you can't...just don't hurt Aaron," Tom asked. He had folded the towel and placed it on the counter. Greg was nowhere to be seen, and Debby's stuff was gone. Rachael was happy to rush to the bedroom.

Tom's straightforward words brought thoughts and emotions she was trying to ignore to the surface. She picked up her Kindle and attempted to rebury them in her book. She was half-reading and half-dozing when Aaron came in 45 minutes later.

"Not on your computer?" she asked. She didn't mean for it to come out coldly, but it did.

Aaron flinched. "No, not on my computer," he said. "Are you OK? Was it my game?"

Rachael burst out laughing, which turned into a laughing cry that ended with a loud, piteous sob that she hated herself for.

"Aaron. It was not your game. Your game is lovely — though Greg is getting intense," Rachael admitted.

Aaron sat on the edge of the bed like Rachael would bite if he came too close.

"I don't know what happened," she said after a long pause. "We just stopped communicating, and I have felt so lonely."

Rachael moved to Aaron and with calm breaths — guilt stabbing her as she left out her infidelities and issues with Greg — she really talked to Aaron for the first time since their move.

39

MOUNT PRINCETON HOT SPRINGS

Rachael loved the feel of her back pressed into Aaron's chest as his hand draped across her, absently drawing little circles on the inside of her thigh. The setting sun caressed their skin as the sound of the babbling river drowned out all but the horniest of birds. They had spent the afternoon having a lovely couples massage, and now they sat and watched the sunset from the heated natural pools on the side of the flowing river.

Aaron kissed the back of her neck and nibbled at her ear.

"I love you," he breathed. Rachael could live in those words, the way he said them. She tilted her head back for a kiss and Aaron obliged with a tenderness and knowledge that only years of being together could create.

"I love you, too," she responded.

The sun slipped behind the mountain and the sky blushed slightly, pinks and purples quickly being overtaken by the vast night sky.

"I'm starting to shrivel," Aaron stated as the Milky Way came out in its full glory.

"Me too." Rachael moved to get up. But Aaron stopped her, pulling her back down and kissing her until she was senseless. Dinner that night was simple but elegant and they fed each other and joked like newlyweds. Aaron had even called ahead and ordered a special dessert that came out with her name on it and a single red rose drawn underneath.

"Red is my favorite color," Rachael said, delighted.

"And double chocolate Belgian cake is your favorite cake," Aaron smiled.

Rachael moved to sit next to him as they shared the dessert, the candle burning low on their little table. The textured inky black of the pine forest melted into the clear star-filled sky. She felt herself blush as Aaron's hand wandered between her legs, lightly brushing and exploring. His other hand brushed her cheek and she turned toward him.

He tasted of chocolate cake, his mouth warm and tender, as he pressed it against hers. His hand moved from between her legs to her back to bring her closer. Rachael leaned into him and closed her eyes, one tear slipping down her cheek.

"Why are you crying?" Aaron's voice was soft.

"Because I love you so much," Rachael breathed. "This is too perfect."

"I love you too," Aaron responded. "Nothing is too perfect for you."

They spent the night talking and making love. Their bodies moved in familiar patterns as they brought each other to a climax again and again. Aaron promised not to ignore her, and Rachael promised not to stop communicating. They said they would make more time for each other. They spoke of nothing, of emotions, and of how happy the future was going to be.

But all things come to a close.

Too soon, Rachael found herself back home. The sound of the washing machine erasing the weekend from their clothing set the backdrop for the click of Aaron's keyboard. Rachael sat at her desk and scrolled through Facebook, her eyes unfocused as she watched her own reflection in the screen.

plink *plink*

40

EMAIL – MAY 16

Dear Underdark Party,

I apologize in advance, but I need to cancel our next two sessions. Work has been extremely demanding and I do not like to run when I cannot give you my full attention or preparation. However, I would like to start back in June with a long Sunday session before continuing with our usual Fridays. With two weekday sessions for some social encounters, assuming you live through the Sunday. Please return this email with your free dates.

However, I will not leave you high and dry. Rachael and I played out her bit while the party has been separated. I made her write it out, but we did sit together and roll it, so it is honest. I have also included a scene setting for our long session at the end of the email. I hope to see everyone the first Sunday in June.

Hi guys, Rachael here. Sorry in advance. My writing is terrible — and I am trying out some first person. Yay?

In the dragon cave: My short legs prevented me from reaching the entrance very fast. Or so I thought. Really, Isa was making me drag my feet, assuming the dragon would chase whoever stole the crystal and leave me unattended. Obviously, it didn't work well and now I am trapped here with the dragon. Isa takes control of our shared body completely. Isa has been saving her energy, and the most powerful sleep spell I have ever felt comes out of my lips. The dragon is out like a light.

I leave Isa in control of my body as she begins searching the treasure pile. The going is slow, and I notice that certain items are glowing. I can feel Isa start to panic, as the specially prepared sleep spell is going to wear off the dragon soon.

"I could help you search if I know what you are looking for," I thought.

"It will still only be one set of eyes." Isa sounds scared.

"We were not supposed to get stuck in here with it, were we?" I ask, but Isa doesn't respond.

But I feel the oddest sensation as Isa gives me control of one eye, funneling the vision from that eye to my consciousness alone. I see the image of a wand in my memories. Oddly, I can even feel it in my palm. The handle crusted with red and black crystals, the wood dark, smooth, and unnaturally crooked.

At this point, we've climbed with some difficulty to the top of the hoard — the spell that Isa cast first thing upon entering the cave made all the things imbued with dragon magic glow.

"There is no way it would be on the bottom," Isa hissed. "It is one of his prized treasures."

As if speaking it made it true, I notice an outcropping of rock, glowing. Isa nudges the body to it. Six small items, including the wand, are delicately placed on the top of the rock and covered in a layer of dust.

We take a long look at the dragon and then grab the wand and the two items next to it, not even registering what they are. Isa pulls a drawstring bag that I don't even recognize out of our many layers of clothing. The leather is covered in burned patterns (I rolled a 2, it could be an extra spotted cow for all I know). The items vanish into it and the bag folds into our layers of clothing.

Isa takes full control of our body once again and sprints for the entrance of the cave, her magic prodding for any openings. There are none, impenetrable. We don't stop looking as the dragon wakes up very slowly; we can hear the sounds of it stirring and stretching.

"There is no way out," the dragon groggily purrs.
"I didn't take your things," Isa says angrily.
The dragon's booming laughter fills the cave. "I don't believe you and will eat you for trying."
"Let me talk to him," I ask Isa in our mind.
"No," Isa says firmly.
"Heal him. Do something nice and maybe he won't hurt us," I plead.
Isa pushes me further aside. She can't defeat a dragon. I can hear it in her thoughts as her mind races for ideas and spells. I gather all my will, every little scrap of it that I can...and roll an eight! YES. I kiss my dice and drop my will meter to almost empty.
I gain control just as the dragon is coming for us. I throw out my fastest control spell, Tasha's Hideous Laughter, and the dragon did not save. I declare that I don't have to role-play out what I did, but this dragon is laughing so hard he is crying. Dragon tears have magical properties, and I quickly heal its injured eye with his own tears as a medium. The dragon only laughs for a short time. It is confused that I haven't moved and more confused that his eye doesn't hurt anymore, though it is not working.
I haggle my life for a song. The dragon accepts. I roll a seven, but Aaron lets me make up a ballad on the spot, and if it's good enough the dragon won't eat me. It is a ballad unrepeatable, it was so good – or possibly long and whiny, I tried really hard.

After three more songs of various rolls, the dragon tells me his name is Horase and my songs will be a part of his treasure. He lets the door melt and I have to use my remaining will to keep Isa from running, as we would not have made it.

I am taken through many hallways by some of the white gorilla things with long arms. They lock me in a room with no roof made of ice and filled with furs, armor, and clothing with some frozen body parts still in them.

After Isa and I have a thorough check for escape — impossible — we find as many body-part-less furs and layers as we can and hunker down. Interestingly, on a regular and fairly often schedule, the gorilla things bring me the warmest, sweetest liquid I have ever tasted. I have named my gorilla things "Goodall." It's a pun and science! And I am happier every time I see them. Man, this drink is good. *hic*

The End

Scene setting for our next session:

The beating of fists against packed snow thrums from underneath the howls and cheers of the Goodalls. The party walks tall and proud along the path lined by the creatures. The line funnels them back into the dragon's hoard. They find themselves circled by five Goodalls as they enter, two in front, two in back, and one in the lead.

The pile of treasure has been rearranged, parts organized, and parts restacked to become the dragon's bed once more. It must have taken hours. The dragon probably spent the night accounting for his treasure instead of searching for them.

"We live down these tunnels," the Goodall in the lead directed them to a hidden hole in the ice. "We are loyal to the master. But some have wandered off recently, and you must go down to solve our mystery. Lilly is safe in the master's care. The first part to finding her is to get to the top of the building we are currently in." The Goodall was hard to read, his eyes never blinked but a forked tongue whipped out of his mouth often, licking the shiny blue surface.

Would you like to go up or down first?

Choose your path wisely.

Sincerely, Aaron

P.S. My apologies again.

41

FORT COLLINS

HAUNTED GAME CAFÉ

Rachael reached for the colony in their *Dominion* game, showing her 11 gold and ending the game. She would bet money that she hadn't won, but she didn't play to win.

"I need a beer after this," Tom stated as they all started separating money and victory points out of their decks.

"Dungeons & Drafts?" Glen asked.

"Sounds good to me," Debby added.

"I think I would rather go to Coppersmith's," Rachael added.

"Really?" Aaron asked.

"It is a Saturday night. It might be fun to play pool or darts or something different than board games," Rachael defended. That might not be entirely why she was suggesting it, but it was true.

"Something other than board games," Debby said, seeming to try out the words in her mouth.

Rachael finished sorting her cards. "Fifty-three VP's," she stated. A solid score for her, though not a winner. The week had been a winner after their amazing weekend at Mount Princeton. Aaron had come home early, or at least on time, every day.

They went out together twice for dinner and had made delicate love four times.

"You love Dungeons & Drafts," Aaron said, concerned.

"I do," Rachael admitted. "But I am all about trying new things right now. I love games because you love games." She reached for his hand as he finished sorting his cards and squeezed it. "Come with me?" she asked.

"I'm out," Debby said. "Glen, would you like to come to Dungeons & Drafts?"

"I'd love to," Glen said, blushing a little. Debby gave him a look. "You remember you and I play for the same team?" she asked. Glen turned beat red. Glen was a mutual gaming friend of theirs they met through Debby. He was on the short and heavy side with a hint of Mexican descent. His age that indeterminable one that happens somewhere between 31-45 that makes you scared to ask.

"I forgot," he said awkwardly, though he didn't seem to notice his own awkwardness. "Thirty-two," he said.

"Ouch," Debby said sympathetically. "Fifty-seven," she said her score.

"Twenty-three," Tom looked at the heavens. "My strategy was shit. I am down for Dungeons & Drafts."

"Seventy-nine," Aaron said, almost sorry. "I win again?"

"I'm not playing *Dominion* with you," Debby stated.

"I will add that to your list of games you won't play with Aaron," Rachael laughed.

"And I will try a new bar," Aaron said, still unsure.

Rachael cheered inside.

42

DENVER

PERFORMING ARTS CENTER

"I just honestly didn't like it," Aaron said. They were in the car waiting in the longest line known to man, the exit to this overpriced parking garage far in front of them.

"What about it didn't you like?" Rachael asked, honestly curious.

"I didn't find the main male character believable," Aaron said. "His acting was OK, the writing was OK, but the storyline just led you right to the answer. It was really obvious."

"I think the play wasn't about having a twist. I think it was supposed to be about the interactions getting there," Rachael responded. "And I think if you had been in Jason's shoes you would have been shocked that Apostla murdered their only daughter."

"It was obvious," Aaron insisted.

"It was a twist on a Greek tragedy," Rachael argued. "Just because it was set in space doesn't mean it is going to be less tragic. You could guess that someone dies by the hand of someone they love from the poster."

The car inched forward. A car near them reparked, the

couple walking in the direction of the elevators going up to the bar level.

"That is not a bad idea," Rachael said, commenting on the couple.

"We have an hour drive home," Aaron pointed out. Rachael sat for a moment, the car inching again.

"My point is that we miss things when they are close to us or we don't want to see them," Rachael got back to the point. "And Greek tragedies often incorporate that."

"I won't disagree with that last bit," Aaron said. "BUT I do think you would need to be blind to have missed Apostla's aria about being jealous of her daughter and wanting to kill her."

"Wanting to do something and doing it are two different things," Rachael said absently. Her mind wandered to some of her recent choices that seemed so far away after these last two weeks.

"Well, I don't want to ever drive down to Denver to sit for an hour in a parking garage again," Aaron stated, inching forward again after letting another car in front of him. He was much too nice. The car was quiet for a bit.

plink

"You have been getting a lot of messages," Aaron commented.

"They are from Greg mostly," Rachael said, frustrated. "I wish we had never had lunch. He needs to get a girlfriend."

"That is really nice of you, sweetie," Aaron said. "He is just lonely. He has told me how grateful he is to have you as an ear to talk to. I think Colorado is really helping him with some of his anxiety."

"Greg has anxiety?" Rachael asked.

"It is not my place to talk about it. But he has had trouble with girls in the past. I hope you try to set him up again," Aaron continued. "Maybe one of your work friends that you did your martini afternoon with. When is your next one?"

"I am not sure," Rachael said absently. The messages she got from Greg went mostly unreturned and most of them were not something she would share with Aaron. What was Greg sharing with Aaron?

43

FORT COLLINS

KITCHEN

"I promise it will just be a few hours. You know how important this project is to me, and we have done so much together in the last two weeks," Aaron said. He kissed her forehead and messed her bed head. She had woken up alone and found him dressed and having coffee in the kitchen on a Sunday morning.

"I know. I am sorry I have been insecure. You have been wonderful." And he had. The show last night, trying pool at a new pub last week — he hated it but was a good sport. The dinners and coming home early. Although the sex had already started to drop off, it was tender and loving when it happened.

"I need you to be honest with me," Aaron said, kissing her lips softly again. "But I am going to be honest with you, too. I just like being home and working on my projects. We will find a balance. A few more weeks of testing this program, and once the demo is made and approved it will be smooth sailing."

"We will find a balance," Rachael promised. "I will talk to Karen tomorrow and get some things going on my own time. And I am going to audit that evening summer class on astronomy. The professor got back to me and said it was fine."

Rachael knew she was babbling. Aaron knew it was coming from a good place and kissed her firmly to stop it.

"I love you," Aaron said. "I will do everything I can to make us both happy."

He was quickly out the door. Rachael went to pour a cup of coffee, but he had only made enough for himself.

44

FORT COLLINS

SOCIAL BAR

"What is an underground cocktail bar?" Rachael asked. She absently pulled down on her skirt.

"Stop that." Karen swatted at her hand. "And it is not as exciting as it sounds — it is literally just a cocktail bar that is located underneath a building. But I saw it in *The Coloradoan* over the weekend. Really good write-up, apparently in the top 10 bars in Fort Collins."

"Cool," Rachael added, a little disappointed that it wasn't a secret speakeasy or some historical theme.

"Hey." Karen waved to a few other women all waiting outside a lit staircase. They waved back. The ladies' night out with her coworkers was not yet a regular thing, but it was a thing now. Rachael hadn't gotten a new dress yet, and Karen said this was her last martini night until she went shopping. There had only been two martini nights so far — Elliott's the first, and the second she missed as she and Aaron were reacquainting.

The bottom of the stairs opened up to industrial-themed décor, with a flair of steampunk and the '40s. The male bartenders even dressed in what looked to Rachael's untrained eye as the appropriate vests. As she looked around the busy little place, she scanned for faces she recognized and was relieved to not see any.

At ease, she went to the bar and asked for a recommendation. The drinks were not as artfully poured as at Elliot's, but her martini was fab and came in a fun glass with an explanation of the era it was from. Usually she loved stories, made up or historical, but Karen was prodding her toward their table.

"I'll come back with more appreciative friends," she promised the bartender as she began to move. It wasn't far to their claimed spot. The lovely leather booth was set in a corner of the room, already full of her coworkers, and she sat on the remaining chair. Her back to the bar, she took a sip and listened as her coworkers started to gossip about some of the clients.

Halfway through her drink, she felt a hand on the back of her chair. It brushed her shoulder.

"Why, what a lovely table of ladies," Greg's voice purred. Rachael didn't turn around.

"Why, it's Greg, isn't it?" Karen asked with a hint of surprise.

"It is. Has Rachael been talking about me?" Greg asked. "Mind if I pull up a chair?"

"Go right ahead. And not really, I just remember seeing you drop her off a few times," Karen answered. "I have a way with names and faces."

Greg deftly, with one of his beefy arms, lifted one of the heavy industrial-looking chairs.

"Here, you can sit between us," the woman on Rachael's right offered and excitedly moved over a little. Rachael squeezed closer to Karen so he could fit.

"So, how do you know Rachael?" The words sounded innocent, but Rachael knew fishing when she heard it. She happily piped up.

"He is Aaron's younger brother and on the market," she announced.

"This is girls' night," Karen chastised. "No boys invited."

"I just happened to be here," Greg admitted. "I never pass up a chance to pester the love of my brother's life. So, girls' night." Greg turned on the charm, and that easily became the focus of their little group. The conversation turned to gyms and food. Of their group, the two single ladies and Karen asked the most questions.

Rachael was careful not to chug her martini, but didn't spare it any time, either.

"I'm out, I will be right back." Rachael picked up her glass.

"First one to finish buys the next round," one of her coworkers laughed.

"That would have been me, then," Greg picked up the banter. "And I am happy to oblige. What would you all like? Here, Rachael can help me with the orders."

That fast, her little plan to ditch the group backfired.

"No, you don't need to do that," she said, but it wasn't even heard as the group was already requesting orders. Karen handed him a pen and Rachael headed to the bar, intending to close out her bill and leave before he had finished writing.

It took 30 seconds too long for her to get the attention of a bartender. She really needed a flashier dress.

"I didn't get your order." Greg came up behind her, his hand closing around her elbow as he trapped her against the bar.

"I am actually not feeling well. I think I am going to close out and go," she said. Greg's hand came up and pressed against her forehead. She flushed, knowing she was caught in a lie.

"You don't seem feverish. Although you have not responded to any of my Facebook messages." He made a tut-tut noise. Before she could respond, he turned to the bartender, releasing her arm, and handed him the list of drinks.

"And a Sex on the Beach for Rachael here," Greg added to the order. Rachael didn't really know what that was, but she did not want it from Greg.

"Greg. You need to leave me alone," she said quietly. "Aaron and I are getting things worked out. I shouldn't have led you on." She didn't look at Greg, she kept her eyes on the rows of bottles backlit by bronze and soft yellow lights.

"You just don't know what you want yet," Greg stated after a minute, and then his voice dropped seductively. "But we need to talk in a more private situation."

Rachael felt the hairs on the back of her neck stand up. She did not, no matter how sexy his voice, have any interest in that.

"Why don't you come over for dinner tomorrow? I am making Aaron's favorite," she asked.

"I was thinking a little more private than that," Greg laughed. The bartender started putting drinks on the bar.

"I will start taking these over." Rachael grabbed two and walked to her friends.

"I am so sorry, Karen. But I just got a call from Aaron and he has locked himself out," Rachael said, as tragically as she could manage. "Do you want me to tell Greg to shove off before I go?"

"Don't you dare," Karen said. "You could just make Aaron wait."

"He has a conference call for work tonight. I really can't." Rachael needed to leave now. She could see Greg with an armful of drinks heading back to the table.

"OK, see you tomorrow then."

Rachael was already moving. She could feel Greg's eyes on her as she made the long way around him to the door and disappeared into the evening.

45

FORT COLLINS

DINING ROOM

The late morning sun streamed through the dining room window. The day was beautiful. Rachael had a brunch hash in the Crock-Pot and the stuff for mimosas on the counter. A glass-and-a-half of bubbly was already missing out of the bottle. Aaron had spent all evening Friday and all of yesterday preparing for the game. New foam cutouts and painted miniatures were set up on the center of the table, all the whites and blues of snow.

She was nervous to see Greg, though the bubbly had calmed her a bit. She would add orange juice soon to slow down. Greg had not sent her another message. But she had seen him drop Karen off at work on Friday. Karen had not been shy saying he was an amazing lover. She might even be willing to go on a second date — though she thought it was odd that he wanted to see her office. Rachael did too, but was happy Greg was moving on.

By noon, everyone was seated with food. Drinks of choice and banter abound.

"That was some craptacular writing," Tom said as he popped a beer opened and sat down in front of his character sheet.

"Thanks!" Rachael said cheerily, toasting him with the last of her bubbly with a tad of OJ.

"Another mimosa?" Debby's voice was judgmental.

"We all can't be godly Christian lesbians from the Bible Belt," Rachael intoned as she popped the cork of a fresh bottle. The delightful popping sound that accompanied bubblies opening filled her kitchen briefly.

"I'll take another for the road," Greg said, making to move from his spot to come help. It was the first time he had had the opportunity to talk to her. Rachael was delighted that when Greg arrived first and early, Aaron had pulled him aside for some Q&A about his most recent leveling choices for Craig. Craig had enough homebrew in him — his character was not from the standard rule book — that he was hard to balance.

"Don't you already have a beer?" Debby asked. "Let's get started."

"Rachael will bring you one when you need it," Aaron assured his brother.

They were in their usual positions around the big table, their character sheets in front of them. Phones in various states of activity strewn about along with various copies of the player's guide. Aaron sat at the head of the table behind his oversized DM screen, which was covered in generic D&D art from the books. Rachael and Tom sat across from each other on either side of Aaron. Greg and Debby, with Debby next to Rachael, faced each other, and Martin took the other table head. Debby spread out the most. She had her pink and purple swirled portable dice tray assembled and all of her dice turned to their highest number — dice training.

Though Rachael had done the same with her two sets — both sets blood red, but one with swirls of black and the other with swirls of white and gold flecks. She did a quick double-check that her mimosa was full and the bubbly back in its cooling vessel before folding her legs under her in the big padded dinner chairs. They really had gone all out for their dining room.

The sound of Tom rolling the low numbers out of his dice trickled on the table. She took another sip as Aaron cleared his throat.

46

ICE DRAGON'S REALM

POPPY

Magic flows like water. If you close your eyes, you can feel it connecting everything together. Spells can be used by all creatures for battle, for understanding, and even for control.

— AARON, DUNGEON MASTER'S NOTES, CS11.

Poppy let her eyes wander the large room. When they were in here last, she was so focused on looking through the treasure that she didn't take the time to look around. The sheer ice walls sparkled and refracted as the sun tried to get through their thick layers. The ceiling was so high she could almost not make it out, and along the walls and in a few places on the floor, she could see little holes and ice doors a dragon could never fit in.

"How many of you are there?" Poppy asked the Goodall in the lead.

"Usually around 100 to serve the master," the Goodall responded. "It was he who created us."

"What is Lilly's state of mind?" It was Eismus that asked.

"Metagaming," Rachael mumbled. *"Using outside knowledge of the storyline to make in-game decisions."*

"It is a fair question," Martin defended Tom. *"We know Lilly's mind has been invaded by someone else. We also — as her friends — would want to check on her."*

"How is Lilly?" Craig asked. "Is she well?"

"She is well and her state of mind is sedate," the Goodall answered.

"Sedate," Eismus repeated. "If we rescue her first, will she help or hinder our second quest?"

"We are rescuing Lilly first," Craig stated flatly.

"I hate it that you asked that question, Eis, because I was thinking it," Poppy admitted.

"I cannot answer your question. But choose soon, I would recommend," the Goodall added.

In the end, Craig would just not budge and it was not much of a discussion. Poppy did not take Eismus' bait at the split-the-party suggestion and instead started looking for ways up.

"We are going up first," Craig stated to the Goodall.

"Good luck to you then," the Goodall said. "Somewhere in this chamber are several sets of...what would you call them? Stairs? Ladders? Steps? Climbing steps? Something anyway. Only one of the paths makes it to the top."

And with that, he used his long arms to reach up into the ice wall and begin to climb. Poppy watched, fascinated, before he disappeared into a barely visible slit in the wall. 4aDeer walked right up to where the Goodall climbed up and inspected the ice.

"Handholds, small lip," he stated. Poppy saw his hand and the very tip of his fingers disappear into the ice as he investigated.

"We know what we are looking for. Let's split up and see if we can find more of these." Eismus started to move along the wall. Poppy doubted her helpfulness but started searching anyway, the few handholds she found way above her.

"Maybe we are looking for the wrong thing," Poppy said. As if Craig had a similar idea, his booming rock body jumped up just a little way into the air to catch one of the handholds...it crumbled under his weight. Their four guards didn't seem bothered. They were standing between the party and the dragon's hoard.

"Craig too heavy," 4aDeer stated.

"4aDeer states obvious," Eismus mimicked 4aDeer's voice.

"Finish the search before we run out of time," Poppy hissed. She searched her mind for anything she could change into that either climbed ice or could make her own handholds in the wall.

At the back of the passage 30 minutes later, the now crabby party met back up with no luck finding a more condensed set of handholds. They all just seemed random.

Poppy looked around, frustrated, and noticed a piece of ice sticking out of the ground about the perfect size for her bum. With a frustrated sigh, she let herself sink down.

"What is that?" Craig asked. Poppy looked in the direction he was pointing. A slab of ice was sticking out of the wall. She hadn't noticed that before. Excited, Poppy stood to investigate it. As she moved forward, it began to sink back into the wall.

4aDeer grabbed it, trying to keep it out, but it sank back, disappearing completely into the wall behind it, magically enchanted, no doubt. Poppy tapped 4aDeer for a lift and ran her hands over the surface it came out of. Perfectly smooth.

"Maybe it is on a timer?" Craig asked.

Poppy wrinkled her nose and went back to sit on her ice slab to think, but Eismus beat her to it, his long legs stretched out as he sat.

"It's back!" Craig cried. Poppy jumped aboard 4aDeer to inspect. Behind her, Eismus stood to join them and the rock started sinking back in.

"Sit back down," Poppy yelled.

"Why?" Eismus asked.

"Just do it," Poppy said, and Eismus did. The stone started coming back out.

"It is pressure triggered!" Craig said. "Do you think it will hold me?"

"One way find out," 4aDeer deadpanned. Craig didn't need much more encouragement, and with quite the huff and puff — rocks were not really meant for climbing — he was able to gain purchase and stand on it.

"We need to find more pressure platforms," Poppy said, excited.

"I will be right back," Aaron said to the party. Less than a minute later he came back with a painted Styrofoam tower. Jenga blocks, painted blue, were flush with the painted wall on the side he faced toward the party. He pushed out the one closest to the ground.

"Wow," Martin said. "How long did it take you to make that?"

"Hopefully less time than it takes you to solve the puzzle," Aaron answered smugly.

"Right," Martin answered.

Poppy studied the wall looking for outlines, but there were none. However, you could see patches of darker blue where the ice seemed to be thicker.

"The ice is thicker in places," Eismus echoed her thoughts. "I bet that is where the ice comes out of. But there are so many of them. And how do we get the others to come out?"

"Stand up," Poppy said to Eismus. "Let's see if the ice stays with weight on it."

Craig wobbled as it began to slide back in. "Sit back down!" he said loudly. Eismus sat.

"Do you see anything, Craig?" Poppy asked.

"I don't. I will keep looking," Craig answered.

"More ice." 4aDeer's voice came from a little distance away, and suddenly more slabs of ice started coming out of the wall.

Eismus left his slab to come look, forcing curses and a hasty descent from Craig. Poppy hurried over and found several slabs in the ground, all with symbols they didn't recognize. OK, puzzle time.

They started stepping on tiles, and random patterns of tiles started appearing on the wall. They found a pattern that gave them the first three steps, a big gap, and three more. Eismus, the most acrobatic of them, climbed up the first three steps looking for another plate or something to push.

"Wow, every time we try a pattern, you push out the corresponding pattern of blocks on the 3D model. That is incredible!" Tom exclaimed. The model was about five feet high. As incredible as it was, it was also time-consuming. Rachael had started helping push them back in to speed up the process.

"Thank you," Aaron said brightly. "Now, I am not giving any hints. You can do this."

"We could put treasure on the tiles to hold more down," Craig suggested. With a glare, their guards deterred that idea right away.

"Eismus, do you see anything to push on or a rune to trace or anything?" Poppy called desperately.

"It is just smooth wall," Eismus responded back, frustrated.

With a cry of anger, Craig moved off his ice plate and slammed his fist into the ice. Chunks went flying, his fist creating a nice hold.

"I have an idea," Craig suddenly said.

Aaron closed his eyes and took a deep breath, "I will make you roll for every single handhold."

"I better get rolling," Greg said.

Poppy watched as the big rock mage began "climbing" the wall.

"Hey, I can't get down," Eismus yelled at him. The block Eismus had used to get to the one he was on disappeared with

Craig's abandonment of the slab. But Craig just continued his slow ascent.

"Why would dragon make this?" 4aDeer asked.

"I don't think it matters why," Poppy answered, still thinking.

"Who did dragon make for?" 4aDeer tried again.

"This is so frustrating. Why didn't I make a smarter character?" *Martin ran his hands angrily through his hair. He had figured it out.*

"Metagaming," Rachael stated.

Poppy thought about the question to the sounds of Craig's bashing fists and ice crashing to the ground. It wasn't a bad question. Dragons could fly, so who would need to climb up the wall that wasn't the long-armed minions? Eismus had needed to jump about three feet to get from one step to the other. The slabs were also strong enough to hold Craig and very wide.

"Frost giants!" Poppy squealed. "Twenty feet tall, live in snow areas, and are known to ally with dragons. These are frost giant steps!"

"What do we know about frost giants?" There was a shower of ice and then a thud that shook the ground. Craig had made it about 15 feet up before he came back down with a crack. Some rock off his bum was left on the ice cavern floor as he joined the conversation.

"Roll me intelligence," Aaron was beaming at the group.

No one could read the frost giant's language or knew what the symbols were. But frost giants were as intelligent as humans, agile, and lived in small clans. They were not well known for building, but their cities were almost Roman in their layout and order. And their religion was an offshoot of the seven gods of order and war.

"Maths here," 4aDeer said, his voice more frustrated than his character should have been.

"There is." Eismus suddenly caught on to the longer and shorter lines on each ice plate.

Craig and 4aDeer had to force three of the Goodalls to stand on pressure plates to bring the total to the prime number of seven. Each standing on plates whose symbols also added up to prime numbers. When the last correct plate was stepped on, a low hum filled the air with some soft, slow clicking. A serpentine pattern of slabs, each about three feet apart, appeared in the cave wall, glowing blue and steady. The party hesitantly left their pressure plates.

"Yes," Poppy jumped up and down, excited. "Time to climb the wall."

The Goodalls didn't follow them as they began the steady jump from plate to plate, Craig and 4aDeer taking turns helping the little gnome, Poppy. About halfway through, the steady clicking began to get faster.

"I think that means hurry," Poppy stated. "We don't know what is at the top. I was trying to save my abilities, but I am slowing us down." She easily changed into the sure-footed polar bear and the party doubled its pace.

Poppy bounded over the threshold at the top. The final stairs were cut into the thick roof, winding up to a brightly lit square that most likely led outside. No door covered the opening, and despite the recent snow, the ground around it was well packed down. The wind howled, pushing her slowly across the slick surface of snowpack and ice.

Poppy yelped as she felt something slam into her side. Her paws scrambled for traction. She was suddenly thankful for the incredibly thick wall, as there was no danger of falling off the edge. She gained enough traction to spin around and dive forward as a club aimed for her center. It had probably been a club that had hit her side the first time. It missed her center but crashed into her haunches. Poppy roared both in pain and warning to her party.

Eismus heard the warning and shot out of the entrance, rolling, with a spell on his lips. He was followed by 4aDeer, with

Craig bringing up the rear. Distracted by Poppy, her attacker's backside was hit by Eismus' firebolt, and he turned his attention to the new arrivals.

Poppy took in the situation. She had to squint. The sky was painfully blue and the sun reflected off the endless white. Her attacker was a huge frost giant who carried a wicked-looking spiked club made probably of iron, chunks of ice stuck randomly to its spikes. The wind was incredibly powerful up here and continued to push her slowly away from the frost giant, who seemed unaffected by the constant blowing, though that would mean it was pushing the rest of the party toward it. Its attack had sent her flying far away from the door. There was no danger of currently falling back in.

She pressed forward to get back into range as 4aDeer's axe bit into it and Craig's earth spell pinned it in place. She jumped the final few feet and tried to swipe at it with her big paw, but the wind was too strong from this side and her aim not true, and her paw missed.

With a hiss of pain, the frost giant's club threw her backwards again, and Poppy let her bear form hit the ground before she shifted back into being a little gnome.

"That club hurts," she yelled into the wind, praying it didn't steal her words. Fire, earth, and axe all took swipes at the frost giant, and Poppy set into a steady walk forward to keep her out of the giant's range but in her spell range.

"Why didn't I take Control Winds," Debby moaned.

"What did you take instead?" Rachael asked, excited to do something other than watch a D&D game.

"Wrath of Nature." Debby shook her head.

"Ouch, there is like no nature here at all," Tom added. *"You can't even cause a rockslide because it is all snow and ice."*

"Thanks for that, Tom," Debby snapped. *"It would have been useful in the Underdark."*

"The frost giants are continuing despite the sidebar." Aaron was matter-of-fact.

Debby focused her mind and summoned minor elementals of the fire variety to combat ice. They appeared on either side of the frost giant, who screamed with rage and turned into the wind, his club crashing against 4aDeer's side.

Eismus and Craig both blasted the giant with spells, fire, and green bolts flying from their fingers, respectively, followed by Poppy's elementals, the little fireballs tiny but hitting. The frost giant was looking a little worse for wear, but Poppy's excitement was swallowed as two more giant shapes were moving toward them, and fast.

"Incoming from the rear," Poppy yelled, and she cast a wall of fire behind Eismus and Craig.

4aDeer's axe arched and slashed the frost giant's chest, his momentum carrying him around in a circle. The now fast-moving axe bit deep into the frost giant's side, blue blood freezing before it hit the ground.

One more stream of spells from Eismus and Craig finished it off. But Poppy's barrier didn't keep the next two away for long, and one of them was a mage. The party now had the wind fighting against them.

Craig took the brunt of the first attack; his already injured body was knocked backwards. Poppy readied a group heal. 4aDeer charged into the wind, trying to get to the mage, but it slowed him down too much and his axe grazed off the leathers of the frost giant standing in front of Craig.

The battle was long and bloody on both sides. Poppy felt her energy draining as she alternated between heals and spells to help the party. Her thorn whip lashed out at legs. She cheered as her gust of wind countered the endless pushing just long enough for 4aDeer to flank his frost giant and gain the advantage with the wind now at his back. Craig focused on the mage frost giant while Eismus split his attention. It was a plink from the remaining of her elementals that felled the last one.

"Well done," a voice boomed from above them as the third frost giant's bleeding shell was finally effected by the wind and crashed to the ice. An extra big gust of wind flattened the party as the dragon landed in front of them. "I can't wait for it to be my turn. Your display of cunning and skills is impressive for little mortals."

The party moved closer together and Poppy unconsciously put a hand on 4aDeer to calm him. But his battered body didn't have any fight left in it. The dragon's tongue came out and ran around the scales of its mouth, a mass of sharp teeth peeking out.

Poppy turned to Craig.

"Do you have anything of Lilly's," she asked.

"I do," Craig admitted. "Though she did not give it to me and I want it back."

"Eww, eww, eww," Rachael backed away from the table.

"Why does your mind immediately go to dirty things?" Greg faked an offended laugh.

"Because you are a boy," Debby got in on the teasing.

"Not all 'boys,'" Martin stressed the word boys, "are dirty."

"Why don't we find out what it is he has before continuing this discussion?" Aaron said excitedly.

Craig opened up his pack and rummaged down to the bottom. He glanced at the dragon, who was just sitting and watching with interest, and then dramatically at the group, before pulling out a glove.

"When she lost the other one of the set, she threw this one away," Craig said. "And I wanted to keep something of hers. Lilly has hot and cold moments." If rocks could blush.

It was the dragon that sighed. "To have love again."

"Ah, ok," Poppy said, taking the glove. She was unsure if that was romantic or creepy.

She had reserved just enough energy for this spell. The morning had already been eaten away by the wall puzzle. Only a day remained to save Lilly. The scrying spell was flawless with the item, and her personal friendship with the object of its focus. They bandaged up the worst of their wounds and then, under the dragon's watchful eye, fought the wind toward Lilly.

FORT COLLINS

DINING ROOM

"I'm phreeee!" Rachael exclaimed excitedly. She almost clipped Debby in the side of the head with her arms.

"And I think we need a break to get some food into Rachael," Debby said, annoyed. She didn't like alcohol and she didn't agree that liquor and gaming went together.

"Relax, Debby," Rachael said. "I'm getting some water and will finish the hash. But the first half of this game was extremely tedious for me."

Martin and Tom stood and were talking. Greg was already in the kitchen. Time to face the music. At least it sounded like Greg was on the right track, dating someone else.

"Hey," Rachael said as she brought her bowl up for a refill. "I'm glad you and Karen are hooking up."

"Yup," Greg said. "I figured it would make you more comfortable, and Karen seems like a sharer."

Rachael wasn't sure what he meant by that, so she didn't comment.

"What are you lovebirds going to do now that you are back together?" Aaron's voice came from behind her as he made himself a very light mimosa with what was left of the supplies.

"Don't forget, the dragon has an aspect now of reverence of your declaration of love you can use your inspiration on."

He didn't wait around for her to answer and quickly darted back to his DM screen, loath to leave it during game time, even extra-long sessions.

"I had forgotten about that," Rachael stated, a bowl of food in one hand and a pint of water in the other.

"You gonna be cool with a moment or two?" Greg asked a little quieter now. She could hear Debby and Aaron moving on to a new topic in the background. "You seem pretty adamant that Lilly is distancing herself from Craig, even though nothing happened in-game."

Rachael turned to him, a little of her pint of water sloshing over her hand. Greg took the glass from her. "I was always cool with it IN-GAME. Lilly is falling for Craig and it is tragic. I love tragedy. But I am not Lilly," she lowered her voice. "And I might be trying to figure my life out. But anything with you is the wrong answer. I am not a prize in your sibling rivalry."

Rachael didn't know what to expect from Greg after her blunt words, but it was not the predatory smile that spread over his face. Or his hands that had picked up a paper napkin from the counter and gently wiped the remaining water off her hand and wrist.

"Are the lovebirds hatching a plan?" Debby let her voice fill with irony as she pushed between them to get to the sink. Debby never missed anything, and Greg must have known she was coming up behind her.

Greg's laugh was hearty, but Rachael didn't trust herself to speak. What was he playing?

48

ICE DRAGON'S REALM

4ADEE

Elemental dragons have grown large and heavy in their lifetimes. They much prefer to exercise their minds. But if a puzzle does not spark their interest, then it is gone before it can ignite. But rest assured, when piqued, puzzle or person can be burned in their memory for eternity.

— AARON, DUNGEON MASTER'S NOTES, CS12

L illy was in bad shape. 4aDeer wished he had some way to help her. After defeating the frost giants, the journey to Lilly had been cold and miserable, but fast. She was down a huge hole in the top of the ice wall, obviously wide enough for a dragon to easily get down, but then the hold narrowed at the base. Claw marks around the ends and wearing on the narrowed part painted a vivid picture of the dragon easily picking things up and putting them in, like a dragon cookie jar.

They had tied all of their ropes together and slid down, discovering the final drop into the "jar" needed no rope. They were short more than 15 feet for the first part but had managed to get Lilly's attention, and 4aDeer got her or Isa, whichever one it was, to cast the invisible pillow that had saved 4aDeer earlier.

"See, it all worked out," Eismus said, still defending his choice to not carry any rope. Lilly had fallen unconscious after her cast. The battered and bleeding group stabilized her and lay her down in the bed before taking care of their own wounds.

"We have no rope now," Poppy exclaimed. "We literally can't retrieve it because of your shortsightedness. And what if the only way out of here is back up?"

"See, that is one of the pitfalls of D&D," Martin intoned. "We knew something our character didn't and acted on that knowledge."

"Pitfalls," Rachael exaggerated the words. "Because we had to use the rope to go into a pit."

"It was an unintentional almost pun." Martin rolled his eyes.

"I'll pay my fine for this one," Greg said. "I think we would have been pushed down by the cold and our injuries alone."

"It should have at least been a discussion," Martin insisted.

Rachael started singing The Twilight Zone. "But if it had been a discussion, then it would still have been a discussion about out-of-game knowledge."

"We could have phrased it..." Martin started.

"But if we had to phrase it, then it is still being controlled by out-of-game knowledge," Rachael interrupted.

"By that logic," Aaron shot in. "Every discussion in D&D brings in out-of-game knowledge because you are not Lilly but Rachael. Lilly doesn't have her own knowledge. In my opinion, a big part of D&D is phrasing things and the challenge of setting yourself in a different mindset to make decisions."

"I agree with Aaron," Tom added. "Although I do think in this case, we should have had a discussion. BUT we were also cold, miserable, and injured, and possibly would not have taken the time to have it with our goal so close."

"Let's just play the game?" Debby asked. "We can work on our finer points of metagaming in future discussions."

"Will your missing rock ever come back, Craig?" Eismus changed the subject.

"I can remake it with earth magic, but it takes a lot of energy," Craig answered.

"So, you could make an entire limb?" Eismus mused.

"I made you an ear, so yes," Craig reminded Eismus. He hadn't left Lilly's side since they entered, and the group sat down to eat and drink. They were surprised when an ice door slid to one side, exposing a tunnel and a Goodall. The Goodall didn't seem surprised to see them.

He was, however, distraught that Lilly was not conscious. He had a steaming mug of something in his hand.

"She needs to drink," he stated. His eyes wandered the room looking for direction, but his body remained unnaturally still.

"What is it she needs to drink?" Poppy asked slowly.

"The master's drink," the Goodall said helpfully.

"Leave it here and we will make sure she gets it," Eismus ordered. The Goodall's tongue came out and licked its eyes in quick succession. Faster than anyone could react, it leapt toward Lilly and grabbed her by the throat and stuck a long finger in the side of her mouth. With practiced ease, it started to pour the liquid into her.

Craig slammed his fist into the side of the Goodall's head. It flew the short distance to the wall and hit it with a crack, its body, unmoving, landed on the floor. The now empty mug rolled into the middle of the room.

Lilly took a deep breath and started coughing, her hands on her neck, the pile of blankets she was under shuddered with each one. Craig put his rock arm around the pile, not worried about his cold skin with all the layers between them.

Lilly looked up, grateful. Her eyes glazed and her face flushed.

"There is plate in here," was the first thing she said. "I love how much everything sparkles!"

4aDeer jumped up with excitement and started rummaging through piles.

"Do you, dear?" Poppy's voice was soothing. Craig gave Lilly some water and real food. She had not had anything but the liquid the dragon was giving her since last night.

"I need to pee," she said. 4aDeer absently thought that was very practical. He continued to sort clothing. He hated sorting or any kind of cleaning, but he was encouraged by the bits of metal he continued to find.

"I really do," Rachael added. *"Quick pee break."*

"You just sat for four hours and did nothing. Why didn't you pee during break?" Debby exclaimed.

"I was eating and drinking," Rachael said as she disappeared toward the bathroom.

"While she is out, let's start rolling the stuff you would like to dig through and investigate, if that is not too forward of me to assume," Aaron said.

They rested for an hour, getting what strength they could back. The liquid was unidentifiable but obviously salty, sweet, and had some sort of mind-altering drug in it. All but Lilly shed their sweat and blood-soaked layers and replaced them with dry, although not very clean, layers from the piles in the room. No valuables were found, though everyone added a new hand weapon or two to their collection. 4aDeer could not stop smiling as his body was covered in pieces of armor. A few pieces matched every here and there, but most of them even different metals from completely different armor concepts.

As their rest came to a close, Eismus walked over to Lilly, sitting on the side not occupied by Craig to meet her eyes.

"I have a question for Isa before we head out," Eismus said. "The dragon accused us of stealing more than one thing."

4aDeer looked at Lilly's face. It was still flushed, her eyes glassy.

"Did either of you take something else?" Eismus asked very seriously.

"Lilly does not steal," 4aDeer stated. He had known Lilly for over 10 years now. IF it wasn't a part of the job, she wouldn't take it. Eismus didn't respond.

"We...took...things," Lilly's double voice said slowly as if recalling a memory from long ago. "I love how shiny the room is."

"We know," Poppy patted her as she went by.

"Let's go. When she is more herself, we can ask again," Craig said. He cradled Lilly to his side as the party moved out the door the Goodall had come in.

The way was twisty and slanting down, with only a few splits. They decided to take the splits that continued down, in the direction of their second quest from the dragon. Lilly's steps grew stronger, but her eyes remained glazed.

"Goodalls coming," she said and giggled. Not two seconds later, they ran into three of the creatures coming toward them. 4aDeer hefted his axe, but Lilly stepped in front of the party.

"I am looking for more of the sweet juice," she cooed. The Goodall in the lead bobbed his head.

"I will bring it to your room," it said.

"I am not in my room," Lilly stated.

"I don't know where else to bring it," it stated.

"I don't know either," Lilly said wistfully.

"I hate to break up this bizarre little exchange." Eismus reached for Lilly and pulled her back into the party. "But we are on a mission for the master."

"We know of it," all three of the Goodalls said at the same time.

"A little help?" Poppy added. "We are lost in your home."

"We will take you to where you need to be. But Lilly must

not be without the comfort of her juice. We will go there first," the first one answered.

"She is not…" Craig started to say, but 4aDeer cut him off.

"Lead on," he said. Lilly slipped in behind him, her footsteps sure. He could hear Poppy whispering to Craig, good gnome. Smart gnome. They needed a guide. Lilly didn't have to drink anything. They just had to pretend to agree.

The monotony of the ice paths and endless white was wearing on 4aDeer, the walls of slick clear-and-blue ice seemed almost identical. The echoes of their own footsteps and the slight odor of lizard and metal. He was itching for a fight, despite feeling bruises and scrapes from their earlier encounter.

The pathway split. The Goodall took the path angling slightly up, and it opened up into a completely white cavern with firelight licking the walls and casting shadows on the snowy surface. The smoke from the fire rose up through a collection of holes that occasionally dripped back down on the fire, hissing and sizzling and giving the room the scent of wet wood.

The Goodall motioned for them to stop and went behind the fire. He took a steaming mug out of a metal holder.

"What is in this stuff?" Poppy asked the Goodall as if they were good pals, just out for some gossip.

"Master's essence," the Goodall answered.

"She is not drinking that," Craig stated. But Lilly had already stepped around the fire and had the mug in her hands. Too late to move, the party watched her take a big sip. The Goodall smiled and bobbed its head.

"This way," it said and led them back out. Lilly followed blindly, and 4aDeer put himself directly between her and Craig. Craig was not happy and looked like he wanted to murder the Goodall. He didn't want him to hurt Lilly by accident or kill their guide. 4aDeer was determined to get out of here. Lilly had survived with however many "essence cups" she had had before this one.

Craig apparently calmed, although 4aDeer had to catch Lilly as the drink began to zap her clarity again.

"Give her to me?" Craig asked. And 4aDeer obliged. The almost empty mug was pushed out of Lilly's hands. She didn't seem to notice.

They walked for a solid hour, some branches in the tunnel lighter than others but all mind-numbingly similar. 4aDeer knew he could not find his way back.

Eventually, they arrived at an odd crossroads. The biggest one they had seen. It looked like a snowflake with at least six different tunnels leading out.

"We have been leaving from this crossroad," the Goodall stated. "I must go fetch Lilly another drink. I will find you here?"

"Yes," Eismus answered, even though the Goodall had been looking at Lilly. It bobbed, licked its eyes one more time, and then went back the way they came.

"Wait, you just said, 'we have been leaving,' " Poppy called after it, but it did not return. "Rats. Missed opportunity. Now what?"

The party searched for clues. Craig sat Lilly down on the ice near the middle so he could help, and she began mumbling to herself, her glassy eyes turning to the ceiling. Twenty minutes later, the party still had nothing.

"Same symbol as on the rock in the cave. Symbols every-where. Cymbals make noise. I love noise? I don't love noise. I love dragons. I love dragons? I am a dragon? I am a dragon symbol. Same symbol as on the rock. 4aDeer's hot rock. Craig is a rock. Craig be hot rock?" Lilly's double voice was the only sound in the chamber.

"Craig can be your hot rock." Craig came over to soothe her.

"There is just nothing here," Eismus said. He made a childish stomp and looked up at the ceiling as if the gods were at fault. "Hey!" he shouted. "There is a symbol on the ceiling.

"Same symbol as on the rock. Symbol burned. But fire sounds better…" Lilly's double voice.

"Craig, can you do something to make her be quiet. I need to focus on this symbol on the ceiling."

Lilly made a polite hiccupping sound. Craig gave her water and bent down to rub circles on her back.

"Same symbol as on the rock," she said knowingly. "No sparkles here."

"I think Lilly knows something," Poppy said. "We need to move before the Goodall comes back."

"Just kill it," 4aDeer said. "Bored."

"What do you know?" Poppy asked Lilly.

"Same symbol as on the rock," Lilly said, and then managed to swallow more of her babbles. She looked up and nodded at the symbol.

"Can you take us to it?" Poppy asked.

"Sparkles," Lilly said, and then bit her lips together and shook her head.

"No sparkles or guiding us to what you are saying?" Poppy asked.

"Rock," Lilly moved her hands over Craig's knees, thighs, and hips.

"Same symbol as on 4aDeer's rock," Lilly patted Craig's hard quad muscle.

"Right," Poppy said. "4aDeer, where is your rock?"

"I don't have a rock," 4aDeer said, confused.

"Think," Poppy hissed. "Rack that brain of yours. Are there any rocks we have come across in this cursed ice land that you paid special attention to?"

4aDeer racked his brain.

"Big rock in cave," he finally said. "Cave from first night."

"Hot rock," Lilly said excitedly as she used her hand that had not moved off of Craig's quad to stand.

"Isa used the big rock you found to create heat for us the first night," Eismus said.

"It must be that one," Poppy agreed. "But how does that help us now?"

"The cave was in that direction." Craig pointed down one of the passages.

"How do you know," Eismus demanded.

"I am an earth mage," Craig started to lecture. "My magic is rooted in the core of the ground. My sense of direction is impeccable."

"Bored now. Moving," 4aDeer stated. He set a fast pace in the direction Craig pointed.

It was a much shorter walk than trudging through the snow above. The ice tunnels turned into rock tunnels, some natural-looking and others chipped out. Other smaller, dug-out passages showed signs of life and little tufts of white hair that could belong to Goodalls came in from various other directions. Most of the day was gone now. They needed to escape the Ice Dragon's Realm soon, or Isa would escape from Lilly's mind and leave her a vegetable.

"Or not," Eismus said. "She is recovering but clearly going to be out of it for the next 24 hours. Maybe the dragon was trying to find a way to 'cure' her so Lilly could stay as his treasure."

"I don't want to risk it," Craig stated. Poppy nodded in agreement, and the party broke into a heedless run; Craig, in the lead, followed his instincts in the direction of the first tunnel.

Unable to hear anything over Craig's booming footsteps and 4aDeer's clunky metal set, they didn't notice as more and more Goodall came out of side caves and jogged behind them. It wasn't until they ran into a massive natural cave, stopping to get their bearings, that they heard the mass of rustling behind them.

"Ahh!" Poppy screeched. She had been bringing up the rear.

The party turned, all but Lilly, who swayed a little. She had stopped babbling; the run seemed to have helped moved the dragon's liquid through her system a little faster.

4aDeer drew his axe to charge.

"We don't want to hurt you," the Goodall said.

"We just want to stay...alone." The last word sounded more like a question.

"Individual," another Goodall piped up.

"Unattended," another. "Onliest," another. "Solo." Soon the cavern echoed with voices. Their words bounced off the walls.

"Unique." It was Lilly's double voice that whispered in the last echoes of the Goodalls.

"We won't hurt you." Poppy didn't hesitate. "Just show us the way out and we will be gone."

The first Goodall pointed at a boulder. 4aDeer walked to it and moved it to one side.

"Our own selves must flee," the Goodall said. "Your eyes have doomed us."

"Come with us. We run for safety," Lilly offered. It was the most put-together sentence she had spoken in hours.

She didn't wait. She charged through the opened door. Craig, cursing that he had not held onto her, boomed after her. Poppy changed into the shape of her polar bear again as the mass of Goodalls flowed into the cave opening.

Eismus and 4aDeer shared a look before bringing up the rear, Eismus magically moving the boulder back behind them.

49

FORT COLLINS

DINING ROOM

"And that is the perfect place to stop for a dinner break," Aaron said.

"How much of this was planned?" Tom asked.

"Well," Aaron said carefully, not wanting to give anything away. "I pushed pretty hard at the beginning of this for things to go one direction. But to be honest, once you had Lilly, there were a lot of ways this could go and you didn't choose any of them."

"I'm sorry, sweetie," Rachael said as she leaned over and gave Aaron a kiss. He started moving pre-drawn maps out from underneath the 3D layer that was the dragon's hoard they had just escaped.

"I also didn't expect so many low rolls on your cognitive checks," he said to Rachael. "Or a natural 20 on your rapport with the Goodalls. If I had to guess, tonight will be short. The party will either wipe right at the beginning or get back to town, and I will have to end because I will need new material."

"I am OK with that," Rachael said. She had done a great job maintaining a happy buzz for most of the afternoon and early evening. "Maybe we can have some snuggle time tonight if we end early."

"Ugh, I don't need to know about your sex lives," Debby said dramatically. "Chinese food good for everyone?"

"I brought a salad," Greg added.

"Chinese is great for me." Tom went and got the menu.

Rachael got another glass of rosé, the perfect middle wine for when you don't know what you are planning on eating, and stepped outside. She took a deep breath of fresh air, not that her house was stuffy. They had a few windows open, but six people sitting around a table all day would always lead to some B.O. Seeing the green of their messy little unkept garden made her happy.

"Rachael, you out here?" Debby's voice joined her on the back porch. The sound of the hot tub in ready mode cycled on. The sun was just setting. The backyard was facing the wrong direction to see it, but some colors still started to warm up the sky.

"What's up, Debby?" Rachael asked happily. She loved playing D&D, the made-up worlds, the quests. She always knew what to do and Lilly was so brave.

"Greg is hitting on you." Debby was always so straight-forward.

"I know," Rachael said. She turned around and shut the sliding glass porch door. Debby took a sip of Diet Coke and Rachael took a sip of wine, feeling her mood drop a tad.

"He is using the game to do it right under Aaron's nose." Debby sounded disgusted.

"It is my fault," Rachael said tonelessly.

"Aaron didn't cancel last week because of work." Rachael gave Debby a quick update on her emotional state, though no real details. "And although I never tried to encourage him, I also didn't stop the flirting until too late. And now I am trying to make it stop and I just don't have control," Rachael finished.

To her surprise, Debby turned and gave her a hug.

"Greg needs to leave you alone. I don't think it is right that you didn't discourage him right from the start. But I understand being lonely." Debby took another long sip of Coke. "God, if I understand nothing else, I can understand that. When I escaped from my church world to be who I feel I am inside, my family and most of my friends cut me off completely. I didn't realize how even my emotionally abusive relationships with all of them were at least company."

"I didn't know," Rachael started.

"Bah," Debby's voice was gruff. "It is in the past. FoCo has been amazing to me. Still no solid girlfriend, but I'm dating and have more friends than I can count. I am still amazed that more gaming women aren't lesbians."

"Maybe in San Francisco?" Rachael said unhelpfully.

"You straights and your stereotypes." Debby shook her head. "Look, I know we are not super close and I am more Aaron's friend than yours, but if you need someone to talk to, let me know."

Rachael felt a tear in her eye. She brushed it away and leaned down to give Debby a hug. The sliding door opened.

"Are you trying to convert our little Rachael?" Greg asked as he and Martin joined them. Martin puffed on his e-cigarette.

"I thought you quit," Debby said to Martin; both women ignored Greg's comment.

"No, just changed to the electronic. Much better for the environment," Martin answered as he blew out a puff of smoke.

Debby very animatedly let Martin know how she felt about that, and Rachael easily slipped into a conversation about leveling Craig with Greg. It was a safe topic and one full of speculation about what Aaron would and would not allow as well as whether they were going to level after this marathon Sunday.

Eventually, Tom and Aaron joined them outside with

Chinese food in hand. When Greg returned with his salad, the group had sat, a space between Debby and Martin left for him. Aaron's chair was close to Rachael's, and when he wasn't using his hand, he rested it on the top of her leg. The group ate their dinners in the lovely spring air as the sun finished setting, the topics mostly leveling up characters and what various DMs did with unused prepared materials. Rachael was happy.

"Martini night on Tuesday this week." Karen had come over to her desk to point out the email she just sent.

"I need to go shopping still," Rachael said. "Besides, it says 'Martini Night' and not Girls' Night."

"Boss man said that if I am using official channels, we have to be inclusive of both sexes." Karen had a slight edge to her voice. "Assholes. And anyway, I want to bring Greg."

"Well, I will have to catch you next week. I have plans this evening, and then tomorrow I need to go dress shopping," Rachael said. She had been afraid of dress shopping. Greg's messages were just a little too creepy and she was uncomfortable wandering the mall alone.

"What are you doing this evening?" Karen asked politely, but a little disbelieving.

"I need to go to CSU and register to audit a class," Rachael said, a little embarrassed.

"What? Why?" Karen asked. "You don't need any more qualifications to work here."

"No." Rachael splayed her fingers and moved her palms

around in front of her. "It is an astronomy class. I am trying to find a hobby that has nothing to do with Aaron that I can enjoy."

"Oh right, you are still on that kick." Karen lost interest immediately. "OK. Well, enjoy."

Rachael watched Karen walk off. She would need to do something nice for Karen soon, but right now she was too excited to know that Greg would be busy. She could go dress shopping.

The day rushed by and Rachael worked late. The bus to campus didn't come until 6:30 p.m. She was surprised that at about 4:45 p.m. Greg walked into the office, his eyes scanning the rows of little cubicles.

"Greg!" Karen's voice was excited from across the room. Rachael couldn't help but look herself, and her eyes accidentally met Greg's. He grinned. She gave a halfhearted wave.

"Are you amazing, picking a girl up from work, or what?" Karen asked dramatically.

Greg gave a theatrical bow.

"Rach, need a lift as well?" Greg asked offhandedly.

"She is working late, has to sign up for something or some-thing," Karen chattered. Rachael wished she hadn't said that, but at least Karen wasn't specific about her activity. Greg gave a disappointed little nod before Rachael focused back on her computer. She felt his eyes on her for another minute before Karen, with all the drama she could muster, left on Greg's arm.

FORT COLLINS

COMPUTER ROOM

"Aaron, look." Rachael came down the stairs sprouting her find from her dress shopping earlier. When she got into the middle of the computer room, she did a little twirl like she was 12 again.

It had taken hours, and she had probably tried on 50 dresses, but she had ended happily with two and no creepy messages from Greg to make the experience weird.

The one she was showing off was the slinkier one, and she had an ulterior motive. Despite ending the campaign early and her amazing mood, Aaron had not been interested in sex at all. It had now been five days, not really that long in the grand scheme of things, but long enough, taking their earlier conversations into account.

"Aaron," she said again, preparing to twirl. The dress was blood red — her favorite color, and one that gave her plain brown hair some depth. It was a halter top, though the halter was a crisscrossing of skinny straps. The top of the dress hugged her breasts, propping them up with a ridiculous amount of cleavage that would be pornographic if it was not for the straps. The clingy material formed to her body like a glove. BUT what she loved the most were the layers of gauzy reds and blacks that created an empire waistline over top of the clingy material, obscuring and hiding her less-loved shapes. The dress ended just above her mid-thigh, and she had found little black flats that matched both her dresses.

Aaron finally looked up.

"That is a sexy dress." Aaron whistled but didn't get up. "Is that for girls' night?"

"It is, or maybe for us, too." Rachael blushed a little and rolled her hips as she walked toward his computer chair. Aaron pushed his chair away from his desk, and she straddled him, kissing his nose and moving her pelvis in obvious motions. Aaron kissed her neck a few times and rested a hand on her hip. She ground her hips down and was surprised to feel nothing down there."

"I just have a lot on my mind." Aaron kissed her again. "I love the dress but I spent too much time on my game and this work project."

Rachael squeezed her eyes shut for a moment.

"Don't look so disappointed," Aaron said. He kissed her again. "I love you. And we have been going at it like rabbits since Mount Princeton. If I didn't know you were on birth control, I would think you were trying to get pregnant."

Aaron laughed.

Rachael tried to laugh with him. "I guess you are right. It was worth a try."

"Try it again later," Aaron said seductively. "I promise it will work."

Rachael went upstairs and put away both dresses. She didn't try it again later. Instead, she sat down at her desk and woke up her computer. Email, calendar, Facebook. She had a Facebook message waiting for her, blinking in the little window on the bottom right of the screen.

Greg: I like red, too.

A cold chill ran its way down her back.

52

UNDERDARK

EISMUS

A mortal tavern is much the same in the Underdark, with a few exceptions. Its walls and tables are made of stone, along with a few long benches and the bar. The number of wood chairs is surprisingly high, though each one balances precariously with signs of many repairs. Cups and dishes are made of cheap metals that crash dramatically to the floor, adding to their collection of dents.

— AARON, DUNGEON MASTER'S NOTES, CS13.

T he town tavern was completely packed. Lilly's slightly intoxicated voice rang out in song in time with the complicated beating of her drum and the thumping of the Goodalls' hands on the floor.

Their feet flew over rock and snow
The bright cave entrance so close
But with a roar of ice and a hiss that was not nice

The dragon cut off their flow
But the double voice of the bard and drow
Broke through the day, a pitch of acid tar it flung
And 4aDeer, his axe ever near, leaped into the fray
The very earth shook, the snow rushing to look
It's noisy rush delayed, by fire
Cast by Eismus' desire to win the day
Goodalls and adventurers side by side
The dragon's wails never seemed to die
White bear in the lead, picking up speed
Thus the party did succeed.

Lilly's hands blurred as they hit every part of her pony keg drum, creating higher and lower pitches before dramatically stopping. Her breath in could have taken all the air out of the pub, it was so loud.

That's the Goodalls' addition
to the Elm City's tradition
Of drink'n at the well

The last lines were punctuated with drumbeats, except for the final verse that was shouted more than said. It was almost drowned out by the cheers of Elm City having its name mentioned in a song for the first time.

Eismus lifted up his own tankard of the piss that passed for ale in the Underdark and drank it down. It hadn't happened quite like that. Only half the Goodalls had made it out alive. Turns out dragon "essence" — he still didn't want to know what was in it — really messed you up, and Lilly had been sharing minds with not only Isa but the dragon and his psychic-linked minions.

The Goodalls they had rescued had somehow slipped through the psychic net; probably the dragon didn't even pay them mind anymore. Literally. The dragon couldn't follow them into the caves but used Lilly to flush them all out into the open for the slaughter. It had been a mess, Craig's love for Lilly pausing the dragon just long enough for them to scatter.

They had taken Lilly straight to the temple. The priest, surprised to see them, held up his end of the bargain, though the dragon's juice delayed everything by a day. Craig didn't leave Lilly's side, even to sleep, for 36 hours.

Poppy used the time to talk to the town about integrating the Goodalls and came to an agreement. The Goodalls were given their own house just outside of town and they worked an even number at each temple, learning about life as an individual.

Eismus took another deep drink of his beer. Poppy had even offered for all of them to move into the Goodalls' house to help the transition. He was so tired of being around those stinky animals.

The only upside to the house was that it was constantly protected by the Goodalls, who were fiercely loyal to Lilly. The items Isa had stolen from the dragon were powerful, and Poppy had found the bag before Lilly and Isa were separated. The wand Eismus had taken, though he was still exploring it to see exactly how it worked. Poppy wore the green and gold ring of unknown abilities, and a new sparkling red, black, and gold necklace was hidden under 4aDeer's plate. Oddly, the neckless had burned anyone else who touched it. Including Craig.

A heavy hand patted his back. "Why so blue, Eis?" Craig asked. He practically beamed at Lilly as she sang for the crowd.

They should just get married and get over it. Eismus was sick of seeing that blossoming too.

"We share our house with filthy animals, the Dragon Temple is being difficult, and we are no further in our questing," Eismus spat. Poppy was seated with him, quietly listening to Lilly and the very drunk and rowdy tavern-goers, her serene little personal space unaffected by the energy of the public.

"I feel like the town keeps getting fuller and fuller," Poppy stated. "Even the market stalls are swelling. I need space. I miss my forests. Lilly is settling in a little too well." She looked concerned as Lilly drained yet another tankard of ale across the room and laughed.

"How is the Dragon Temple being difficult? I thought we were done with them after that mess," Craig asked.

"Well, um," Eismus picked up his beer and took a long, slow drink.

"Where is 4aDeer?" Poppy suddenly asked. As if the moment was planned, a scream came in from the front door. The crowd died down, slowly, but die down it did.

"My husband," the woman said as the crowd got quiet enough. "He has been killed!" She screamed again, and Eismus could see blood on her hands and the front of her skirts.

"That's not possible," someone very drunk and very loud said. "This is neutral ground."

"But it is true," the woman wailed. "Someone help me!"

Eismus was by the woman's side. "Take me to him."

Eismus found 4aDeer standing outside the woman's home, his axe out, keeping anyone from entering. Eismus gave him a questioning look.

"Heard bad noises," he said. "Crime. Not just anyone should look."

Eismus once again wondered at the intelligence in the orc but passed it off. The woman had probably said something. She was probably the murderer. Eismus noticed Poppy slide in next to him and was very grateful to not be going in alone, not that he would tell Poppy that.

The first thing Eismus noticed was the smell of metal, blood, and stink that filled the room. A large pool of blood had started running downhill on the uneven flooring from a body. The body was flat on the floor, his chest so bloody from the multiple stab wounds that you couldn't tell he was human. His eyes were wide open and his throat was jaggedly slit, as if his attacker had been shaking.

Eismus covered his mouth and nose with part of his shirt, as did Poppy.

"I came home after my morning shopping and found him like this," the woman began crying. Eismus looked around and found fresh shopping dropped haphazardly by the door.

"Is there even a governing force here?" Poppy asked. The woman just shook. Poppy bent down and took the woman's bloody hand in hers. "Here, let's get you to a friend's house. Is there anyone we can look for?"

It was later. The temples sent a guard each to watch the house while they decided what to do. This shouldn't have been possible. The party sat in the dining room of the house they shared with the Goodalls. Eismus wrinkled his nose as he picked a tuft of fur out of his favorite chair. Someone needed to start cleaning and it was not going to be him.

They needed a plan, both for the murders and this living situation. Eismus took a breath, but before he could speak...

"Teehee." The little laugh announced the arrival of Minksey before her body appeared. "You are the most entertaining thing to happen down here in thousands of years."

"How so?" Lilly asked. She had been hit hard by the murder. This was supposed to be a safe haven for "her" Goodalls, as she had said. The silence had been awkward after that; the party's goals continued to fracture.

"How so? Teehee." The fey did a little flip in the air. "What a silly question. Your adventures, and now an impossible murder. Not even a hard one to solve. The human man refused to leave his wife for that blonde that he got pregnant, so if she couldn't have him, no one could."

"Did you just solve our murder for us?" Lilly asked slowly. "Do we owe you anything for that?"

"Shut up, Lilly," 4aDeer and Eismus said at the same time.

"Teehee. I guess I did," Minksey laughed. "And I guess you do."

"For fuck's sake," Tom said, looking right a Rachael.

"I will take my inspiration, please," Rachael said to Aaron.

"We don't owe you anything. It wasn't our murder to solve," Eismus said vehemently.

"It was your fault, though," Minksey said. "I would run along to the Temple of the Fey if I were you. Negotiations are not going well." With that, she blinked out of existence.

The group booked it; Craig picked up Poppy so her short legs wouldn't fall behind.

Minksey was the queen of understatement. The table the town had set up between the two temples for the meeting was a pile of melted metal and hot red rock. The fey priests were on a slow retreat toward their own temple, the dragon priests steadily advancing with murder in their eyes.

Minksey popped back, settling herself on Eismus' shoulder. "This is your fault."

"How?" Eismus demanded.

"What makes something neutral?" she asked sweetly.

"Balance," Eismus said. There was an awkward silence.

"Is the entire party hearing what she is saying or just Tom?" *Martin asked.*

"The party can hear it," Aaron answered.

"Gave dragon priests power," 4aDeer's voice was devastated.

"Bingo," Minksey said. "Now you owe me two things."

53

FORT COLLINS

LIME LIGHT FITNESS

R achael was excited for her spin class this morning. At least there would be something between her legs making her sweat. She banished the thought and found her favorite bike. She loved Lime Light. They let her pay per class, and this particular spin class blocked out the world. It was just loud music, rave-like lighting, and an instructor telling you what to do.

She adjusted all the various settings on the bike to fit her before clipping on her rental shoes and her water bottle. Sandy, a middle-aged mother of two, came up on her left with a smile and polite, "How are you doing?" Rachael responded in kind and looked for Katherine, who usually rode on her left. She sucked in a breath as she saw a man's beefy shoulder move in to take Katherine's bike — they weren't really assigned. Just human habit assignments.

"Good morning," Greg's voice purred. Rachael froze.

"Hello there, Greg." She wanted to scream.

"Who's your friend?" Sandy asked, eyeing Greg appreciatively.

"This is my brother-in-law, Greg," Rachael answered. "Who I did not invite or ask to sit next to me."

Greg waved to Sandy. "Sorry if I took someone's bike. Rachael was just telling me how much she likes the spin class, and I have been looking around for something to add to my lifting." Greg sat straight up on the bike, stretching his chiseled arms.

"No problem." Sandy didn't look away, but a spot of heat rose to her cheeks.

Before Rachael could leave or say anything else, the instructor dimmed the lights and turned on the music.

"Let's get ready to ride!" he screamed over the bass. Rachael focused on the music and the instructor. Greg was with Karen. It was possible that Greg just happened to find her spin class. It was not a big secret or anything. But it still gave her the creeps, especially after that message about liking red too and the way he touched her on the Sunday marathon game. None of this was feeling right.

The class was over way too soon. Rachael dripping with sweat, the lights were slowly raised as a new instructor took them through a cool down and stretch. The original one walked around the room and took a moment to speak to each person in turn. Rachael risked a peek at Greg as the instructor came over to him. He was also sweating — at least he was human. But he had taken off his shirt. She could see every muscle in the side of his well-defined abs and narrow hips.

He twisted his waist toward her as the instructor moved on. He had known she was looking.

Rachael skipped the final stretches, intending to not wash her bike and just run.

"Don't forget to wipe down your bikes," the instructor said loudly. She was not alone in trying to skip out early and was shamed into grabbing some paper towels and spraying some cleaner on them. She found Greg already wiping down her bike when she got there.

"It is a really good class," Sandy finished whatever she had been saying to Greg. "May I use those?" she asked Rachael.

Rachael handed them to her with a smile. "Of course you can. I will see you next week."

Greg fell into step beside her as she walked back toward the locker room — she didn't actually need to use it. She had walked here and she was planning on walking home.

"You are a good-looking guy. It is hard not to notice, but me noticing is not a signal," Rachael said. They were two steps from the locker room. "Greg, you can't keep just showing up in my space," Rachael blurted out.

"I'll give you a ride home," was Greg's answer.

"I would like to walk. It is a lovely day," Rachael responded, praying it hadn't started raining as predicted.

"Then I will walk you home," Greg answered. He crossed his arms and leaned against the door. Only one way in and one way out. Rachael cursed. She might as well pee while she was in here. She did her business and washed her face. She took a minute to look herself in the eye.

"You will continue to tell him to fuck off," Rachael told her reflection. "He will get the message and leave you alone."

He was still leaning against the wall with his arms across his chest when she came out. He fell into step behind her. The parking lot was huge. Most of FoCo was made up of these mini strip malls, and Lime Light was in the corner of one about a mile from her house. She searched the lot for Greg's car. Finding it, she pointed to it.

"It was really nice of you to offer, but your car is here and I would rather walk alone," Rachael stated.

"No, you wouldn't," Greg laughed. A few drops of rain started to come out of the sky. "Get in my car." Greg didn't ask. "I just want to get you out of the rain. Here," he handed her his keys. "You seem to think I am going to do something to you. Now, I can't even start my car."

Rachael took the keys, and they ran for the car as the rain suddenly started to come down hard. It was Colorado; if she didn't want a ride, she could always just wait 15 minutes for the sun to come back out.

Rachael unlocked the car and settled into the passenger seat. Greg pulled a protein shake out of the back seat and offered her one.

"You are right, I am afraid you are going to do something to me," Rachael said harshly. "You don't respect what I say. You send me creepy Facebook messages. You show up in places in my life where you are not invited," Rachael continued. Greg sat and listened. Such a good fucking listener.

"I'm sorry you feel that way," Greg said. He took a gulp of his shake. The rain continued to hammer on the car. Blurry outlines of other gym-goers running for their cars crossed her vision.

"You are sorry I feel that way?" Rachael repeated slowly.

"I didn't mean for the messages to be creepy, and the last one I sent you was by accident. But it had been so long since you messaged me back that I assumed you had blocked me. As far as today, I might have had a feeling this was your spin class, but I didn't know and I didn't want you to think I was trying to bum a free class by asking."

Greg was full of explanations.

"Wasn't it nice to spin with me?" It was a question, but the inflection was not quite right. "We talked about that at lunch."

"You took Katherine's bike," Rachael deadpanned.

"She didn't show up today anyway," Greg defended himself.

"You need to ask about that kind of stuff," Rachael turned to him. He was on his side of the car and honestly looked sheepish. She handed him his keys. "Take me home, please."

"Is it ok if we stop at the grocery store first since it is right next to your house?" Greg asked. Rachael nodded, feeling bad.

"Look, I'm sorry," she said. "You are just doing some creepy stuff and what you said after we kissed. I have two sisters, and I understand that emotions can get jumbled."

Greg didn't respond, just pulled the car out of its spot. The five-minute drive was quiet and uncomfortable. Rachael could not wait to get out of the car and, when he parked, practically opened the door before the car was even stopped. She froze as his hand grabbed her forearm.

She tried to pull away, and he clamped down, pain lanced through her muscle. He easily pulled her back into the car. She didn't close the door.

"It is true. I have sinned in the past." Greg's voice was low. "I wanted what Aaron had so badly that I went to jail for it."

The hand squeezed her arm harder.

"But that is not what is happening now." Greg's face was right in front of hers. He licked his top lip. "I want to kiss you so badly. I am hard for you right now. Not because you are my brother's wife but because you are you. You might have had your little second honeymoon, but I know my brother and he will go back to putting your needs second, to not touching something that should be touched every day."

Greg released her arm as if he had just forgotten he was holding it. She lightly rubbed the spot he had grabbed with her other hand.

"When you wise up, I will be here, the better of the brothers."

Rachael fled.

FORT COLLINS

KITCHEN

A ll the water in the world didn't make Rachael feel clean. When the water started to run cold, she finally got out. Her forearm ached. She couldn't really see it without her glasses or contacts. She tried to put her contacts in but found that she was shaking.

With disgust, she shoved on her glasses and dressed in her rattiest undergarments. She squeezed herself into a pair of jeans and a plain but comfortable black sleeveless tank. She snuggled into her soft dark red hoodie — the dark red color making her feel more comfortable and the long arms keeping her from looking at her pulsing forearm. She took a deep breath and put on some Celtic hoop earrings and matching choker. Her mother's voice in her head repeated for the thousandth time, "No outfit is complete without something to frame the face."

"Aaron," she said as she came down the stairs.

"In the computer room," he answered absently.

"We need to talk about Greg," she said, her hands still shaking.

"He just messaged me saying that you ran out of his car

upset." Aaron stood and came over and enveloped her in his arms. "What is wrong?" he asked.

"Aaron, it's Greg that is wrong," Rachael cried into his shirt, so grateful to finally be able to talk about this. Aaron nudged her face out of his shirt, and she looked up at him.

"Did Greg do something?" Aaron asked.

"When I tried to leave the car, he grabbed my arm really hard," Rachael said. She sounded like a four-year-old complaining.

"What did you do right before he grabbed your arm?" Aaron asked in a slow, calm voice.

"I'm not a kid," Rachael spat at him, anger suddenly welling up from her gut. Greg had scared the piss out of her.

"Did you accuse him of a bunch of things he didn't do and then try to make it sound like he was in the wrong?" Aaron asked very quietly.

"You already talked to Greg," Rachael said very quietly. "You already picked a side."

No, this isn't happening, Rachael thought. Aaron was her support, her rock.

"Look, we haven't talked about it," Aaron explained. "But Greg was in juvie when we were in high school, and if I didn't pull him out of his spiral back in California, he probably would have gone to jail. Bad things happened to him in juvie, and he is terrified of going to jail. Even one accusation against him and he will get picked up. You can't just upset people, especially family, and then expect them not to react."

"He left a mark on my arm." Rachael felt like her voice wasn't hers.

"He is strong, and we both know you bruise easily," Aaron pointed out. "He is family. I have invited him over for dinner tonight so the two of you can make peace."

The silence between them was unbearably thick.

"I'm sorry," Rachael heard her own voice say. "I will do my best to be more civil."

"It is only as big a deal as you make it," Aaron said. He brought her in for another big hug and kissed the top of her head. Rachael nodded.

"I'm going to go out for a bit." Was her voice really that calm?

"I need to work anyway," Aaron said. "I can do it from home. Do you have anything to make us for dinner tonight?"

Rachael just stood, her hand absently rubbed at her forearm and pain ran up her arm at every touch. Was this really happening?

"Earth to Rach," Aaron said. "You are spacing out again — off in some fantasy world?"

Rachael felt a tear leak out of her eye.

"Don't cry, sweetie." Aaron hugged her again. "I promise we will snuggle and watch a movie tonight after we smooth things over."

Rachael felt herself nod. She didn't remember picking up her purse or putting on shoes, but at the bus stop, both were there.

FORT COLLINS

DUNGEONS & DRAFTS

The pub was packed. Rachael hadn't been here for weeks, but she didn't know where else to go. Really, it was the closest place, other than work, that felt like home. Bob and Bobbie were both working the bar along with the guy from a few weeks ago. He noticed her first as she waited calmly in the little space between the cash register and the pint draws.

"A little damp?" He chuckled, and Rachael noticed that she had not been spared from the rain on her walk from the bus stop to the bar. "What can I get you?" he asked when she didn't respond to his banter.

"A large glass of Malbec, please." Rachael's voice was still far away. The bar was busy enough that they had opened the upstairs.

"Something going on?" she asked as she paid for her wine.

"No," the bartender answered. "Just the rain bringing everyone in from the park."

"Right," Rachael said. She had forgotten about the park. About half the tables were full of gamers and half the tables were full of park-goers. The sound was more voices than dice, but the music was low, and she usually kept dice in her purse so she could add to the sound of dice if she wanted. The climb to the top floor was a steep one; hence, the balcony was usually closed during peak drinking hours, but she managed without spilling her wine and easily found the back booth unoccupied.

Everything was quieter up here. She absently rubbed her arm and pulled out her dice set, carefully placing each one with its highest value number up. Her eyes looked at them, unfocused, as the clicks of dice and plastic chips under the rich blanket of laughter began to center her.

She hadn't noticed she had finished her glass of wine, but she was suddenly unbelievably angry that it was empty. She wanted to hit something or throw something or scream. She settled for grabbing her dice and pelting them over the railing.

"Hey," a few voices responded to the little dice making contact. One guy looked up, a die clearly floating at the top of his beer. She waved at him unabashed, hoping that he would come up and confront her, but he just waved back and looked back at his game.

"There is no throwing things off the balcony." Scottish.

"Shoot me then," Rachael deadpanned. She looked over at David. He looked fresh, a few raindrops on his dark button-down, his hair slightly messy. He had a beer in one hand and a glass of red in his other.

"Is that Malbec?" Rachael asked.

"Is that weird? I asked Scott what you were drinking."

Rachael thought of Greg and she felt her mind start to disconnect again.

"Do you have any dice?" Rachael asked David. She still hadn't sat down herself or invited him to join her.

"I feel like this is a loaded question," David said, looking over the edge at where she had just thrown hers.

"Does it matter what I do with them?" Rachael challenged. David came the rest of the way to the table and put down the two drinks. He pulled a single D20 out of his pocket.

"This is the only die I have on me," he said solemnly. "Once I give it to you, it is yours to do with as you wish."

He was next to her then. One of his hands ran along her back and hooked onto her waist. The other held out the die.

Rachael didn't lean into his arm but took the die. It was heavy, made of some type of silver metal with black lines running along it, and the numbers were pink. Not pink.

"Is that rose gold?" She brought the die up to her glasses; the prescription might be a tad old.

"And Damascus steel," David didn't try to take the die back. She rolled it around in her fingers before turning and rolling the die on the table. David's arm left her back as they turned. It clinked up against the sweating beer glass and landed on a two.

"Ouch," David said.

Rachael picked up the wine glass and drained half of it, letting it come to rest in her cupped hand. Her index finger tapped the glass.

"I am bad company again," she stated.

"Are you ever good company?" David asked.

"I don't know anymore," Rachael confessed. She picked up the die again and rolled it. It landed on a one.

She drained the other half of her Malbec.

"I've been avoiding this place," Rachael said. "I made up with Aaron, and we had an entire week of bliss before it all started again. And then he picked his brother over me," she stated it like facts. Like she wasn't a part of the situation. She picked up the die and rolled it again, eight.

David didn't sit. He didn't drink his beer. He just stood near her but not in her space, close enough that she could easily reach out and run a hand down his chest, but far enough that she could move back if he tried to run a hand down hers.

"Why are you here?" David asked.

"Because I can't go home," Rachael answered. She tapped the glass again, twice.

David picked up his beer and took a sip.

"What are you doing here?" Rachael asked.

"Hoping you were here," David answered.

"Really?" Rachael couldn't stop the sarcasm that dripped from the word.

It was two steps, the exact distance they were apart, and then it was nothing. David's hands reached her first, one hand cupping the side of her cheek and neck, the other settling along her lower back, supporting her frame.

The kiss was short but passionate. David's every movement was confident but demanding; his teeth lightly bit her lower lip as he pulled back.

"You're crying," David stated.

"I'm unhappy," Rachael returned. "Will you kiss me until I don't remember?"

David picked up his die and rolled. It landed on a 20.

"I should have gotten us a taxi," David stated as they entered his apartment, both drenched despite his coat. Rachael was unsure if her shiver was the cold or anticipation.

"We are just going to take it off anyway," she said.

"A kiss is not a contract," David stated. He took off his raincoat; his shirt was much dryer than hers.

"But it's very nice," Rachael finished the *Flight of the Conchords* quote. She took off her glasses to clean off the water drops. She was pretty sure it wasn't raining in David's apartment.

Her hands grasped for a scrap of dry clothing.

"Use this." David's voice came up behind her and he started kissing her neck as he handed her the shirt he had just been wearing. She leaned back, the shirt falling to the floor along with her glasses as his hands unzipped her sodden hoodie.

He stepped back to pull it off of her and she hissed with pain as the sleeve pulled against her forearm.

"What hurts?" David asked, his voice husky.

"My left forearm," Rachael was honest. There was no reason

not to be. The moment broken, she bent down to take off her shoes and wet socks.

David flipped on the lights in his hall. He was bare-chested, the surfaces wet enough to glow. She could feel the heat in her face and imagined she looked like a drowned rat.

"You are incredible," David breathed, his bare feet silent on the hall runner as he approached again. She lifted up her left arm. Rachael looked at it for the first time. The perfect shape of Greg's hand was blooming in purple and ugly yellows.

"Do you want to talk about this?" David asked. His words were even, but she could see a storm in his eyes. She started to cry. Why couldn't Aaron's eyes look like this?

She answered him by pushing her body against his. Her lips moved against his, her tongue tracing the middle of them, begging for entrance. He resisted briefly before his arms came around her again. His hands pulled her tank up and off and pushed her breasts out of her bra. She pushed against him again, her nipples pressing into the hard contours of his chest.

Both of his hands moved down to her butt, and he squeezed.

"Up." His command was filled with need. She gave a little jump, and her legs caught on his hips. A small excited whoop escaped her lips as he began carrying her farther into the apartment. Her tongue drew circles from his neck to his ear. He set her down on his kitchen table. His mouth once again claimed hers, their tongues dancing. His swollen manhood strained against his pants. Her legs had still not unwrapped from around his waist and she pulled them in tighter, grinding against the hard surface.

He groaned and pulled back; his hands undid her bra clasp and he removed the garment before moving to his own pants. Rachael tried to move to undo her own pants, but his hands lightly clasped around her wrists, being very careful of her injury. She looked up into his eyes, and he shook his head.

"Patience," he whispered. Rachael shivered as he guided her

back onto the table. She fought the cold hard surface of the table for a moment before relaxing onto it. David's strong hands briefly put pressure on her crotch before exploring up her body, his mouth kissing the lines they left behind until they reached her breasts. He breathed a stream of cold air on each of her nipples before moving back down to kiss her stomach.

Her hips bucked as his mouth and hands caressed her navel. A soft moan escaped her as he moved one of his hands down to give her hips something to grind against. She felt the release of the button at her waistline and then David's mouth made little circles with his tongue as he kissed the zipper down. His hands easily hooked into the sides of her wet pants.

There is no romance in getting a wet pair of jeans off, and after enough wiggling and shimmying, the jeans finally landed on David's floor.

"I'm gonna need a rest after that," David's voice was both full of humor and lust.

"You better not." Rachael sat up and scooted her still under-pants-covered bottom to the edge of the counter. Her mouth met with his chest, her tongue tracing lines and kissing down as far as she could bend toward the center of his stomach.

David put a hand under her chin and brought her face up to meet his again, their lips locking before he pushed her back onto the table.

"Are these *Dragon Ball Z* underpants?"

"I wear them when I want to feel stronger..." Rachael started to explain. But words left her abruptly as David's hand pressed against the cloth. She could feel the material absorbing some of her juices. His fingers played a few more times before she lifted her hips; her underwear joined her pants on the floor.

David's mouth kissed her stomach again and then kissed down toward her nether region. His mouth blew cold air over her slit and moved to the inside of her thigh before kissing up and up. She moaned as his tongue pressed into her opening, one long lick moving aside her lips and pressuring her clit. He did it again slowly before his tongue started darting out, caressing the little nub. His hands found their way up her body and back down it before landing on the sides of her hips and pulled her forward.

His tongue was like magic. Rachael reached for something to grab onto, but there was nothing, so she settled for running her hands through his hair as her hips bucked against his ministrations. She felt her insides start to pulse and need escaped from her mouth.

She cried out in disappointment when his mouth left her so close, but his hands pulled her forward. His hard dick slipped deep inside of her, his hips moving back and forth so the motion never stopped. Rachael used her arms to sit up, her eyes looking from his flat, hair-covered stomach up to his face. His bushy eyebrows were relaxed, his eyes filled with heat as he rocked her, slowly at first. Her first almost crest faded into a buzz of sensation. She found the ledge of the table with her hands and grabbed, using her own grip to match his strokes. He grunted. His length pressed against her internal organs, and with a free hand, he put two fingers lightly against the top of her slit. Their rocking sped up, his fingers making the nub pulse.

Her breath came faster. High-pitched noises escaped from her throat, and then the world stopped for a moment. Her body constricted as she climaxed and the euphoria destroyed her other senses. She felt David's strokes speed up as her orgasm tensed around him, and soon after his own fever pulsed inside her.

He didn't stay inside this time. His length slid out of her so his mouth could reach her stomach and give a final lick down to her oversensitive slit. He stood and held out his hand, and Rachael took it to stand next to him.

"I need a towel," Rachael said automatically as she felt their juices begin to drip down her legs. David's warmth was briefly gone before he wrapped his arms around her stomach again and handed her a towel. She stuck it between her legs and leaned back. David's still half-erect member pushed into her butt. She wiggled it.

"Ready for seconds already?" David growled.

Rachael looked out the big window that surrounded the apartment. The world was a blur of drab colors, all the same runny, inky texture. She looked at her vague reflection in the glass — almost see-through, with someone's shape cradled behind her.

She turned from her reflection and pressed her lips to David's.

It was hours later; the sun had gone down, and David was softly snoring, the blankets of his bed twisted and wrapped around them. There were very few surfaces in David's apartment that hadn't been explored in some fashion or another. Rachael was sore and tired, loath to return to reality.

She watched her phone once again light up as another text message came in. It had been happening for about 15 minutes now. Her stomach growled audibly. The sex had been mind-numbing. Except for a few short naps and a break to watch a video on something she had always wanted to try that turned into funny video show-and-tell, they had been at it for hours.

The screen lit up again; she found her glasses on the floor next to the bed. Rachael slowly untangled herself from the blankets, careful not to disturb David, and, butt naked, padded over to his dryer — all her clothing had been washed and dried.

She folded it, still slightly warm from the drying cycle, and helped herself to David's shower. There was nothing of hers here. She didn't know why she was looking. She thoroughly lathered up with his soap, enjoying the new smells that surrounded her. His bathroom was as nice as his apartment, open with a raindrop shower and a directional nozzle.

Cleaned, dried, and dressed, Rachel exited the shower. David still slept. She used the light on her phone to make her way out and flipped on the lights to the big open living space. Her phone lit up again. David's things were very neat and very orderly; nicely framed pictures of what she assumed was Scotland and collector's D&D paraphernalia dotted the walls as if a professional artist picked their locations.

His furniture was all modern and matching. A large bookcase shaped like a poorly played Tetris game held an eccentric but impressive collection books. Rachael's glance found D&D manuals of almost every edition, hardback expensive-looking copies of all 15 of *The Dresden Files* books, and a few computer *Programming for Dummies* books thrown in at the bottom with a stack of game mats. Scattered at eye-level mostly, in front of his fantasy and science fiction hardbacks, were painted miniatures in little protective cases. She picked one up. The paint job was absolutely incredible. Damn it, Aaron and David would probably get along so well, Rachael thought.

Her phone started buzzing quietly in her hand. She put down the miniature and looked at Aaron's picture. He smiled up at her from their vacation to Durango last year, his face plastered in a permanent smile as they took the slow historic train to Silverton. Rachael liked trains too.

"What am I doing?" Rachael whispered to herself. The phone stopped ringing, and she sat down on the closest chair and read through the messages.

Aaron: I forgot to tell you what time Greg was coming over.

Aaron: I just noticed the time, you have been out for quite a while.

Aaron: I hope everything is OK. Greg will be over at 6.

Aaron: Greg is here, I am worried about you. I guess Greg didn't stress how upset you were when he messaged me.

Aaron: I love you, just let me know you are safe.

Aaron: Just be safe.

Rachael wanted to throw the phone. Fuck this entire situation. She sent a quick text back.

Rachael: I am safe. I love you too.

That was all she could think of to write. "I've been having incredible sex with a stranger who looked like he wanted to kill the person who hurt me, and you didn't even notice I was gone until dinner wasn't getting made" just wasn't as poetic.

Rachael stood and found her purse, flipped off the light, and let herself out. The rain had stopped. The air was crisp and cool. Rachael kicked at sticks as she walked back to Dungeons & Drafts. She stuck her finger in her pocket and was surprised to find David's D20 still in it.

She hesitated for a moment. It was obviously important to him and valuable. She should take it back. She found herself moving it to one of the zipper pockets in her purse. She could always leave it with Bob and say she found it on the ground.

FORT COLLINS

DIRK AND DIRK REALTY

"You have that look about you again," Karen said. Rachael had made coffee this morning. "And Greg told me you and Aaron had a fight. Was the makeup sex magical?"

Rachael felt at least three different emotions bubble to the surface at the question. Anger, lust, and fear being the front-runners. Karen must have seen something in her face.

"That is a confusing look for you," Karen voiced.

"I am so angry," Rachael started to say, but then she remembered that Karen was sort of dating Greg, and she left it at that.

"Relationships can be tough," Karen tried to sympathize.

"I came home, latish," Rachael said. "I played a few rounds of *Splendor* at Dungeons & Drafts and had some food. Then caught the last bus home. Greg was gone by the time I arrived. Aaron had an episode of our show cued up for us. He didn't apologize. He didn't ask where I had been. He didn't say anything. We watched our episode and then he let me know that he thought I was being childish and adults don't avoid their problems. But if I needed time to process family history that he would give it to me."

"And then mad makeup sex?" Karen's voice was hopeful.

"Then we went to bed at the same time, which was nice, but that is all we did."

"That is really not what your face is saying, girl," Karen stated. "My sexdar must be off."

Rachael shook her head and moved her hands in a gesture of "beats the hell out of me."

"So, what is this family history that is causing all the drama?" Karen asked in a low voice.

"Greg went to juvie in high school and apparently, whatever he did, he started doing again a few years later in California. So, Aaron brought him out here." Rachael was happy to pass that on.

"He went to juvie for stealing," Karen nodded.

"What did he steal?" Rachael asked. She didn't believe for a second that he went to juvey for stealing, but she was curious what lies he was spinning Karen.

"Women's undergarments," Karen giggled. Maybe she wasn't lying.

"How do you know?" Rachael asked, really curious now.

"He told me," Karen said, excited. She knew something about Greg that Rachael didn't. Rachael let Karen tell the detailed story of Greg's telling of his personal history for the rest of break. Fuck Greg. When she sat back down at her desk, she had never typed so loud in her entire life.

FORT COLLINS

ELLIOT'S MARTINI BAR

Rachael laughed with her coworkers as Matilda finished telling the story of her little girl making cookies. It honestly wasn't as funny as Matilda thought it was, but Rachael was enjoying her happy hour.

"I am so glad we got this together," Matilda said, wiping a tear of humor out of her eye before it could affect her makeup. "I even love it that there is a dress code."

Rachael was excited to be wearing her new royal blue cocktail dress. It was quite simple, coming down to her knees with a thick belt of material that brought in her waist and melted into a halter top. It had some white beadwork and a slit that showed off her cleavage and the top of her chest. She had kept it simple, not changing up her work bun, but added a delicate headband of white stones and flowers. A silver teardrop fell off each ear.

"Between the husband and the kids, I just don't get to be around adults very much anymore," Matilda continued. The group laughed again, and the stories turned to complaints about husbands. Rachael added her own complaint about Aaron never willing to cook that was met with much agreement, except

Akane, who took the time to brag about her husband's prowess in the kitchen.

Rachael was thinking about her second martini. She had already decided she wanted to try every drink on the menu eventually. She even took pictures of it and was marking them off as she went.

"Greg?" Karen's raised voice made her look up.

Greg must have come straight from work. His sleeves were rolled up over his biceps and his dress pants were slightly mussed from the day's work.

"Karen," Greg said, coming over to the group. When he was closer, Karen stood.

"What are you doing here?" she asked, her tone unfriendly.

"I was in the neighborhood and saw you were out and thought I would join you," Greg answered.

"I told you that I was going out with the girls," Karen said. "I didn't invite you to join us."

"Well, I am here now," Greg smiled. "Hi, Rachael, what's up?"

Rachael's skin crawled. To her surprise, Karen took a step forward and put a hand on Greg's chest.

"Look baby, here is the deal," she said. "I know I said we could go steady but go steady doesn't mean it is OK to drop in on my social engagements. This is a girls' happy hour with my girls. So, take the hint and scatter."

The threat was clear in her voice. Greg looked down at her hand and then took one long, hard look at Rachael. Rachael shook her head and looked down at the menu.

"Don't even try to kiss me goodbye," Karen said. "I will call you later and maybe you can make it up to me."

The ladies cheered Karen's victory, and another round of cocktails was ordered immediately to celebrate. Rachael cheered with them but couldn't regain quite the joy she was feeling. Once again uncomfortable waiting at the bus stop, she caught an Uber home.

FORT COLLINS

24 HOUR FITNESS

"What are your goals in joining 24 Hour Fitness?" asked the generic personal trainer in his bright red shirt with the blue "24" on the pocket. He sat at a computer filling out her new membership information.

"To avoid my house and my old gym that my stalker found me at," Rachael answered.

"I don't think I have a drop-down for that. Are you OK?" The man raised an eyebrow and turned from the computer screen.

"Sorry, my sense of humor can be dark," Rachael said humorlessly. "My old gym didn't offer a boxing class and I would like to hit things. You are also on a major bus route and I don't have a car at the moment."

The man nodded and turned back to his computer.

The week was mostly over. She and Aaron had officially settled back into their old routine of work, eat, work on their own projects separately, and then sleep. Aaron had not mentioned Greg again, and that was that. The dynamics in the house were peaceful. But Rachael was anything but.

Greg picked up Karen every day. Every day he took the time

to come over and ask Rachael innocent questions. He also dropped subtle hints, details of her life he shouldn't know or details of his she didn't want to know. She didn't see him outside these interactions. There were no more messages from across stores or random appearances in her life. Except for one misspelled "u up/" on Facebook that she had not been up to see.

She would be damned if she cried anymore or let Greg control her life. She absently rolled David's D20 around in her fingers and finished the oral members' questionnaire.

"Do you want to set up your free personal training sessions now?" the trainer asked.

"Yes, and I want them to be with someone who can teach me how to punch," she said.

60

THE UNDERDARK

CRAIG

Although the bulk of Elm City's inhabitants are traders just passing through, the little town does have local residents who get along well enough in their own little economy. But they remember a time when the temples had more magic and their community was much more.

— AARON – DUNGEON MASTER'S NOTES, CS14.

The party had rushed to the defense of the fey and helped them maneuver into their own temple, wards coming to keep the dragon priests at bay.

"I don't know how this happened," they fey priest said, his spidery hands ran over the magic that protected the temple. "The balance has been there for hundreds of years. They must have gotten some sort of item that increased the temple's power as a whole."

"That must be it," Eismus agreed quickly. "Is there something like that for your temple?"

Craig had his big hand over Lilly's mouth before she could say anything. They could be honest later. They needed to figure out how they could help now. Lilly fought against him, but he easily overpowered her, his big arm firm across her chest, one finger almost uncomfortably in her mouth. Craig enjoyed the feeling of her that close and that safe under his protection.

"Yes, but it was lost long ago." The priest's shoulders dropped.

"We are experts at finding things," Eismus said. "Maybe if you tell us about it, we can help restore the balance."

"You still have not completed the quests I gave you," the fey priest sniffed.

"Sorry," 4aDeer stated.

"We didn't know those were time-sensitive," Poppy tried to smooth over. "But this is something time-sensitive, and we want to help. We brought the Goodalls here to be safe and now they are not."

Craig nodded. Making it important to the party as well would make the priest more likely to give them the quest. Lilly squirmed in his arms, but he just held on tighter. They had to fix this. And Eismus was actually correct for once in his way to go about it.

"Fine," the fey priest sniffed. "It can't hurt anything." They all moved into the large room with the giant desk. Craig picked up Lilly, so she stayed with the group. The fey priest quickly pulled a few things out of a drawer and beckoned them forward. Craig let go of Lilly but kept his eyes on her little fuming form. She moved to the other side of the room, arms crossed over her chest, to look at the desk from as far from Craig as she could get.

"The Dragon Temple's eyes are glowing," the Priest began. "The last written history of that happening is back when they had a dragon's heart power crystal inside it." He opened a book and showed them a drawing of the cube they had just procured from a dragon.

"We also originally had a dragon's heart power crystal," he continued. He flipped the pages a few times until a similar drawing opened up. This cube was more purple and green, and the shape inside looked more like a tree.

"The two crystals were removed at the same time by one of our great and powerful forefathers — Alexander von Higgensbain. He felt that the temples were too powerful and should return to the people. However, without the magic to sustain them, our gardens and magic failed, and Elm City's population shrank to what it is now. Honestly, that is how we could find you a house so easily, so many abandoned. Alexander von Higgensbain died of scurvy a few years later, unable to admit he made a mistake or that his mistake caused the loss of the power crystals. You see, the adventurers he trusted to take the crystals away were robbed and slaughtered."

The fey priest dramatically closed the book, and it boomed around the room.

"The only clue to its whereabouts is the occasional flicker of energy we feel when it is being used, but exactly where we cannot pinpoint."

"Are there any patterns to when you feel this energy?" Eismus asked.

"The only correlation we can find is when the slavers come through," he answered. He took a moment to study a painting hanging on the wall. "And the last few times we sent adventurers in to retrieve it," he admitted.

"Is it evil? Is it killing people?" Lilly asked.

"It is just a power core, the magical heart of an ancient dragon. It can do anything in the hands of the wrong person." The fey priest hesitated and then looked at Poppy, handing her three pieces of paper.

"These are for your eyes alone, druid. Trust no one, especially not the drow." He didn't acknowledge Eismus but turned back to his desk. He raised his voice dramatically, "Go now, find the core and save us all."

———

They found themselves in the tavern, the papers on a small table in the back corner, far away from other patrons. Lilly had a mug of ale and was keeping her distance from Craig across the table. Craig just shook his head. Her mood was once again cold toward him.

The papers included a list of names, a detailed map of a cave system, including part that looked like a maze that they didn't recognize, and a blank piece of paper. They had passed the paper around to see if it reacted to any of them, and when it hadn't, Eismus had snatched it up before anyone could object. He was currently casting spells on it to see if it was just hidden. The map and the list of names both sat on the table in front of them.

"What happened to 'don't trust the drow?' " Craig rumbled, watching the drow's unrestricted attempts to make something appear on the paper.

"He must have meant other drow," Poppy stated. "Even if we are not all agreeing on stuff at the moment, I trust our party."

"I think we are all in agreement on this," Lilly cut in. "I know I have been distant, but we need to fix this. What is this a map of? Does anyone recognize anything on it? Eismus, put that down and look at the paper that actually has something on it."

Eismus took a deep breath but did as he was told. The party studied the map. Poppy pulled out her little map and put it off to one side. She had added all the details from their most recent adventure to it.

"Is that the same warning as on the cave troll's lair?" Poppy asked, comparing their drawings.

"That does look a little like it," Craig agreed.

Lilly picked up the list of names and scanned through it. "Grogith Gotlittle is on this list."

"Who is that again?" Tom asked.

"The cave troll," Greg filled him in. "Keep better notes."

"But 4aDeer is the newest name added to the list, and we don't actually know what the list means," Lilly said, disappointed.

"We should conduct interviews and see what they have in common," Poppy recommended.

"If we ask too many questions though, 'people' will know we are onto them, and if 'people' know, they will change their habits," Lilly explained.

"Good point," Craig agreed with her. She shot him a dirty look.

"What? I was agreeing with you," Craig said defensively.

"You shouldn't just agree with me because I said it," Lilly shot back.

"I just think it is a good point as well," Eismus responded.

"Children!" Poppy exclaimed. "Did we ever decipher the letter we had to deliver to Grogith?"

Lilly reached into her bag and pulled it out.

"Did not," 4aDeer stated.

"Maybe we should start there," Poppy recommended.

"Do you think it has anything to do with this?" Craig asked skeptically.

"I think it is too much of a coincidence not to," Poppy stated.

Lilly put the list of names and the blank page in her pack but left out the map with the letter. She cast comprehend languages and touched first the letter and then the map.

"The words on the map I will translate into Common for us, but the letter must be code," she stated. "It was worth a try." She sat down and did a rough sketch of the map, translating the text into Common.

"What if not letter?" 4aDeer asked.

"Like a location?" Eismus asked.

"A meeting?" Craig added. Lilly suddenly stopped her writing and looked up.

"I overheard a group of regulars talking about a festival," Lilly suddenly said. "Could it be an invitation?"

4aDeer picked up the message and moved it around a bit before handing it to Eismus. "Message not flat," he stated.

Craig took the message from Eismus and did the same thing.

"That is really clever, Aaron," Greg said. *"That must have taken a really long time."* *He looked directly at Rachael.*

"It did," Aaron said, pleased that his optical illusion had been found.

"I was even more pleased that Rachael rolled so high to copy it — otherwise, you would have never seen it."

They passed the letter around, everyone turning it this way and that until the little pictures all lined up and made a 3D sentence. "At the festival, 11, 21, and 8. Don't come alone."

"When is this festival you heard about?" Craig asked.

"Tonight!" Lilly exclaimed. "I don't have anything I can wear!"

"I doubt many people will be dressed up," Poppy said, looking around the tavern. "Most of the town is working-class and travels. And we don't know what kind of festival it will be."

"Oh," Lilly sounded disappointed. She paused for a moment. "Especially as I just cast comprehend languages and it lasts an hour, I am going to wander around and see if I can learn more about the event. I just assumed we are going."

"I think that is a safe assumption," Eismus said. "4aDeer, let's go talk about being civil and at least cleaning your plate armor as you have basically been sleeping in it. You smell foul."

Craig started to follow Lilly, and she shook her head. "Go with Eismus," she said.

"I don't want to leave you alone," Craig stated.

"I am a badass dwarf," Lilly hissed vehemently. "And I am a bard. This is what my character is designed to do. Fuck off."

"That was uncalled for." Martin didn't like it when people swore.

"Moving on." Aaron's voice was very even.

The event was common knowledge, although mostly being talked about in all the various languages the party did not speak down here. It was apparently an annual thing that happened in the main market square. People dressed up in their best and spent the night drinking and dancing. Even folk from other towns came in to be merry.

The town had been slowly swelling with people for the last week. Tension was high with the murder and the Temple of the Fey literally barricaded, with dragon priests prodding its defenses at all times. There were whispers of cancellation, but when they investigated the market square, it was being hung with garlands and little lights, and a stage was being erected.

"OK, here is the deal," Rachael said, excited. "I want to wear a dress and keep my leathers inside my pack, as my pony keg drum is currently full of ale so I can't use it for storage. We can sit here and play that out. Or I can just describe to you what I am wearing."

"Just describe it and I will tell you how much less money you have," Aaron said.

Rachael looked put out. "I was expecting an argument or a roll-off or something."

"Nope, I don't think anyone cares what you are wearing," Aaron said bluntly. Martin even looked up, the air in the room thick with tension. Aaron loved details.

61

FORT COLLINS

DINING ROOM

"I need some air. Anyone want to join me?" Debby asked. The hint was received and the room was cleared — all but Greg, who stayed put.

"Greg, why are you still here," Rachael asked.

"He has every right to be here," Aaron answered.

"You love game details," Rachael turned to Aaron. "Why does it not matter what I am wearing?"

"Because we have spent half of this session listening to you snap at Greg and treat him poorly for no reason other than you refuse to make peace and apologize." Aaron, sweet Aaron, who never raised his voice, raised it now.

"Aaron, you don't understand," Rachael started. "He held Lilly against her will. He put his hand over her mouth so she couldn't talk and trapped her arms to her sides so she couldn't get away. You and the rest of the party just went with it."

"It is just a game, Rachael. Lilly makes bad deals. She wasn't assaulted," Aaron said angrily.

"But I was," Rachael said the words without emotion. She didn't sound like a little kid this time.

"I didn't mean to hurt you, Rach," Greg stood. "It was a misunderstanding."

"This is why I wanted us together before game night," Aaron said quietly.

Rachael shook her head. "Aaron, this is not about Greg. This is about you not defending me, your wife. The person you promised to protect and cherish."

She didn't look at Greg or Aaron.

"I will agree to a truce tonight, for the sake of the campaign. But this is a D&D game, not a love story, and Craig must stop smothering Lilly." Rachael's finger hit the table to punctuate each of the last three words in her sentence. "She is her own person."

She looked over at Aaron, who was pale but nodded to himself. Rachael took her wine glass to the sink and emptied it, replacing it with a glass of water. She walked to the side of the kitchen, her voice fueled by anger.

"I am going to go outside and drink this and imagine my beautiful fucking dress. My dress is going to let me blend in with the rest of the ladies who you, Aaron, described. It will give me freer movement because women are just little things who come out and play when you let them." Rachael paused to see if Greg or Aaron had anything to say. "Right then, have your shit figured out."

Rachael walked quickly but purposefully to the sliding glass door to her porch. She could see Tom, Debby, and Martin all standing in a circle. The talking stopped as she slid open the door.

"And those Broncos," Tom said lamely.

"Talking about me?" she asked sweetly.

"Is everything OK?" Tom asked the obvious question.

"How much did you hear?" she asked.

"Mostly your speech at the end," Debby said. She held up her hand for a medium five. "You go, girl."

Rachael gave it to her.

"Honestly, things are not fine at all," Rachael said. "But I don't need to burden you with family drama, and I think we have an understanding for the evening."

"Greg needs to back off," Martin said. "He is smothering your ability to play Lilly's attributes."

"I could hug you, Martin." Rachael smiled at him. "The long and short of tonight is — there is some shit in real life that all the Chambers have brought with them to the table. Literally."

"Ah, to game with family," Tom said, looking wistful. "Nope, never done it, never want to do it. Maybe a girlfriend someday, though."

Rachael finished her water. "Shall we see if things are settled?"

They were. Aaron had taken the opportunity to get out his newest 3D model, complete with decorations, although the food stalls were dice and the stage an immaculately painted bridge from the first session.

Rachael felt Aaron's and Greg's eyes on her as Aaron set the scene for the party and each person went around the table describing their attire. Craig kept his distance from her for the rest of night, and the party, if a little more solemn than usual, finished the encounter.

Rachael smiled and waved everyone off with cheer. She left every plate on the table, her movements staying with Debby or Tom until she and Aaron were alone in the house.

She turned to Aaron. Their half-lit living room cast shadows into every corner. The sounds of the house were accompanied by some honest-to-God crickets.

"It's late," Rachael said. "I will sleep in the guest room."

"Is that really necessary?" Aaron asked quietly.

"Are you going to listen to me?" Rachael asked. "Are you going to tell me why it is OK that Greg drives a wedge between us?"

"It is not OK that he does that," Aaron said. "You are the one who won't apologize. You overreacted and scared him and worried me. Can we find middle ground?"

Aaron stepped forward and took Rachael's hand.

"It is just a stupid fight. No one is hurt. I am sorry I didn't support you. Greg is sorry he scared you and overreacted — you heard him say it earlier."

Rachael let him take her hand and wrap his arms around her. She didn't really want to sleep alone tonight, especially not if it was by Greg's design.

"Fine," she whispered into his shirt. "I apologize for not making peace before campaign night," Rachael specified. "I will apologize in person next time I see him. But do not invite him over without talking to me first."

Aaron began to rock her and she let him, but no tears came out of her eyes and her body didn't mold to his like it used to.

"Never again," he promised.

He held her in his arms that night. He didn't initiate anything, and she didn't either. She watched the ceiling. The little shadows of the trees from the distant streetlamp danced until sleep found her.

62

EMAIL FROM TOM TO RACHAEL

Hi Rach,

Please do not tell Aaron I sent you this and delete it after you
have read it. But I have noticed Greg popping up in your
conversations a lot, and Aaron mentioned the arm grabbing
incident, and after last night…I know it is not my place, but this
shouldn't be kept quiet.

Greg went to juvie pretty much for stalking a girl. Here is the
short version of what happened.
Greg had a big crush on this girl named Ashley. He had had a
crush on her for years, anyway. Ashley primarily dated
computer guys — I have no idea why — and she asked out our
super dense high school version of Aaron, who didn't put two
and two together and said yes. Or if you ask Greg, Aaron did it
on purpose. Anyway, Greg got super obsessed with her and,
even after Aaron and Ashley's short high school romance was
over, he continued to show up at all her activities and her stuff
started going missing. In the end, they found it all in Greg's

bedroom. We are talking about little things like undergarments all the way to a copy of her house key. It was pretty creepy.

Anyway, the family pressed charges and he went to juvie for a few months, where he was beaten up by a guard pretty badly. He was unconscious for three days.

Aaron feels like a lot of that was his fault. You already know his family is super close and means everything to him. I am still surprised sometimes that you don't have a bun in the oven.

Anyway, that is pretty much it. I hope this helps.

Tom

P.S. I don't know why Aaron got him a job out here. Aaron just said staying in California was a slippery slope with all his old friends in the area and he deserved a fresh start.

63

FORT COLLINS

24 HOUR FITNESS

Rachael was breathing hard by the end of her spin class. She had spent her 30-minute personal training session learning how to wrap her hands and punch with straight wrists. And then tried out a new spin class. She missed the rave-like lights and atmosphere of her old class, but the music was loud and the class based on intervals, her favorite way to spin.

"Hey," another woman got her attention. "Did I see you punching the bags before class?"

"Yes." Rachael's breath still came out in little gasps. "I used my 30-minute free personal training session to learn the basics."

"Right on," the woman said. "I was actually going to recommend Holly to you — she is great. She teaches during lunchtime hours. Her boxing class is at noon today."

Her new friend's name was Alexandra, but she went by Alex for short. She was a few inches taller than Rachael, with long red hair that was currently up in a trendy braid and matched her pale complexion. Her gym outfit was as trendy as her hair and coordinated perfectly with her bright blue and purple shoes. Rachael was unsure if she hated the woman because she seemed to have hardly broken a sweat or because she was drop-dead gorgeous.

"I am actually headed out for today," Rachael responded.

"I am, too," Alex said. "I am sorry if I seem overly friendly, I just love making new workout buddies!"

"Sorry," Rachael rushed. "I am not trying to be rude. I just need to catch a bus. This gym is not in walking distance to my house."

"Can I give you a ride home?" Alex asked.

"No, it is fine." Rachael turned her down. "It was nice to meet you. Maybe I will see you in another class."

Rachael forced her very wobbly leg muscles to walk two blocks over to catch a different bus than the one outside 24, just in case Greg came by, but she had been careful not to post anything about her switch of gyms to social media or leave a paper trail.

FORT COLLINS

DUNGEONS & DRAFTS

Rachael had stretched a little on the bus on her way over and was starting to recover from her spin. She felt good after punching the bag, really good. Her hands ached a little, but it was a satisfying ache.

Dungeons & Drafts was hopping with gamers. There were only a few tables still available.

David's die was in her pocket today. She rolled it around in her fingers and scanned the crowd.

"Rachael," Bobbie called. Rachael turned to the bar and waved.

"Long time no see," Rachael said.

"I thought I saw you get in on some games last Saturday, but it was so busy," Bobbie said.

"I was in for a bit," Rachael admitted. "Aaron has been working really hard. He is working today and tomorrow for the final push on this project, and I don't like to play games by myself."

"Indeed," Bobbie said. "What can I get you? And I'll give it to you for free if you would be willing to fill in and teach some games this afternoon. David called in, and whatever business that he is in town for needs him this weekend."

Rachael squeezed the die in her hand and let it drop into her pocket.

"Do you have any scotch?" she asked.

"Scotch?" Bobbie questioned.

"If I am filling in for a Scot, I might as well drink like one," she stated.

Bobbie laughed and poured her a dram out of a bottle from the middle shelf. Ugh, the smell of it burned her sinuses.

"Table eight would like to play Five Tribes," he scooted her off.

Rachael threw her gym bag into the office and sent a quick text to Aaron, not that he would get it at work. And she settled in with the three strangers.

"Think of this as the adult version of Mancala," Rachael started. The sip of scotch she took burned her throat and brought color to her face, but it was not bad.

65

FORT COLLINS

DIRK & DIRK REALTY

K aren was late to work. That in itself never happened. It didn't seem to matter how outrageous her night was or how late or how much of whatever she drank came out of whatever end. She was never late.

Rachael sent her a quick text.

Rachael: Just checking on you, queen of punctuality.

Karen: Sorry, I am on my way. Greg and I broke up and my car won't start. On the bus now.

Rachael: I'm sorry! I will have coffee waiting for you when you walk in the door.

Karen: You are a sweetie. Just wait 'til I tell you what happened!

Karen: You were right to warn me.

Rachael read the last message twice but could think of no response. She waited another 15 minutes before putting the pot on so it would be as fresh as possible. Karen came in with all the noise and drama of the queen she was.

She sank artfully into the office break room chair and accepted the coffee and a cupcake Rachael had grabbed off the communal table.

"He said your name while we were doing it." Karen didn't beat around the bush.

Rachael blinked. "What?"

"I thought something was weird." Karen leaned into the table. Rachael did the same. "He always wanted to come up to the office. He constantly asked if you were going to be there for drink night. He even asked if I wanted to go on a double date with you and Aaron. Please, can you imagine me on a double date?"

"I'm so sorry." Rachael didn't know what to say.

"You should be saying, 'I told you so,'" Karen said. "You told me there was something off. You even refused to set us up. And then he just happened to show up at Elliot's 20 minutes after I tagged you in a selfie saying we were there. Aaron's brother is stalking you."

Rachael just sat there, unsure how to respond.

"He is?" Rachael wasn't sure if it was a question or a statement.

"I can't believe you don't see it," Karen said. "You need to go to the police or at least tell Aaron."

"Aaron doesn't believe me." Rachael's jaw locked and the stubborn line formed across her lips. "Greg is manipulating the situation. He is very good at it."

"How long has this been going on?" Karen's voice was quiet. One of the supervisors popped his head into the break room.

"Fuck off, Jerry," Karen said. "We will both work extra this week to cover it." Jerry blinked and backed out.

"Weeks, maybe more," Rachael admitted. "And I know it is my fault and I am dealing with it."

"You are not dealing with it. That psychopath dated me to get to you. Oh my god," Karen stopped. "That is why you stopped talking to me or telling me things about your life. You didn't want it passed onto your stalker. I can't believe this."

"You didn't know," Rachael said. "I didn't really realize it myself until recently, or at least I didn't admit it was a thing. It was just little things at first, and then he just started showing up everywhere. And then he showed up at my spin class and grabbed me." Rachael swallowed down her anger.

"He grabbed you?" Karen exclaimed.

Rachael rolled up her suit top jacket to show the last fading purples of the handprint bruise.

"Did you take pictures of that?" Karen asked.

"No," Rachael looked confused. Karen grabbed her phone and made Rachael lay out her hand and started taking pictures of the light, fading bruise.

"Everything is hearsay," Karen said. "And I can attest, Greg is good at 'say.' "

"Please don't do anything," Rachael said. "It is beyond wonderful to just have someone to talk to who believes me."

Karen pursed her lips. "I won't say or do anything unless it escalates. But you talk to me, woman, and if you need anything, any time, I will cancel as many dates as I need to. Oh, and girls' night on Wednesday next week — margaritas. Invite only and booking necessary."

"I am in. I even have a new dress," Rachael said excitedly. "Is red a good color for margaritas?"

"Red is a good color for everything," Karen answered.

66

FORT COLLINS

COMPUTER ROOM

Rachael was scrolling through books on Amazon. She needed a light read. Something that could take her mind off her life and make her laugh. She could see part of Aaron's reflection in her computer monitor, his desk a little behind and to the side of hers. Maybe she should play one of those stupid role-playing romance games Facebook advertised.

"You choose," the advertisement read over the picture of a hot, anime-styled man. "Hit on him or slap him." Rachael briefly wondered why both options seemed so violent. She did a quick google search for two-player games. She didn't need a distraction from life; she needed to do something fun.

"Aaron?" she questioned. It took him a few minutes to take off his headphones.

"What's up?" he eventually answered.

"Do you want to play something together?" she asked.

"Like what?" Aaron asked.

"I don't know," Rachael said. "We have several two-player games and *Lego: The Lord of the Rings* is on Steam. It has a two-player mode. Or we haven't played *Worms* in ages." Rachael's voice lightened as she remembered killing her own worm with the kickback from the bazooka she had tried to kill Aaron's with. A game would be perfect.

"I'm not really feeling like playing a video game right now." Aaron had slipped one earphone back in one ear.

"What do you feel like doing?" Rachael asked.

"I am watching Geek and Sundry's YouTube channel," Aaron said. "I guess I could put it on the big TV and we could watch it together."

"I guess we could watch it together," Rachael repeated the words in her head. "No, never mind, I will entertain myself," Rachael shook off the idea. Aaron's headphones covered both his ears again.

FORT COLLINS

DUNGEONS & DRAFTS

Rachael, tipsy from happy hour margaritas, had the taxi drop her off at Dungeons & Drafts. Aaron had let her know he was working late, and she should feed herself. She sent him back a high-angled selfie of her in her red dress, the angle showing lots of cleavage, and captioned it, "This is what you are missing."

She was super overdressed for the pub. She eyed the front door. She would just take a peek, and if David wasn't there, she would take a little walk in the park to sober up and then maybe go to the gym until Aaron was going to be home.

She opened the door just enough to slide through and looked around. Every head had turned when she opened the door — it was that slow of a night. The bartender she didn't know well gave her a nod, and a few men at the bar gave her an appreciative once-over.

"Can you make a margarita?" she asked…Scott. Was his name Scott?

"I can probably make something that is close enough, but I am guessing you had some better ones already."

"Har har," Rachael said. "Not the usual attire for D&D, is it?"

"Nope." Scott got to mixing.

"It was an after-work girls' happy hour thing."

"Sounds like fun. Why aren't you still there?" Scott asked.

"Honestly, I saw Greg's car in the parking lot, and it made me nervous," Rachael said. Scott probably didn't know Greg or anything about her situation, but she had a habit of being more honest with strangers.

"I'm sorry to hear that." Scott handed her the drink, clearly confused but trying to be polite. She paid.

"I saw the umbrellas out front still up," she said.

"I'll wait a bit longer to take them down. We just put in a new set of chairs in the back where the sun sets over the park. Here." He handed Rachael a towel. "I don't know if this is clean or not, but feel free to head back."

Rachael did. She set her clutch and her drink on the table and did a little wipe down of the high-backed bench. The view of the park was lovely, the evening warm enough, but she was very alone back here. She watched as a figure walked from the park and up the little hill toward Dungeons & Drafts. As it got closer, it was clearly male, shoulders back, chest out. David's impeccable posture. She willed him to see her.

She had not really come here to see David. Karen had helped her realize that if Greg and Aaron worked at the same company then it was very likely Greg knew every time Aaron was not home and Rachael was. It was always possible he was just in Old Town for the evening. But if he was looking for her and she was home alone...she just didn't want to be in that position.

Having David see her looking smoking hot instead of crying pretty much in her 'PJs was an added bonus.

He almost missed her but looked over just as he started to pass. She felt her insides melt as their eyes met. She stood slowly, smoothing and pulling at her dress as she did.

"I have your D20," Rachael stated as they walked toward

each other. "But I have it tucked away in my other purse, and I forgot to move it to this one."

"I gave you that die to do with as you will." David's hand wrapped around her waist, pulling her in close. Short whiskers brushed her face as his mouth claimed hers.

"Tequila?" he asked when they parted for air.

"Margarita happy hour at work," Rachael stated.

"Your husband let you walk around unaccompanied in that?" David growled.

"You don't like it?" Rachael mock pouted.

"It makes you look like sin itself." David kissed her again, short and hard, his hand moving down from her back to squeeze one butt cheek. Rachael's breath caught in her throat as they parted. She could feel his dick starting to come to life in his pants.

"Did you need something in D&D?" Rachael breathed.

"I already found it." David picked up her clutch for her and finished off her margarita.

David's apartment was dark, and he easily asked Alexa to turn on "mood lighting." Half the lights came on, some purple and green making inky shadows over all of his things.

"That is new." Rachael stepped out of her little flats. "Alexa, turn on mood music," she demanded.

"Playing smooth jazz," Alexa stated. A piano started plinking out aimless patterns that floated through dissonant chords and relaxing melodies.

"This is something else," Rachael said, looking around the apartment. David came up from behind her, his hands on her hips, his thumbs rubbing little circles. His mouth came down on her neck, delicate kisses sending little tingles of pleasure everywhere they touched.

"I want something different," Rachael's voice was husky.

"Demanding today, showing up at my pub in that," David growled. He spun her around, undressing her with his eyes before pulling her in for another kiss and moving them backward farther into the apartment. She pulled back first, wiggling her butt where his hands currently rested.

"Do you have any rope?" she asked innocently.

Ten minutes later, Rachael looked at her handiwork.

"I was thinking this would go the other way," David sounded unsure. She loved the waver in his voice. He was naked, his hands tied to his headboard and his feet loosely bound together. Rachael was down to her undergarments, a red lacy set that she had ordered online just for this dress. Although, when she ordered it, she assumed Aaron would be taking it off of her.

"I think this is a nice look for you." Rachael carelessly undid her bra and slid off her panties, tossing them to the side. She slowly crawled on top of him, letting her breasts drag against his chest as she moved up his body. She stopped dangling them just out of reach of his mouth.

"Tease," David breathed.

Rachael moved back down, kissing his stomach like he had kissed hers, trailing her tongue down to his erection. She kissed and nibbled at the skin where it met his crotch, and again on the other side. She put her tongue along the underside of the base of his girth and gave it a long, slow, thick lick to the tip. She could feel him wiggle underneath her and relished it.

Again, she put her tongue at the base and slowly licked up, like a giant popsicle. This time, she kissed the head before swirling her tongue around the tip and putting it in her mouth. There was no way she could fit all of him, and she wasn't even going to try. She went down for one longer lick and left as much saliva behind as possible.

She looked up at him, his head propped up comfortably on pillows, his eyes closed, mouth slightly open, and body wiggling to participate.

"Open your eyes," she breathed, and he did. She gathered her breasts up in her hands and pushed them together around his shaft, twisting her own nipples as she slid down. His length was long enough that she could look down and engulf the tip in her mouth. David moaned as she slid her breasts up and down on his long, hard shaft, sucking at the salty moisture that came out of the tip.

Rachael moaned around his tip one last time before crawling up his body again, kissing and nibbling every part before she made it back to his mouth. She pressed her lips to his and immediately invaded his mouth with her tongue, the appendage exploring his mouth as much as it had done his body. She crawled up, pressing each nipple in turn to his waiting mouth before dragging them back down his body.

She could feel his manhood rub against her slit as their hips met. She stayed high, letting just his tip rub lightly back and forth. She rocked then, her eyes closed, her arms holding her up, and her nipples rubbing against David's chest. Moisture began to build as her senses kicked into overdrive. She opened her eyes. David had been watching her.

"You are unbelievably hot," David breathed. His hand strained at the bonds to touch her. Rachael felt her body respond to his words, fire stoked in her core. She leaned down and gave him a chaste kiss before positioning herself above David's hard arousal and ever so slowly inched herself down. She could feel David's hips pushing up, wanting her to go faster; his hands strained against their bonds but she kept it slow. The control was almost as hot as the sex. When she finally fit all of him inside her, she began to rock her hips forward in small motions, for her alone.

"More," David groaned, his hips screaming for freedom.

Rachael pushed herself up and down a few times, automatically responding to the request, his dick sliding in and out of her. But that wasn't what she wanted.

"Don't stop," David breathed. Rachael did stop. She bent down and put a finger on his lips.

"Patience," she said, and then slowly began to rock. Her clit rubbed against his base in little circles that turned into bigger circles that sped up as her strokes started to get longer and grind harder into his body. She felt him tense as he released inside of her; her muscles clenched at his sudden swell in size, but she couldn't stop. She wouldn't stop. Everything was in just the right place.

Her breath came out short, gasping as she moved, and then stopped and then moved again; her summit tensed her entire body and filled her senses. Her hips made small movements, throbbing and rubbing a few last times before everything was suddenly too much. She didn't move off of him and just collapsed down, their combined bodies filling something that was desperately empty.

68

UNDERDARK

LILL

Elm City is in the middle of an immense cavern in the Underdark. The ceiling is barely visible. It is often easy to forget you are in a giant cave. Dull crystals create enough light to push away most of the darkness from its orderly, straight streets. Oddly, every building has a shingled roof, the richest of them shingled in the light grey of slate and the poorest collapsed beyond repair.

— AARON, DUNGEON MASTER'S NOTES, CS16.

L illy wiggled her hips as she folded up the dress she had worn to the yearly party the night before. The thick green material had contrasted perfectly with her red hair and matched her brilliant green eyes. The festival had been amazing! They had found numbers hidden in the vendor booths, met all kinds of people, and learned there were a surprising number of local miners, quite a few of whom were on the list of names Master Corath had given them. Most importantly, they had observed and found access to Grogith Gotlittle's little Underdark mafia, although 4aDeer did have to knock two of his men unconscious. They had not wandered town yet to see if there was any fallout from that.

There was a knock at her door. Well, really the door to the room she shared with Poppy and a few other women who lived in the house. The others who had been pulled in here with them were still around, working and surviving until they could return home.

Craig's rocky form filled her doorway. Lilly took a calming breath.

"We are gathering downstairs," Craig said carefully.

"I will be there in just a moment," she replied quickly and shut the door. Craig wanted to apologize, but she wasn't ready to hear it.

She finished repacking her travel pack and strapped her pony keg around her waist. Then she loaded the pony keg strap, her belt with her warhammer and the various hand axes and knives she had collected, as well as her drinking mug. She leaned left and right, checking her center of gravity. With a full pony keg, she most definitely tilted to the left, so she swung her pack on the right and headed down. She was the last to arrive.

"Why does it sometimes take you five minutes to open a wine bottle and other times two seconds?" Tom asked as Rachael sat down with her glass of white.

"Sometimes I am just imagining how Lilly would start her day," Rachael said happily. She had brought the bottle over to the table this week and pretended to fasten it to her belt.

Martin chuckled. Aaron shook his head and began speaking. "You wake up late, but fresh and rested from the party. Grogith Gotlittle has agreed to speak with you after your successful networking and, unknown to Grogith, deciphering during the party."

"I just want to make sure that we are all on the same page, as some of us were drinking last night, Lilly," Eismus almost sneered.

"It is what I do," Lilly smiled brightly.

"We learned that Grogith is or was playing both sides of the temple's political power struggle. We learned that the power spikes the fey are feeling are located east. This map we have been given was found on the body of an adventurer who had come through town looking for the Temple of the Fey's power crystal, and his body was found by Grogith, whose cave, we already knew, is located on the northeast side of town," Eismus reminded the party.

"Our mission, if we choose to accept it," Craig's deep voice boomed dramatically.

"Cave troll, make tell us all," 4aDeer's hand started fingering his axe.

"Right," Lilly said. "Let's stop by the market and pick up a few days' rations as we head over."

Early teatime found them knocking on the cave troll's giant wood and iron door. Lilly scanned it, looking for markings, but turned up only years of scratches and dings. The door opened slowly as Grogith tried to open it with his foot.

"Some help," he said. "You are early and I am still taking scones out of the oven."

4aDeer mechanically helped with the door. The massive, ugly cave troll was now in a white apron covered in flour.

Lilly entered first, her eyes adjusting in surprise to the bright light of the interior. Glowing crystals lined the center of the top of each cave and to the edges where the walls met the ground. The inside, though it still smelled terrible, was decorated with plush, dirty furniture, blankets, and...were those doilies?

"Welcome to my home," Grogith said, his tusks preventing his hideous face from a full smile.

"These are beautiful doilies," Poppy said, motioning to one.

"Feel free to pick it up and admire the craftsmanship. I have them imported all the way from the surface," Grogith said, excited that they were taking an interest. "I have to get the scones out before they burn. Careful when you are looking at the doilies, though. The green ones are poisonous to anyone with pores on their skin."

Lilly immediately dropped the one she was looking at.

"I think it is brown," Craig said, and he reached down to pick it up for her. It was.

A few minutes later, the cave troll was back with a silver tray covered with little scones that even Poppy could pick up with her hands, and one big one for Grogith, supposedly. The tray also had on it a giant teapot, five little glasses, and one Grogith-sized glass. He seemed to have this down to a science.

After they were settled on various pieces of furniture with tea and a scone each, Grogith spoke.

"Despite only being here for a few weeks, you seem to have earned the trust of some powerful people. It is only a lucky few who are granted an audience with me."

"We are humbled by the honor," Lilly said. She took a bite of scone. It was delicious. She didn't want to know what was in it, though. "This scone is incredible."

Grogith laughed. "I think it tastes even better because people expect it to taste bad. That is the nature of expectations."

"We ask questions?" 4aDeer was seated on the edge of a stool, struggling with his own tusks and the delicate teacup.

"If that is why you are here," Grogith responded. "You have come at an interesting time, for me especially."

"We are new but have enjoyed the benefits of Elm City being a neutral ground," Eismus stated.

"I also enjoy neutrality," Grogith assured them. "Otherwise, adventurers like yourselves would be knocking on my door trying to slay the evil cave troll."

"That is terrible." Lilly's comment would have been sarcastic if she wasn't so earnest.

"To that end," Eismus continued. "We would like to restore the Temple of the Fey with its original crystal."

"We are just putting all our cards on the table, just like that?" Martin asked.

"I could roll something instead," Tom started to backpedal.

"Nope," Aaron said. *"You know my RP rules — if you want to roll it, you can't play it out first."*

The cave troll sighed.

"I don't have the map," Grogith answered.

"But if we found the map," Poppy took over. "Would you be able to tell us where the starting point is?"

Grogith sat up and narrowed his eyes.

"Do you have the map?" His voice was commanding. Four voices piped up "yes," and one low rock rumbled "no." Grogith looked at Craig and shook his head.

"You should have eaten your scone," Grogith said as six heavily armed men suddenly ran into the room from attached corridors. The party was taken completely by surprise. One charged Lilly and knocked her over, his knee pushing into her back as he held her hands away from her weapons at the small of her back. She could hear other members of her party struggling and yelling but, very quickly, they all seemed to be subdued.

"Why are you really here?" Grogith asked again.

"We didn't know about the power balance, and the dragon priests paid us to get their crystal back and so this entire thing is our fault and we want to fix it," Lilly blurted out.

"We also promised the Goodalls a safe home," Poppy added.

"I just want to go home," Eismus said. "Why did I say that?"

"Where is home?" Grogith asked again. Four different answers spilled from their mouths.

"Who are you working for?" Grogith continued the interrogation.

"The Temple of the Fey," all four of them said.

"What do you intend to do once the balance is restored?" Grogith's face was starting to look puzzled. "Go home," three voices answered. Grogith looked at Lilly.

"And what about you, bard?"

"I do want to go home, but I also really like it down here," Lilly stated honestly. "I have no idea what I want."

"If you stay down here, what do you want to do?" Grogith motioned for Lilly's captor to let her up but not let go of her.

"Sing at the tavern. I want to meet more dragons. I want to be something more than I am." Lilly sounded surprised by her own words. "Where is this coming from?"

"It is the truth potion I cooked into the scones," Grogith answered.

There was silence for a moment as Grogith thought. He finally moved back so he could see everyone again.

"I have eaten the bodies of many adventurers who tried to retrieve the Temple of the Fey's crystal. But it is at the end of the map, and if Master Corath decided to give it to you, he must truly believe in your abilities."

"Who is Master Corath?" Rachael whispered to Debby, scanning her notes for the name.

"It's the name of the fey priest that no one here ever bothered to ask," Aaron shook his head. "I don't know why I name things sometimes."

"He said he had no one better to give it to, and it couldn't hurt," Lilly nodded with confidence.

Grogith looked at the floor.

"Release them — except for the orc. I do not trust him to remain calm after being trussed up. Escort them to the start of the east upper tunnel wing, let us see how true their hearts be."

"At this point, everyone is going to level up." Aaron stopped the party. "I would like to do that as a group this time, as six is a big level for most of us, and then with the time left, I will set the scene for the east wing."

FORT COLLINS

DINING ROOM

R achael read through the spells Lilly could pick up at level six and listened to conversation around the table. Debby had the hardest job; the druid's shape-changing ability was still useful but not as powerful as she leveled. She had to decide if she wanted her role in the party to be more of a healer or damage dealer.

"What are you thinking for Lilly?" Aaron asked. Rachael looked up from her player's manual.

"I want to stay utility, but some of my spells are just useless at the moment," Rachael said. "I really want unseen servant to be useful, but he just can't do anything."

"He did a good job cleaning our gear before the party," Tom jumped in.

"Haha," Rachael said. She would have shoved Tom, but he was across the table.

"Any suggestions, sweetie?" Rachael asked Aaron.

"Don't sweetie me," Aaron said. "I know you hate leveling your own character, but I won't do it for you."

Rachael smiled and put down her player's manual to stand. She clasped her hands in front of her to bring her breasts together and leaned over the DM screen with as much cleavage as possible peeking out of her usual black sleeveless top.

"Please," she said and batted her eyelashes. Aaron laughed and gave her a kiss on the forehead.

"Nice try," Aaron said. Rachael dropped her eyes in mock defeat and released her arms and her cleavage. Her eyes were drawn to a drawing — no, a painting — in Aaron's notebook.

"Is that Lilly?" Rachael asked. She looked up at Aaron; he blushed and rushed to close the notebook.

"No, let me see it," Rachael said. She snatched the notebook out of his hands. It easily opened again to the painting; this page was obviously opened often. Though the notes were from an old campaign session weeks ago.

"I will take it back if you turn any pages," Aaron warned.

"Aaron, this is amazing," Rachael said. Her eyes took in his work. It was Lilly. She was curled behind the stone of the Underdark, her long red hair was caught in an invisible breeze that also seemed to be blowing some of the Underdark itself. One exaggeratedly long arm reached in the other direction. The painting was serene, detailed, and incredibly thoughtful. Rachael felt a little twist in her heart.

"Beautiful," Martin said from behind Rachael.

"You painted Lilly?" Debby asked. "Why didn't you show it to us?" Debby reached for the notebook and Rachael gave it to her to pass around.

"Don't turn any pages," Aaron said again.

"We won't, Aaron, relax," Debby said. "This is lovely. I wish I had someone in my life who loved me enough to paint a portrait of my D&D character."

"I love it that Rachael and I can play together," Aaron said apologetically. "I didn't paint it for people to see, just for me. I think about Rachael a lot when I should be working on other things, and so I started painting this whenever I needed to focus. Now that it is done, I just like to look at it sometimes."

"Sometimes? The binding is completely broken here, the page is going to fall out soon," Tom stated. He handed the book back to Aaron, who quickly closed it and buried it under other papers behind his screen.

"Why don't you tell me when you are thinking about me?" Rachael asked quietly. Aaron didn't move from his spot.

"Because I see you all the time," Aaron said simply. "I will give you one leveling hint." He changed the topic, and Rachael could feel ears straining for some insight into the campaign's future.

"There will be combat in the future," Aaron said dramatically.

"Really? That is your hint? There will be combat in a D&D game?" Tom asked sarcastically.

"Choose your skills well," Aaron said, and then chuckled as everyone went back to reading and making decisions.

Rachael sat and picked up her handbook, but the words were hard to focus on. Aaron loved her so much. Why couldn't she feel it?

FORT COLLINS

GROCERY STORE

Rachael squeezed a few avocados and placed them in her basket. Aaron's work project had hit a snag in testing, giving him some time home while it duplicated the failed test. Aaron was at work now, dealing with the new results. They had had a lovely afternoon together on Saturday ending with beers at Equinox, his favorite brewery, with Tom and some of his gaming crew. It had turned into a mini pub crawl and both of them had gotten smashed.

Rachael licked her teeth and bit her bottom lip. The intoxication had relaxed them both, a lot. Even when Greg magically appeared in pub number two, it hadn't even bothered her, as Aaron's hands never seemed to leave her the entire evening.

Lacking in passion or skill, the drunk sex had been much needed after their fight days ago. That still wasn't resolved but it didn't hurt anymore.

"It honestly looks like you are going to have sex with that avocado." Greg's voice pierced through her memories.

"Hi, Greg," she said. She put the avocado into her basket. "A supermarket shopper now? I thought you lived downtown and only shopped at trendy health stores."

She didn't wait for his answer, just moved on. She was basically making two meals a day for Aaron to eat at the office. She hoped this project was worth it.

"I like to be diverse." Greg moved in beside her. "Having company over?"

Rachael looked down at her basket, with its massive number of greens for extra salads and sandwiches.

"Yup," she said brightly.

"You shouldn't lie to me," Greg said, echoing her bright fake tone. "We work at the same company. I know that he is basically sleeping at work since the testing came back with code errors."

"Code Monkey think maybe manager want to write goddamned login page himself," Rachael sang, ignoring Greg's comment completely. "I think whoever is running the contract just doesn't understand that compiling scripts takes time."

"It's a foreign contract," Greg said. "They just don't think the same way we do."

Rachael felt heat flush to her face as she remembered David pushing her up against the cold of his glass window, her nipples instantly hardening as he whispered unintelligible Scottish words in her ear.

"What did I say to get that reaction?" Greg's voice was lude.

"I have been watching *Outlander*," she lied.

"I didn't know you watched TV shows like that," Greg said. "Learning anything you would like to try?"

"Not that I am willing to share with you." Rachael was suddenly very tired of his company and she still needed about six more things.

"Greg, why are you here?" She stopped her scanning of aisles for what she needed and turned to face him.

"I am here to keep you company," Greg stated, moving forward. Rachael stepped back.

"I do not want your company. You are stalking me, and you

need to leave me alone." She didn't yell but she pitched her voice to carry.

"Funny," Greg said. He turned to face the shelf. "Then I am doing my own shopping."

"Great," Rachael said. As quickly as possible, she gathered the remaining of her shopping. Greg didn't address her, but he was always in sight. The definition of a stalker.

Her final item was a bottle of V8 for Aaron's desk. Her basket was heavy. She should have grabbed a cart.

"You are being silly. Let me carry that for you." Greg came up behind her and put his hand, fingers spread, against her stomach. As he reached down to take the basket, his hand slipped down, brushing her crotch.

Rachael didn't think. She turned and kneed him in the crotch. They dropped her basket, and a few of the items on the top tumbled out. Greg sank down to his knees, his hands protecting the family jewels.

"You have no right to touch me," Rachael said calmly. She picked up her fallen groceries as well as the V8. It was a struggle, but she managed to hold it all. Greg was still lying on the floor. A few customers were staring, and she could see an employee running toward them.

"Is everything OK?" he asked, looking at Greg, who was starting to recover.

"This pervert followed me through the store and then used my heavy basket as an excuse to grope me," Rachael told the employee.

"She just kneed me in the crotch." Greg's voice was both angry and pained.

"Well, I would bet the store security camera and you can have some time together to discover who is right. I am done shopping," she said and headed for the checkout. "If you follow me, Greg," she said as she left, "I will call the police, damn my marriage to hell."

71

FORT COLLINS

KITCHEN

R achael had just finished putting groceries away when Aaron opened the door.

"You are home early," Rachael said.

"I got a call from Greg at the office," Aaron said.

"And what kind of drama is master manipulator inciting now?" Rachael asked with false cheer.

Aaron took a breath to speak and then thought better of it. Instead, he walked forward and gave Rachael a hug, one of his hands moving to the back her head as he tucked her to his chest.

"Tom says if I can't be impartial, the best thing I can do is stay out of it," Aaron's chest rumbled.

Rachael felt anger burn in her stomach. It was at least better advice than accusing her of something. She was sure that is what Aaron rushed home to do. That, and making sure his psychotic younger brother didn't get reported to the cops.

Rachael let Aaron hold her for as long as he needed.

"Can you stay for dinner or do you want to go get something before you head back in for more testing?" she asked.

"I am tired of salad at my desk," Aaron said. "Let's go grab a burrito."

"That sounds lovely," Rachael said calmly. "I would love to hear about your day."

72

FORT COLLINS

DIRK AND DIRK REALTY

"You did what?" Karen screeched. Rachael was pretty sure the office was just used to these noises by now. Rachael smiled to herself. She was taking control.

"It felt really good," Rachael said. "I have been going to boxing class once a week and I made a new friend named Alex. She has been giving me pointers, and I think just going out and being around other strong women, like you and our office nights out, is helping me be more independent."

"That is wonderful," Karen said. There was a short pause — Karen waiting for something.

"How were your dates?" Rachael just liked to make Karen hang for the question sometimes. It was the standard Monday question.

"Friday night. Let me set the scene," Karen started as she launched into an epic tale of romance and wine with an adorable private investigator. "But this story gets better."

Karen paused for dramatic effect again. "I. Canceled. My. Sunday. Date."

"Was Mr. PI that good?" Rachael asked, scandalized.

"Actually, I didn't sleep with him," Karen said, embarrassed.

"I hired him for a job and told him if he could get it done this weekend I would give him a chance at a second date on Sunday. We had it and it was lovely. There will be a third. The man does not want to give it up easily."

"Oh, wow," Rachael said, surprised at both the third date and the job.

"Let's go to my desk." Karen motioned for her to bring her coffee.

"Break isn't over," Rachael pointed out.

"Don't care." Karen was already out the door.

Rachael refilled her own coffee mug and Karen's before heading to her office. Unlike Rachael's little cubicle, Karen's office had a little window and real glass walls and a door; it was good to be a manager.

"Why don't we come here more often?" Rachael asked.

"Because I like to think that my underlings enjoy the view as I walk past," Karen stated. She woke up her computer, set a business card in front of her, and typed in an address on the address bar.

"This," Karen said as the website loaded, "is a phone tracker. And I had Mr. PI, as you called him — I like that — install it on Greg's phone so you can see where he is and where he has been."

"Is that legal?" Rachael asked.

"Mr. PI wasn't clear on that," Karen answered. "But he is stalking you, and that pushover you married isn't doing a thing about it."

"Aaron has a lot on his plate," Rachael defended.

"OK, so today. Let's see," Karen pressed on the "see map" button that had appeared on the loaded website.

It took a moment for Rachael to orient herself and figure out what the different symbols meant, but it really functioned just like Google Maps. Lines showed the phone traveling and pins showed places it stopped. Green pins were places he stopped for

10-29 minutes, yellow 30-59 minutes, orange 60-89 minutes, and red 90+. You could click on the pins to see the exact amount of time.

"So, if I am reading this correctly," Rachael said slowly, "he was outside my house for 45 minutes this morning." Karen didn't say anything. Rachael took control of the mouse and started clicking through past days. Eventually, Karen's hand rested on hers, stopping her clicking.

Rachael hadn't noticed that Karen had moved out of her chair or that Rachael had sat in it.

"I didn't know it was that bad," Karen said, the fun out of her voice. "You should get help."

"He watches my house at night. Almost every night." Rachael felt like her voice was far away. "He watches me walk to the bus. He already knows I joined 24. He has been in their parking lot during my boxing class. He knows everything."

Rachael suddenly felt very small.

For once, Karen was at a loss for words. Rachael picked up the card and walked back to her desk, her coffee forgotten on Karen's desk. Greg was picking and choosing their encounters. Was he manipulating her to change her life? Did he know about David?

She opened the website one more time and looked up the date she had met David. Greg's phone hadn't left his house. She found their second meeting at Dungeons & Drafts. Greg never made it to the pub. And she clicked on their third. Greg's phone went from Old Town to her house, where it sat until after midnight.

Rachael nodded to herself. At least she still had something of her own. Even though she said she was done with tears, she felt one slip out of each eye. She scrubbed them away. She was making her own choices. Right?

UNDERDARK

CRAIG

Very few creatures evolved in the Underdark. But certain creatures were summoned, brought, or escaped and have now flourished. The tunnels are riddled with monsters, undead, and unimaginable creatures still bound to their dead masters' biddings.

— AARON, DUNGEON MASTER'S NOTES, CS17.

Craig looked down at the huge square maze that spread out before them. The party had been escorted through Grogith's doily covered home and out a back door. It took about 30 minutes and an amazing number of stairs, but now they stood on a rocky outcropping that overlooked, well, everything they had to get through.

Booms and crashes echoed through the endless cavern and bits of stone slammed into the ground. Lava ran through the sections of the maze and hissed as it came in contact with water.

Screams of creatures, hungry and in pain, created jagged tears in the constant low rumbling of moving stone.

"Can anyone see well enough to plan ahead?" Poppy asked.

"On second thought, let us not go to Camelot. It is a silly place," Eismus said, his eyes large.

"I see enemies," 4aDeer was chomping at the bit. Craig didn't blame him, he was ready.

"Let's go," Lilly cried excitedly.

The start was anticlimactic as they pulled out the map, got it orientated, and planned the shortest route. With the information they had from past attempts at the maze, the maze itself shouldn't be too hard to solve. In some ways, they were fortunate that Grogith's appetite included the bodies of those who failed. However, they did not plan on being the next stew in his cauldron. The party watched each other's lips and verbally repeated the route over and over until there would be no mistakes. Lilly took a moment to pull out a scroll of find path and cast it on herself just in case.

The crystal was thought to be in one of two locations. How or why it was there had been forgotten when the makers of the maze perished generations ago. The route they chose hit both locations, the close one first because you never know, and the far one because it is never that easy.

Four different sets of steep ladders led down into the maze, and they all descended one at a time into the entrance farthest on the right. Combat was immediate. Craig had gone down first. The skeleton-like scorpion the size of a large dog slammed into him before his feet even hit the ground.

If he had not been made of rock he would have fallen. As it was, he stayed upright, and fire began raining down on the creature. A cave fisher, it was called, now that he had a moment to look. Correct that, two cave fishers. The party hacked and slashed their way through creatures, saving their big spells and energy for the unknown future battles.

Craig positioned himself behind Lilly. She didn't even acknowledge his presence. Poppy took point. Their marching order needed no discussion. Poppy was slow but incredibly thorough. She spotted two traps before too long. They ended up going back for the bodies of the two cave fishers and tossed them onto the traps to spring them. The mechanisms went off with a twang, twang.

The noise startled a group of bats that squeaked and hissed before flying up and out of sight. They pushed on; Craig could see sweat pouring down Lilly's face. He didn't feel the heat, but obviously, it was warm. He was still paying more attention to her face as they rounded a corner. The orange glow of flowing lava reflected off her sweat-covered cheeks and in her eyes.

"It would be beautiful if it wasn't so hot," Lilly said over the noise.

4aDeer's battle cry moved Craig's eyes forward as the giant orc jumped over a small wave of fire. Three, no, four giant fire beetles crawled their way out of the lava. Lilly and Craig both hit the deck to keep from being singed by the fire wave, and now three more beetles were coming. Craig loved lava — liquid earth. The fire made his spells a little unstable, but he could work with it. The waves of fire came slightly staggered and he was able to move around to avoid them.

Ice spells began whizzing over his head, and Lilly's pony keg drum added to the cacophony. He took a minute to grin as Lilly's first bardic inspiration infused his very being. He channeled his earth magic into the lava behind the beetles, one already looking worse for wear, and released the heat into the air, leaving 25 small balls that he sent flying into the beetles like machine-gun fire.

After the next volley, he pinned the two still up in place. The very ground rose up and snagged their spindly beetle legs. Lilly's and 4aDeer's battle axe and hammer smashed their skulls.

"We still have to get over the lava," Lilly said. Even Poppy was sweating, her delicate gnome features seeming unused to the activity.

They didn't need to get out the map; 4aDeer was already feeling along the wall. One of the adventurers who had died here had made it past this lava pit and recorded it. Along the side were two chains, one to stand on and one at waist height for balance. 4aDeer led this time and Eismus spelled all of their hands with a layer of cold. It would be too cold if they were not gripping lava-heated metal.

Inch by inch, the party slid along the chain until they got almost to the end.

"BROKEN," 4aDeer bellowed. Craig needed to see details.

"HOW FAR?" he yelled, his second word almost being swallowed up by a burble of hot lava below them.

"FOUR FEET," 4aDeer yelled back.

"FOUR FEET BROKEN OR FOUR FEET LEFT," Craig yelled back.

"FOUR FEET BROKEN," 4aDeer confirmed.

Before Craig could try to move toward the broken part, Poppy's thorn whip grew out of the side of the wall. Craig could not see what it attached itself to, but the line started moving again.

"HURRY," he thought he heard a high-pitched gnome voice yell.

Craig was last, with Lilly right in front of him. He watched her start to cross, her small dwarf hands struggling for purchase on the thick, spiky thorn whip when it started to tremble.

"The spell is running out," he called to Lilly. She looked back at him and nodded before reaching up with one of her hand axes. With one chop, she cut the thorn whip. It dropped, Lilly swinging with it, and she grabbed for the unbroken chain on the other side. She missed the top one but, feet painfully close to the lava, gripped onto the bottom. The thorn whip disappeared soon after.

Craig watched as she very slowly shimmied her way the last several feet and landed with a thud, her feet smoking. Eismus immediately moved to remove the ice spell on her hands and hopefully cool her feet.

Craig summoned his earth magic and once again pulled the earth out of the lava. He created a path just long enough for him to also cross over the broken part. His boom from his jump down fit in perfectly with the sounds of the maze, and the small amount of chain left to the end groaned as his weight returned to it.

They didn't rest long. They had a long way with no information to go. They headed out at a jog; Poppy transformed into a dire wolf to keep pace but loped at the back, conserving energy. Stalactites and stalagmites dotted the man-made path, but they didn't stop to investigate, just kept up the ground-eating jog. Too soon, they came upon the series of pounding stones.

"Look, the first chest!" Eismus exclaimed. There was indeed the outline of the first chest behind the pounding stones. A howl of pain pierced the cave, and Craig turned around to see the dire wolf covered in little worms, biting hard and lashing onto its fur.

"Shit," 4aDeer shouted. "Not natural caves," he yelled and tried to axe off some of the wormlike creatures.

"Piercers," Eismus yelled. The wriggling bodies were just mouths attached to grey bodies that fed on blood. "We must have run past 20 of them disguised as the stalacgrocks and woken them all up at once."

The dire wolf didn't make it long before all the worms suddenly popped off, and the body of a little gnome druid was curled up in its spot. 4aDeer, heedless of his own safety, charged all 20 of them, swinging wildly. The necklace on 4aDeer's chest glowed red and a few of the piercers dropped harmlessly off him. Craig shot out a wave of earth, pushing the remaining back before they could jump again.

"Smash them in the rocks," Lilly yelled. She had not turned to help Poppy but had not let her eyes move off the pattern the pounding rocks were making.

"We will get smashed in the rocks," Craig yelled back. "We don't know the pattern."

"We can't take on 20 of those things at once." Poppy raced for the stones.

4aDeer was already running, having come to the same conclusion.

"On me," Lilly cried. She rushed them to a far stone and waited 'til it went up again.

"Now in front," Lilly cried. The group sprinted to the next square, the rock coming down behind them so loudly they couldn't hear the squelching of the piercers.

"Left," Lilly's voice. Craig sprinted and spun, sending a bolt of green energy at one of the piercers that had not yet been squished. "Front." Craig's life became a series of sprint and fire. Fortunately, all the piercers died halfway through. Unfortunately, their progress slowed as Lilly had obviously not been able to look much farther. They sprinted from one square to another a few times, Lilly guiding them back and forth as she searched for the pattern. Craig's rock legs were burning, and Poppy was sagging against 4aDeer's knee.

"Last one. Front," Lilly's voice was gone but they all moved, if a little slowly. The stone coming down was almost too close to call.

Lilly just sat. She didn't look around, just opened up her waterskin and drank heavily before pouring herself what was probably a warm pint and downing that. Craig looked around, waiting for something to attack them, but nothing came.

"I need a breather and I'm not even there," Rachael stated.

"No breathers." Aaron's voice was excited. "I was sure you were going to die on those piercers. What horrible perception rolls."

"Saved by Lilly's scroll of find path," Martin said. *"I don't remember you picking that up."*

"I bought it on one of our supply runs during, like, our second session and forgot about it. And it wasn't really meant to be used like that. It gave me a little bonus, but it was mostly my rolls." Rachael did a short, quick breath on her nails and polished them against her shirt.

"Later," Aaron insisted.

"I think he has something different to kill us with," Tom laughed.

Eismus opened the chest. The rest of the party had spells ready for whatever baddies might come out of it. When nothing did, Eismus crept forward and looked inside.

The inside was filled with treasure and precious stones. As a group, they decided to take a short rest — eating and drinking and dividing up the gems as equally as possible, still hoping but not expecting the crystal to show up.

It did not. Poppy handed her heavy wealth to 4aDeer and Craig offered to carry Lilly's. She gave him a flat look and added the heavy bag to her pack.

"Just an offer as friends," Craig said. Lilly picked up her pack once and twice, feeling its weight in her arm before shouldering it. "If it is slowing me down, I will ask you, if you don't mind," she responded.

"Why not just let me do it for you?" Craig asked.

"Because I am my own person who can take care of myself and make my own decisions," Lilly's voice was hard and she met Craig's eyes evenly. "It doesn't matter how much you think you know," she added.

Craig's eyes narrowed.

"What does that mean?" Greg asked Rachael.

"Why are you asking me?" Rachael said. *"Lilly said it."*

Greg looked at her for another minute before shaking his head and moving Craig's piece away from Lilly's.

The rest of the table was quiet after the awkward exchange.

"With the boom of thudding rocks now behind you and the air

cooling every step farther from the lava you get, you notice the stone of the maze has some pink and white moss growing in places. Someone has tried the maze recently enough that their footsteps have disturbed the growth," Aaron described.

They took another look at the map and double-checked with Lilly's cast. The footstep went ignored. They repeated the directions to each other one more time. Marching order was only disrupted by Lilly and Eismus switching places, and they were off.

They took the time to find piercers, which were easy to kill off in groups of one or two. Twice, skeletal spiders dropped from the roof to surprise them, but otherwise, the path was clear, though filled with turns. They came to a place where they should have been able to turn left, but there was no left turn. Eismus found the secret catch, sticking his hand through a terrifying hole filled with slime that made his hand sticky.

"It's just really annoying," Aaron said after Tom asked a third time if he felt anything sinister.

They had to pass *The Labyrinth's* unoriginal but required two door riddles, complete with the red and blue guards from the iconic movie. They got the logic puzzle on the first try.

"What kind of magic spell to use," Debby sang.

"Slime and snails, or puppy dog tails?" Rachael picked up the song, almost singing the right notes.

"Then baby said," Tom sang.

"Dance magic, dance," Martin didn't sing. He deadpanned the words but added some jazz hands on the second dance. "4aDeer doesn't sing," he justified himself

Still chuckling, the party arrived at the back of the maze. They simply turned a corner and a giant courtyard was hidden behind it. Water fountains tinkled on either side of a raised dais. A knot of purple and black scales started moving against each other and a massive flap of scales and membrane lifted into the air. With the sounds of slime and clicking, the membrane pulled back like a grotesque opening tulip. Tentacles grew and just kept growing from its center. It didn't make a sound, the head just bobbing as if being fluttered by a breeze.

"Is that a painted neothelid miniature?" Greg asked. He picked up the 3D part snake, part Japanese tentacle monster, part flower that was a neothelid from the D&D monster manual.

Martin tried to take it from Greg next.

"Do that after," Aaron said, swatting at Martin to put it down.

For a moment, the giant monster seemed to float in the air, but the party shook their heads and realized they were seeing things.

A high-pitched and almost pipe-like roar escaped from the neothelid's gaping cavity, and 10 little stirges jumped forward. Stirges were little, annoying, bloodsucking creepers that latched on until they were full and then exploded.

Craig's dodge was not good, but he kept his footing as the chaos of battle began. He could see 4aDeer leap and swing for the tentacles. A few of the stirges turned from their attempts to latch onto the party to latch onto the big purple worm instead. Craig shot a few more of the little shits before sending a big spell at the neothelid. He jumped away from another string of tentacles, barely managing to stay on his own feet.

He felt a body bump into his leg and looked down to see Lilly dodging away.

Now close to him, she chanted something. Her hand reached out and her palm made contact with his leg. He felt his concentration narrow as his exploding earth spell came to the forefront of his mind. Craig charged and cast his spell; dust and rock showered down on the party, momentarily obscuring the vision of all. When it returned, Craig had to blink as multiple copies of each of them were hanging around the worm in various locations. Lilly must have used the distraction to cast an illusion. Confused, the worm started lashing out at their copies instead of them.

Thunder wave shook the ground as the little druid cast one of her big spells at the confused worm. The battle raged, and Craig found himself low on energy, both physical and mental. He used his last spell to heal 4aDeer, who was taking a mad beating. Craig knew he had gone down at some point but couldn't put it together.

"I'm out," Craig said.

"Most of the tentacles are gone," cried Poppy. She was running low too, and suddenly the dire wolf was back. It leaped into the giant worm. Craig looked for Lilly and found her and her warhammer jumping from piece of the thing to piece of the thing, avoiding its spitting poison and thrashing body as best she could.

4aDeer went down again. Craig ran to him, pulled him out of the way, and began stabilization. 4aDeer came to with a start just after the neothelid gave its death wail and crashed to the earth. The ground shook under its weight. The group gave a cheer as they looked for movement.

Poppy didn't transform back to a gnome but whined at 4aDeer's pack. Lilly seemed to know what she wanted and rummaged through it to find some of the potions. She looked for a healing one and found it. Not much, but enough to hopefully get 4aDeer back on his feet.

The group bandaged themselves, healed, and drank what small potions they had, leaving the bigger ones for emergencies. They were as refreshed as they were going to get. No more monsters had appeared; it seemed they had won!

"Don't jinx it," Poppy hissed at the mention of the word "won."

"Look for the chest," Eismus said. The party did, splitting up and wandering the courtyard. The tinkles of the fountains continued. But there was no chest. They met back in the middle.

"I need to rest," Lilly said. "I have one spell left if we have an emergency but that is it."

The group all mumbled their similar states. Some of them walked to keep from getting stiff while others sprawled on the ground. Lilly's singing voice was clear but soft, her song helping them heal and recover. They still halfheartedly looked for the chest.

"Inside purple worm?" 4aDeer said, still lying on the ground. It had been about an hour.

"Gross," Poppy said. "But it is the only place we haven't looked."

Craig stood, breaking open the purple worm was something he could do. 4aDeer's strength would be exceptionally useful if he could help. Craig started pushing and pulling the still warm and soft neothelid's coiled body.

"We should have kited it around the room. There was enough space for it," Eismus declared.

"No run, running for cowards," 4aDeer stated.

"KITE," Eismus said again, spelling out each letter of the word. "When you run from things with purpose. You get your enemy to chase you around the room so that you can hit it, but it can't hit you as easily. It is a very specialized skill."

"4aDeer no run from anything," 4aDeer stated again.

"We are not really a good matchup, are we?" Eismus asked.

Poppy and Lilly chuckled and 4aDeer slowly stood to help Craig. With the two of them pushing and pulling, the giant worm's knot became loose enough that a three-foot-tall gnome could explore. She came out a few minutes later with the Temple of the Fey's crystal, the little tree in the middle and everything. It was attached to a base with some sort of long wiring sticking out of it.

"No chest?" Craig asked.

"No chest. Just this," Poppy confirmed. She gestured to the wiring. "It goes under the neothelid. I think it maybe connects to the fountains?"

"May I look at it?" Eismus asked. He took the entire contraption from Poppy before she could answer. He began examining the base that the crystal was resting on. The lines that connected it were pulled as tight as they would go.

"Maybe there is a switch or something. Let's just check one more time," Poppy begged. It was not a bad request. The party spent another solid 30 minutes moving around the worm and checking every nook and cranny of the space. Other than some odd scratching from some of the stone that made up the ground near the fountain, the courtyard was well and truly empty.

"I feel like we are missing something," Martin said, frustrated.

"I feel like we are missing something, too," Aaron nodded thoughtfully.

"So, we are missing something." Debby gave Aaron a hard look.

"I don't know. I'm not even there," Aaron laughed.

"You are the equivalent of God in this game. You are everywhere," Tom added.

"I thank you for your worship but I have nothing for my followers. That is why God gave man free will and the ability to explore," Aaron said as if preaching, his hands raised.

"And women," Rachael added. "Did we ever figure out the blank paper?"

Head shakes around the table.

"Let's just get on with it," Martin said unhappily.

"I bet we couldn't kite it," Lilly went back to the original argument. "I bet it was tasked with staying curled around that thing."

"Still would have been worth trying." Eismus didn't back down on his opinion. "I think just taking it off the base is our only option. Ready?" he said as he pulled the crystal off its base.

The tinkle of the fountains stopped and so did the boom of the rocks and most of the sounds in the maze. It was eerily silent for a heartbeat before the sounds of beating feet and monsters roaring and yelling started getting closer and closer in their ears.

"Oh shit," Eismus whispered. "Did we just turn off the maze and tell every monster in it our location?"

"Yup." It was the grimmest yup Craig had ever heard.

"Teehee." Minksey's voice came from the direction of one of the fountains. "Teehee. To me if you want to live. But you will owe me a favor, a big favor. That will make three in total. The magic of trinity."

The party didn't have a choice. They ran for the fountain, the scratched stone now covered by another. The hole was just big enough for 4aDeer to squeeze through if he held his arms above his head.

They jumped in biggest to smallest, no party member left behind. The opening slid closed behind them.

"Teehee. Follow me," Minksey rhythmed, and with no other options, the party followed the little fey's voice.

Rachael was so grateful this session was mostly combat. She wouldn't have made it through a social encounter with Greg. She loved Aaron's game and she had moments of fun tonight, but overall, she felt trapped. Being forced to interact with Greg while he was stalking her was painful. This should have been a night of triumph and celebration. They had come together really well as a group and defeated some long odds.

She was trying hard to be strong, but it was terrifying knowing that Greg had probably been watching her sleep for weeks. She was pretty sure Aaron had given him a key when they moved here. Had he taken any of her stuff like he did to Ashely?

Rachael had taken the bottle of wine out with her. She had it resting on the closed hot tub and she leaned against the house, too agitated to sit. Her finger worked David's D20 in her pocket. She glanced over as the sliding door opened and closed. Tom nodded to her. She offered him the bottle, and he shook his head.

"Everything OK?" he asked.

"No," Rachael almost laughed. "I kneed him in the nuts when he 'happened' to be shopping at the same time as me for the same things. Aaron came home to tell me off. I could see it in his eyes, but instead, he held me and said he would stay out of it."

Rachael took a long drink straight from the bottle.

"He has a key to our house," Rachael said quietly. "Do you think he has a collection of my stuff?"

A curl of smoke came from beside her and she looked over. Tom had a bent and old-looking cigarette in his mouth.

"I didn't know you smoked," she said.

"I did a lot in high school. It was Aaron who got me to quit," Tom answered.

The night was filled with crickets and bugs and rustles and a low murmur from inside the house. The session had gone really late, but it had been intense. Some of the best communication and teamwork they had ever done.

"I wish I could do more," Tom finally said. He reached for Rachael's bottle and took a long swallow before handing it to Rachael to do the same. The porch door opened again, and Greg's muscle-bound form seemed to crowd the space. Or maybe it was just Rachael.

Tom, to his credit, didn't move and kept himself between Greg and Rachael.

"Hey, guys," he said. "What's going on?"

"Not a lot, just enjoying the quiet of the night," Tom said, emphasizing the word quiet.

Rachael took another long swallow from the bottle.

tap tap tap "I am headed out to my car." Debby's voice was muffled by the glass, her nose flattened against it. Greg grinned at her and went back in.

"I would try to just escape to my bedroom," Rachael said. "But I am pretty sure he watches me sleep — or maybe I am being egotistical and he is watching Aaron sleep."

Tom's light laugh was forced and short.

"I'm sure that is it," Tom agreed.

FORT COLLINS

THE HOUSE

Rachael got up with Aaron's alarm; he yawned and stretched.

"It is so much easier to get up in the mornings when we leave the windows opened," he stated.

"I like having them closed," Rachael said; it was not a discussion.

"This is my last weekend working." Aaron rolled out of bed and looked at her sideways. "We should do another little trip like Mount Princeton."

"Greg would probably just follow me up there too," Rachael thought bitterly. "That would be wonderful," she said, her voice as bitter as her thoughts. She wanted him to ask why she was in a bad mood.

"I hate it when you wake up in a bad mood," Aaron stated. He disappeared into the bathroom.

"Do you want to know why I am in a bad mood?" Rachael asked through the door.

"No," Aaron's voice. "Greg probably did something last night that you disagreed with."

Rachael sucked in a breath and held it, counting down from

12 slowly, to calm her voice. The toilet flushed and the door opened.

"I really don't want to get in the middle of whatever argument you are having with Greg." Aaron stripped out of his undergarments and started to dress for the day.

"He is stalking me," Rachael said. She wanted to tell Aaron about the app she put on Greg's phone. But Aaron would take it as a betrayal, and worse, what if he told Greg and she was back in the dark? Knowing Greg's location at least gave her some degree of control.

"Rachael." Aaron pulled a wrinkly, powder pink button-down over his head that only looked manly because of his dark brown khaki shorts. He took her hand like she was a child. "Greg is not stalking you." He paused. "I know Tom said something to you about his past. Don't make this all about you. Greg might have some boundary issues, but he is working them out."

Rachael swallowed hard. "Don't make this all about me?" Rachael repeated.

"Yes," Aaron gave a little laugh and kissed her on the forehead. "Greg said he has been messaging you for weeks to apologize himself and was trying to apologize at the grocery store. Greg came out here for a fresh start, and you are turning his past on him. It is why I didn't want you to know about it."

"I am making this all about me?" Rachael said quietly. "He is stalking me. It isn't about me. It is about him forcing himself into my life, our lives."

"Rachael, you are being dramatic." Aaron stood and rubbed his bald head. The prickles of almost a week's growth made a scratching sound against his palm.

"What if I have proof that he is following me around." Rachael started shaking, desperate for Aaron to understand.

"Rachael, if you put a tracker on his person, I will be more worried about you." Aaron started moving for the door. "Please don't do anything stupid. Greg said he is worried about you and

I am too. Your personality has been changing. The word Greg comes up in our conversations a lot. Maybe Greg isn't the one having the problem."

Rachael sat completely still. She heard Aaron move through the house. His car started and pulled out of the driveway, the sound of the engine disappearing into the distance.

Rachael slowly got up, pulled on some 'PJs, and looked at her phone; she had installed the app that would show her where Greg was. He, or at least his phone, was still at home.

She went to the bedroom curtains and opened them wide. The morning sun dazzled her vision. She replayed her conversation with Aaron over in her head once, pretty sure it could not have gone worse. And then she tucked it into a box and shoved it to the back of her mind.

Aaron was sure of his brother's innocence; he would not be strong for her. She needed to be strong for herself.

FORT COLLINS

DUNGEONS & DRAFTS

Rachael would call her day so far successful. She had managed to pull herself together after her talk with Aaron. Boxing had been challenging, but the instructor had twice told her that her hooks were looking much better, and now she was walking to Dungeons & Drafts in the beautiful sunlight.

Her gauzy, light purple shirt stopped just below her waistline and her long legs sprouted a short pair of khaki shorts. She had chosen her dice earrings for the day, the dice eternally hanging in limbo.

She was excited to see that Greg's phone was still at his gym. If Scott was tending bar, she was going to ask him to make her something summery and head to the back outdoor seating again. Maybe she would grab *Splendor* on the way out and see if she could catch someone for a quick game.

The pub was very dark compared to the outside world, and she had to stand in the doorway and let her eyes adjust. The usual set of chairs, tables, and patrons slowly came into focus. She could see David's head with a group seated around a table in the middle. David might be able to get away to say hi, but he was probably running a game today. She caught his eye and nodded before finding Scott at the bar. Scott managed to come up with something unnamed but interesting.

"You should really go somewhere that specializes in mixed drinks if you are looking for creative," Scott said as she paid.

"I like seeing what concoction you'll come up with next," she batted her eyes.

"This is literally the happiest I have ever seen you." Scott looked confused.

"It happens to all of us eventually." Rachael took her drink and headed over to the racks of games. *Splendor*, with its yellow edges, was easy to find. She felt eyes on her back. A tingle ran from her navel to her groin, her memory feeling David's hands and kisses.

Game in hand, she found the back mostly unoccupied. The low glass walls keeping drinkers in had been recently cleaned and a couple was seated near the edge, their heads bent over a game. There was just enough breeze to rattle some chimes and rustle game pieces, making it annoying to game in but not impossible. She set up *Splendor* for two and sat back with her drink, enjoying the sounds drifting up from the park and the pub.

"Expecting someone?" Greg's voice startled her.

"Not really," Rachael said honestly. "It's Dungeons & Drafts; if you set up a game, usually someone will come play it with you."

"May I join you?" Greg asked.

"No," Rachael said firmly. Greg took the seat next to her anyway.

"I can't believe I never thought to check for you here before," Greg said. "How are things with Aaron?"

"None of your business," Rachael said, her voice slightly raised. "You need to leave me alone."

"That app you put on my phone doesn't mean anything,"

Greg continued softly, as if talking to a wounded animal. "I know you don't trust me, but you will. I promise. You will see."

Rachael stood up, intending to leave.

"Just sit and play a game with me," Greg said. "Is it that fucking hard? We already see each other for game night, and it was wonderful of you to get Aaron's and my weekly dinners going. I haven't been this close with him since, well, it has been a while. I just want to spend some one-on-one time with you too."

"Greg, you are stalking me," Rachael said calmly. "You are a manipulative, jealous bastard, who only gets off on control. And when I say you need to leave me alone, you should respect it, or I will get a restraining order, fuck Aaron and the campaign."

She moved out from behind the table as Greg stood, his bulk partially blocking her path to the exit. "I should have sat facing the other direction," she thought to herself. "Too late now."

"Please move," she asked. Greg's slimy smile didn't change. Rachael readied herself for whatever was coming and walked quickly past him. She felt his hand dig into her shoulder, clasping it painfully hard as his other hand came up and squeezed her bottom.

"Is everything all right back here?" Scottish. David and Bob rounded the little corner with the young woman who had been sitting out back with her date. Greg's hand remained in a vice-like grip on her shoulder, though he stopped fondling her butt.

"No," Rachael's voice was calm and even.

"Everything is fine," Greg answered cheerily. "Rachael and I were just talking about some sensitive issues and things got a little heated."

"I want to leave." Rachael's voice didn't change. She couldn't meet anyone's eyes. Greg made everything sound like it was so fucking dandy.

"I think you should let the lady leave." Bob's voice took on the tone of a drill sergeant.

Greg's grip relaxed and he started to rub her shoulder as if he had just planned on giving her a back massage. She pitched forward to get away.

"It's going to be OK, Rach," Greg said. "I'll talk to Aaron and get it sorted. Everything will work out in the end."

Rachael didn't look at anyone as she hurried away from the pub. She had no idea where she was going but it needed to be somewhere very public.

She was both relieved and disappointed that David didn't follow her. She couldn't stop looking around for signs of Greg. Hopefully, Bob and David waylaid him for long enough that she could make her escape. A few blocks over she pulled out her bus pass and got on — she didn't know where she or the bus were headed.

She absently rubbed her shoulder, feeling the relief of the public bus. Suddenly, she thought of the app on her phone; what if he had one on hers? She scrambled desperately in her purse for a pen and something to write on. The business card David had given her slid out. She added a few numbers to it, did a quick search for the nearest phone store, and then powered down her phone.

FORT COLLINS

KAREN'S APARTMENT

"This is nice," Rachael said. Karen's little apartment was in the middle of Old Town. It was a big room with a loft and a separate bedroom off the kitchen area, across from a huge bathroom. The entire place was filled with plants and quite orderly. The blue/grey furniture was accented with pinks and green and rested on top of light wood flooring. Her toes dug into a shaggy area rug, the shades of grey, white, and brown meant to look like rocks.

"You thought it would be a mess," Karen nodded sagely.

"Your love life is a mess," Rachael tried to defend herself.

"You have lost your right to talk." Karen looked pointedly at the simple, prepaid phone in Rachael's hand and motioned her to sit on the couch. They both sat.

"You have no idea," Rachael said quietly. She clasped her hands together to keep them from shaking.

"Come here," Karen said. A rolling sob ripped out of Rachael. The tantrum was short, noisy, and very unflattering. Karen quietly made little noises of comfort that Rachael could barely hear. As she quieted, Karen left her and returned with two glasses of something ruby red.

"It is a fruit bomber called Pour Pour Me," Karen said, cracking a smile at the name.

"I'm so sorry. I said I wasn't going to cry anymore," Rachael sniffed, taking a big drink of the sweet red.

"Don't be," Karen said, and then quoted, "That's the thing with dames, sometimes all they gotta do is let it out and a few buckets later there's no way you'd know."

"Did you just quote *Sin City?*" Rachael asked.

"You know so little," Karen said. "Actually, Mr. PI and I had our third date and we watched it — not really my type of movie, but I really liked that line. It spoke to my heart."

"Is there gonna be a fourth date?" Rachael asked. Karen looked down and blushed a little.

"Let's talk about you," Karen said. "I need to get caught up so we can hatch a plan to kill Greg."

Rachael half cried and half laughed. "My last bucket is draining a little slow." She took a drink of wine and composed herself. She related everything that happened before Karen picked her up from the phone store, including her reason for getting the phone.

"Now," Rachael continued. "Here are the facts. Aaron is guilt-ridden about Greg's past and will not see the bad in him. Greg is escalating; I am seeing him more often and he is getting bolder." Rachael took a moment to rub her shoulder. Karen came forward and pulled Rachel's shirt off her shoulder.

"Ouch," she said. "That is going to be another nice bruise for my — our — collection."

Rachael kept talking while Karen grabbed her phone and took pictures.

"He is right about the tracking information on his phone. He is at our house often enough. I even play in a D&D campaign with the man once a week. Everything is hearsay. And the few online chats we have had, I am sorry to admit, were quite flirty…this was months ago before I knew it would get weird."

Rachael took a sip of wine and looked at the floor.

"We even kissed," she said quietly.

"Wow, really?" Karen said next to her. Rachael nodded.

"You go, girl," Karen said as if stating a fact. "I mean, I wish it hadn't gotten so weird. But marriage doesn't mean what it used to. Aaron doesn't know how good he has it."

"We might not see eye to eye on that," Rachael said. The hand not holding her wine glass traced the outline of David's die in her pocket. David, her secret, her lover?

"Anyway," Rachael continued. "The point is that my options are limited. Have you googled what to do if someone is stalking you? It made me furious. The police don't even take half the claims seriously because all of it is hearsay. And my 'first line of defense' is my family. Well, one of them is the stalker and the other one believes the stalker over me." Rachael's voice became bitter.

"And even if I get the restraining order, assuming Aaron doesn't kick me out, what's to say Greg respects it? Restraining orders are a joke. They will hit him with it after the damage is done. What I need," Rachael's voice got stronger, "is to trap him. I need Aaron to see what he is doing."

"Ugh, really, your plan is for Aaron to save you?" Karen asked.

"No," Rachael said. "My plan is to show Aaron that his brother is sick. Do you have a computer?"

Karen went and grabbed her laptop and brought it back. Rachael quickly searched for the article she read just the other night.

"Wow, you did some research," Karen said.

"I love Aaron, with all my heart. And for better or worse, Aaron loves Greg with all of his," Rachael said. The link loaded. "This is a special clinic just for stalkers. If Aaron sees that Greg is sick, if we can record it and send it to the family, maybe they can come together and help him."

"And if not," Karen said skeptically.

"Then I leave Aaron, change my name, and move," Rachael said. "It was step five or six on most of the lists of how to deal with a stalker."

"That is depressing." Karen took another sip of wine.

"It is," Rachael agreed. She was surprised that the idea excited her more than depressed her. She didn't want to leave Aaron; maybe a change of scenery would even help their marriage. Would he like to move? Was this a conversation they were even capable of having?

"Any ideas on how to trap him?" Karen finally asked.

It took Rachael a moment to remember they were talking about Greg. It didn't matter what she did now; both brothers were going to get hurt.

FORT COLLINS

LIVING ROOM

"**D**id you have fun with Karen?" Aaron asked as Rachael walked in the door.

"I did. We did some shopping and then had some wine in Old Town. Thanks for letting me know you were home."

"You didn't need to come home for me," Aaron said, but his face lit up as she came in for her welcome home kiss.

"You smell," Rachael said as she pulled back but kept her arms draped around his waist.

"And you taste like sweet, cheap wine." Aaron smiled, pulling back as well so they could look each other in the eyes. Rachael tried to freeze the happy moment. It was cheesy but, with Aaron's arms around her waist and the two of them teasing each other, everything didn't seem so bad. She was glad he was in a good mood, however, as she was about to ask a weird favor.

"Could you do something for me, sweetie pie?" she asked innocently, batting her eyelashes and everything.

"I need to know what it is first. I still won't buy you a pony." Aaron laughed and brought her in for another kiss.

"I would like the campaign to start on Friday with no DM — no you. I would like to try an experiment with team building. I want you to watch and listen, but no one will know you are there. Like all out." Rachael let some tipsy excitement accent her words, to lend innocence to her request. "I want you to put in that you are staying late at work. You can come home at your usual time but take a cab so your car isn't here...you will need to sneak out like a ninja."

Aaron laughed at her antics.

"And where will I hide in my own house?" Aaron laughed.

"I was thinking the pantry?" Rachael said with a question mark. "But it might be fun to play some hide and seek this week and find the best view." She let two of her fingers crawl up his chest and caress his collarbone.

"I don't know, Rach," he hesitated. "That just seems really over the top. What could you possibly want to discuss with the group that you think they can't do if I can hear? Much less what I would want to overhear. This already feels bad."

Rachael had been expecting these questions, and so many answers would be the wrong ones. Aaron was honest, brutally open, and hated anything that had to do with deceiving his friends.

"It is not a big deal. I just want to role-play out some personality conflicts that you can use for or against us in upcoming sessions. We did really well last session, and I was reading a blog about the Fate Core system recently, bringing in more character aspect details. But if the players are expecting it, then it is prepared role-playing. I was thinking this group is good enough to try that concept out with."

Aaron moved one hand off her waist to smooth down his goatee, his face set in his thinking frown.

"I do love the concept of bringing in surprise aspect details, but I don't see why I can't just put headphones on and you record the entire thing so I am not actively listening," Aaron said.

"Because people will know that something is going on. If

there is even the barest hint that you are home, we won't speak as freely," Rachael insisted.

Aaron looked down at her. "This is really important to you?" he asked.

Rachael nodded so hard her head hurt.

"Ok, we will give it a try. I have my doubts. But I also see your point," Aaron acquiesced.

Rachael jumped with joy and moved in close, pressing her mouth hard into his. To her surprise, instead of breaking it off, he kissed her back.

"I thought you had to go in to work tomorrow?" Rachael breathed.

"I think I can spare some time for the two of us." Aaron put two fingers under her chin and kissed her long and gently before leading her up the stairs to the bedroom.

FORT COLLINS

DUNGEONS & DRAFTS

Despite the beautiful morning, Rachael found herself inside the pub running a one shot for a college-aged group of men who had recently seen *Stranger Things* and wanted to see what it was all about. She did not, in any way, shape, or form, want to be alone anywhere today, especially her house. She had called Bob to see what had happened with Greg after she left yesterday and to apologize.

He had brushed off her apologies and said that Greg had not caused any trouble and left pretty soon after she did. When she offered her assistance for the day to make up for it, Bob jumped on the chance.

"What do I need to roll again to make a perception check?" one of the guys asked. His eyes seemed incapable of staying on her face for very long. Rachael had chosen a tight pair of jean shorts and a low-cut, long-sleeved blouse with the shoulders cut out for her D&D teaching outfit. The black blouse was accented with silver buttons that matched the silver on her ears, wrist, and the little crystal teardrop that came down to midchest. Maybe not her smartest choice in hindsight, but she was very comfortable.

"A D20," Rachael answered sweetly. "Pretty much everything is a D20 unless it says otherwise." In her left hand, David's D20 danced in her fingers as it slipped in and out of her shorts pocket.

The day didn't go by fast. The group finished their one shot at around 1 p.m. and Rachael took a break for some greasy bar food before her afternoon session at 2 p.m. She needed to send some texts from her real phone but was afraid to turn it on.

"A penny for your thoughts?" Scottish. Rachael grabbed the napkin and wiped greasy burger juice off her chin.

"Bob said you were out today." Rachael turned on her spinny bar stool, and David's hand lightly pressed on her knee to stop her, facing him.

"I am. I actually called Bob to check on you after yesterday and he told me you were here," David answered. "I wish I had your number."

"You came to check on me?" Rachael asked, surprised. David's hand moved a little way up her leg and then back down to her knee.

"I spied a damsel in distress," he said dramatically. His hand left her knee, and he sat down in the seat next to her and faced her slightly.

"But really, are you all right?" David asked, his voice low.

"Yes, I'm fine," Rachael answered. She started to reach for her burger again when David's hand reached over and squeezed her shoulder. She winced.

"Is that who bruised your arm, your husband's brother?" David's voice was dangerous. Rachael wanted to lie but couldn't.

"Yes, but the situation is very complicated," Rachael answered.

David waited for her to explain, and Rachael suddenly just wanted him to go away. She needed to fix herself, her life. She needed to be more independent, not lean on another man.

David would rush in to save her. And just the knowledge that someone cared about her that much gave her strength.

"Here," she said. She reached two fingers into her tiny shorts pocket and pulled out his D20. "Take this back. I was going to return it yesterday, but the day didn't go according to plan."

"What if I don't want that back?" David asked.

Rachael looked deep into David's eyes. The die had been a symbol of her independence. But to David, it was a promise — a promise that she didn't know if she wanted to keep.

"I can't keep it right now," she finally said. She took his loose hand in hers and turned the palm up, placing the die in the center. She curled his fingers around the D20. "I need to work on myself."

FORT COLLINS

DIRK AND DIRK REALTY

Rachael sat in the break room and turned on her cell phone for the first time all weekend. She needed to get the group's phone numbers off of it. It cycled to wakefulness. She hadn't missed much, just a few text messages from Greg as if nothing had happened on Saturday. She had blocked his Facebook weeks ago.

After getting all the numbers off of it, she left it on. Karen handed her the prepaid phone.

"Remember, we can't tell them it is canceled because A," Karen listed off, "that is something they will double-check with Aaron and expect an email about. And B, if it doesn't work, you are in the clear to try and trick him again."

"Debby first," Rachael nodded her agreement.

Rachael: This is Rachael.

Rachael: Do not share this next message or phone number with anyone.

Rachael: Underdark starting late Friday evening — 7 p.m. instead of 6:30 p.m.

Rachael: We won't be home so please, please don't be early.

Debby: Everything OK?

Of course Debby was at her phone.

Rachael: I need to have a chat with Greg before the game starts.

Debby: Ok, good luck. Will aim for 7 p.m.

Rachael: Thank you! Please don't discuss it anywhere — in person or on the computer.

Debby: Got it, you have family drama to sort so we don't have a game interruption and you don't want it all over social media.

Debby: Every family has problems. Don't feel so bad.

Rachael: Thanks, I think.

"Ok, Tom next," she said after reading the conversation with Debby to Karen.

Rachael: This is Rachael.

Rachael: Do not share this next message or phone number with anyone.

Rachael: Underdark starting late Friday evening — 7 p.m. instead of 6:30 p.m.

Rachael: We won't be home so please, please don't be early.

She waited a minute or two to see if he was by his phone. He wasn't. Tom was a wildcard. He could ruin everything if he tried to protect Aaron.

Rachael: That is the lie we are telling the rest of the group. I want Aaron to see Greg for who he really is.

"I wouldn't have added that," Karen shook her head. Rachael remembered back to her conversation with Tom after their last session.

Rachael: If Greg behaves, the campaign will run as usual. I am not trying to hurt anyone.

"I think you are making it worse," Karen said.
"You are so helpful right now," Rachael wanted to scream at the woman. "Do you want to write the texts?"
"It's your stalker," Karen responded, gesturing to Rachael as a whole.
"Martin should be easy," Rachael said. "He doesn't really talk to anyone outside of the campaign."

Rachael: This is Rachael, I lost my phone. Using this one for the week.

Rachael: Please keep both the phone number and the next information to yourself.

Rachael: Underdark starting late Friday evening — 7 p.m. instead of 6:30 p.m.

Rachael: We won't be home so please, please don't be early.

"And our favorite person last," Karen said. "Back to your real phone."

Rachael: Aaron will be home late on Friday but game is running as usual with some team bonding at 6:30.

Greg: Cool, mind if I come early and bring this new beer I found?

Rachael: Aaron won't be here to try them so there is no reason.

Greg: Gotcha ~_- We will have the house to ourselves then.

"Just don't respond to that," Karen said, disgusted. Rachael took her advice.

"Now we wait and hope everyone does what they say." Rachael could feel the butterflies in her stomach already.

81

FORT COLLINS

LIVING ROOM

Rachael could not remember a more nerve-racking week. She kept her phone on and her schedule regular to keep Greg in the dark. She had bumped into him almost every day. The run-ins were short. On the first one, he actually apologized for Saturday, saying he didn't know what had come over him. Every day he reminded her that he was planning on coming over early and every day she told him to piss off and that she wouldn't be home until the last minute.

"I will know when you are home." Greg winked.

Rachael had walked to the nearest bus and got on it after that. She was learning about parts of FoCo she didn't know existed with all these extra bus rides. She had wanted to travel more, right?

Thursday, a giant bouquet of roses was delivered to her office with a note.

"We were meant to be – G," it read. Karen photographed it. If this didn't work, Karen was going to go to the police, even if Rachael wasn't willing. Rachael gave the roses out to all her coworkers. She didn't have the heart to throw them in the trash.

Aaron had been the only saving grace of the week. He went

from skeptical to full-on childlike excitement as they explored the best place for him to hide. In the end, they actually made a little peephole in the closet under the stairs so he could see the living room and dining room. The walls were thin, and he could hear everything clearly.

The problem with his coding was solved and all testing was green. He still came home late, but they at least watched part of their show together and snuggled, if not more, every night. Rachael wished she could enjoy it as much as him. But knowing the train was going to fall off the tracks really dampened the ride for her.

Friday afternoon she sent Aaron a text letting him know that her phone was running out of batteries. She didn't know what Greg could pull off hers and she didn't want to risk Aaron blowing the plan with some unexpected communication. She called him from work before catching her bus. He didn't pick up; he must have left for the day. Rachael shivered; this was happening.

"Good luck tonight," Karen said. "Call me if you need anything."

And now she was walking up to her house at 6:20 p.m., her usual, predictable time. Greg was leaning on her front door-frame, his beefy arms loosely crossed over his chest. He was dressed in white shorts and a shimmering, black, short-sleeved button-down. He was holding a six-pack of beer loosely in one hand; the weight of the beer didn't even register on his muscled frame. His hair was perfectly styled, his face clean-shaven. He uncrossed his arms and lifted up the beer in greeting as soon as he saw her coming.

"I know you have a key, let yourself in," Rachael said. She hoped her voice sounded chipper and not nervous. Aaron's car was nowhere to be seen. "I need to change, but I will meet you in the kitchen in a few minutes."

"Don't avoid me just because I am early," Greg complained.

"I just want out of my work clothes," Rachael responded. She was careful to watch Greg walk in front of her. She shut the front door behind them and watched his back walk to the kitchen before she quickly changed into her loose gaming clothing, comfortable jeans, and her hoodie. She stuck both phones in her pocket and washed her face before heading back downstairs.

Greg was waiting for her with a beer; she accepted it and walked past him toward the middle of the living room to sit.

"Did you get my flowers?" Greg asked.

Rachael stopped and turned; she nervously looked toward the little hole they had made under the stairs. With Greg's arrival before her, she hadn't gotten a chance to check anything. She and Aaron should have come up with a system of knocks or something.

"I gave them out to the office," she said evenly. "I don't want flowers from you."

"I saw," Greg answered. "And you do."

"How did you see?" Rachael's voice wavered. He could see into the office?

"My birdies showed me," Greg purred. He moved forward to touch her. Rachael flinched but forced herself not to move. Aaron would come out of the closet any minute to confront his brother.

Greg used his hand to pull down one side of her hoodie over her shoulder, exposing the strap of her sleeveless tank and the curves of her breast. The dark purple and green bruise of his handprint was hard to miss.

"I wish there had been another way. You bruise so easily," Greg said. He took another step toward her and wrapped his other arm around her waist. Rachael wanted to cry. Why hadn't Aaron come out yet? She had put herself in this position and now Aaron hadn't followed through. She started to cry.

"Don't cry, my love," Greg said. He put his hand against the side of her face and kissed her. His lips were warm and his mouth large, just like their first kiss. But instead of excitement, all Rachael felt was fear and self-hatred.

"We will be amazing together." Greg's breath was minty on her face. Rachael couldn't think of anything else to do. She slapped him hard and ran out her front door.

He didn't chase. He didn't need to.

82

UNDERDARK

4ADEER

Yes, the fey have their own realm, but the fey also have their finger in every pie, their aim often as directionless as the chaos they cause.

— AARON, DUNGEON MASTER'S NOTES, CS18.

T hey followed Minksey through twisting tunnels of rough-cut stone. She occasionally tried to banter with Lilly, but Lilly had none of her own words to say back.

"Are you sure we should be running?" Tom asked Aaron for the third time.

"I am sure it is fine," Aaron answered.

"She left a note," Greg pointed to the typed paper in the middle of the table.

So sorry, dealing with some stuff. Headed to Karen's, try not to kill Lilly. – Rachael

"That is just really, really weird," Debby said. She started to open her mouth to say something else but just shook her head. "Should we be worried?"

"Karen told me that Dirk and Dirk is struggling with the housing the way it is," Greg stated.

"She has been spending more time with work friends," Aaron said. "I am not worried. It will be a short session tonight anyway. Thank you again for starting late."

4aDeer didn't trust the fey creature and did not want to owe it a favor, but he was grateful for his life. Even the mighty 4aDeer knew he wouldn't have survived an attack by every creature in the maze.

The rough stone walls of the tunnel slanted up and slowly started to mix with dirt and roots.

"I can smell fresh air." Poppy was relieved. They all were when the tunnel spit them out in the overly focused and bright world of the fey.

They paused and 4aDeer watched Craig and Poppy each touch the earth and trees. He forced himself not to complain. The connection to their powers helped them recover a bit. He would have to continue on, dragging his feet.

"I need one thing before I guide you back to Elm City," Minksey stated after Craig and Poppy were finished.

Eismus groaned loudly.

Minksey smiled at him.

"Teehee," she laughed at his frustration. As the fey do. "One of my friends is trapped against her will by a dragon priest. The shift in powers already is being felt in this world. This is not the favor you owe me. But your payment for my safe guidance now that you are no longer being threatened but still lost."

"That is extremely straightforward," Eismus said. 4aDeer nodded in concerned agreement.

"Through the fey wilds to Elm City, Temple of the Fey," Poppy added. "It is not that straightforward."

"Teehee teehee," Minksey tinkled. "Agree," she said.

4aDeer looked around at the party; they all seemed to be nodding.

"Bad idea," 4aDeer stated.

"Do you have a better one?" Poppy asked. 4aDeer thought hard for a moment and shook his head.

"If that journey is more than two hours, we will also need a protected place to eat and sleep," Poppy added to the deal.

"Agree, agree, agree," Minksey quickly agreed.

The walk was quite long, and after exactly two hours, Minksey brought them to a giant tree where they ate and rested their injured bodies. Nothing attacked them under the fey's protection, and they rested soundly. They continued to march the next day. Poppy seemed to start glowing as the fey sun bathed her in its light and 4aDeer became anxious, itching, and unnerved in this world.

They could see a wall of stone looming before them, and as they got closer, patches of the fey greens were withering away, veins of uneven, pulsing, dark purple intertwined in the rock and earth.

"Balance," 4aDeer stated wisely.

"How does this work?" Eismus asked Minksey.

"The Dragon Temple grows strong and sends their energy into our territory," Minksey said, as if that explained everything.

The silence of the group was heavy. Minksey led them true, and soon enough they could see another three-foot-tall elf-like creature trapped in a jagged iron cage. The ground was barren here on the edge of the fey world and Underdark. Evil-looking dark veins pulsed along the ground. They didn't see any guards.

"There is no way it is as simple as letting her out," Eismus said. But after a short debate, 4aDeer moved forward, axe in hand, to bust open the cage.

Two dragon priests materialized seemingly out of thin air, and 4aDeer managed to dodge one but not the other. Craig's and Eismus' spells came from over his shoulder and he felt Lilly's inspiration fill his heart.

"See, Rachael always forgets to cast that during little battles," Martin said. "I think when we are playing someone else's toon we need to be true to the player's intent."

"But Lilly would remember to cast that," Debby pointed out. "It is Rachael who forgets it is a bonus action."

"When Lilly is under our control, she does better than when Rachael is making decisions?" Greg questioned.

"No, that is not what I was saying," Debby shot Greg a look.

"We need to be true to Lilly's purpose, not Rachael's choice," Greg stated.

"That doesn't really sound right," Tom said. "But I think as we are not prepared for the missing individual we should play her bard stats during combat and just let her fade out otherwise.

"I don't like it," Martin said. "I think we need to be thinking of what Rachael would want Lilly to do."

"Missing people is always tricky," Aaron stated. "During combat, we will play by the numbers and Lilly will play to her strengths regardless of Rachael's past choices."

"I can play her during social encounters," Greg spoke up. "We are really close."

"That is a bad idea," Tom just came out and said it. "If we need her during a social encounter, we will figure it out as a group."

Aaron nodded. "Ok, that is settled, the cast of bardic inspiration is good."

Combat was short and sweet. One of the dragon priests was able to summon a single undead minor dragon that chased Eismus around for a bit. 4aDeer was happy to leave him to his "kiting" as he and Craig, with much difficulty, busted open the cage doors.

"Look!" Poppy exclaimed as they finished. "I found a key and a note!"

"Really, we didn't loot the bodies first," Craig said, his breath ragged from breaking things.

"4aDeer smash," 4aDeer stated.

The note was in a language they didn't know, and they decided to wait for "Lilly" to be back before having her cast on it and translate it. Minksey was good to her word and delivered them to the Temple of the Fey. Master Corath had been expecting their arrival and dramatically took the crystal to the base of a giant tree, set in the red and gold walls. 4aDeer ducked as power pulsed through the gold vines.

As they exited the temple the townsfolk cheered. The dragon priests angrily stomped back to their original territory. A woman threw flowers at 4aDeer and then herself as the party was dragged off to the tavern. Much celebration and rejoicing to be had. Balance was restored to Elm City.

FORT COLLINS

MOTEL

Rachael had gotten some odd looks wandering into the lobby with no shoes or luggage. But the man at the front desk let her pay for the room with her memorized credit card and now she was here. She had showered, paced, cried, screamed, and then fallen asleep. She had slept like a rock, secure knowing that no one knew where she was. Blackout curtains closed tight together. But her dreams had plagued her and woken her up earlier than any human should be awake.

Rachael looked at both her phones in the yellowy lamplight of the cheap motel room. She wouldn't turn on her phone; Greg would know where she was. The pay-as-you-go phone was out of batteries.

What did she want? Aaron hadn't meant to abandon her, her mind tried to rationalize, but her emotions were raw. She thought of David and his fierce will to protect her even though they didn't really know each other. She didn't want to rely on any man. The thought both terrified her and empowered her.

She needed to go home and confront Aaron, let him know she was leaving with or without him. And she needed to do it soon before she lost her resolve.

She had the front desk call her a taxi; it was 10 minutes out. A new person was on shift at the front desk and gave her a look similar to the guy who checked her in. She handed him her room key, saying thanks, and waited in view of the front desk for her taxi.

It was a short ride. The driver insisted on seeing her to the door when she said she needed to go inside to get cash. She didn't mind; at this time of night he probably half-expected her to tweak out and not pay. She tried the door and found it unlocked.

It barely opened before it was ripped out of her hands and Aaron's arms were around her, strangling the air out of her.

"I am so sorry," his voice was raw. "I should have been there for you."

"I need to pay the taxi driver," was all she could think of to say.

PASADENA, CALIFORNIA

PSYCHOLOGY CLINIC

Rachael didn't understand why she needed to be here for this. But family was important to Aaron, and she felt guilty for her part in Greg's state of mind. The family had picked this clinic especially for its success in rehabilitating stalkers. Aaron had not asked her to do this. But after hearing him on the phone for hours with his parents, and receiving a few messages from his family herself, she had very unhappily relented.

Doctor Partin, Greg's doctor, had contacted her directly and talked her through the beginning of Greg's healing process. She had been told to dress like she always dressed and be at the clinic at 10 a.m. Aaron was waiting for her at the door of their hotel room. She took one last look at herself in the mirror.

Her eyes had huge bags under them. Her hair was up in a tight bun except for the few pieces that refused to stay. Her black, shoulderless blouse washed out her skin color. Even her ever-present earrings, she had chosen plain silver hoops for today, seemed tarnished. She felt like she was looking at a ghost of herself. She washed her face for the third time. Her skin felt tight against the contours of her face.

"Thank you for doing this," Aaron said. His thanks echoed in her mind; she had lost track of how many times those words had come out of his mouth. She had been ready to leave. To leave everything. But Aaron needed her now. His family, his strength, was fracturing. She couldn't leave him; she didn't want to leave him. She just wanted her life, her Aaron back. Their hands found each other as he led her out of the room.

They arrived at the clinic with the rest of Aaron's direct family. Aaron's youngest sister gave her a hug, but the rest of the family ignored her or visibly frowned. They all walked in together and were shown to a big meeting room where Greg already waited for them. His new white patient uniform bulged over his muscles, and a woman in a pencil suit with a lab coat sat next to him.

"I am so glad all of you could be here for Greg's official entry to the clinic," she said. "It is good to see you in person. I am Doctor Partin. Greg and I had a good chat this morning and he is also excited to be here."

"I am," Greg agreed.

"And thank you especially, Rachael," Doctor Partin said. "I know as the victim it can be very hard to come face-to-face with your fears. But Greg needs direct closure to start recovering and to know that he is still loved and supported by his family."

Rachael didn't say anything; she took slow, steadying breaths.

"A lot of stalker victims blame themselves," Doctor Partin said. "You did nothing wrong."

"Bullshit," a poorly disguised cough from one of Aaron's family members.

Doctor Partin frowned and looked toward the group arranged beside Rachael. Aaron was seated closest to Rachael, his mom and dad, two sisters, and remaining brother all in a line next to him.

"I will say it again, Rachael did nothing…" Doctor Partin started to continue, but Rachael cut her off.

"I am sorry, but I am extremely uncomfortable," Rachael said, her eyes pleading with the doctor's to understand. "Just tell me what you need from me."

"Understandable," Doctor Partin said. She motioned to an orderly to turn on the camera that was just over Greg's shoulder so it would look like she was looking into it while she was talking to Greg.

"Greg," Doctor Partin turned to him. "Your family is here to support you in this process, and Rachael is here to help you begin to let go. I need you to really listen to her words."

Doctor Partin turned to Rachael.

"Please tell Greg how what he did made you feel," Doctor Partin asked.

Rachael shook her head and her lips pressed into a line on her face.

"You manipulated me. You isolated me. You inserted yourself into my life. You created conflict in my marriage and made me feel powerless," Rachael stated facts, her emotions gone with her overwhelming sense of discomfort. "I will not give you the satisfaction of hearing my thoughts, the only part of me I have left to myself!"

Greg's smile was terrible. "You don't need to tell me. I created everything. And I would do it all again. You picked the wrong brother; we will be together in the end."

EPILOGUE

R achael put on her new D&D outfit, the blue cargo pants riding low on her hips, the pockets filled with snacks and emergency supplies. The weather was too warm for sweaters now; she just had on her sleeveless black tank. Little blue glass meeples that Vicky had gotten her years ago hung off her ears, and she wore a matching necklace. She flipped and twisted up her hair to get it off her neck and started laying out snack plates.

This was the first time the group had gotten back together since the Greg fallout. Aaron had installed a camera under the stairs. Instead of sneaking home, he just recorded it to watch later. Tom had talked Aaron into watching it together after the group had dispersed.

Rachael had been forced to watch the tape again with him and then a third time when Aaron called his parents for help getting his brother checked into a clinic. She had to recount everything, from the willing first kiss to the unwanted affections over and over. Each time, she felt Greg's hold on her tighten and she pulled further into herself. Why did talking about things make them more real?

Aaron was so understanding. He had been hurt when she admitted to the first kiss but took all the blame himself and never asked her once to apologize. It was wonderful and infuriating at the same time. She was so angry at herself. Why couldn't he just be angry too? Why did he have to be so damn understanding?

It felt like it had been a year, but really, only two weeks had passed. Rachael found herself struggling to listen to Aaron's sweet words and apologies. He treated her like she was made of glass, ready to break any moment. He didn't touch her unless she asked. He alternated between being hyper-focused on her needs and avoiding her completely. Rachael was numb, but underneath the numb, she seethed with anger.

Rachael felt the giant serving plate in her hands, the decorated rim's smooth patterns cold under her fingers. She had been ready to leave all of this. What she really wanted was to be her own person again. She smashed the dish against the counter. The porcelain and glass shattered almost like a slow-motion action scene in a movie. Pieces flew in every direction. Some hit the floor and broke apart further.

It felt so good to break something. All she really wanted was to feel alive, to walk around town without looking over her shoulder, to be in control again.

Her fingers absently looked for David's D20 as she enjoyed the splatter of ceramic material she had created. But she had given it back to him. She needed to find her own D20.

The front door opened.

"Aaron," Rachael called. "I just broke a plate; will you bring me a broom when you come in?"

"I will. Are you OK?" Aaron's voice.

"I'm fine; it just slipped out of my fingers," she lied.

"We have two new people joining the campaign tonight," Aaron's voce drifted from the living room. "I know I told you about Debby's friend, Hunter. But I just invited David today.

He's the client I have been working for, but his project passed on. He also runs a lot of games; I think he will fit right into the party." Aaron's voice disappeared into the coat closet while he looked for a broom.

"Do you need some help?" Scottish. Rachael froze and slowly turned; she hadn't heard his footsteps coming into the kitchen. David's eyes undressed her in one look. She could feel heat rise to her face and butterflies fill her stomach. She couldn't move or else her bare feet might step on shards of ceramic plate.

"Rach," Aaron rounded the corner, broom in hand. "This is David Douglas."

Rachael held out her hand; David's hand easily covered hers, but the shattered plate prevented them from moving any closer.

"We've met at Dungeons & Drafts," Rachael said, expecting a handshake. David lifted her hand to his lips. Their soft, dry surface brushed her knuckles.

A shiver of pleasure shot through Rachael. Her first spark of life and fire.

"It is good to meet you again." David's accent was thick. Rachael didn't trust herself to do more than nod as she started picking up the pieces of her broken plate.

End of *The Dungeon Master's Wife, Book One*. Find out more about the D&D Underdark campaign in the illustrated *Dungeon Master's Notebook: Aaron, The Underdark* available on Amazon now.

Rachael and Lilly's adventures will continue in book two, available eventually.

This is my first book, and I need your feedback to complete book two. Please take the time to leave a review!

Thank you for reading.

Dear reader,

We hope you enjoyed reading *The Dungeon Master's Wife*. Please take a moment to leave a review, even if it's a short one. Your opinion is important to us.

Discover more books by Kate Messick at https://www.nextchapter.pub/authors/kate-messick

Want to know when one of our books is free or discounted for Kindle? Join the newsletter at http://eepurl.com/bqqB3H

Best regards,

Kate Messick and the Next Chapter Team

You might also like:
Cradle of the Gods by Thomas Quinn Miller

To read the first chapter for free, head to:
https://www.nextchapter.pub/books/cradle-of-the-gods-epic-fantasy-adventure

DUNGEONS & DRAGONS®

Kate Messick
CHARACTER NAME

8th Level - Bard	Scribe	Unknown
CLASS & LEVEL	BACKGROUND	PLAYER NAME
Human	Chaotic Good	over 9000
RACE	ALIGNMENT	EXPERIENCE POINTS

INSPIRATION ■

+3 PROFICIENCY BONUS

STRENGTH **+3** 16

DEXTERITY **-1** 8

CONSTITUTION **0** 10

INTELLIGENCE **+1** 12

WISDOM **+2** 15

CHARISMA **0** 11

SAVING THROWS
- ☐ +3 Strength
- ☐ -1 Dexterity
- ☐ 0 Constitution
- ☐ +1 Intelligence
- ☐ +2 Wisdom
- ☐ 0 Charisma

SKILLS
- ☐ -1 Acrobatics (Dex)
- ☑ +5 Animal Handling (Wis)
- ☐ +1 Arcana (Int)
- ☑ +6 Athletics (Str)
- ☐ 0 Deception (Cha)
- ☑ +4 History (Int)
- ☐ +2 Insight (Wis)
- ☐ +3 Intimidation (Cha)
- ☐ +1 Investigation (Int)
- ☐ +2 Medicine (Wis)
- ☐ +1 Nature (Int)
- ☐ +2 Perception (Wis)
- ☑ +3 Performance (Cha)
- ☐ 0 Persuasion (Cha)
- ☐ +1 Religion (Int)
- ☐ -1 Sleight of Hand (Dex)
- ☐ -1 Stealth (Dex)
- ☐ +2 Survival (Wis)

PASSIVE WISDOM (PERCEPTION)

ARMOR CLASS **10** INITIATIVE **0** SPEED **30**

Hit Point Maximum **43**

CURRENT HIT POINTS **3**

TEMPORARY HIT POINTS **10**

HIT DICE Total 8d8 **0**

DEATH SAVES
SUCCESSES ●●○
FAILURES ●●○

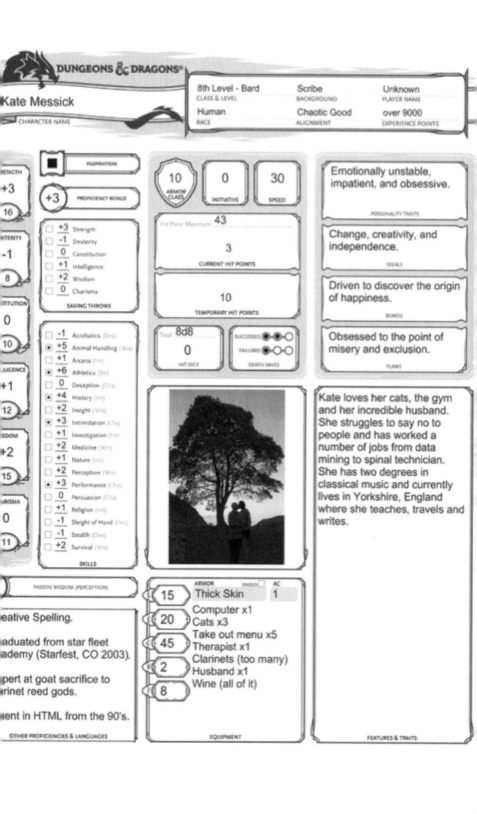

PERSONALITY TRAITS
Emotionally unstable, impatient, and obsessive.

IDEALS
Change, creativity, and independence.

BONDS
Driven to discover the origin of happiness.

FLAWS
Obsessed to the point of misery and exclusion.

FEATURES & TRAITS
Kate loves her cats, the gym and her incredible husband. She struggles to say no to people and has worked a number of jobs from data mining to spinal technician. She has two degrees in classical music and currently lives in Yorkshire, England where she teaches, travels and writes.

OTHER PROFICIENCIES & LANGUAGES
...eative Spelling.

...aduated from star fleet ...ademy (Starfest, CO 2003).

...pert at goat sacrifice to ...arinet reed gods.

...ient in HTML from the 90's.

EQUIPMENT

	ARMOR	SHIELD ☐	AC
15	Thick Skin		1
20	Computer x1		
45	Cats x3		
2	Take out menu x5		
8	Therapist x1		

Clarinets (too many)
Husband x1
Wine (all of it)